WALT DISNEY'S

MICKEY MOUSE

The Chirikawa Necklace

The Chirikawa Necklace

From Italian *Topolino* #230, 1960
Writer and Artist: Romano Scarpa
Inker: Rodolfo Cimino
Colorists: Digikore Studios with Deron Bennett
Letterer: Deron Bennett
Translation: David Gerstein
Dialogue: Jonathan H. Gray and David Gerstein

Caught Out

From British *Mickey Mouse Annual* #6, 1935
Writer, Artist, and Letterer: Wilfred Haughton
Colorist: Digikore Studios

Polar Opposition

From Brazilian *Tio Patinhas* #83, 1972
Artist: Jack Bradbury
Inker: Steve Steere
Colorist: Digikore Studios
Letterer: Deron Bennett
Translation: David Gerstein
Dialogue: Joe Torcivia

Something Turns Up

From *Mickey Mouse* Sunday comic strip, 1950
Writer: Bill Walsh
Artist and Letterer: Manuel Gonzales
Colorist: Digikore Studios

For international rights, contact **licensing@idwpublishing.com**

Special thanks to Curt Baker, Julie Dorris, Manny Mederos, Beatrice Osman, Roberto Santillo, Camilla Vedove, Stefano Ambrosio, Carlotta Quattrocolo, and Thomas Jensen.

ISBN: 978-1-63140-575-4

19 18 17 16   1 2 3 4

Ted Adams, CEO & Publisher
Greg Goldstein, President & COO
Robbie Robbins, EVP/Sr. Graphic Artist
Chris Ryall, Chief Creative Officer/Editor-in-Chief
Matthew Ruzicka, CPA, Chief Financial Officer
Dirk Wood, VP of Marketing
Lorelei Bunjes, VP of Digital Services
Jeff Webber, VP of Licensing, Digital and Subsidiary Rights
Jerry Bennington, VP of New Product Development

www.IDWPUBLISHING.com

Facebook: **facebook.com/idwpublishing**
Twitter: **@idwpublishing**
YouTube: **youtube.com/idwpublishing**
Tumblr: **tumblr.idwpublishing.com**
Instagram: **instagram.com/idwpublishing**

From British *Donald and Mickey* #137, 1974
Writer: Cal Howard
Artist: Tony Strobl
Colorist: Digikore Studios
Letterer: Deron Bennett
Dialogue: Thad Komorowski

The Christmas Tree Crimes

From Italian *Topolino* #370, 1962
Writers: Abramo and Giampaolo Barosso
Artist: Romano Scarpa
Inker: Giorgio Cavazzano
Colorists: Digikore Studios with Dave Alvarez
Letterers: Travis and Nicole Seitler
Translation and Dialogue: Joe Torcivia

A Goofy Look At Snow

From Dutch *Donald Duck* #50/2008
Writer: Jos Beekman
Artist: Michel Nadorp
Colorists: Sanoma with Travis and Nicole Seitler
Letterers: Travis and Nicole Seitler
Translation and Dialogue: Jonathan H. Gray

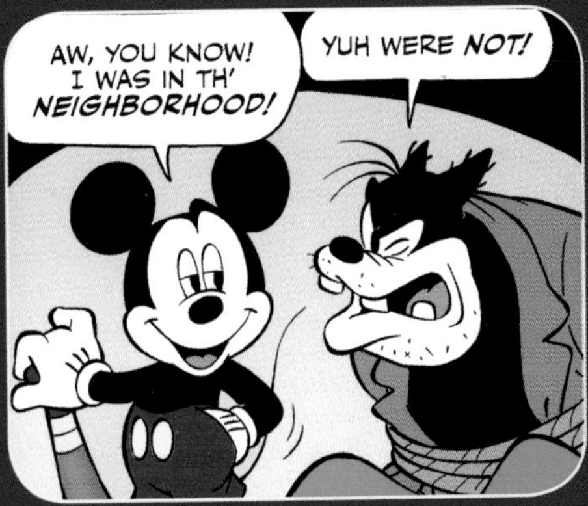
AW, YOU KNOW! I WAS IN TH' NEIGHBORHOOD!
YUH WERE NOT!

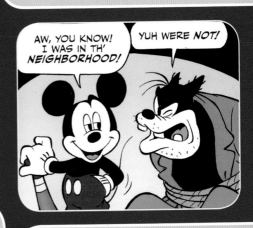

Pot Shot

from British *Mickey Mouse Annual* #1, 1930
Writer, Artist, and Letterer: Wilfred Haughton
Colorist: Scott Rockwell

While We Were Waiting

From Danish *Anders And & Co.* #39/2012
Writer: Maya Åstrup
Artist: Joaquín Cañizares Sanchez
Colorist: Digikore Studios
Letterers: Travis and Nicole Seitler

Series Editor: Sarah Gaydos
Archival Editor: David Gerstein

Cover Artist: Henrieke Goorhuis
Cover Colorist: Arancia Studios
Collection Editors: Justin Eisinger
& Alonzo Simon
Publisher: Ted Adams
Collection Designer: Clyde Grapa

Disney Comics

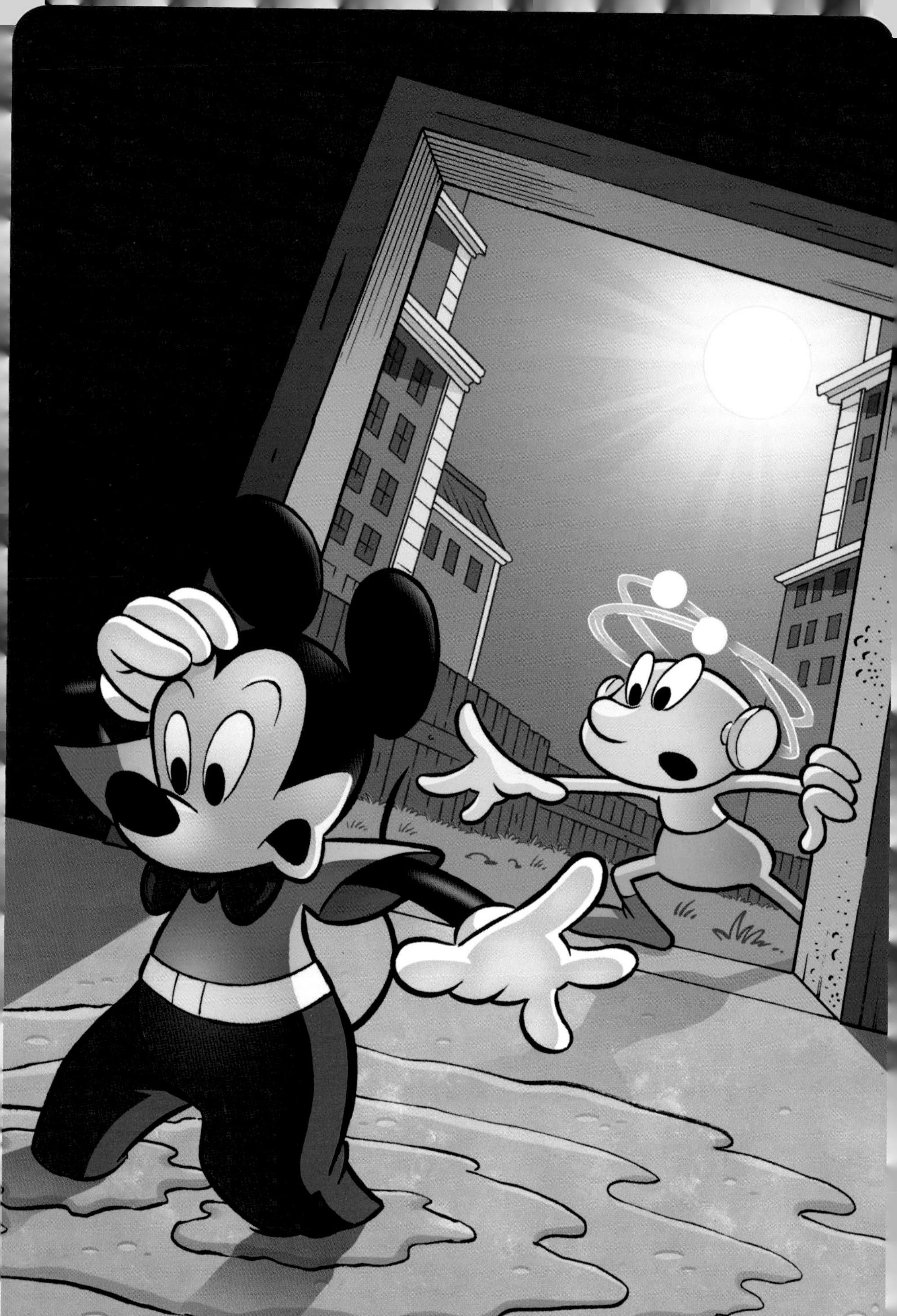

…t by Andrea "Casty" Ca…

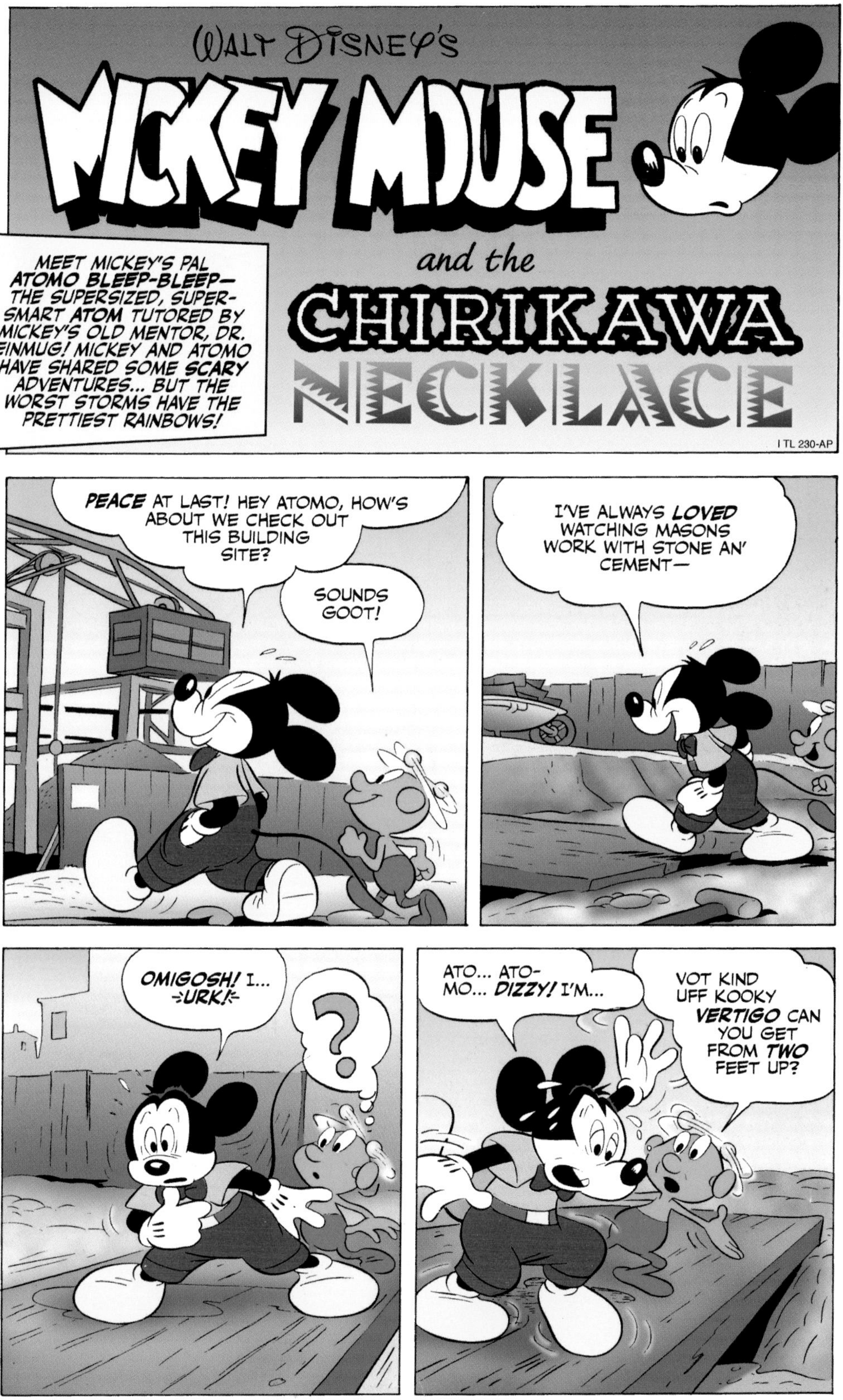
WALT DISNEY'S
MICKEY MOUSE
and the
CHIRIKAWA NECKLACE
MEET MICKEY'S PAL ATOMO BLEEP-BLEEP— THE SUPERSIZED, SUPER-SMART ATOM TUTORED BY MICKEY'S OLD MENTOR, DR. EINMUG! MICKEY AND ATOMO HAVE SHARED SOME SCARY ADVENTURES... BUT THE WORST STORMS HAVE THE PRETTIEST RAINBOWS!
I TL 230-AP
PEACE AT LAST! HEY ATOMO, HOW'S ABOUT WE CHECK OUT THIS BUILDING SITE?
SOUNDS GOOT!
I'VE ALWAYS LOVED WATCHING MASONS WORK WITH STONE AN' CEMENT—
OMIGOSH! I... URK!
?
ATO... ATO-MO... DIZZY! I'M...
VOT KIND UFF KOOKY VERTIGO CAN YOU GET FROM TWO FEET UP?

Originally published in *Topolino* #230 (Italy, 1960)

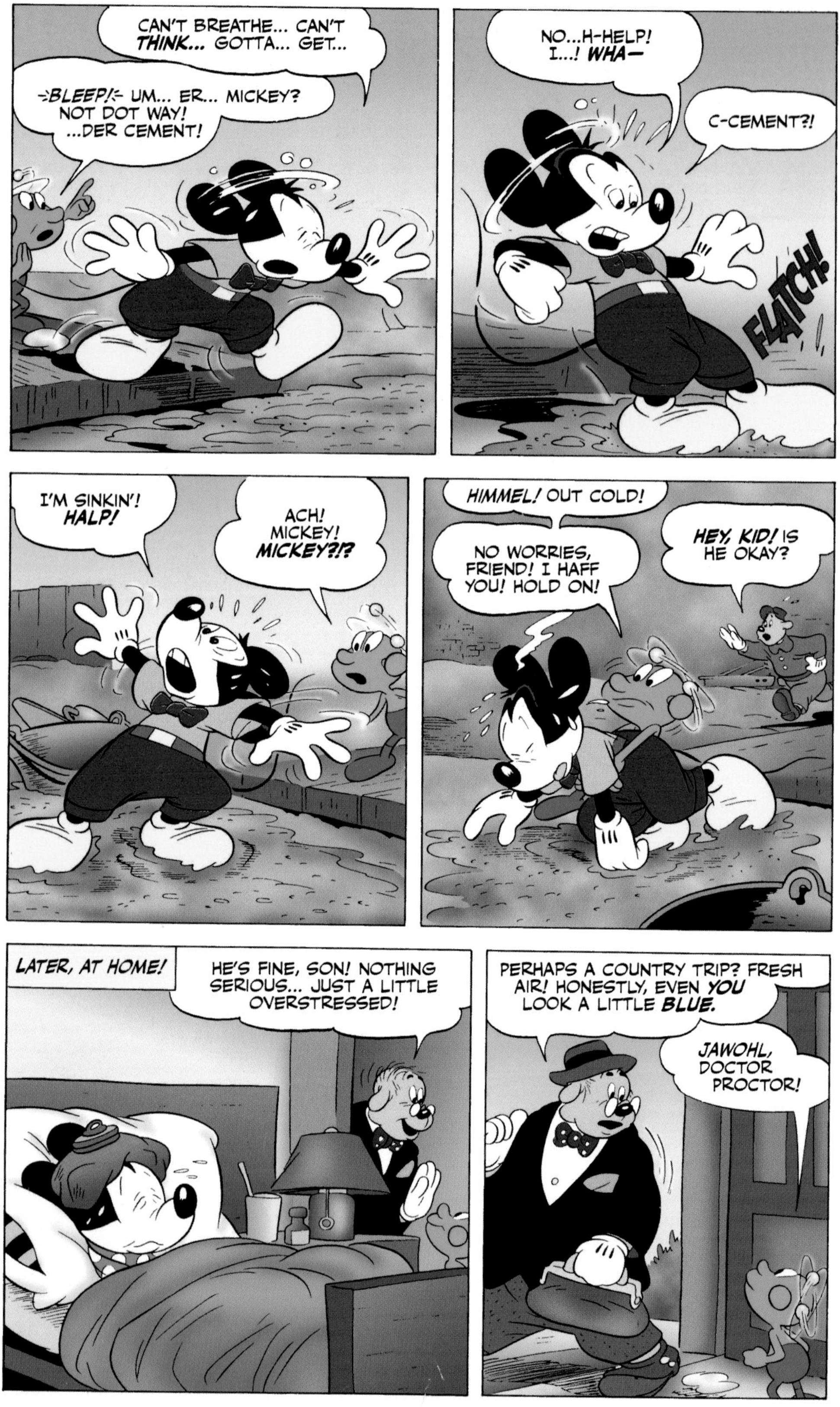
CAN'T BREATHE... CAN'T THINK... GOTTA... GET...
-BLEEP!- UM... ER... MICKEY? NOT DOT WAY! ...DER CEMENT!
NO...H-HELP! I...! WHA—
C-CEMENT?!
FLATCH!
I'M SINKIN'! HALP!
ACH! MICKEY! MICKEY?!?
HIMMEL! OUT COLD!
NO WORRIES, FRIEND! I HAFF YOU! HOLD ON!
HEY, KID! IS HE OKAY?
LATER, AT HOME!
HE'S FINE, SON! NOTHING SERIOUS... JUST A LITTLE OVERSTRESSED!
PERHAPS A COUNTRY TRIP? FRESH AIR! HONESTLY, EVEN YOU LOOK A LITTLE BLUE.
JAWOHL, DOCTOR PROCTOR!

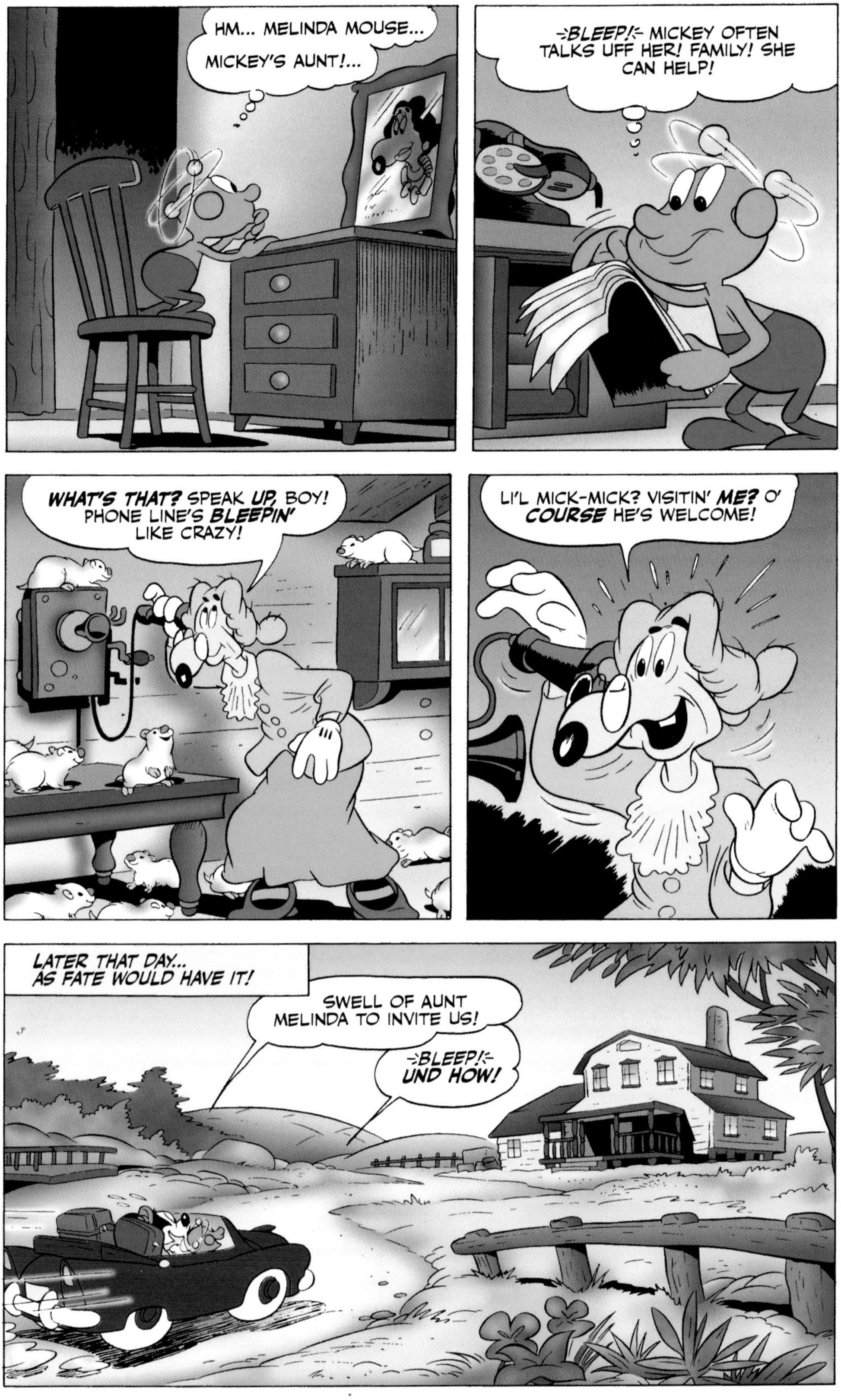
HM... MELINDA MOUSE...
MICKEY'S AUNT!...
-BLEEP!- MICKEY OFTEN TALKS UFF HER! FAMILY! SHE CAN HELP!
WHAT'S THAT? SPEAK UP, BOY! PHONE LINE'S BLEEPIN' LIKE CRAZY!
LI'L MICK-MICK? VISITIN' ME? O' COURSE HE'S WELCOME!
LATER THAT DAY... AS FATE WOULD HAVE IT!
SWELL OF AUNT MELINDA TO INVITE US!
-BLEEP!- UND HOW!

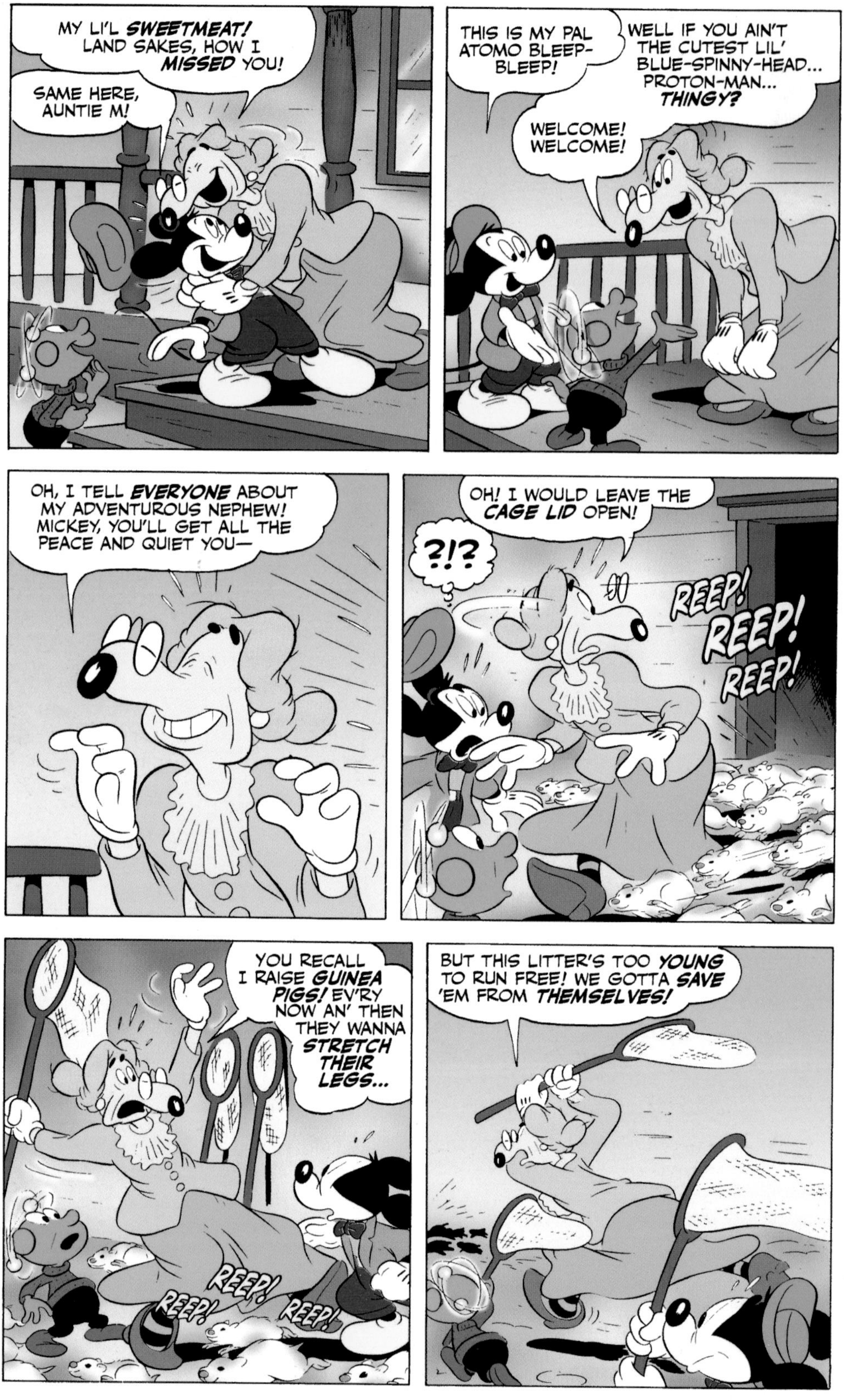
MY LI'L SWEETMEAT! LAND SAKES, HOW I MISSED YOU!
SAME HERE, AUNTIE M!
THIS IS MY PAL ATOMO BLEEP-BLEEP!
WELL IF YOU AIN'T THE CUTEST LIL' BLUE-SPINNY-HEAD... PROTON-MAN... THINGY?
WELCOME! WELCOME!
OH, I TELL EVERYONE ABOUT MY ADVENTUROUS NEPHEW! MICKEY, YOU'LL GET ALL THE PEACE AND QUIET YOU—
OH! I WOULD LEAVE THE CAGE LID OPEN!
?!?
REEP! REEP! REEP!
YOU RECALL I RAISE GUINEA PIGS! EV'RY NOW AN' THEN THEY WANNA STRETCH THEIR LEGS...
REEP! REEP! REEP!
BUT THIS LITTER'S TOO YOUNG TO RUN FREE! WE GOTTA SAVE 'EM FROM THEMSELVES!

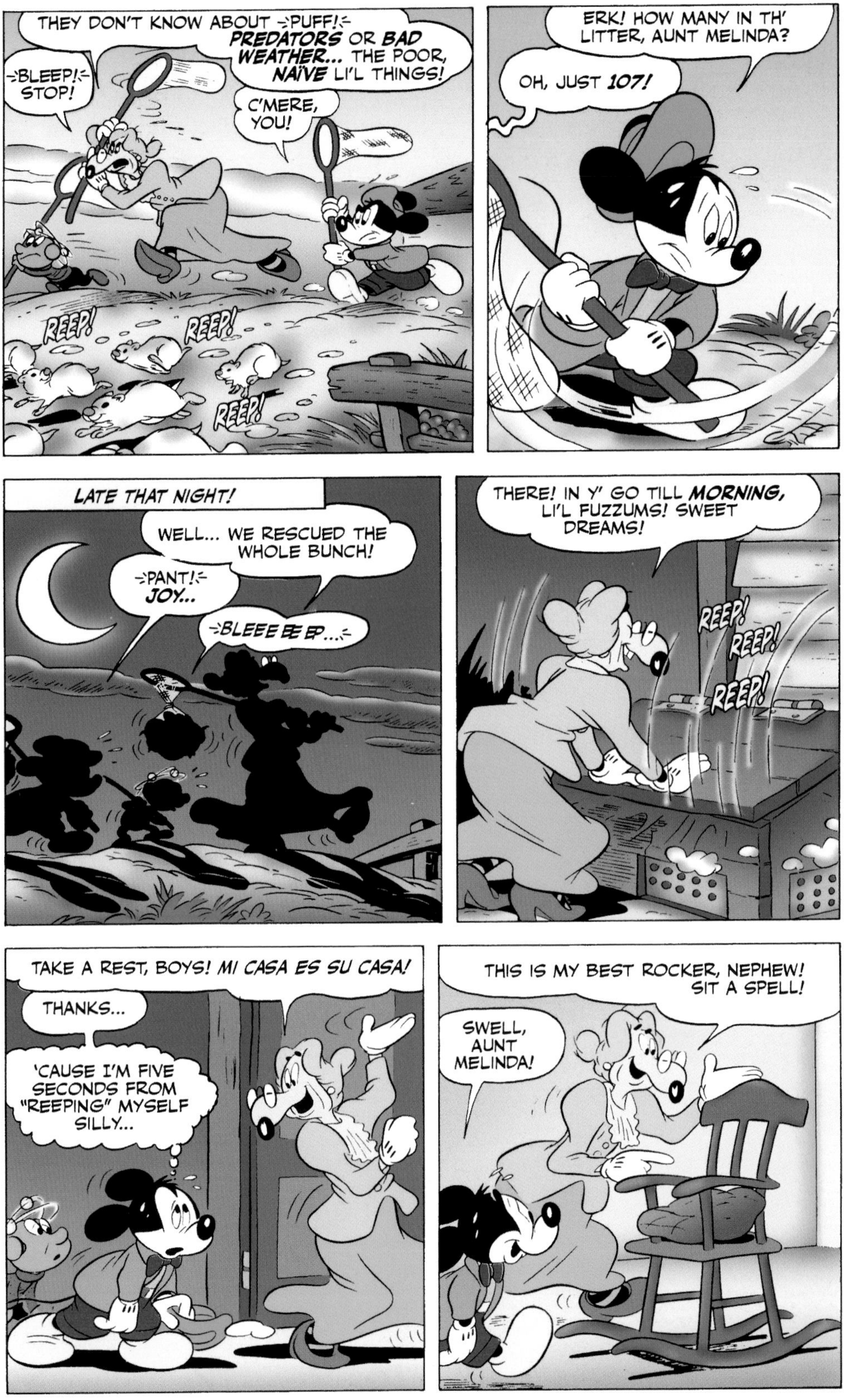
THEY DON'T KNOW ABOUT -PUFF!- PREDATORS OR BAD WEATHER... THE POOR, NAÏVE LI'L THINGS!
-BLEEP!- STOP!
C'MERE, YOU!
REEP!
REEP!
REEP!
ERK! HOW MANY IN TH' LITTER, AUNT MELINDA?
OH, JUST 107!
LATE THAT NIGHT!
WELL... WE RESCUED THE WHOLE BUNCH!
-PANT!- JOY...
-BLEEEEEEP...-
THERE! IN Y' GO TILL MORNING, LI'L FUZZUMS! SWEET DREAMS!
REEP!
REEP!
REEP!
TAKE A REST, BOYS! MI CASA ES SU CASA!
THANKS...
'CAUSE I'M FIVE SECONDS FROM "REEPING" MYSELF SILLY...
THIS IS MY BEST ROCKER, NEPHEW! SIT A SPELL!
SWELL, AUNT MELINDA!

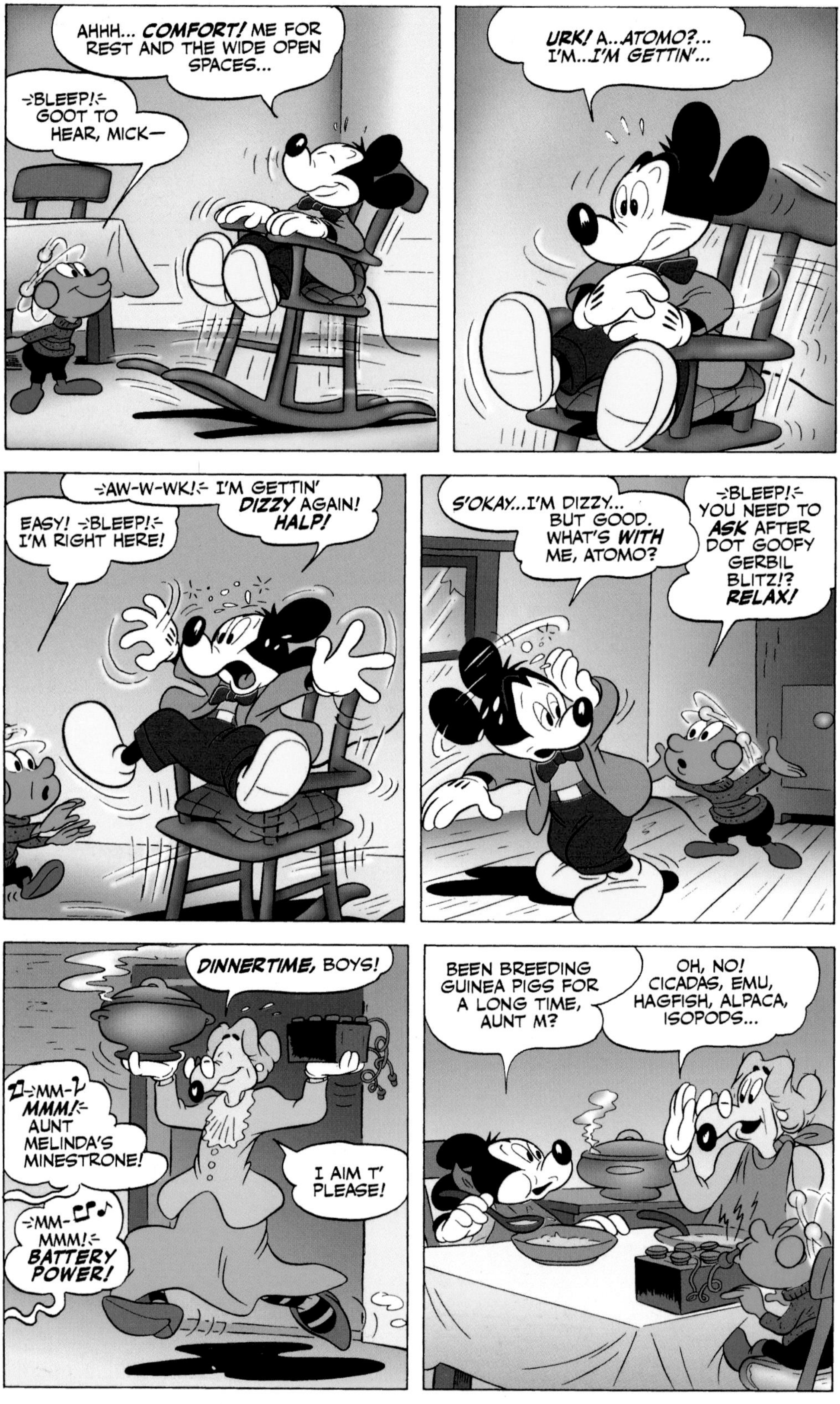
AHHH... COMFORT! ME FOR REST AND THE WIDE OPEN SPACES...
-BLEEP!- GOOT TO HEAR, MICK—
URK! A...ATOMO?... I'M...I'M GETTIN'...
-AW-W-WK!- I'M GETTIN' DIZZY AGAIN! HALP!
EASY! -BLEEP!- I'M RIGHT HERE!
S'OKAY...I'M DIZZY... BUT GOOD. WHAT'S WITH ME, ATOMO?
-BLEEP!- YOU NEED TO ASK AFTER DOT GOOFY GERBIL BLITZ!? RELAX!
DINNERTIME, BOYS!
-MM- MMM!- AUNT MELINDA'S MINESTRONE!
I AIM T' PLEASE!
-MM- MMM!- BATTERY POWER!
BEEN BREEDING GUINEA PIGS FOR A LONG TIME, AUNT M?
OH, NO! CICADAS, EMU, HAGFISH, ALPACA, ISOPODS...

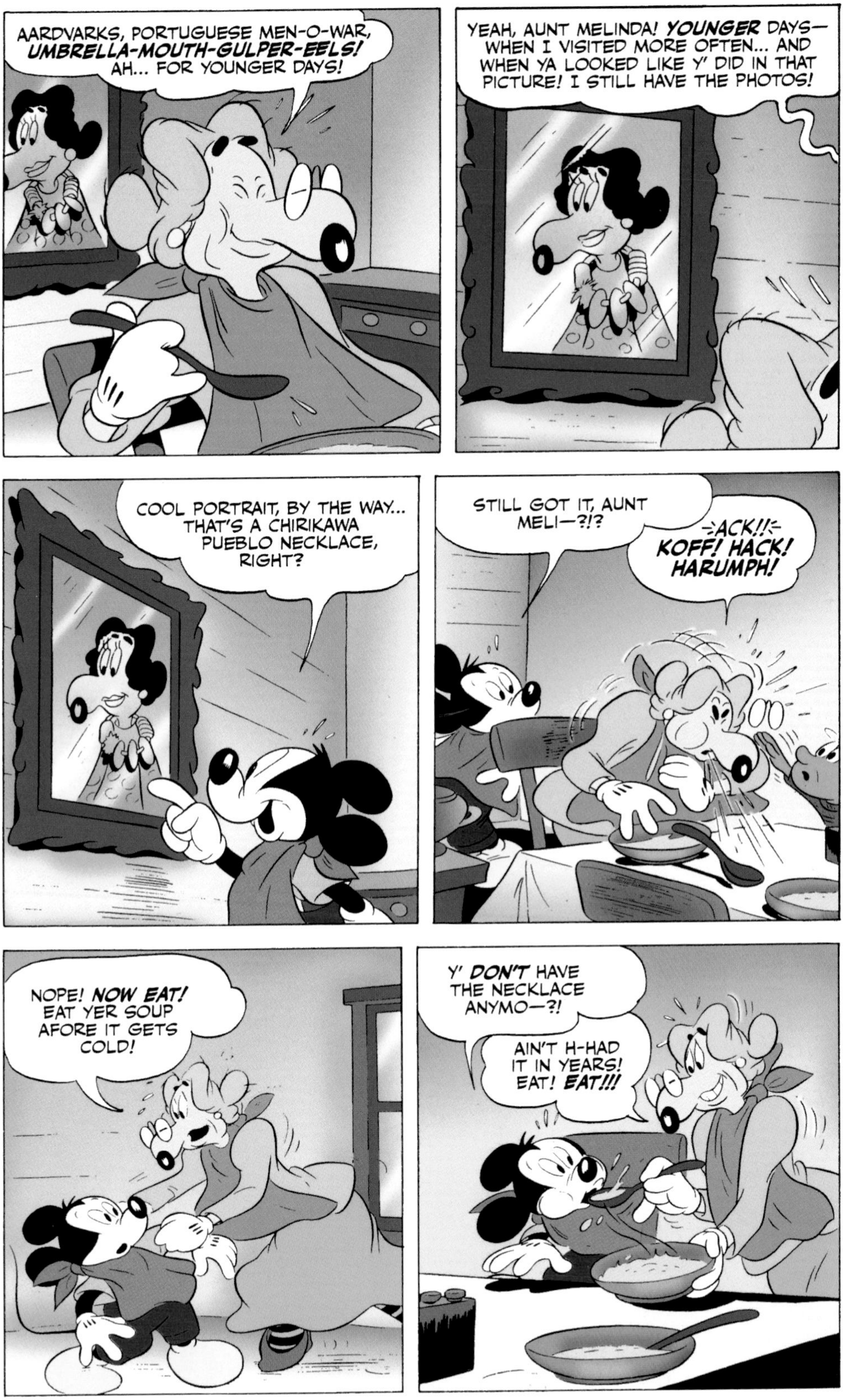
AARDVARKS, PORTUGUESE MEN-O-WAR, UMBRELLA-MOUTH-GULPER-EELS! AH... FOR YOUNGER DAYS!
YEAH, AUNT MELINDA! YOUNGER DAYS— WHEN I VISITED MORE OFTEN... AND WHEN YA LOOKED LIKE Y' DID IN THAT PICTURE! I STILL HAVE THE PHOTOS!
COOL PORTRAIT, BY THE WAY... THAT'S A CHIRIKAWA PUEBLO NECKLACE, RIGHT?
STILL GOT IT, AUNT MELI—?!?
ACK!! KOFF! HACK! HARUMPH!
NOPE! NOW EAT! EAT YER SOUP AFORE IT GETS COLD!
Y' DON'T HAVE THE NECKLACE ANYMO—?!
AIN'T H-HAD IT IN YEARS! EAT! EAT!!!

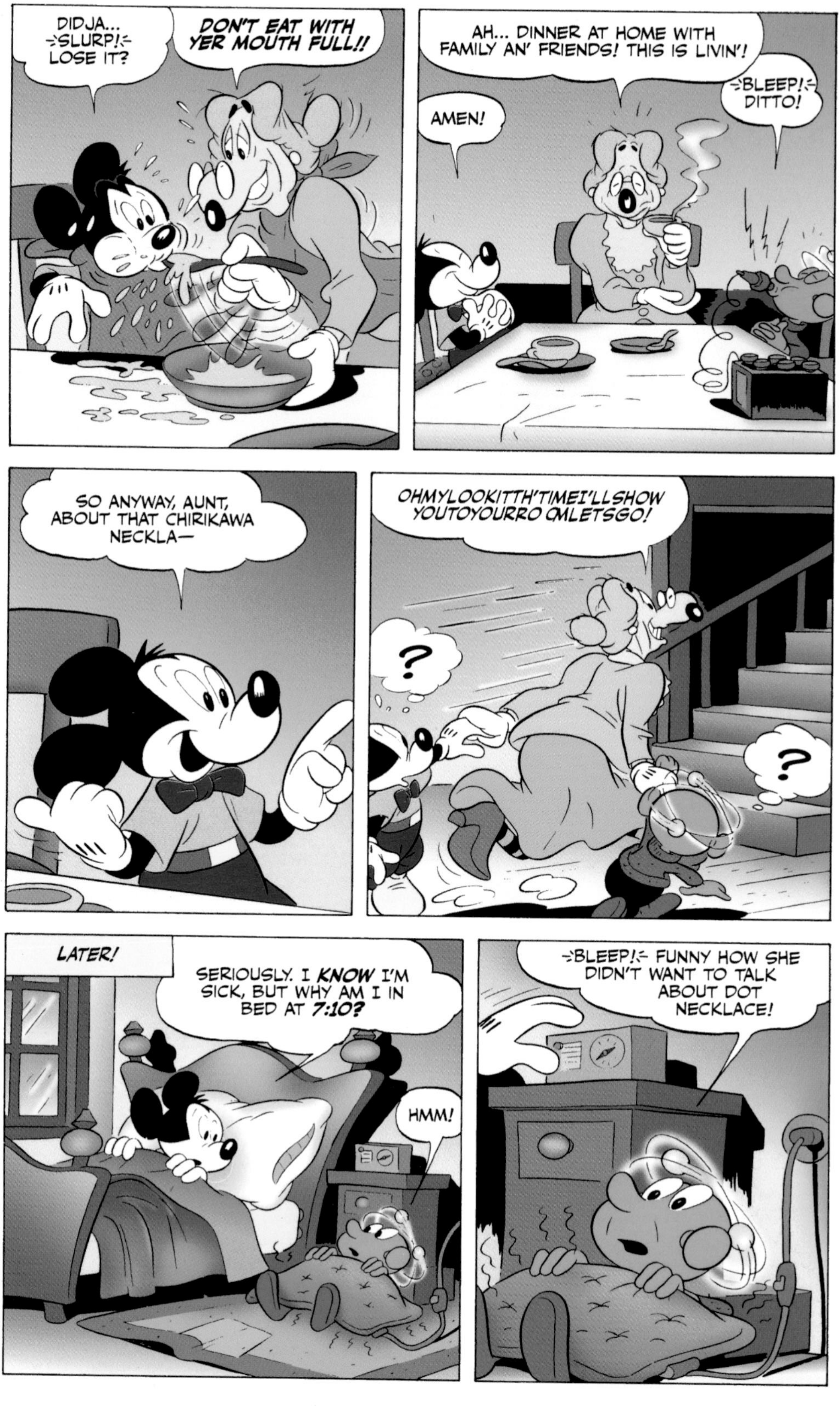
DIDJA... -SLURP!- LOSE IT?
DON'T EAT WITH YER MOUTH FULL!!
AH... DINNER AT HOME WITH FAMILY AN' FRIENDS! THIS IS LIVIN'!
AMEN!
-BLEEP!- DITTO!
SO ANYWAY, AUNT, ABOUT THAT CHIRIKAWA NECKLA—
OHMYLOOKITTH'TIMEI'LLSHOW YOUTOYOURRO OMLETSGO!
?
?
LATER!
SERIOUSLY. I KNOW I'M SICK, BUT WHY AM I IN BED AT 7:10?
HMM!
-BLEEP!- FUNNY HOW SHE DIDN'T WANT TO TALK ABOUT DOT NECKLACE!

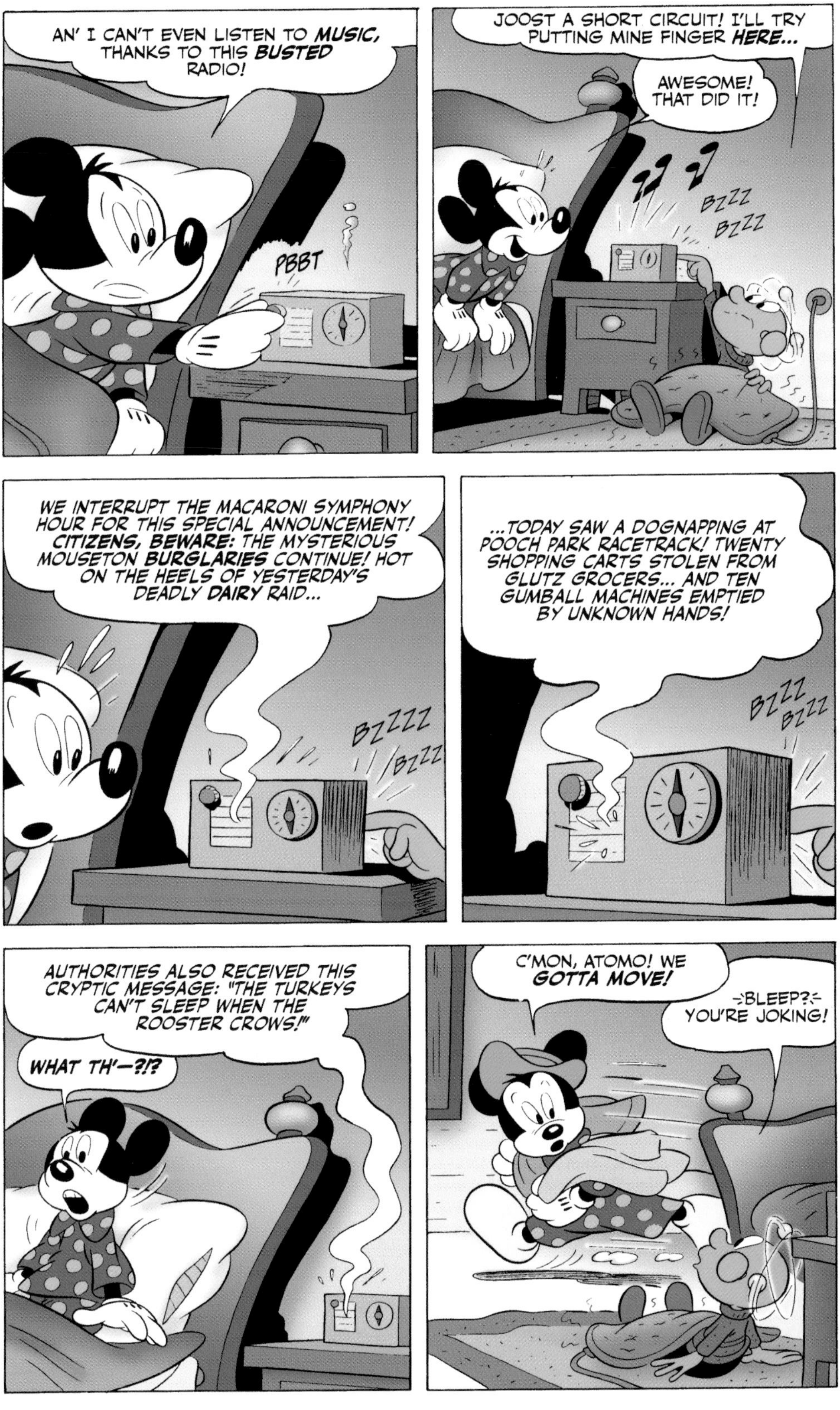
AN' I CAN'T EVEN LISTEN TO MUSIC, THANKS TO THIS BUSTED RADIO!
PBBT
JOOST A SHORT CIRCUIT! I'LL TRY PUTTING MINE FINGER HERE...
AWESOME! THAT DID IT!
BZZZ BZZZ
WE INTERRUPT THE MACARONI SYMPHONY HOUR FOR THIS SPECIAL ANNOUNCEMENT! CITIZENS, BEWARE: THE MYSTERIOUS MOUSETON BURGLARIES CONTINUE! HOT ON THE HEELS OF YESTERDAY'S DEADLY DAIRY RAID...
BZZZZ BZZZ
...TODAY SAW A DOGNAPPING AT POOCH PARK RACETRACK! TWENTY SHOPPING CARTS STOLEN FROM GLUTZ GROCERS... AND TEN GUMBALL MACHINES EMPTIED BY UNKNOWN HANDS!
BZZZ BZZZ
AUTHORITIES ALSO RECEIVED THIS CRYPTIC MESSAGE: "THE TURKEYS CAN'T SLEEP WHEN THE ROOSTER CROWS!"
WHAT TH'—?!?
C'MON, ATOMO! WE GOTTA MOVE!
BLEEP?
YOU'RE JOKING!

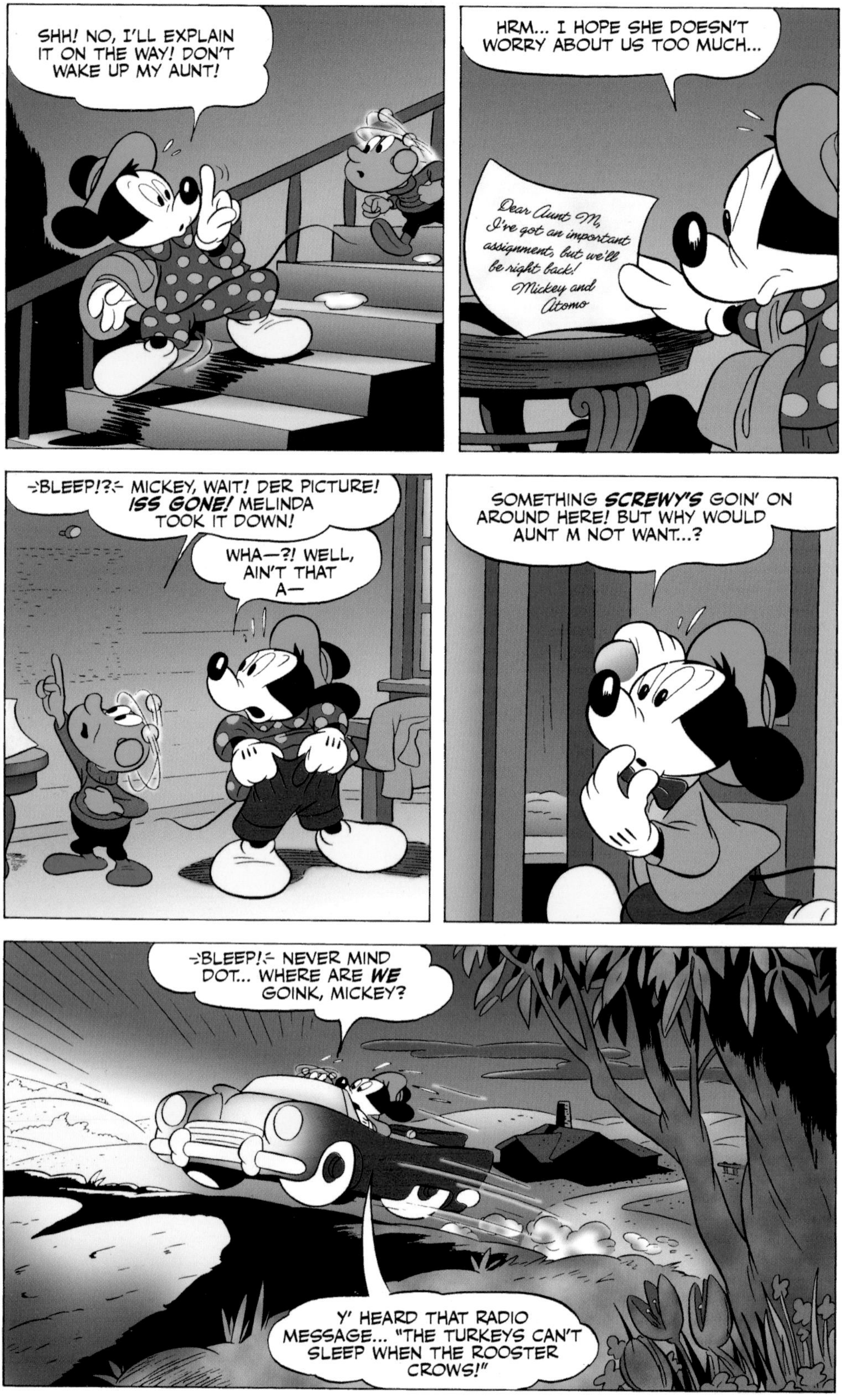
SHH! NO, I'LL EXPLAIN IT ON THE WAY! DON'T WAKE UP MY AUNT!
HRM... I HOPE SHE DOESN'T WORRY ABOUT US TOO MUCH...
Dear Aunt M, I've got an important assignment, but we'll be right back! Mickey and Atomo
⇒BLEEP!?⇐ MICKEY, WAIT! DER PICTURE! ISS GONE! MELINDA TOOK IT DOWN!
WHA—?! WELL, AIN'T THAT A—
SOMETHING SCREWY'S GOIN' ON AROUND HERE! BUT WHY WOULD AUNT M NOT WANT...?
⇒BLEEP!⇐ NEVER MIND DOT... WHERE ARE WE GOINK, MICKEY?
Y' HEARD THAT RADIO MESSAGE... "THE TURKEYS CAN'T SLEEP WHEN THE ROOSTER CROWS!"

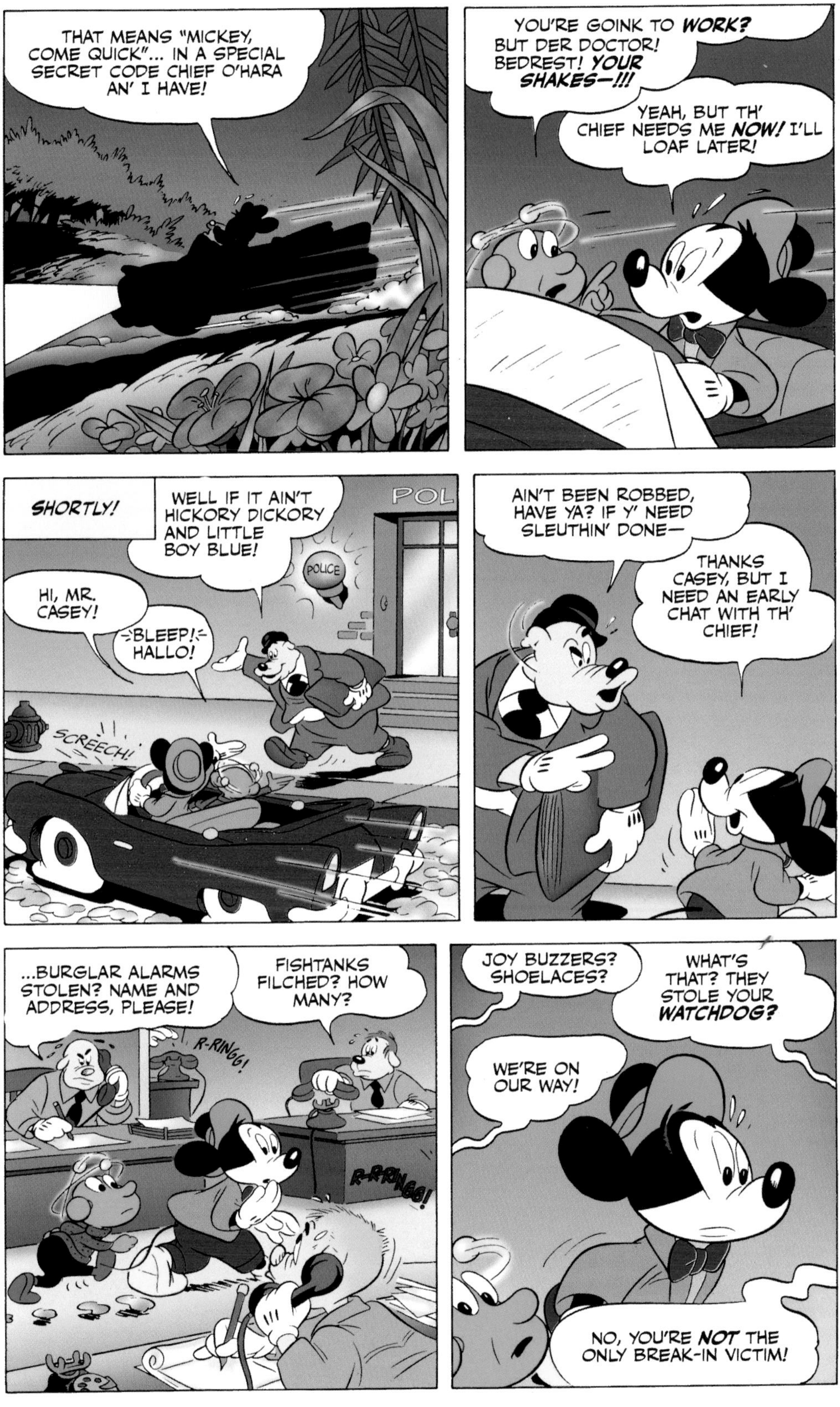
THAT MEANS "MICKEY, COME QUICK"... IN A SPECIAL SECRET CODE CHIEF O'HARA AN' I HAVE!
YOU'RE GOINK TO WORK? BUT DER DOCTOR! BEDREST! YOUR SHAKES—!!!
YEAH, BUT TH' CHIEF NEEDS ME NOW! I'LL LOAF LATER!
SHORTLY!
WELL IF IT AIN'T HICKORY DICKORY AND LITTLE BOY BLUE!
POL
POLICE
HI, MR. CASEY!
BLEEP! HALLO!
SCREECH!
AIN'T BEEN ROBBED, HAVE YA? IF Y' NEED SLEUTHIN' DONE—
THANKS CASEY, BUT I NEED AN EARLY CHAT WITH TH' CHIEF!
...BURGLAR ALARMS STOLEN? NAME AND ADDRESS, PLEASE!
FISHTANKS FILCHED? HOW MANY?
R-RINGG!
R-RRINGG!
JOY BUZZERS? SHOELACES?
WHAT'S THAT? THEY STOLE YOUR WATCHDOG?
WE'RE ON OUR WAY!
NO, YOU'RE NOT THE ONLY BREAK-IN VICTIM!

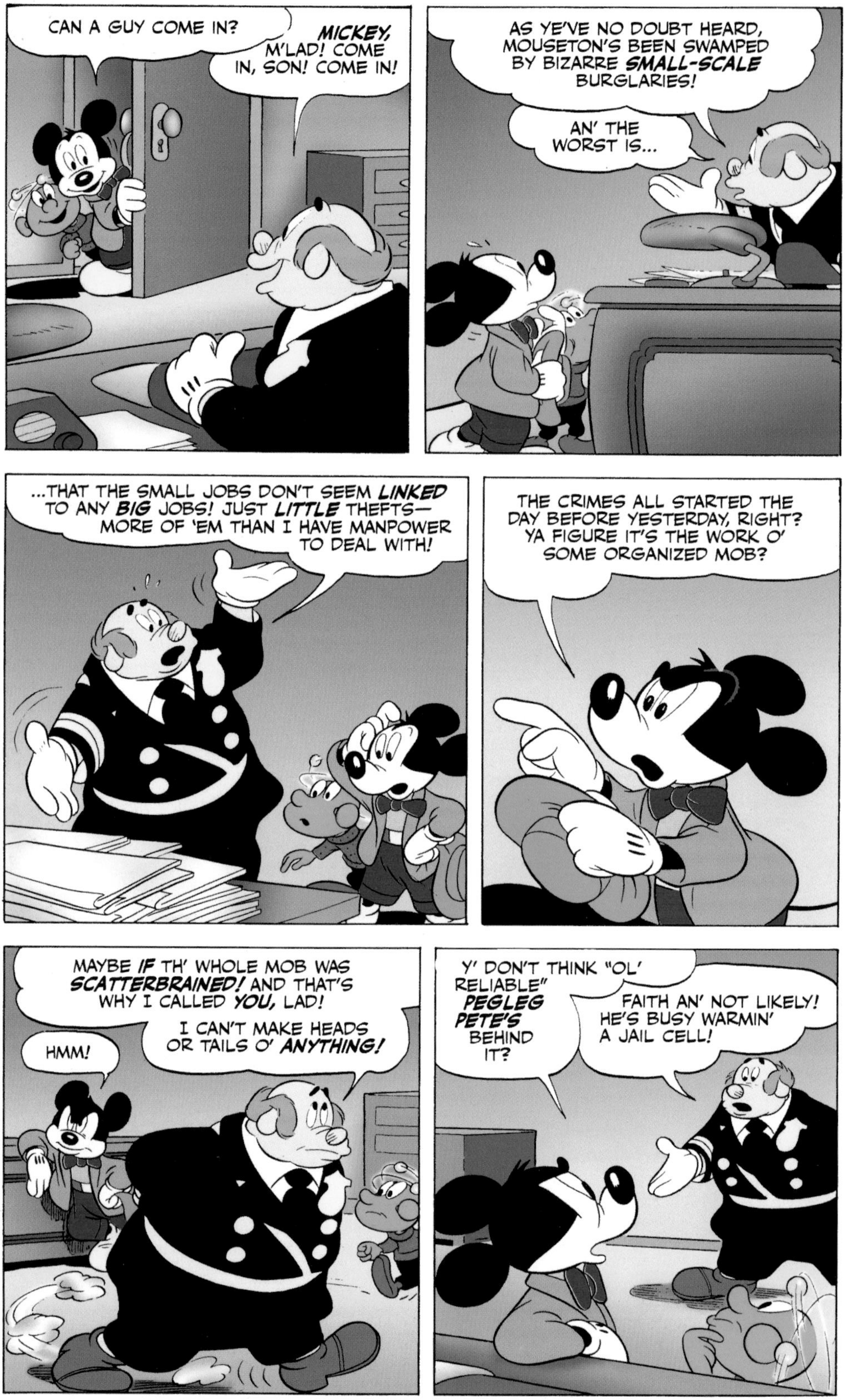
CAN A GUY COME IN?
MICKEY, M'LAD! COME IN, SON! COME IN!
AS YE'VE NO DOUBT HEARD, MOUSETON'S BEEN SWAMPED BY BIZARRE SMALL-SCALE BURGLARIES!
AN' THE WORST IS...
...THAT THE SMALL JOBS DON'T SEEM LINKED TO ANY BIG JOBS! JUST LITTLE THEFTS— MORE OF 'EM THAN I HAVE MANPOWER TO DEAL WITH!
THE CRIMES ALL STARTED THE DAY BEFORE YESTERDAY, RIGHT? YA FIGURE IT'S THE WORK O' SOME ORGANIZED MOB?
MAYBE IF TH' WHOLE MOB WAS SCATTERBRAINED! AND THAT'S WHY I CALLED YOU, LAD!
HMM!
I CAN'T MAKE HEADS OR TAILS O' ANYTHING!
Y' DON'T THINK "OL' RELIABLE" PEGLEG PETE'S BEHIND IT?
FAITH AN' NOT LIKELY! HE'S BUSY WARMIN' A JAIL CELL!

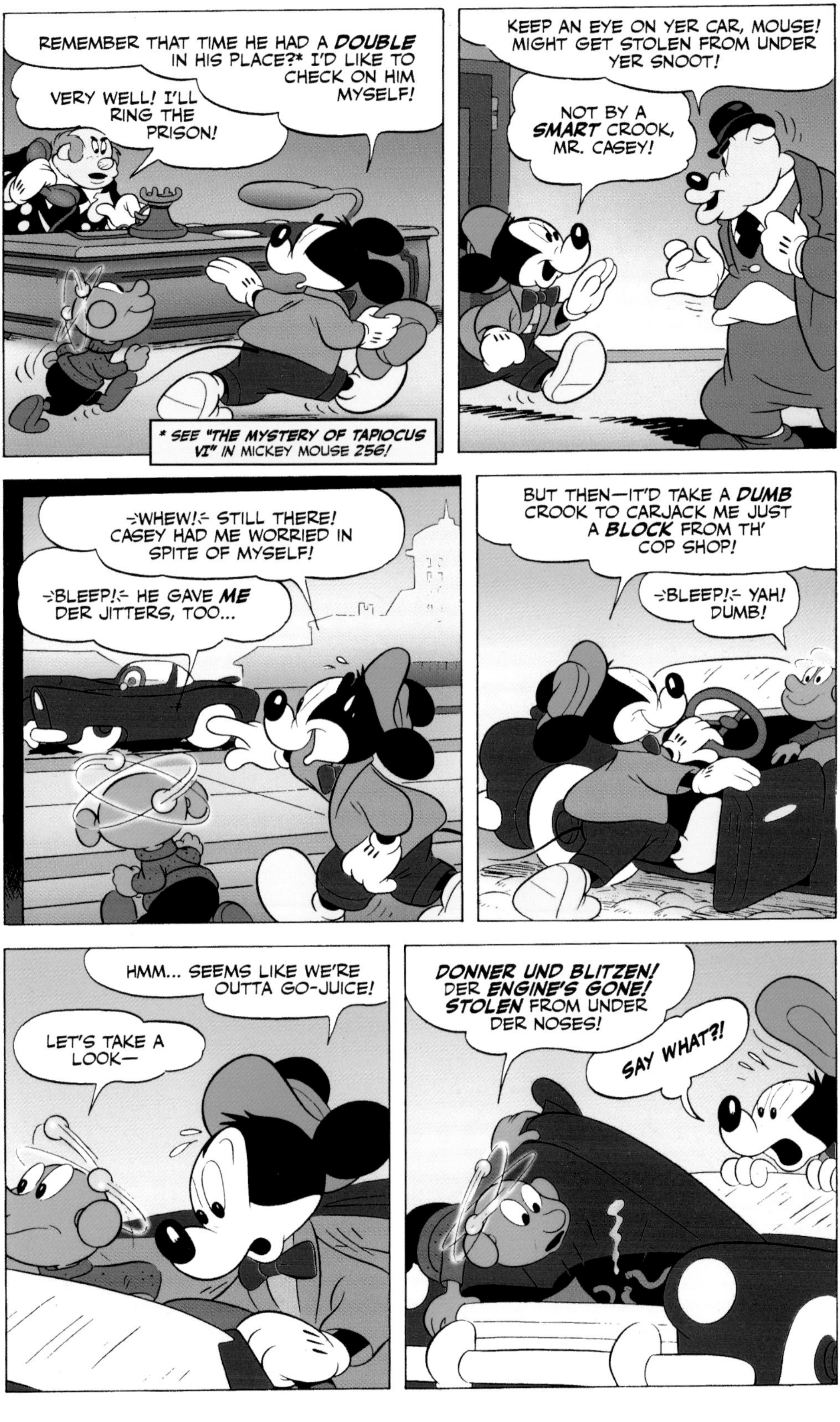
REMEMBER THAT TIME HE HAD A DOUBLE IN HIS PLACE?* I'D LIKE TO CHECK ON HIM MYSELF!
VERY WELL! I'LL RING THE PRISON!
* SEE "THE MYSTERY OF TAPIOCUS VI" IN MICKEY MOUSE 256!
KEEP AN EYE ON YER CAR, MOUSE! MIGHT GET STOLEN FROM UNDER YER SNOOT!
NOT BY A SMART CROOK, MR. CASEY!
-WHEW!- STILL THERE! CASEY HAD ME WORRIED IN SPITE OF MYSELF!
-BLEEP!- HE GAVE ME DER JITTERS, TOO...
BUT THEN—IT'D TAKE A DUMB CROOK TO CARJACK ME JUST A BLOCK FROM TH' COP SHOP!
-BLEEP!- YAH! DUMB!
HMM... SEEMS LIKE WE'RE OUTTA GO-JUICE!
LET'S TAKE A LOOK—
DONNER UND BLITZEN! DER ENGINE'S GONE! STOLEN FROM UNDER DER NOSES!
SAY WHAT?!

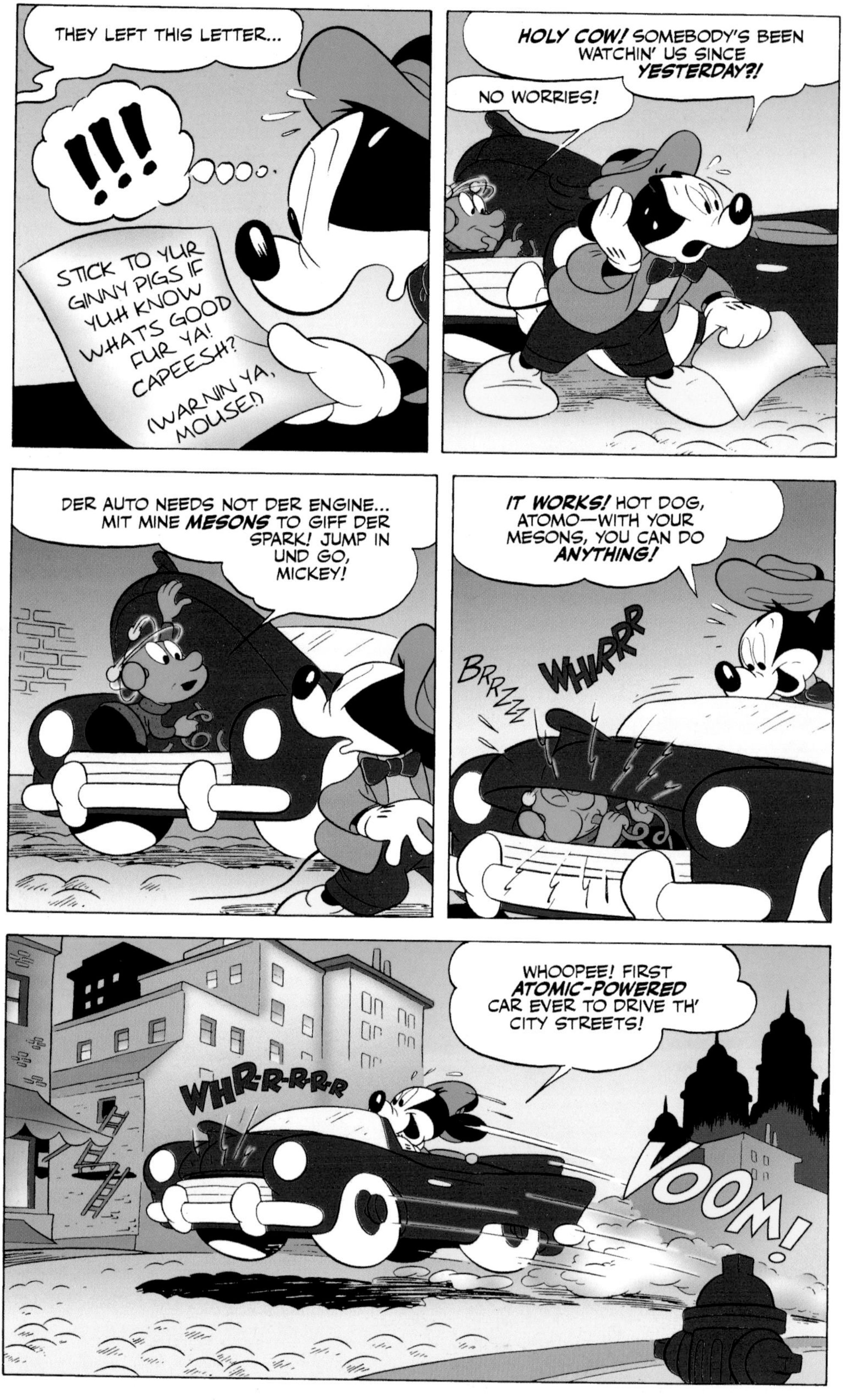

THEY LEFT THIS LETTER...
!!!
STICK TO YUR GINNY PIGS IF YUH KNOW WHAT'S GOOD FUR YA! CAPEESH? (WARNIN YA, MOUSE!)
HOLY COW! SOMEBODY'S BEEN WATCHIN' US SINCE YESTERDAY?!
NO WORRIES!
DER AUTO NEEDS NOT DER ENGINE... MIT MINE MESONS TO GIFF DER SPARK! JUMP IN UND GO, MICKEY!
IT WORKS! HOT DOG, ATOMO—WITH YOUR MESONS, YOU CAN DO ANYTHING!
BRRZZZ
WHIRRR
WHOOPEE! FIRST ATOMIC-POWERED CAR EVER TO DRIVE TH' CITY STREETS!
WHR-R-R-R-R
VOOM!

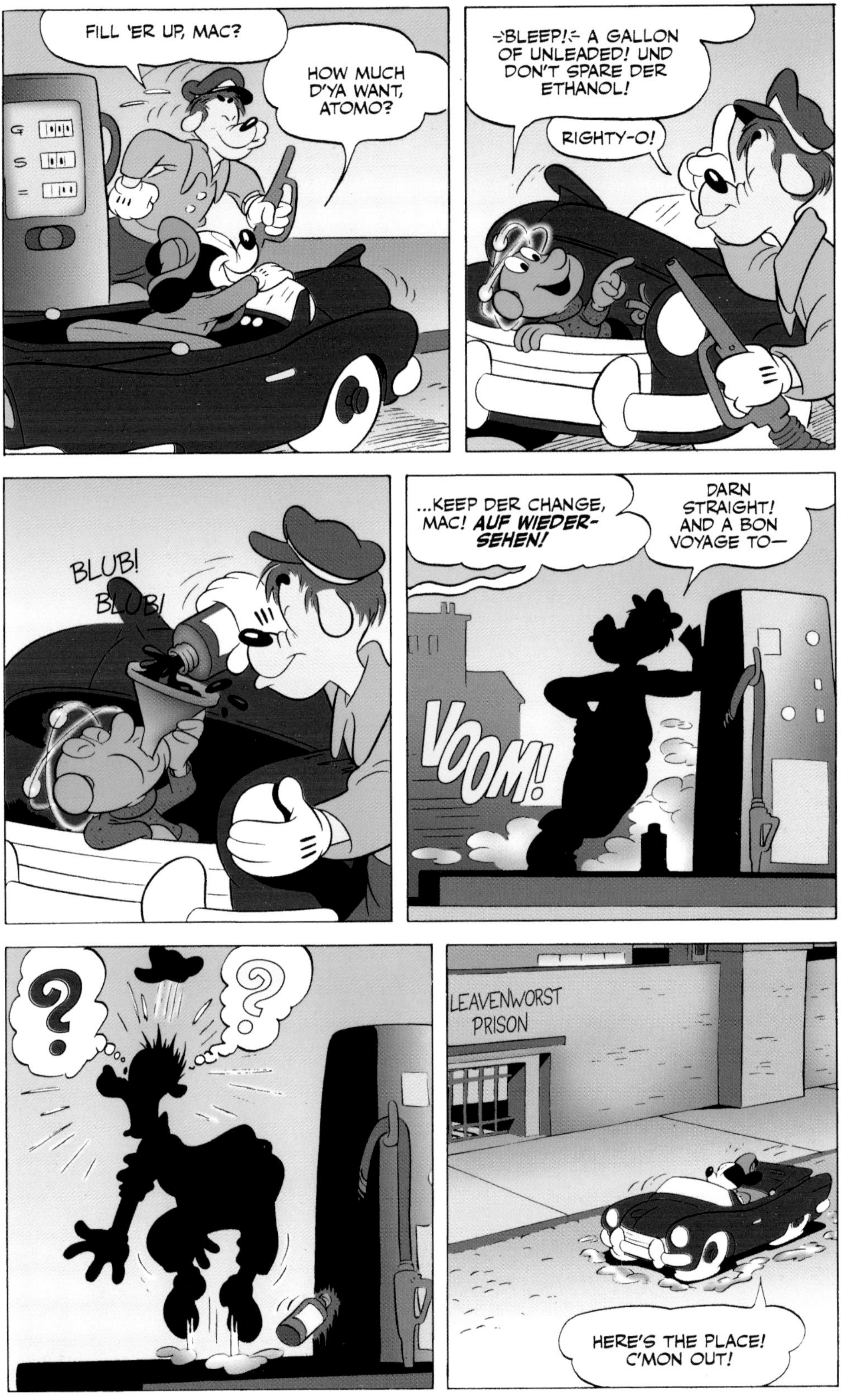
FILL 'ER UP, MAC?
HOW MUCH D'YA WANT, ATOMO?
BLEEP! A GALLON OF UNLEADED! UND DON'T SPARE DER ETHANOL!
RIGHTY-O!
BLUB! BLUB!
...KEEP DER CHANGE, MAC! AUF WIEDER-SEHEN!
DARN STRAIGHT! AND A BON VOYAGE TO—
VOOM!
?
?
LEAVENWORST PRISON
HERE'S THE PLACE! C'MON OUT!

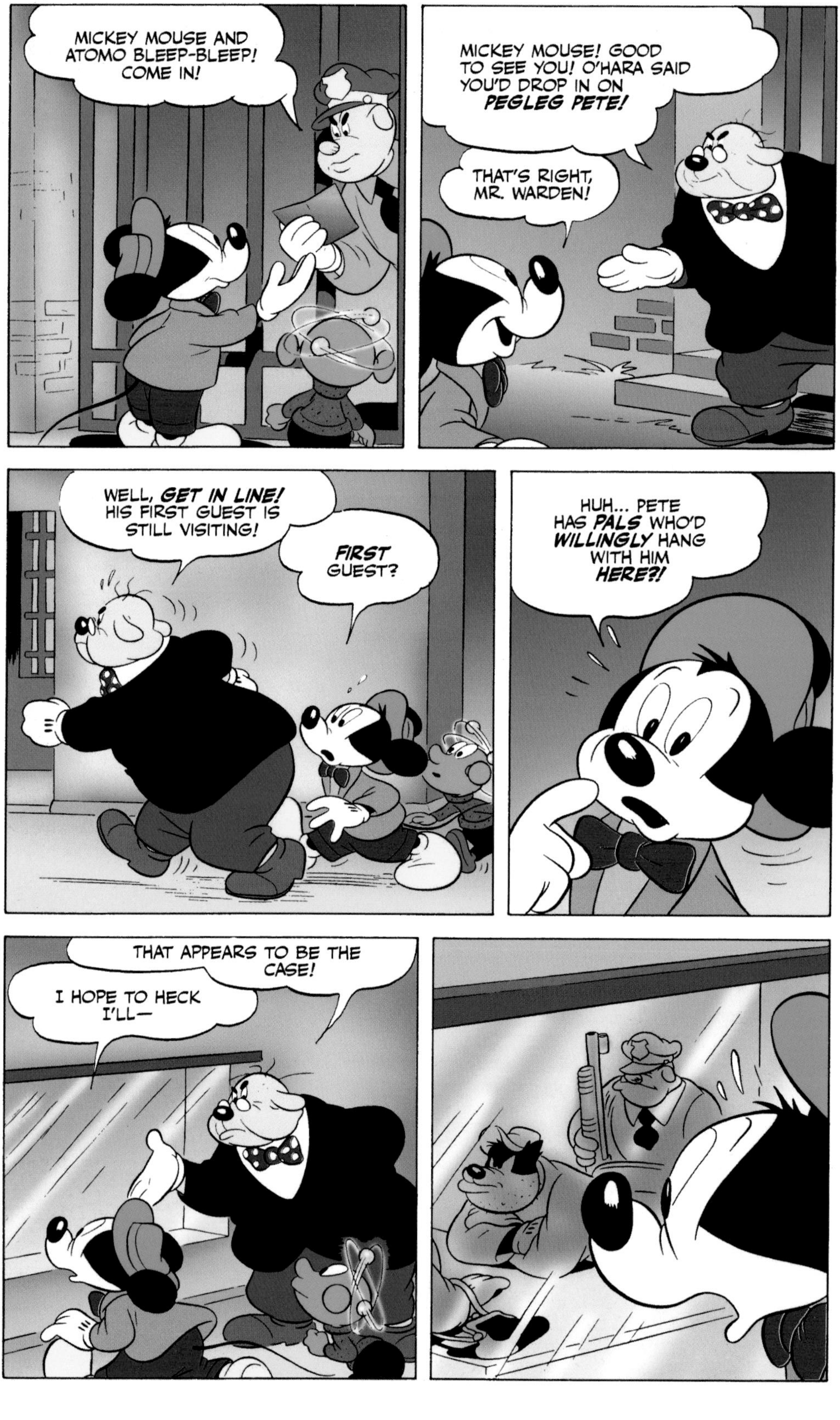
MICKEY MOUSE AND ATOMO BLEEP-BLEEP! COME IN!
MICKEY MOUSE! GOOD TO SEE YOU! O'HARA SAID YOU'D DROP IN ON PEGLEG PETE!
THAT'S RIGHT, MR. WARDEN!
WELL, GET IN LINE! HIS FIRST GUEST IS STILL VISITING!
FIRST GUEST?
HUH... PETE HAS PALS WHO'D WILLINGLY HANG WITH HIM HERE?!
THAT APPEARS TO BE THE CASE!
I HOPE TO HECK I'LL—

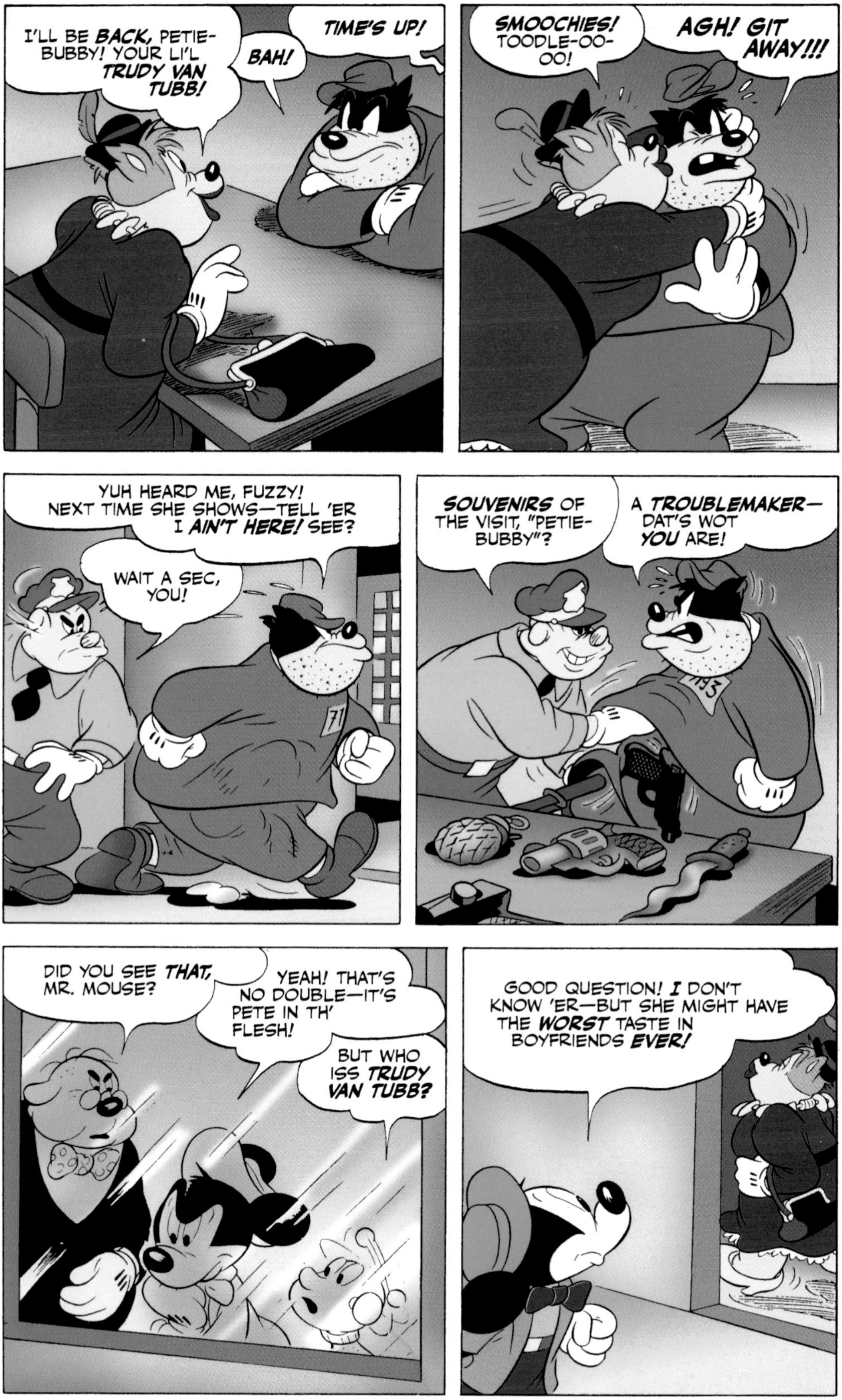
I'LL BE BACK, PETIE-BUBBY! YOUR LI'L TRUDY VAN TUBB!
BAH!
TIME'S UP!
SMOOCHIES! TOODLE-OO-OO!
AGH! GIT AWAY!!!
YUH HEARD ME, FUZZY! NEXT TIME SHE SHOWS—TELL 'ER I AIN'T HERE! SEE?
WAIT A SEC, YOU!
SOUVENIRS OF THE VISIT, "PETIE-BUBBY"?
A TROUBLEMAKER—DAT'S WOT YOU ARE!
DID YOU SEE THAT, MR. MOUSE?
YEAH! THAT'S NO DOUBLE—IT'S PETE IN TH' FLESH!
BUT WHO ISS TRUDY VAN TUBB?
GOOD QUESTION! I DON'T KNOW 'ER—BUT SHE MIGHT HAVE THE WORST TASTE IN BOYFRIENDS EVER!

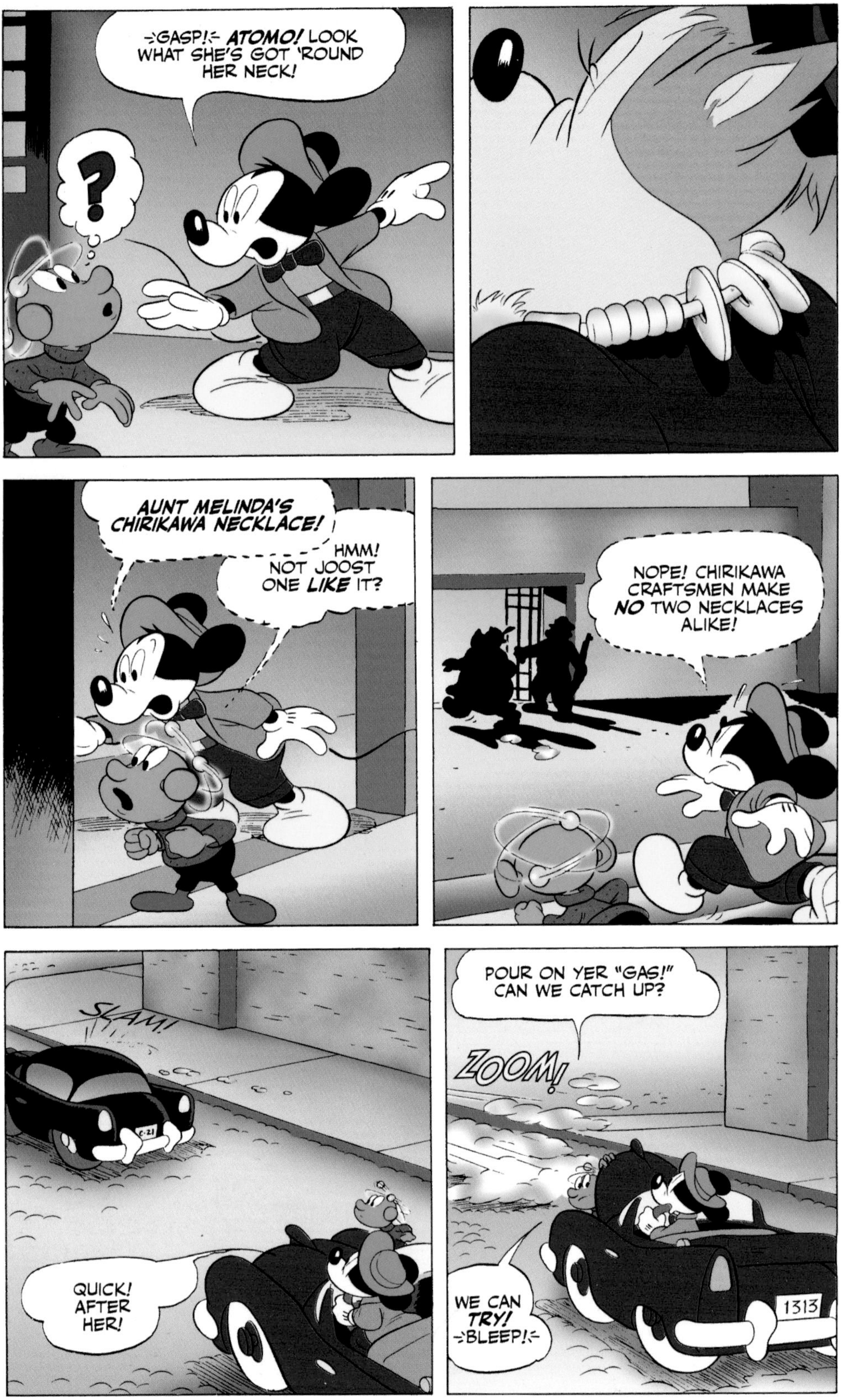

-GASP!- ATOMO! LOOK WHAT SHE'S GOT 'ROUND HER NECK!
?
AUNT MELINDA'S CHIRIKAWA NECKLACE!
HMM! NOT JOOST ONE LIKE IT?
NOPE! CHIRIKAWA CRAFTSMEN MAKE NO TWO NECKLACES ALIKE!
SLAM!
QUICK! AFTER HER!
POUR ON YER "GAS!" CAN WE CATCH UP?
ZOOM!
WE CAN TRY! -BLEEP!-
1313

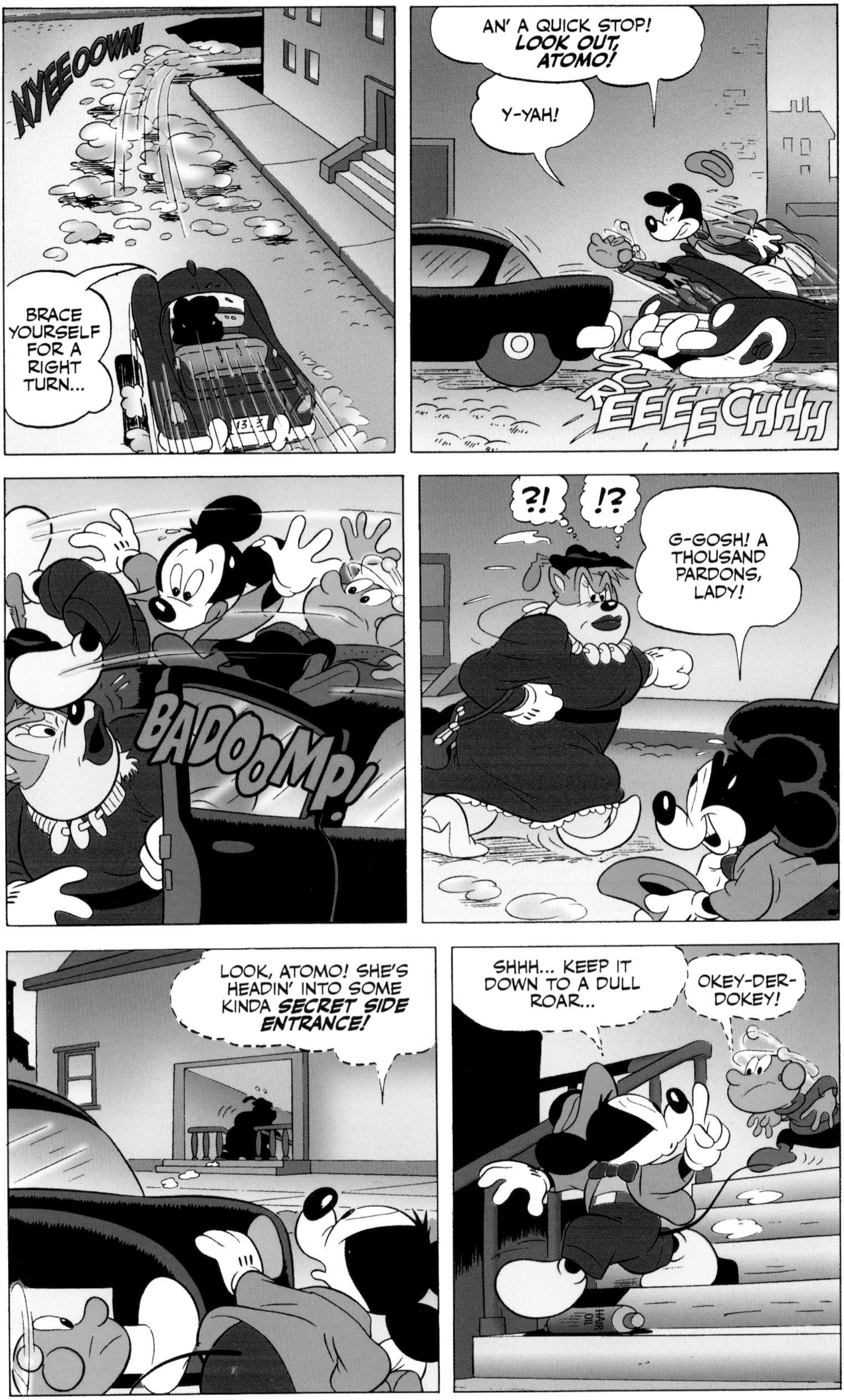
NYEEOOWN!
BRACE YOURSELF FOR A RIGHT TURN...
13 3
AN' A QUICK STOP! LOOK OUT, ATOMO!
Y-YAH!
SCREEEECHHH
BADOOOMP!
?!
!?
G-GOSH! A THOUSAND PARDONS, LADY!
LOOK, ATOMO! SHE'S HEADIN' INTO SOME KINDA SECRET SIDE ENTRANCE!
SHHH... KEEP IT DOWN TO A DULL ROAR...
OKEY-DER-DOKEY!
HAIR OIL

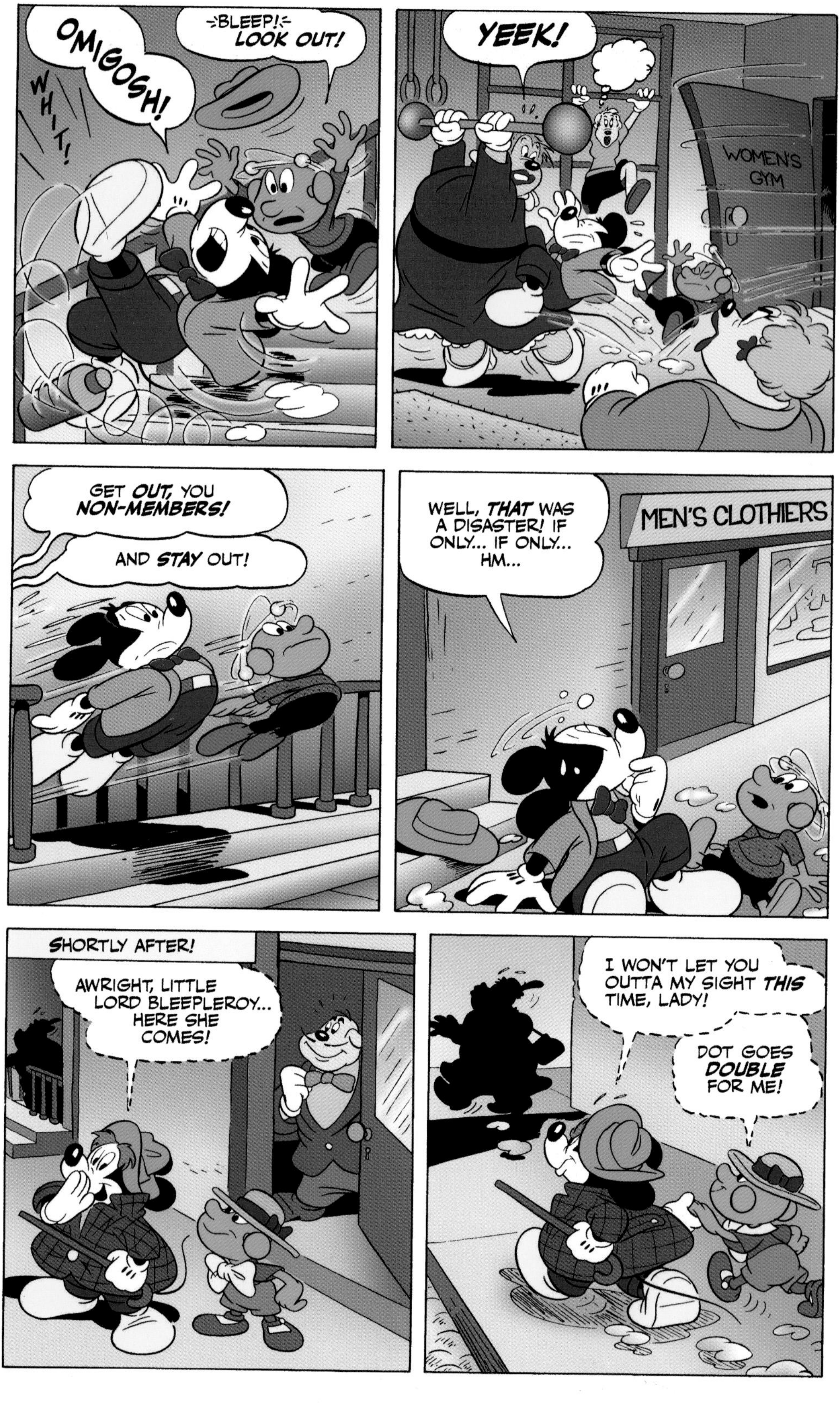
OMIGOSH!
WHIT!
=BLEEP!= LOOK OUT!
YEEK!
WOMEN'S GYM
GET OUT, YOU NON-MEMBERS!
AND STAY OUT!
WELL, THAT WAS A DISASTER! IF ONLY... IF ONLY... HM...
MEN'S CLOTHIERS
SHORTLY AFTER!
AWRIGHT, LITTLE LORD BLEEPLEROY... HERE SHE COMES!
I WON'T LET YOU OUTTA MY SIGHT THIS TIME, LADY!
DOT GOES DOUBLE FOR ME!

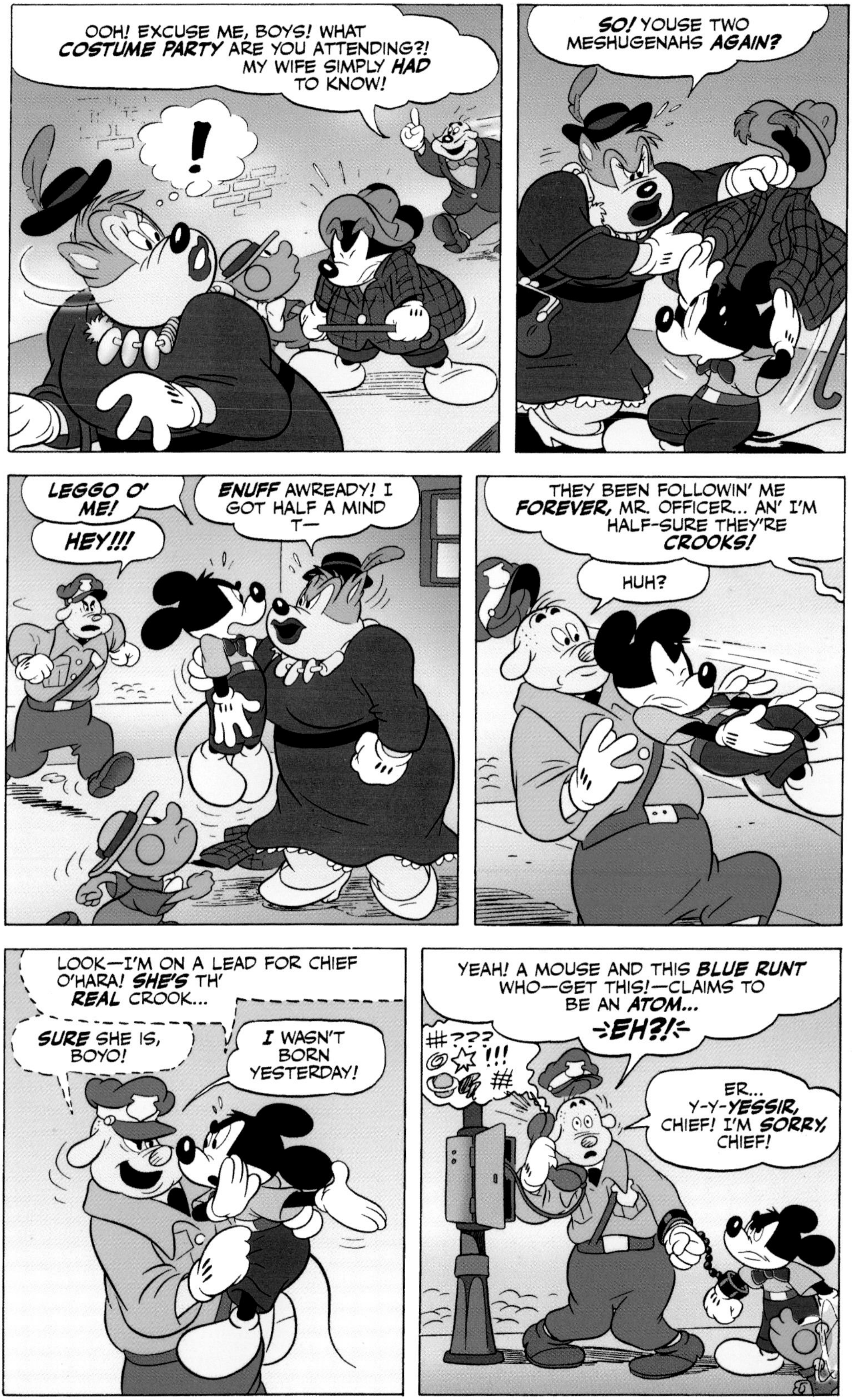
OOH! EXCUSE ME, BOYS! WHAT COSTUME PARTY ARE YOU ATTENDING?! MY WIFE SIMPLY HAD TO KNOW!
!
SO! YOUSE TWO MESHUGENAHS AGAIN?
LEGGO O' ME!
HEY!!!
ENUFF AWREADY! I GOT HALF A MIND T—
THEY BEEN FOLLOWIN' ME FOREVER, MR. OFFICER... AN' I'M HALF-SURE THEY'RE CROOKS!
HUH?
LOOK—I'M ON A LEAD FOR CHIEF O'HARA! SHE'S TH' REAL CROOK...
SURE SHE IS, BOYO!
I WASN'T BORN YESTERDAY!
YEAH! A MOUSE AND THIS BLUE RUNT WHO—GET THIS!—CLAIMS TO BE AN ATOM...
EH?!
#???
!!!
#
ER... Y-Y-YESSIR, CHIEF! I'M SORRY, CHIEF!

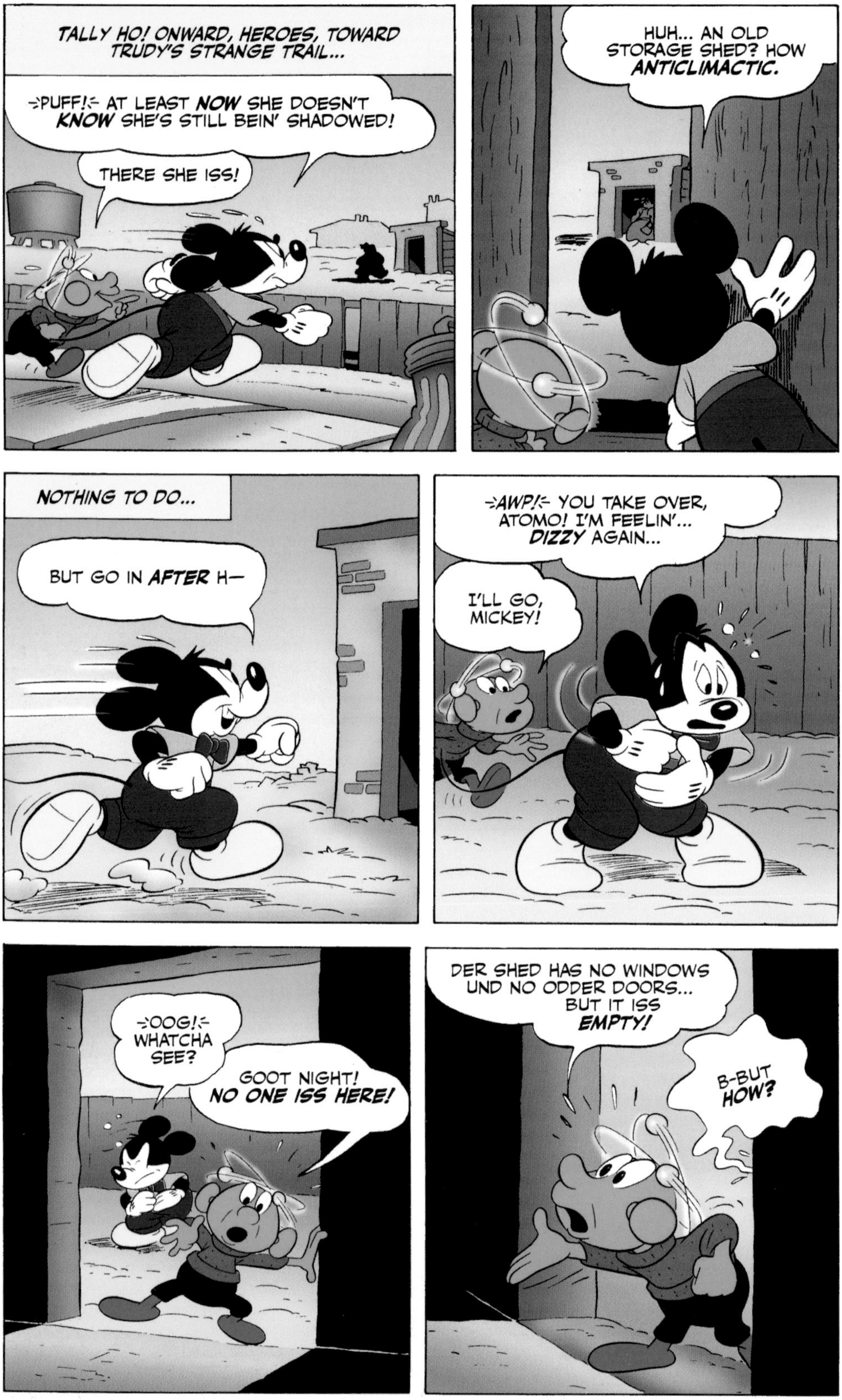
TALLY HO! ONWARD, HEROES, TOWARD TRUDY'S STRANGE TRAIL...
⇒PUFF!⇐ AT LEAST NOW SHE DOESN'T KNOW SHE'S STILL BEIN' SHADOWED!
THERE SHE ISS!
HUH... AN OLD STORAGE SHED? HOW ANTICLIMACTIC.
NOTHING TO DO...
BUT GO IN AFTER H—
⇒AWP!⇐ YOU TAKE OVER, ATOMO! I'M FEELIN'... DIZZY AGAIN...
I'LL GO, MICKEY!
⇒OOG!⇐ WHATCHA SEE?
GOOT NIGHT! NO ONE ISS HERE!
DER SHED HAS NO WINDOWS UND NO ODDER DOORS... BUT IT ISS EMPTY!
B-BUT HOW?

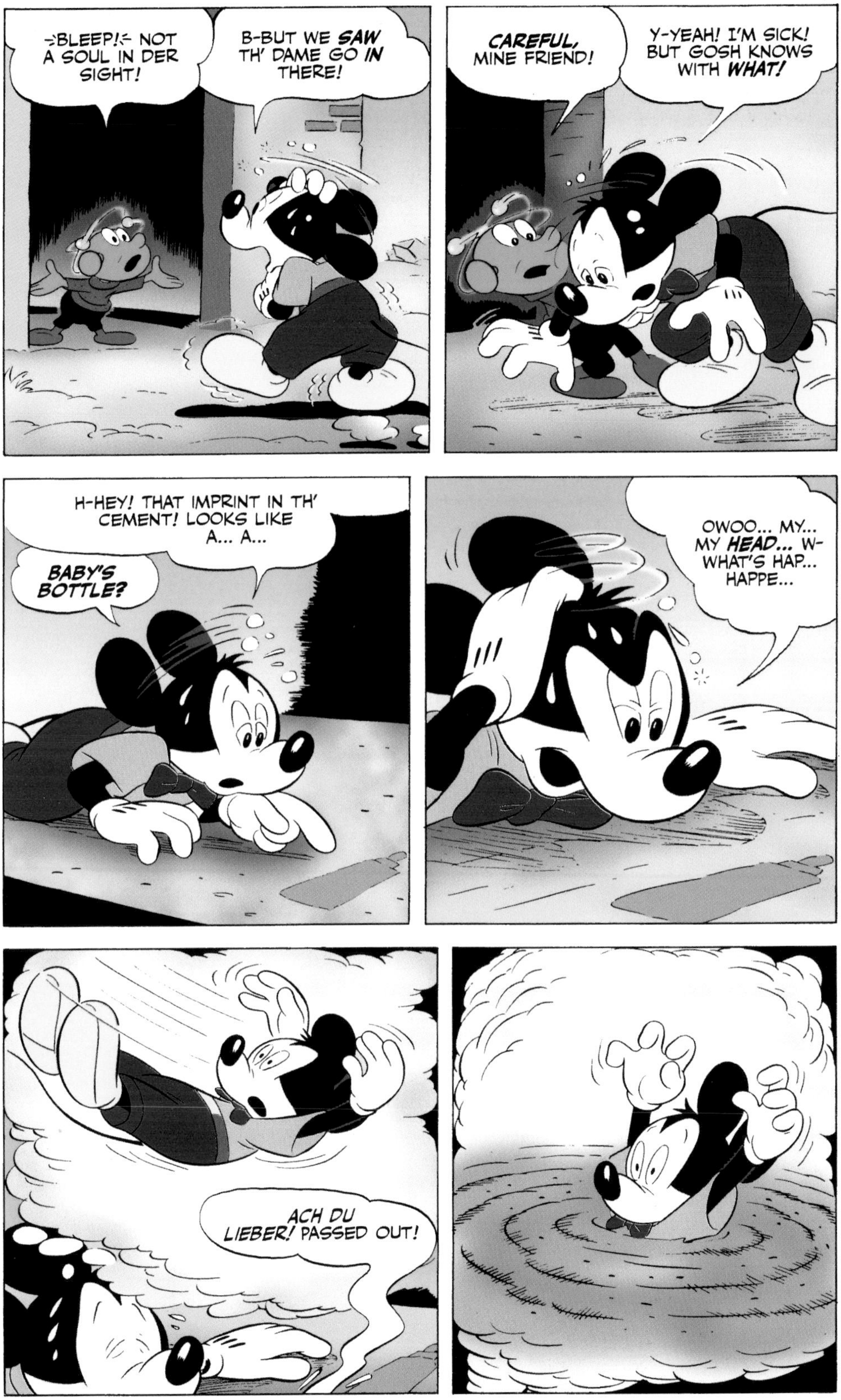
-BLEEP!- NOT A SOUL IN DER SIGHT!
B-BUT WE **SAW** TH' DAME GO **IN** THERE!
CAREFUL, MINE FRIEND!
Y-YEAH! I'M SICK! BUT GOSH KNOWS WITH **WHAT!**
H-HEY! THAT IMPRINT IN TH' CEMENT! LOOKS LIKE A... A...
BABY'S BOTTLE?
OWOO... MY... MY **HEAD...** W-WHAT'S HAP... HAPPE...
ACH DU LIEBER! PASSED OUT!

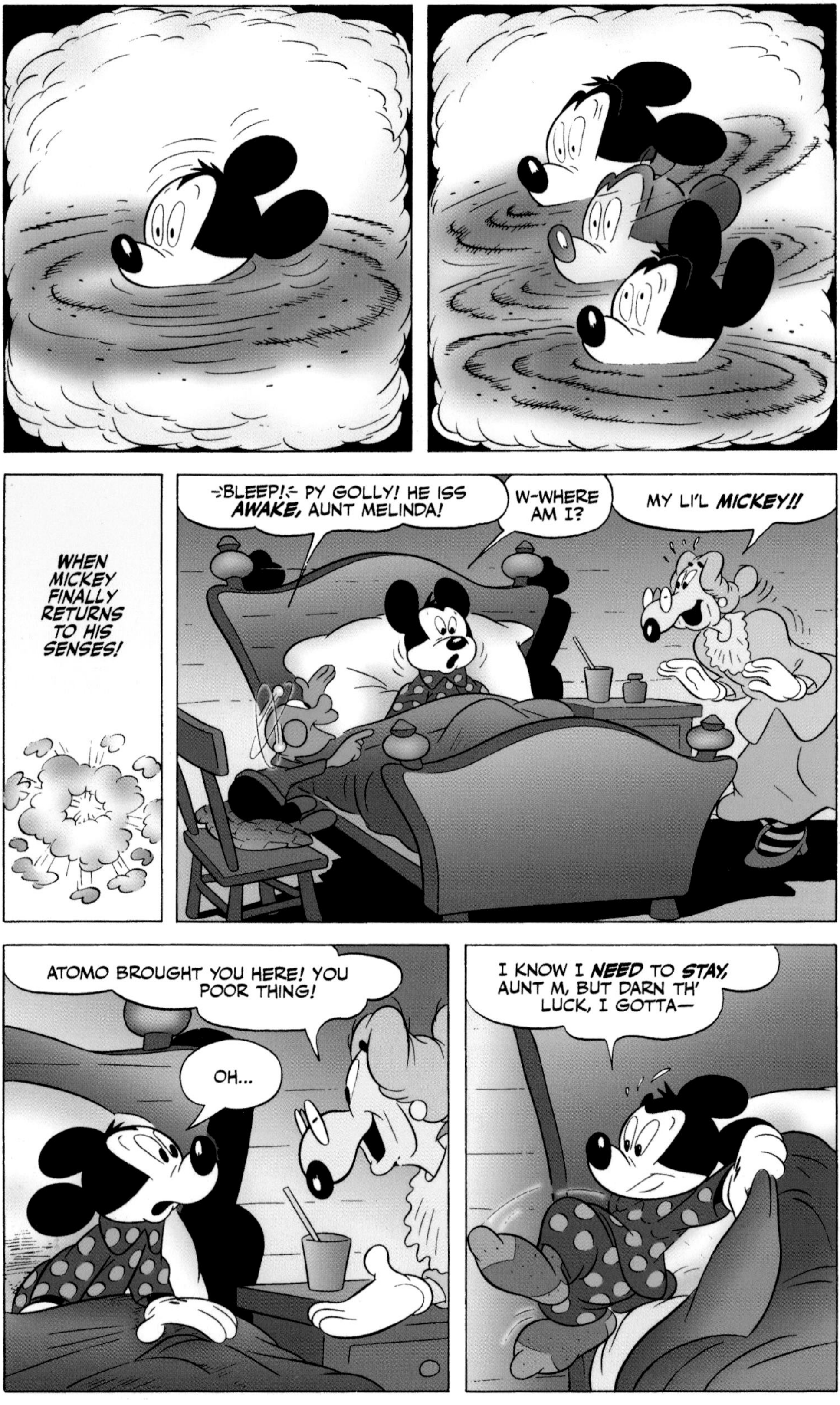
WHEN MICKEY FINALLY RETURNS TO HIS SENSES!
-BLEEP!- PY GOLLY! HE ISS AWAKE, AUNT MELINDA!
W-WHERE AM I?
MY LI'L MICKEY!!
ATOMO BROUGHT YOU HERE! YOU POOR THING!
OH...
I KNOW I NEED TO STAY, AUNT M, BUT DARN TH' LUCK, I GOTTA—

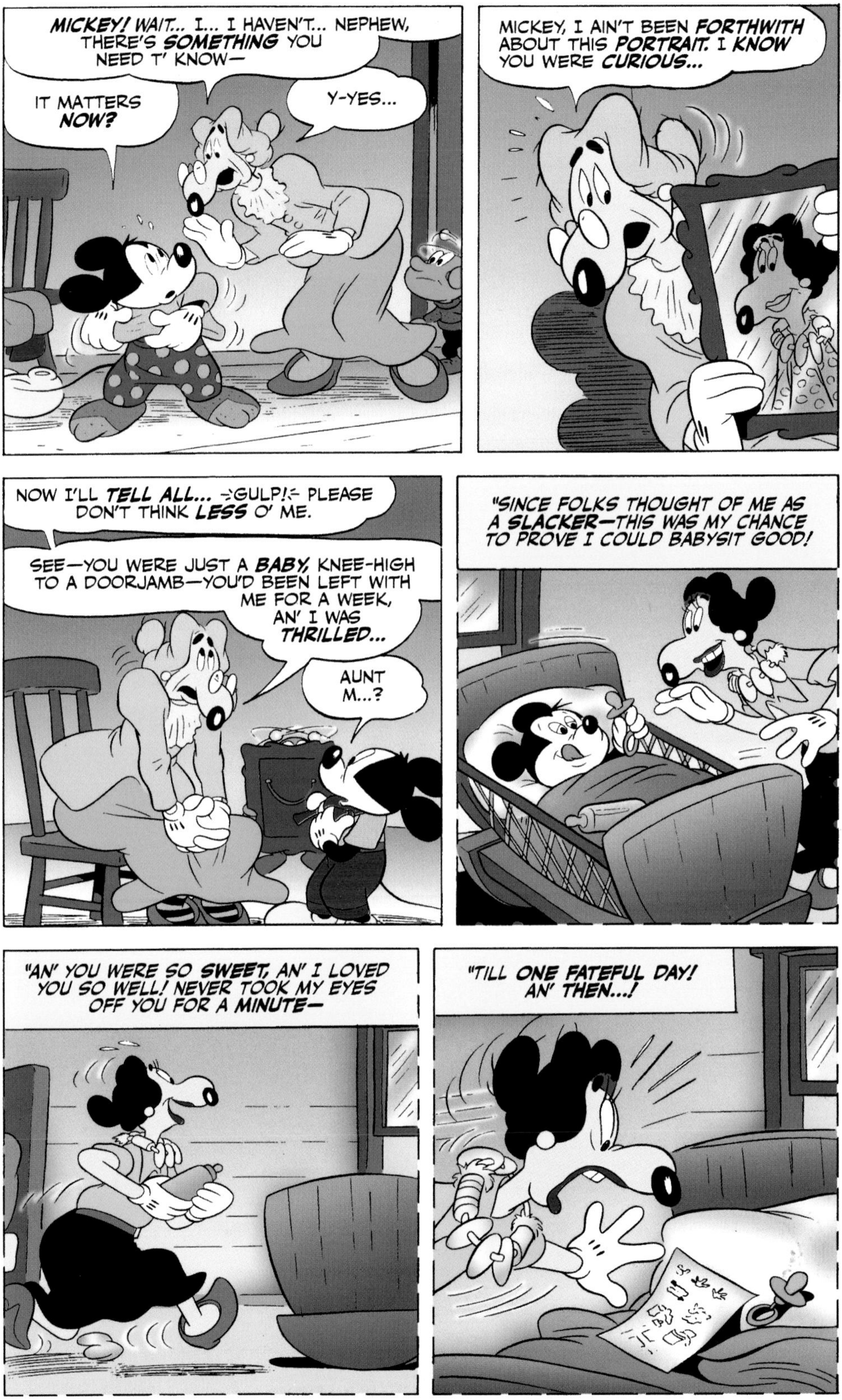
MICKEY! WAIT... I... I HAVEN'T... NEPHEW, THERE'S SOMETHING YOU NEED T' KNOW—
IT MATTERS NOW?
Y-YES...
MICKEY, I AIN'T BEEN FORTHWITH ABOUT THIS PORTRAIT. I KNOW YOU WERE CURIOUS...
NOW I'LL TELL ALL... ⇒GULP!⇐ PLEASE DON'T THINK LESS O' ME.
SEE—YOU WERE JUST A BABY, KNEE-HIGH TO A DOORJAMB—YOU'D BEEN LEFT WITH ME FOR A WEEK, AN' I WAS THRILLED...
AUNT M...?
"SINCE FOLKS THOUGHT OF ME AS A SLACKER—THIS WAS MY CHANCE TO PROVE I COULD BABYSIT GOOD!
"AN' YOU WERE SO SWEET, AN' I LOVED YOU SO WELL! NEVER TOOK MY EYES OFF YOU FOR A MINUTE—
"TILL ONE FATEFUL DAY! AN' THEN...!

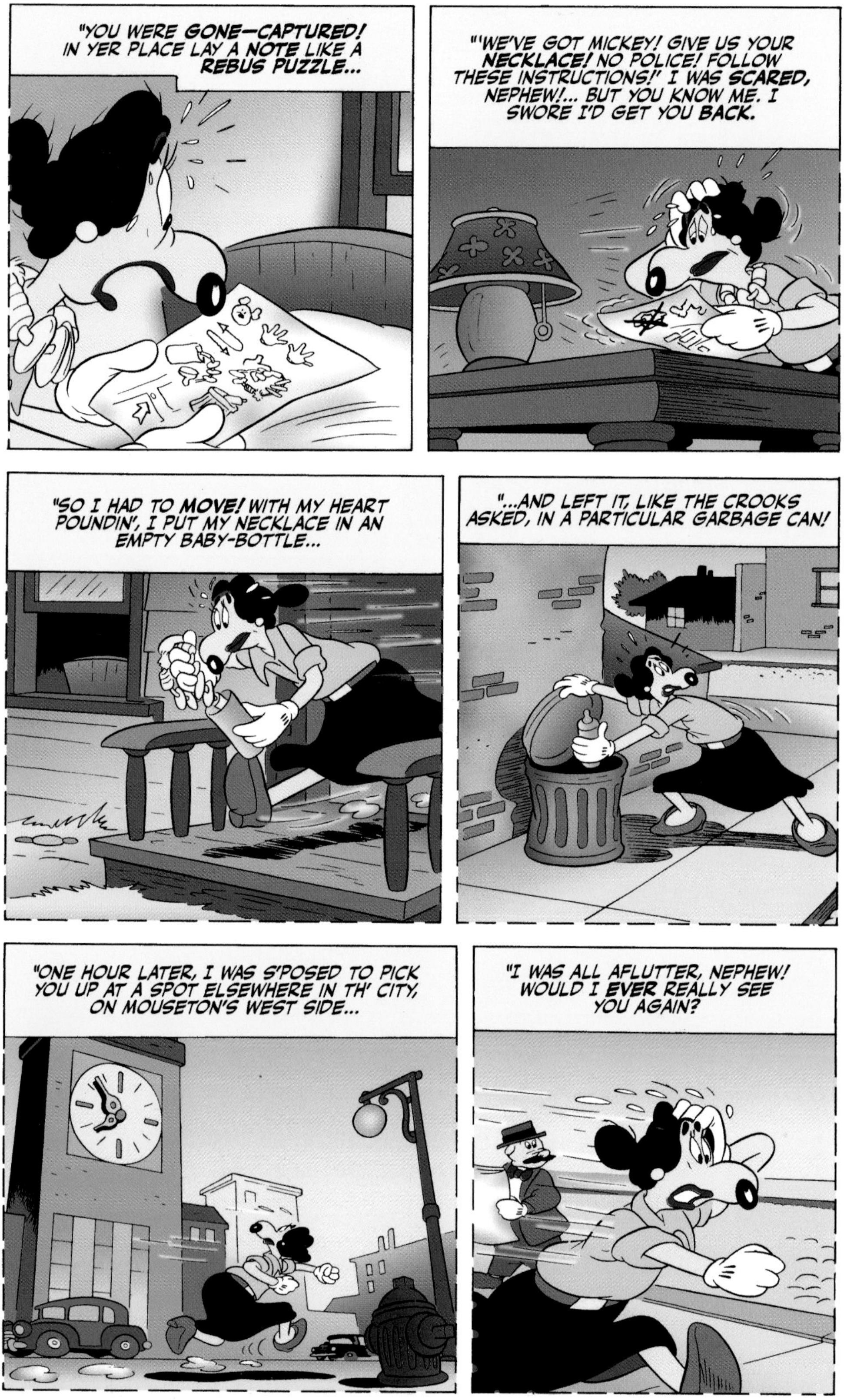
"YOU WERE GONE—CAPTURED! IN YER PLACE LAY A NOTE LIKE A REBUS PUZZLE...
"'WE'VE GOT MICKEY! GIVE US YOUR NECKLACE! NO POLICE! FOLLOW THESE INSTRUCTIONS!' I WAS SCARED, NEPHEW!... BUT YOU KNOW ME. I SWORE I'D GET YOU BACK.
"SO I HAD TO MOVE! WITH MY HEART POUNDIN', I PUT MY NECKLACE IN AN EMPTY BABY-BOTTLE...
"...AND LEFT IT, LIKE THE CROOKS ASKED, IN A PARTICULAR GARBAGE CAN!
"ONE HOUR LATER, I WAS S'POSED TO PICK YOU UP AT A SPOT ELSEWHERE IN TH' CITY, ON MOUSETON'S WEST SIDE...
"I WAS ALL AFLUTTER, NEPHEW! WOULD I EVER REALLY SEE YOU AGAIN?

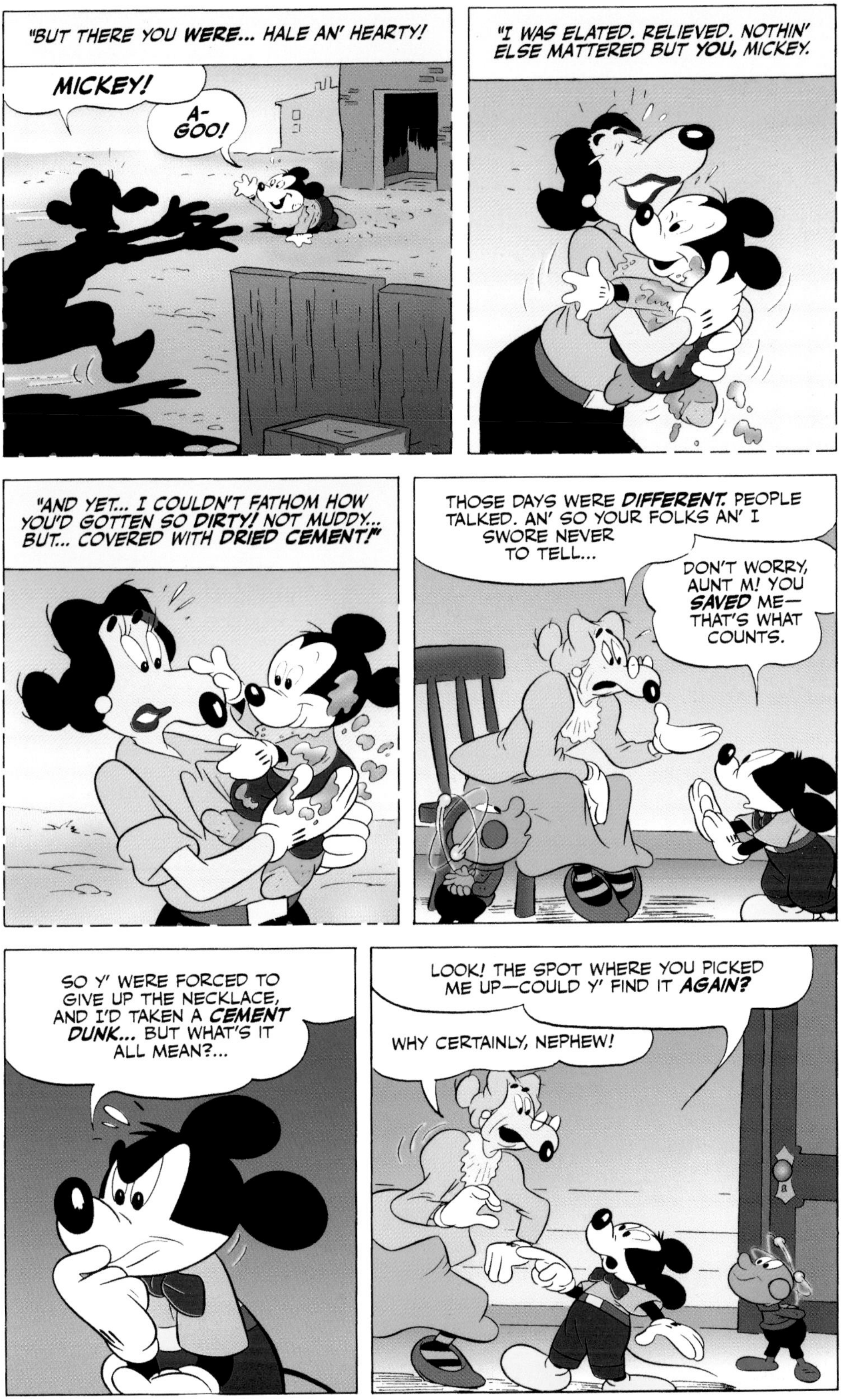
"BUT THERE YOU WERE... HALE AN' HEARTY!
MICKEY!
A-GOO!
"I WAS ELATED. RELIEVED. NOTHIN' ELSE MATTERED BUT YOU, MICKEY.
"AND YET... I COULDN'T FATHOM HOW YOU'D GOTTEN SO DIRTY! NOT MUDDY... BUT... COVERED WITH DRIED CEMENT!"
THOSE DAYS WERE DIFFERENT. PEOPLE TALKED. AN' SO YOUR FOLKS AN' I SWORE NEVER TO TELL...
DON'T WORRY, AUNT M! YOU SAVED ME—THAT'S WHAT COUNTS.
SO Y' WERE FORCED TO GIVE UP THE NECKLACE, AND I'D TAKEN A CEMENT DUNK... BUT WHAT'S IT ALL MEAN?...
LOOK! THE SPOT WHERE YOU PICKED ME UP—COULD Y' FIND IT AGAIN?
WHY CERTAINLY, NEPHEW!

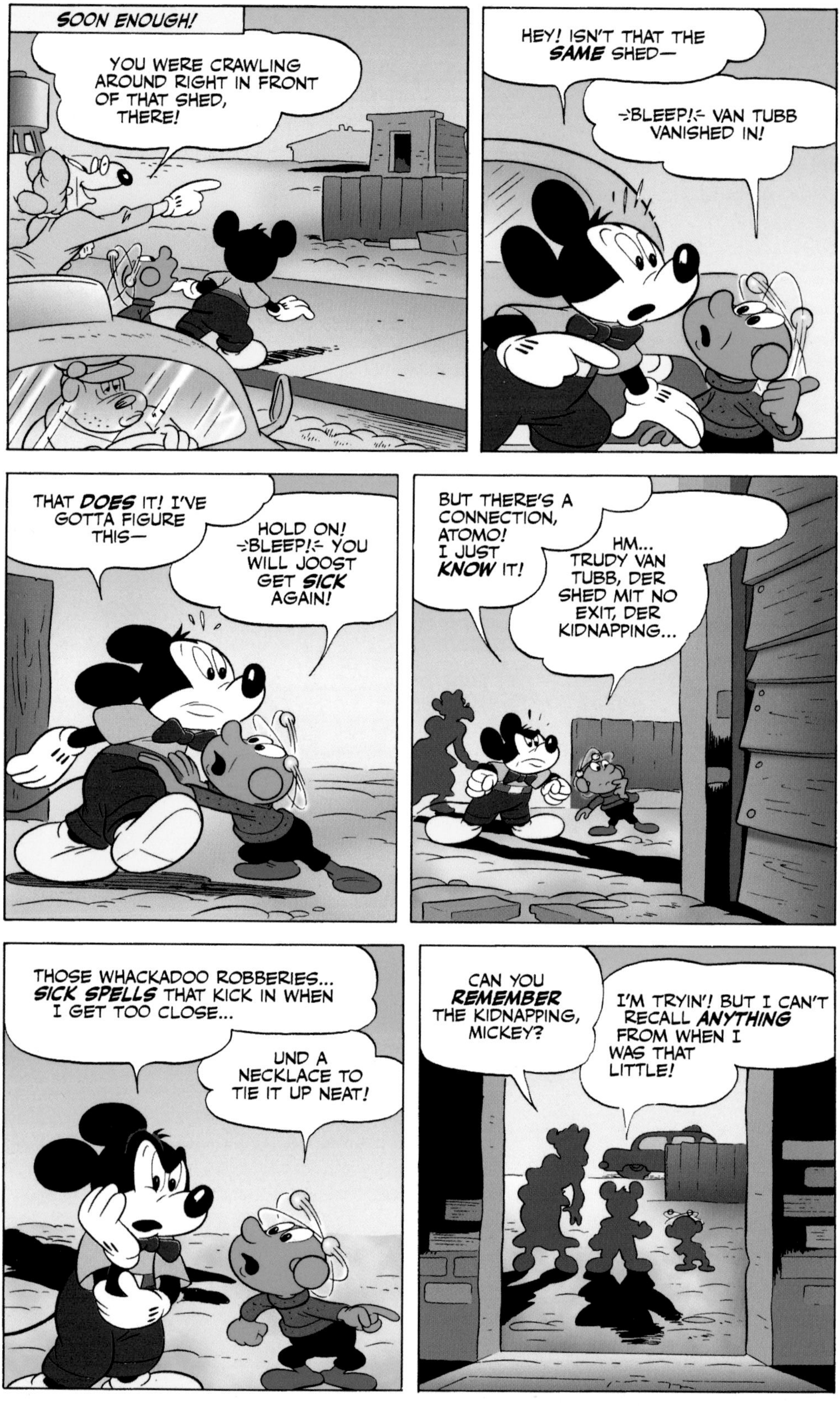
SOON ENOUGH!
YOU WERE CRAWLING AROUND RIGHT IN FRONT OF THAT SHED, THERE!
HEY! ISN'T THAT THE SAME SHED—
⊰BLEEP!⊱ VAN TUBB VANISHED IN!
THAT DOES IT! I'VE GOTTA FIGURE THIS—
HOLD ON! ⊰BLEEP!⊱ YOU WILL JOOST GET SICK AGAIN!
BUT THERE'S A CONNECTION, ATOMO! I JUST KNOW IT!
HM... TRUDY VAN TUBB, DER SHED MIT NO EXIT, DER KIDNAPPING...
THOSE WHACKADOO ROBBERIES... SICK SPELLS THAT KICK IN WHEN I GET TOO CLOSE...
UND A NECKLACE TO TIE IT UP NEAT!
CAN YOU REMEMBER THE KIDNAPPING, MICKEY?
I'M TRYIN'! BUT I CAN'T RECALL ANYTHING FROM WHEN I WAS THAT LITTLE!

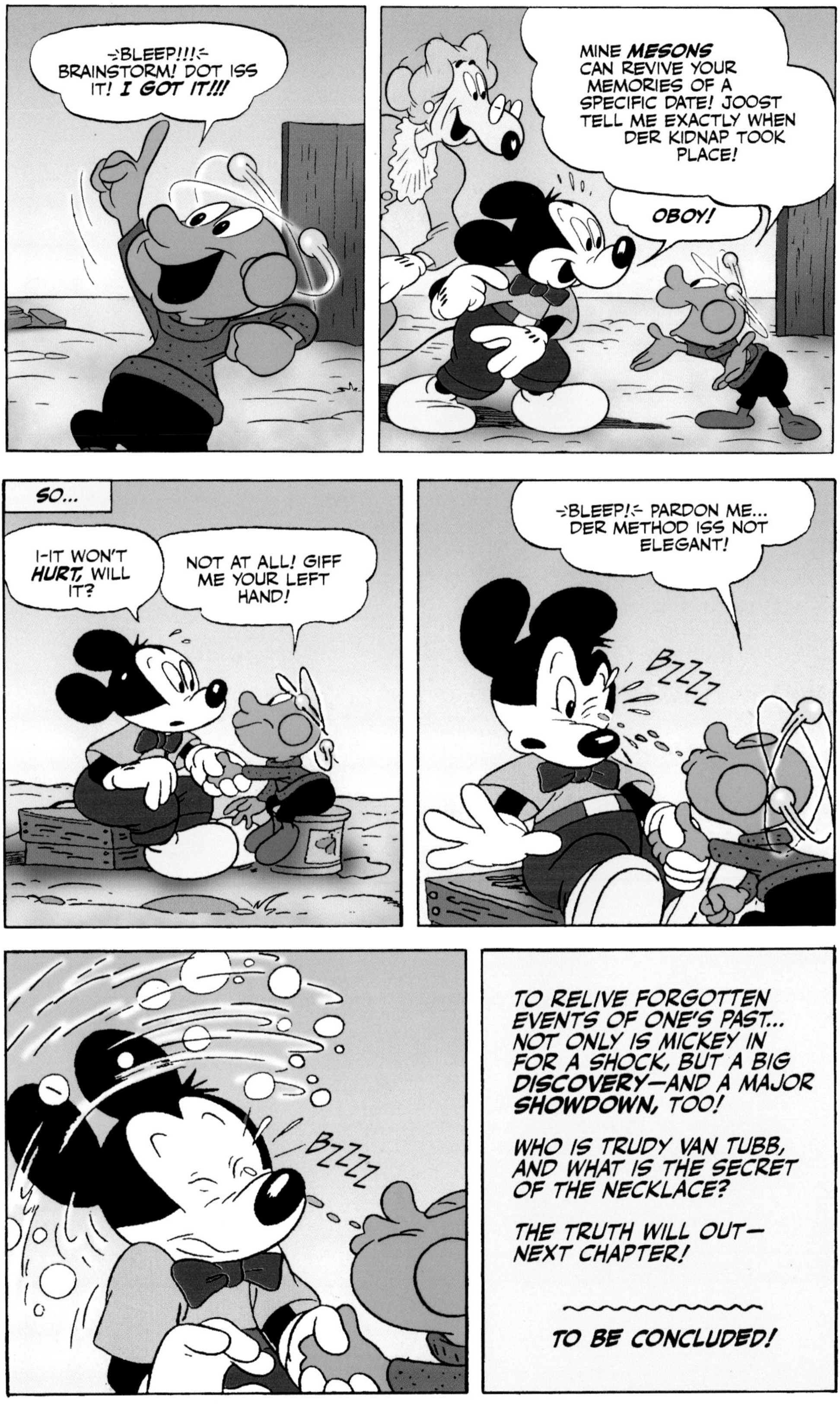

⇒BLEEP!!!⇐ BRAINSTORM! DOT ISS IT! I GOT IT!!!
MINE MESONS CAN REVIVE YOUR MEMORIES OF A SPECIFIC DATE! JOOST TELL ME EXACTLY WHEN DER KIDNAP TOOK PLACE!
OBOY!
SO...
I-IT WON'T HURT, WILL IT?
NOT AT ALL! GIFF ME YOUR LEFT HAND!
⇒BLEEP!⇐ PARDON ME... DER METHOD ISS NOT ELEGANT!
BZZZZ
BZZZZ
TO RELIVE FORGOTTEN EVENTS OF ONE'S PAST... NOT ONLY IS MICKEY IN FOR A SHOCK, BUT A BIG DISCOVERY—AND A MAJOR SHOWDOWN, TOO!
WHO IS TRUDY VAN TUBB, AND WHAT IS THE SECRET OF THE NECKLACE?
THE TRUTH WILL OUT— NEXT CHAPTER!
TO BE CONCLUDED!

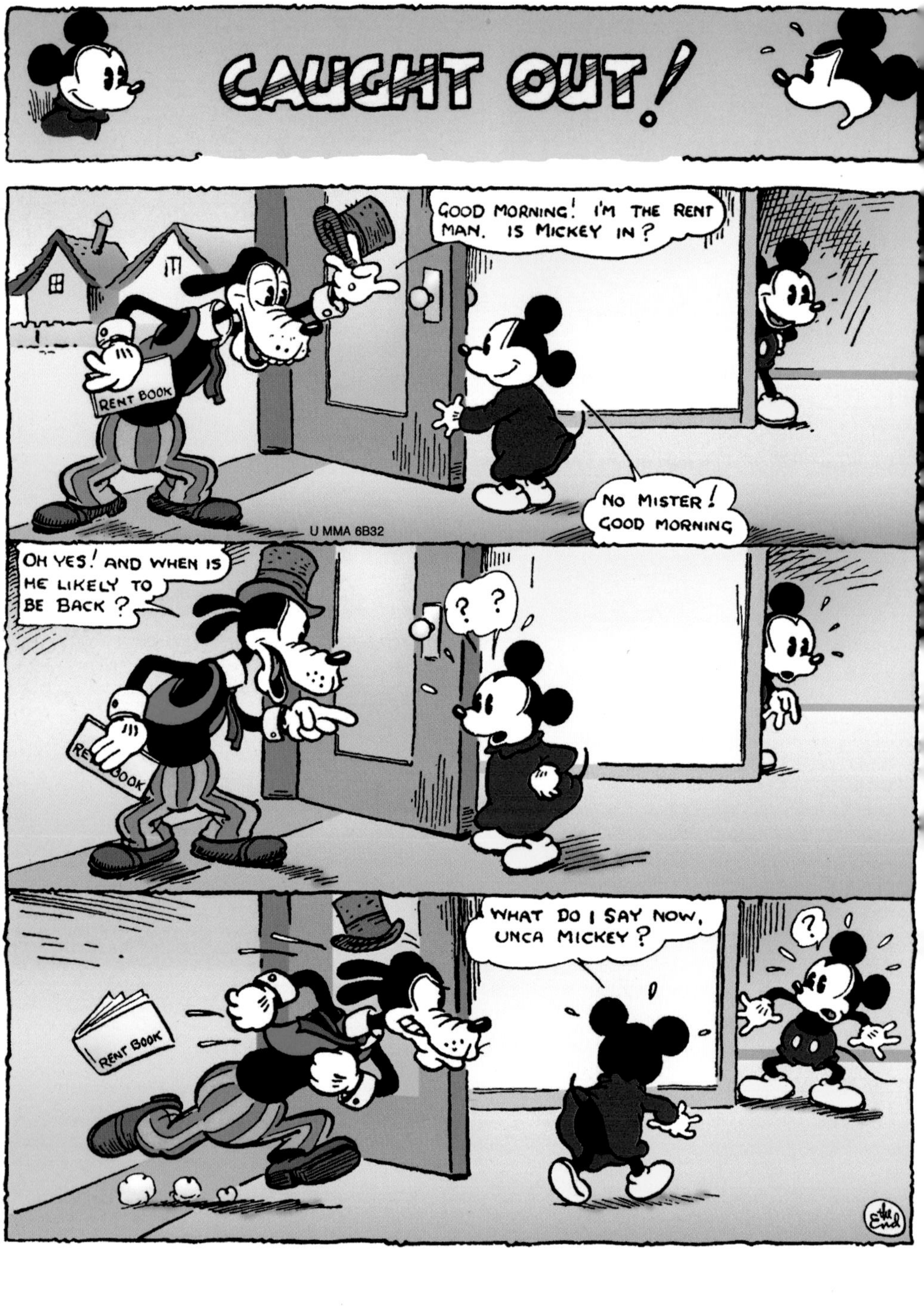
CAUGHT OUT!
GOOD MORNING! I'M THE RENT MAN. IS MICKEY IN?
RENT BOOK
NO MISTER! GOOD MORNING
U MMA 6B32
OH YES! AND WHEN IS HE LIKELY TO BE BACK?
? ?
WHAT DO I SAY NOW, UNCA MICKEY?
?
RENT BOOK
the End

Originally published in *Mickey Mouse Annual* #6 (United Kingdom, 1935)

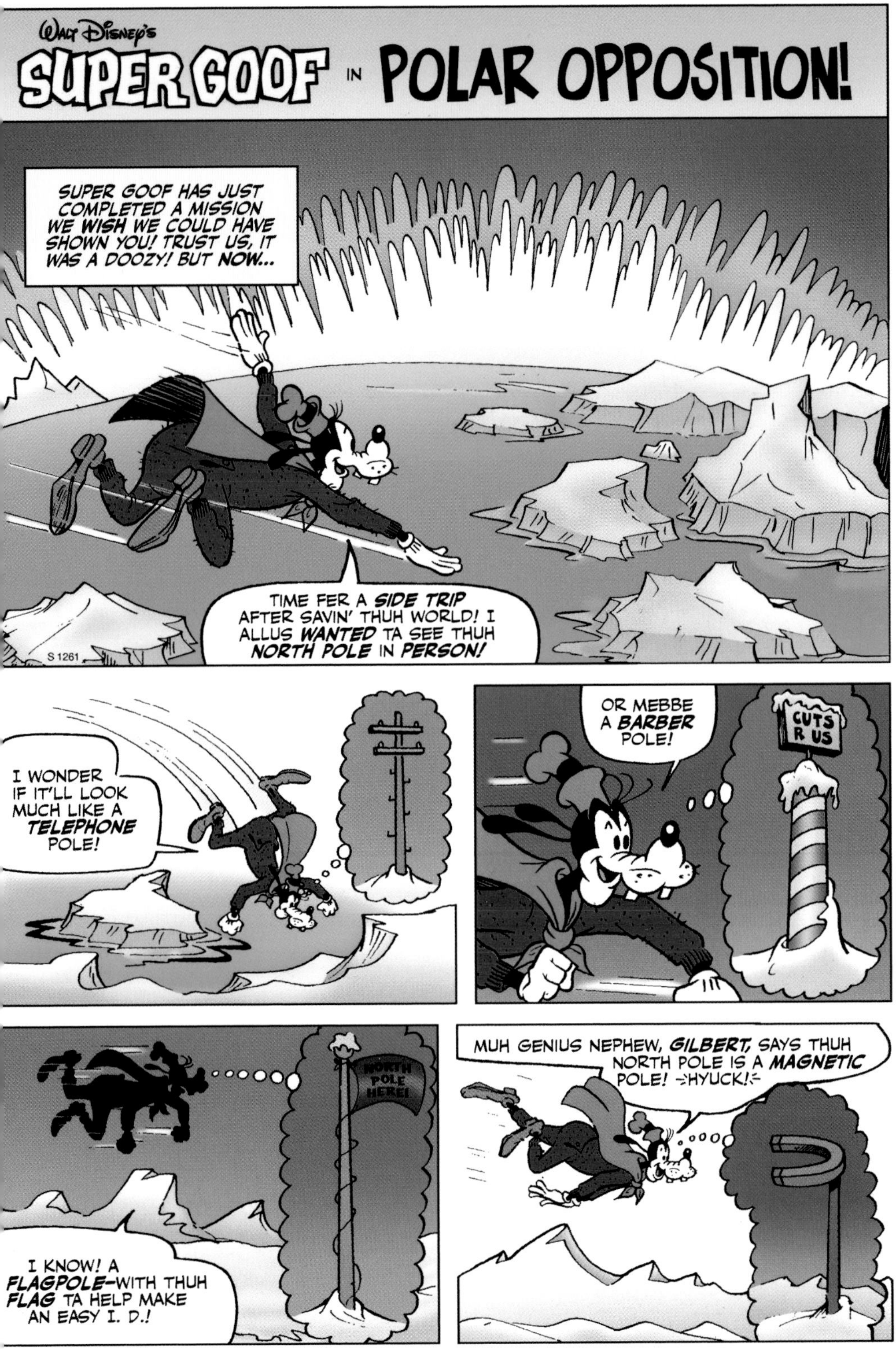
WALT DISNEY'S
SUPER GOOF IN POLAR OPPOSITION!
SUPER GOOF HAS JUST COMPLETED A MISSION WE WISH WE COULD HAVE SHOWN YOU! TRUST US, IT WAS A DOOZY! BUT NOW...
TIME FER A SIDE TRIP AFTER SAVIN' THUH WORLD! I ALLUS WANTED TA SEE THUH NORTH POLE IN PERSON!
S 1261
I WONDER IF IT'LL LOOK MUCH LIKE A TELEPHONE POLE!
OR MEBBE A BARBER POLE!
CUTS R US
NORTH POLE HERE!
I KNOW! A FLAGPOLE—WITH THUH FLAG TA HELP MAKE AN EASY I. D.!
MUH GENIUS NEPHEW, GILBERT, SAYS THUH NORTH POLE IS A MAGNETIC POLE! HYUCK!

Originally published in *Tio Patinhas* #83 (Brazil, 1972)

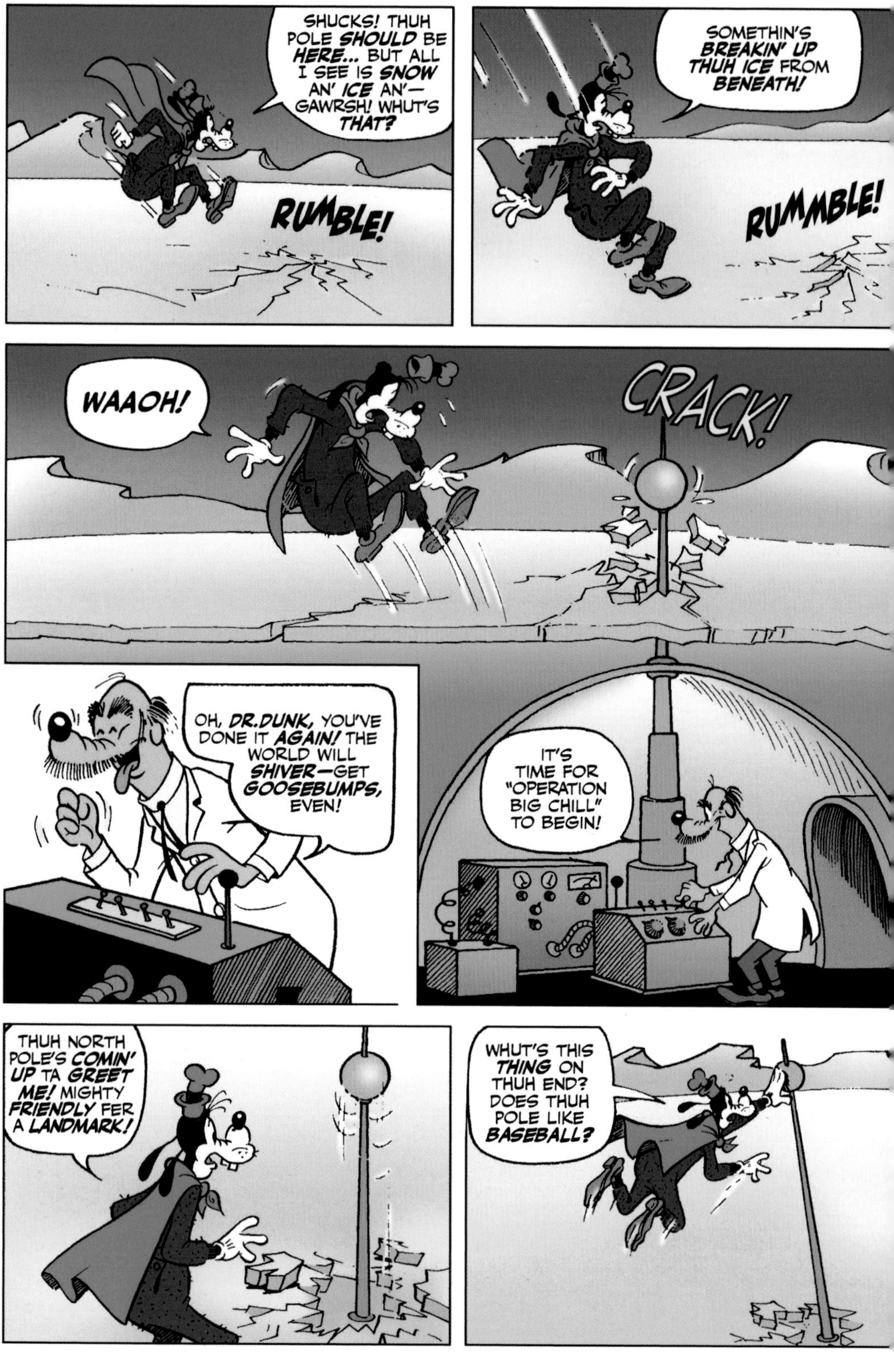
SHUCKS! THUH POLE SHOULD BE HERE... BUT ALL I SEE IS SNOW AN' ICE AN'— GAWRSH! WHUT'S THAT?
RUMBLE!
SOMETHIN'S BREAKIN' UP THUH ICE FROM BENEATH!
RUMMBLE!
WAAOH!
CRACK!
OH, DR.DUNK, YOU'VE DONE IT AGAIN! THE WORLD WILL SHIVER—GET GOOSEBUMPS, EVEN!
IT'S TIME FOR "OPERATION BIG CHILL" TO BEGIN!
THUH NORTH POLE'S COMIN' UP TA GREET ME! MIGHTY FRIENDLY FER A LANDMARK!
WHUT'S THIS THING ON THUH END? DOES THUH POLE LIKE BASEBALL?

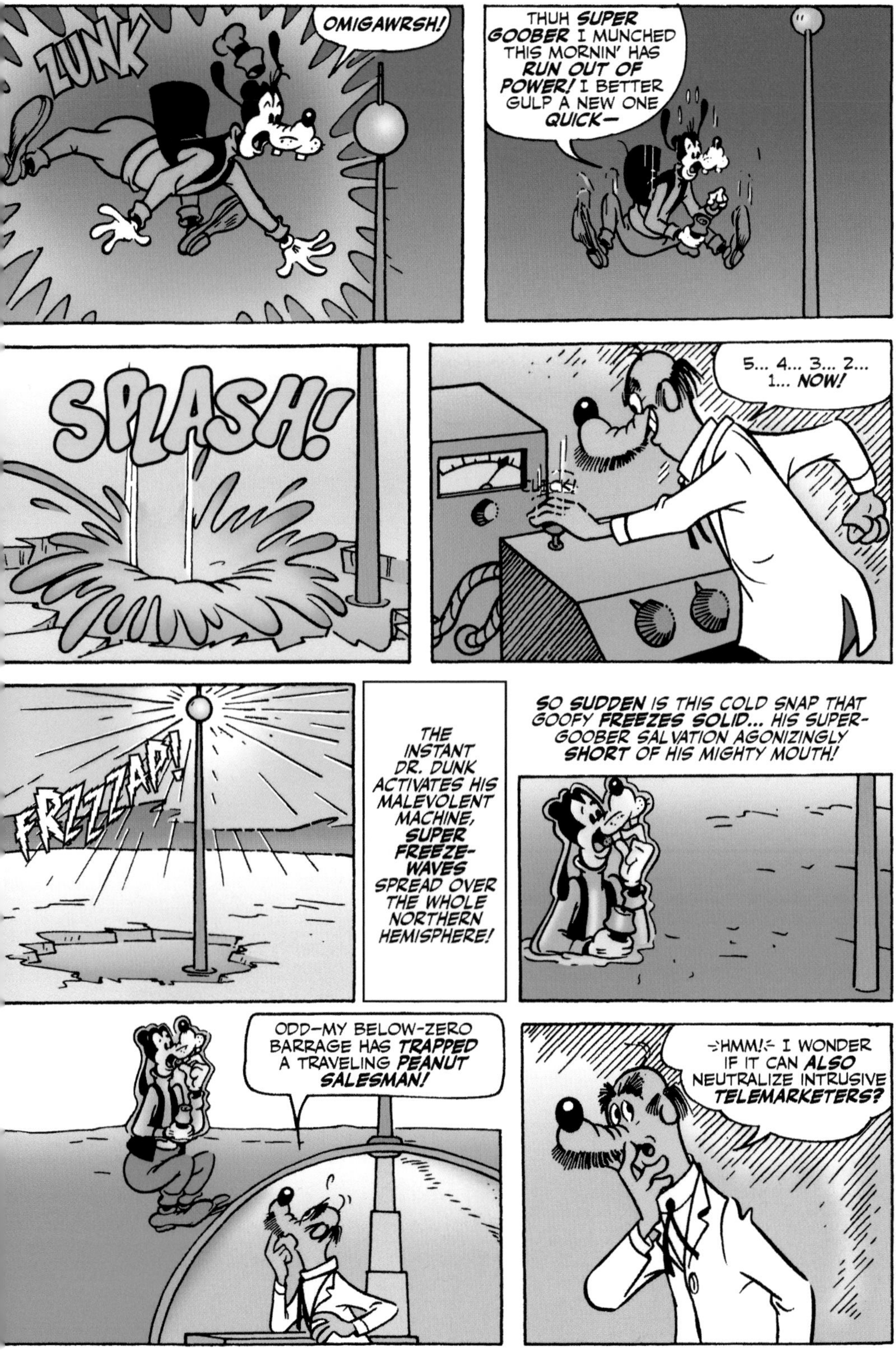
ZUNK
OMIGAWRSH!
THUH SUPER GOOBER I MUNCHED THIS MORNIN' HAS RUN OUT OF POWER! I BETTER GULP A NEW ONE QUICK—
SPLASH!
5... 4... 3... 2... 1... NOW!
CLICK!
FRZZZZAP!
THE INSTANT DR. DUNK ACTIVATES HIS MALEVOLENT MACHINE, SUPER FREEZE-WAVES SPREAD OVER THE WHOLE NORTHERN HEMISPHERE!
SO SUDDEN IS THIS COLD SNAP THAT GOOFY FREEZES SOLID... HIS SUPER-GOOBER SALVATION AGONIZINGLY SHORT OF HIS MIGHTY MOUTH!
ODD—MY BELOW-ZERO BARRAGE HAS TRAPPED A TRAVELING PEANUT SALESMAN!
=HMM!= I WONDER IF IT CAN ALSO NEUTRALIZE INTRUSIVE TELEMARKETERS?

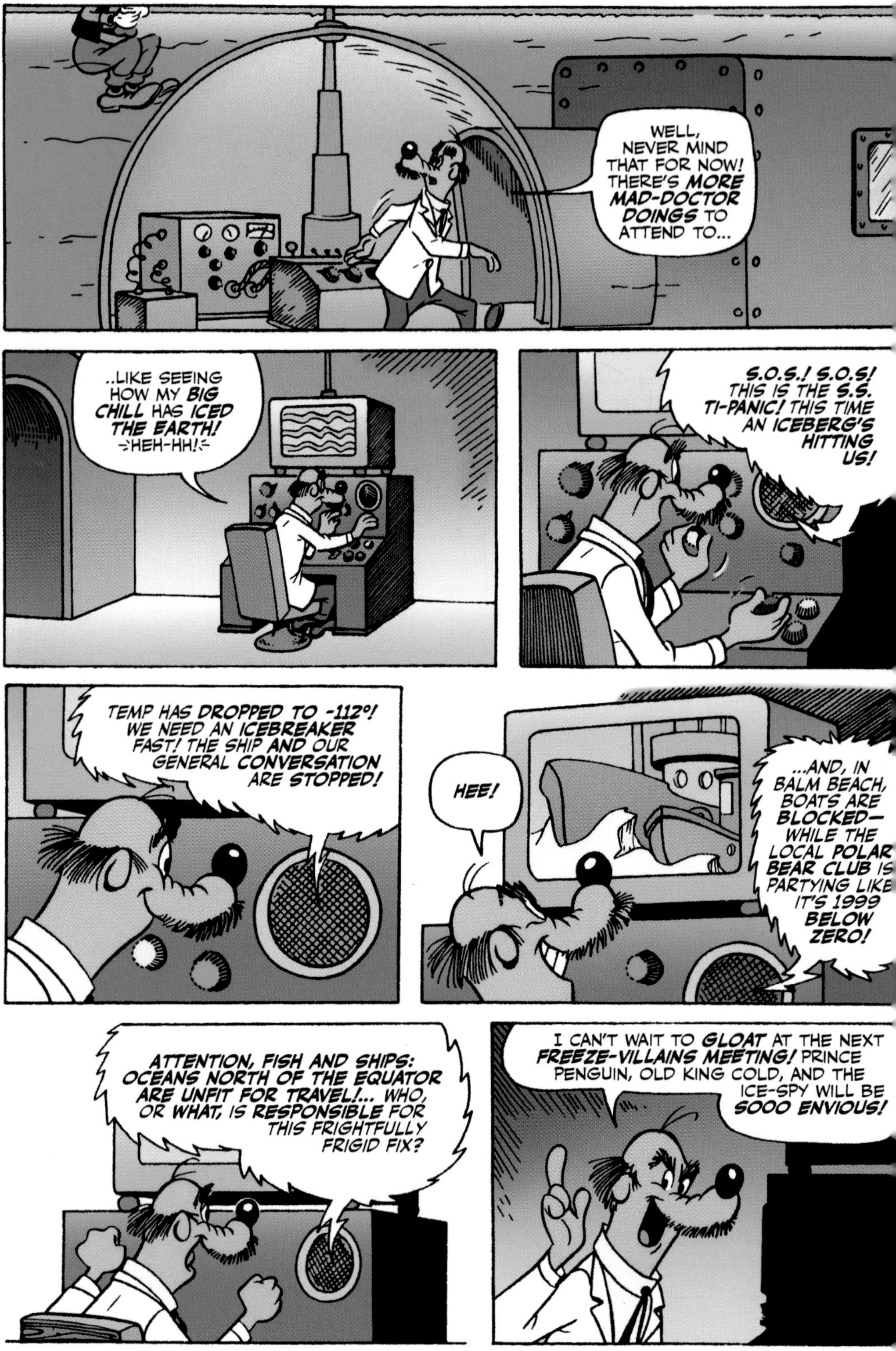
WELL, NEVER MIND THAT FOR NOW! THERE'S MORE MAD-DOCTOR DOINGS TO ATTEND TO...
..LIKE SEEING HOW MY BIG CHILL HAS ICED THE EARTH! -HEH-HH!-
S.O.S.! S.O.S! THIS IS THE S.S. TI-PANIC! THIS TIME AN ICEBERG'S HITTING US!
TEMP HAS DROPPED TO -112°! WE NEED AN ICEBREAKER FAST! THE SHIP AND OUR GENERAL CONVERSATION ARE STOPPED!
HEE!
...AND, IN BALM BEACH, BOATS ARE BLOCKED— WHILE THE LOCAL POLAR BEAR CLUB IS PARTYING LIKE IT'S 1999 BELOW ZERO!
ATTENTION, FISH AND SHIPS: OCEANS NORTH OF THE EQUATOR ARE UNFIT FOR TRAVEL!... WHO, OR WHAT, IS RESPONSIBLE FOR THIS FRIGHTFULLY FRIGID FIX?
I CAN'T WAIT TO GLOAT AT THE NEXT FREEZE-VILLAINS MEETING! PRINCE PENGUIN, OLD KING COLD, AND THE ICE-SPY WILL BE SOOO ENVIOUS!

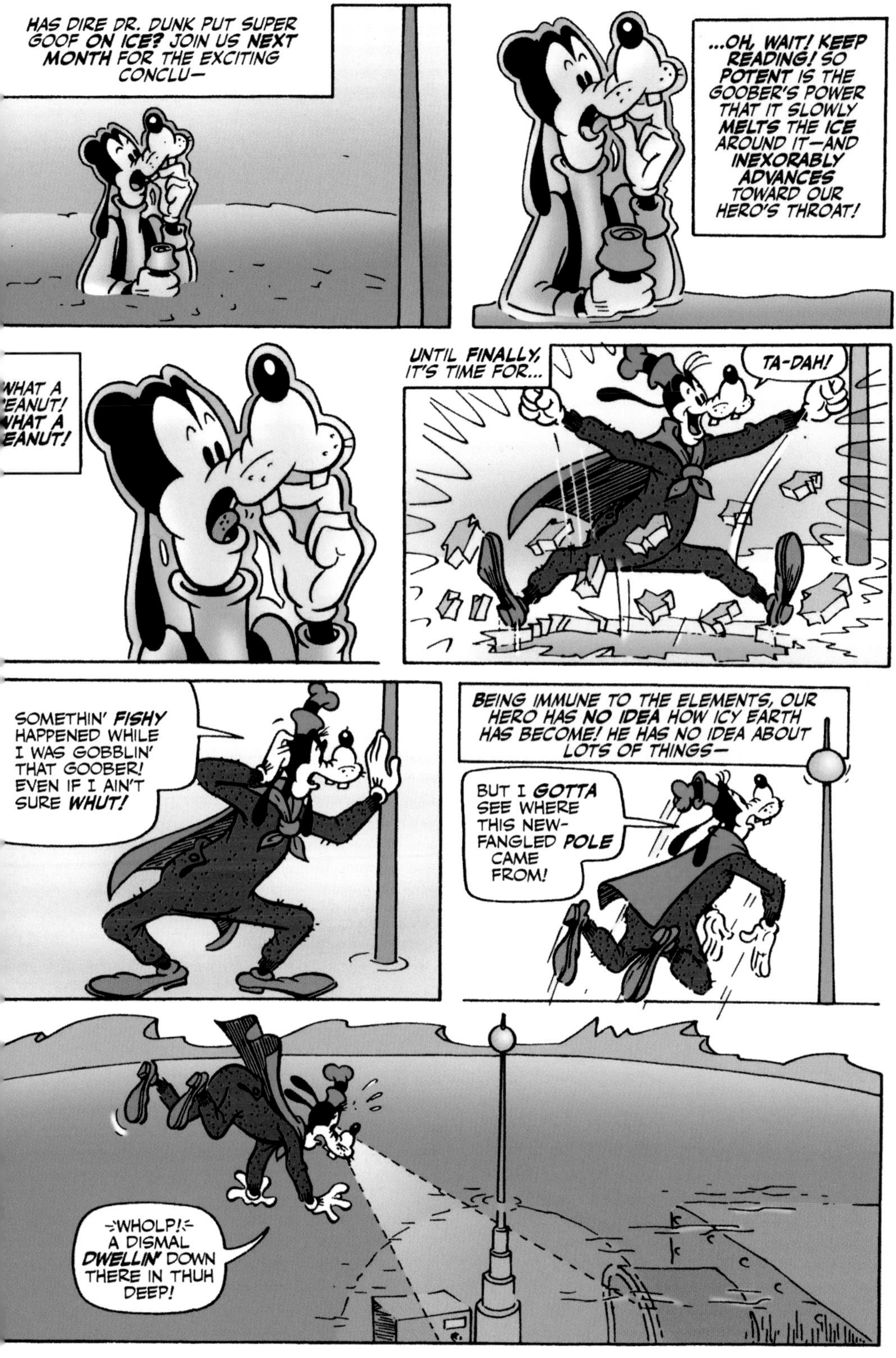
HAS DIRE DR. DUNK PUT SUPER GOOF ON ICE? JOIN US NEXT MONTH FOR THE EXCITING CONCLU—
...OH, WAIT! KEEP READING! SO POTENT IS THE GOOBER'S POWER THAT IT SLOWLY MELTS THE ICE AROUND IT—AND INEXORABLY ADVANCES TOWARD OUR HERO'S THROAT!
WHAT A PEANUT! WHAT A PEANUT!
UNTIL FINALLY, IT'S TIME FOR...
TA-DAH!
SOMETHIN' FISHY HAPPENED WHILE I WAS GOBBLIN' THAT GOOBER! EVEN IF I AIN'T SURE WHUT!
BEING IMMUNE TO THE ELEMENTS, OUR HERO HAS NO IDEA HOW ICY EARTH HAS BECOME! HE HAS NO IDEA ABOUT LOTS OF THINGS—
BUT I GOTTA SEE WHERE THIS NEW-FANGLED POLE CAME FROM!
WHOLP! A DISMAL DWELLIN' DOWN THERE IN THUH DEEP!

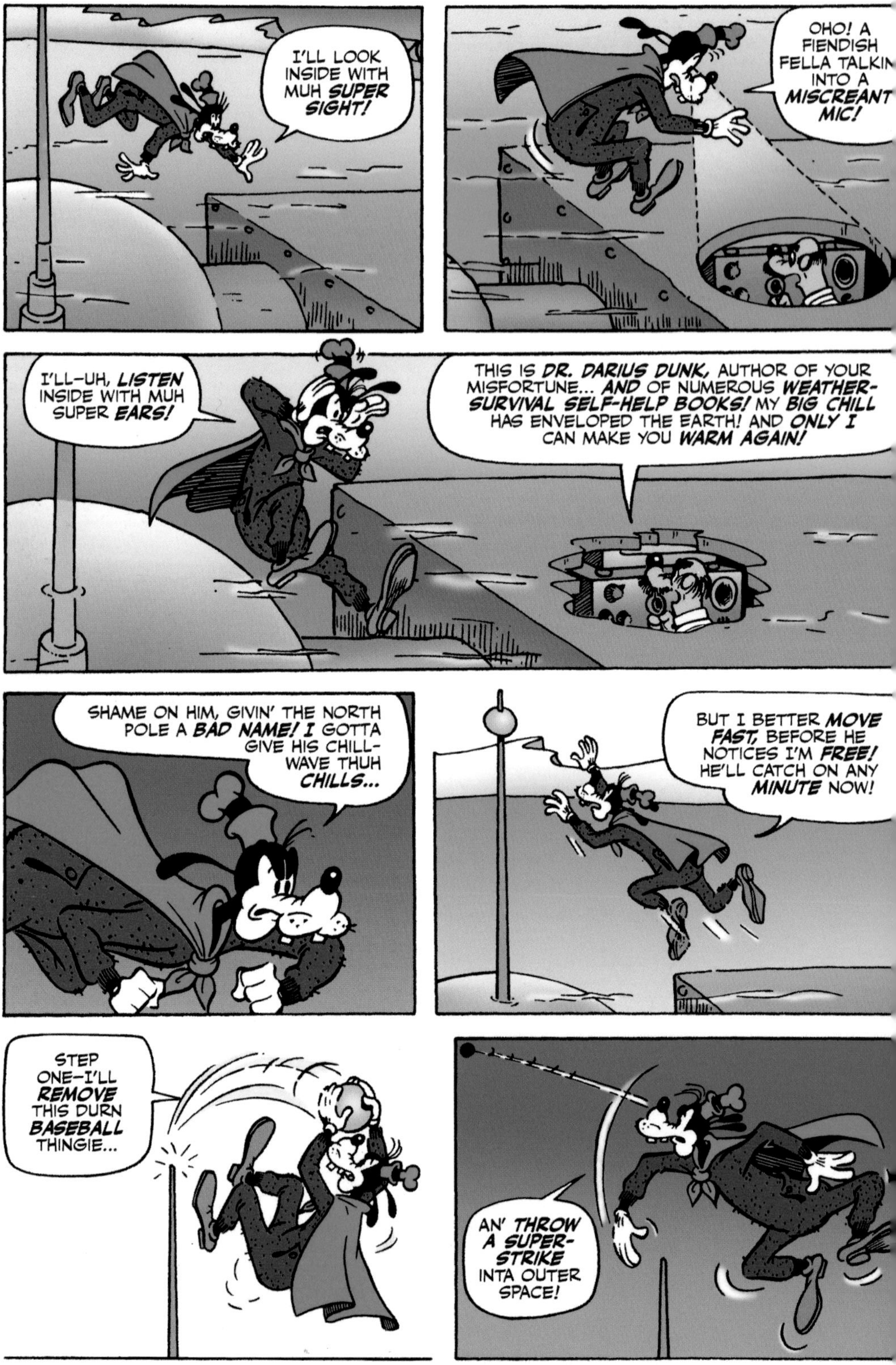
I'LL LOOK INSIDE WITH MUH SUPER SIGHT!
OHO! A FIENDISH FELLA TALKIN INTO A MISCREANT MIC!
I'LL—UH, LISTEN INSIDE WITH MUH SUPER EARS!
THIS IS DR. DARIUS DUNK, AUTHOR OF YOUR MISFORTUNE... AND OF NUMEROUS WEATHER-SURVIVAL SELF-HELP BOOKS! MY BIG CHILL HAS ENVELOPED THE EARTH! AND ONLY I CAN MAKE YOU WARM AGAIN!
SHAME ON HIM, GIVIN' THE NORTH POLE A BAD NAME! I GOTTA GIVE HIS CHILL-WAVE THUH CHILLS...
BUT I BETTER MOVE FAST, BEFORE HE NOTICES I'M FREE! HE'LL CATCH ON ANY MINUTE NOW!
STEP ONE—I'LL REMOVE THIS DURN BASEBALL THINGIE...
AN' THROW A SUPER-STRIKE INTA OUTER SPACE!

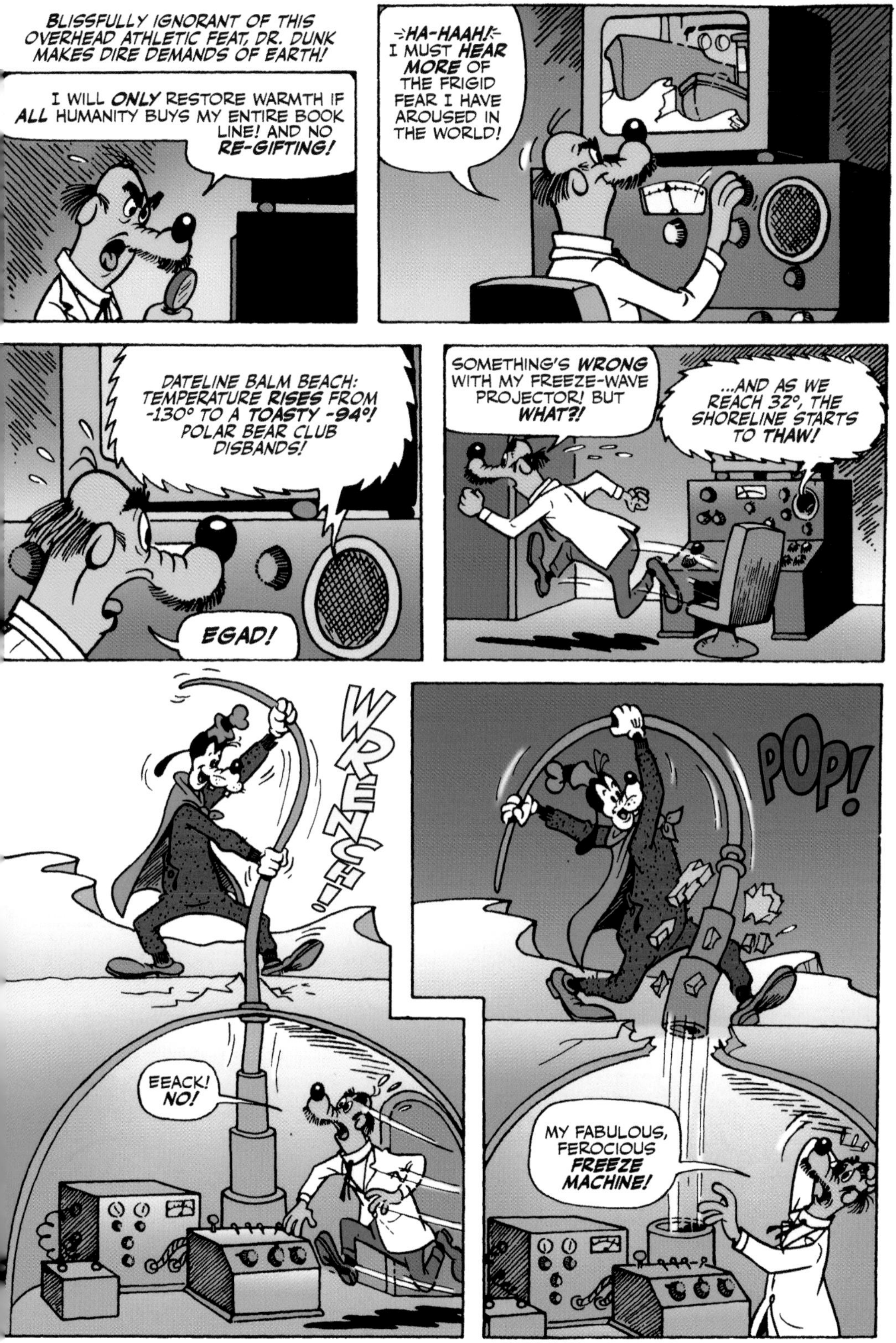
BLISSFULLY IGNORANT OF THIS OVERHEAD ATHLETIC FEAT, DR. DUNK MAKES DIRE DEMANDS OF EARTH!
I WILL ONLY RESTORE WARMTH IF ALL HUMANITY BUYS MY ENTIRE BOOK LINE! AND NO RE-GIFTING!
HA-HAAH! I MUST HEAR MORE OF THE FRIGID FEAR I HAVE AROUSED IN THE WORLD!
DATELINE BALM BEACH: TEMPERATURE RISES FROM -130° TO A TOASTY -94°! POLAR BEAR CLUB DISBANDS!
EGAD!
SOMETHING'S WRONG WITH MY FREEZE-WAVE PROJECTOR! BUT WHAT?!
...AND AS WE REACH 32°, THE SHORELINE STARTS TO THAW!
WRENCH!
EEACK! NO!
POP!
MY FABULOUS, FEROCIOUS FREEZE MACHINE!

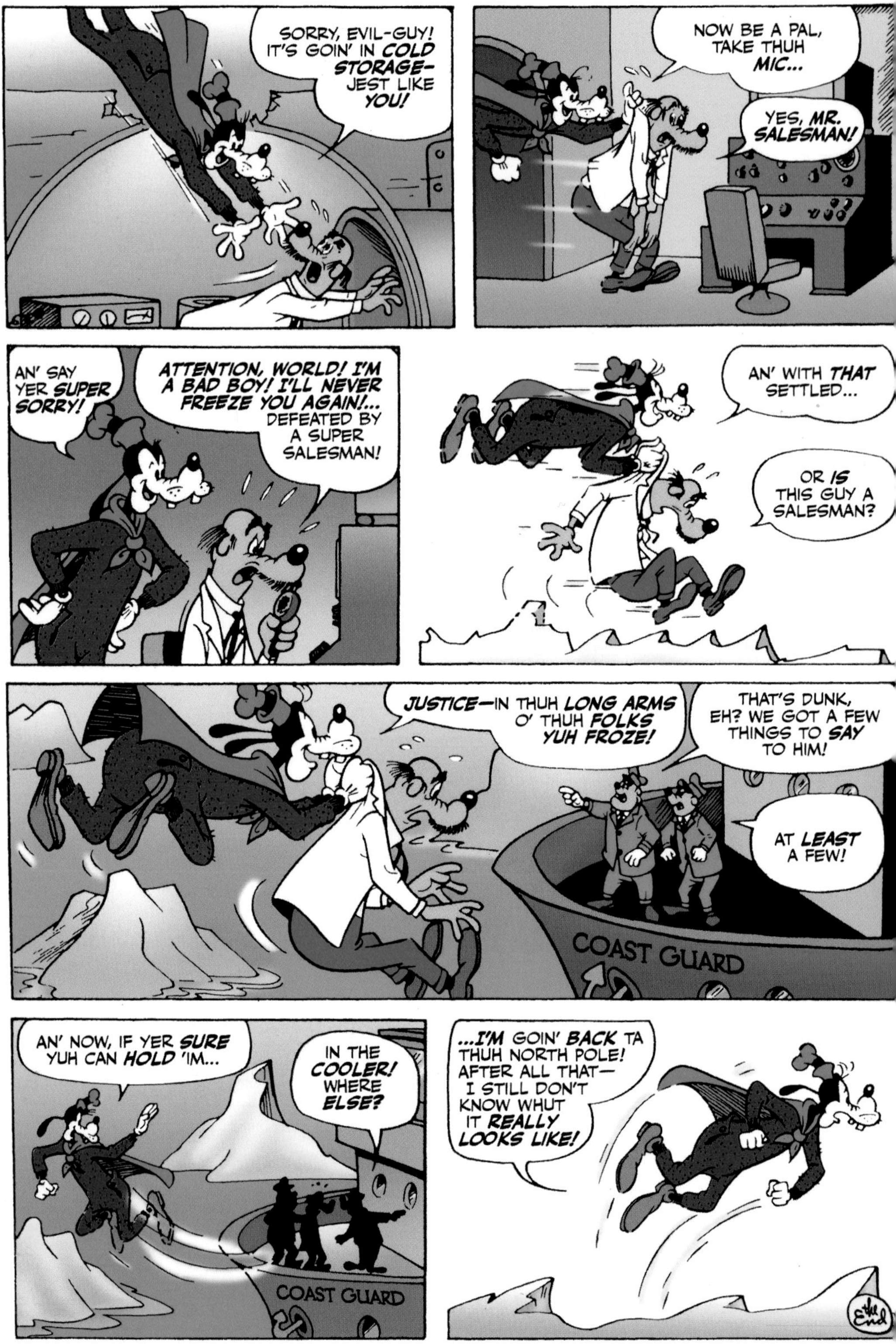

SORRY, EVIL-GUY! IT'S GOIN' IN COLD STORAGE— JEST LIKE YOU!
NOW BE A PAL, TAKE THUH MIC...
YES, MR. SALESMAN!
AN' SAY YER SUPER SORRY!
ATTENTION, WORLD! I'M A BAD BOY! I'LL NEVER FREEZE YOU AGAIN!... DEFEATED BY A SUPER SALESMAN!
AN' WITH THAT SETTLED...
OR IS THIS GUY A SALESMAN?
JUSTICE—IN THUH LONG ARMS O' THUH FOLKS YUH FROZE!
THAT'S DUNK, EH? WE GOT A FEW THINGS TO SAY TO HIM!
AT LEAST A FEW!
COAST GUARD
AN' NOW, IF YER SURE YUH CAN HOLD 'IM...
IN THE COOLER! WHERE ELSE?
COAST GUARD
...I'M GOIN' BACK TA THUH NORTH POLE! AFTER ALL THAT— I STILL DON'T KNOW WHUT IT REALLY LOOKS LIKE!
The End

WALT DISNEY
MICKEY MOUSE
and the
CHIRIKAWA NECKLACE

MICKEY'S BEEN THE VICTIM OF *DIZZY SPELLS* LATELY!... AND THEY HAVE SOMETHING TO DO WITH A NECKLACE, A SHED, AND PEGLEG PETE'S WANNABE GIRLFRIEND, A MYSTERY WOMAN NAMED *TRUDY VAN TUBB!* THE CONNECTION MAY LIE DEEP IN MICKEY'S MEMORIES... AND THE GUY TO FIND IT IS *ATOMO BLEEP-BLEEP*—THE SUPER-EVOLVED ATOM TRAINED BY MICKEY'S OLD MENTOR, DR. EINMUG!

LOOK! ATOMO'S AWESOME POWERS ARE JUST NOW TAKING EFFECT!

"I... I *SEE* IT...

ZING! ZAZZ!

"I'M LYING IN MY CRIB, ATOMO. I... I'M NEAR AN OPEN WINDOW...

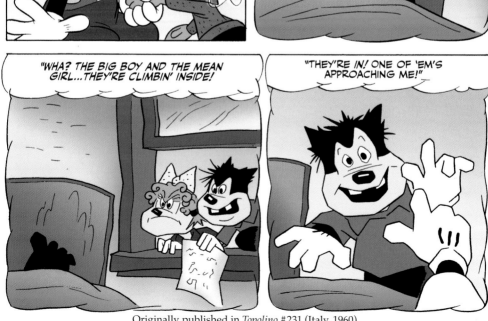

"WHA? THE BIG BOY AND THE MEAN GIRL...THEY'RE CLIMBIN' INSIDE!

"THEY'RE IN! ONE OF 'EM'S APPROACHING ME!"

Originally published in *Topolino* #231 (Italy, 1960)

"OMIGOSH! HE'S GOT ME BY TH' ARM! HE'S CARRIED ME TO THE WINDOW..."

"AND THERE'S A FOOT-POWERED KIDDIE CAR WAITING FOR US ON THE STREET!"

"WE'RE DRIVIN'... ER, FAST-WALKIN' THROUGH MOUSETON..."

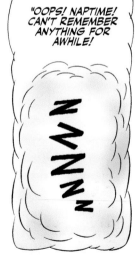

"OOPS! NAPTIME! CAN'T REMEMBER ANYTHING FOR AWHILE!"

"BUT I'M WAKIN' UP NOW... AN' THERE'S THOSE KIDS—HOLDIN' SOMETHING..."

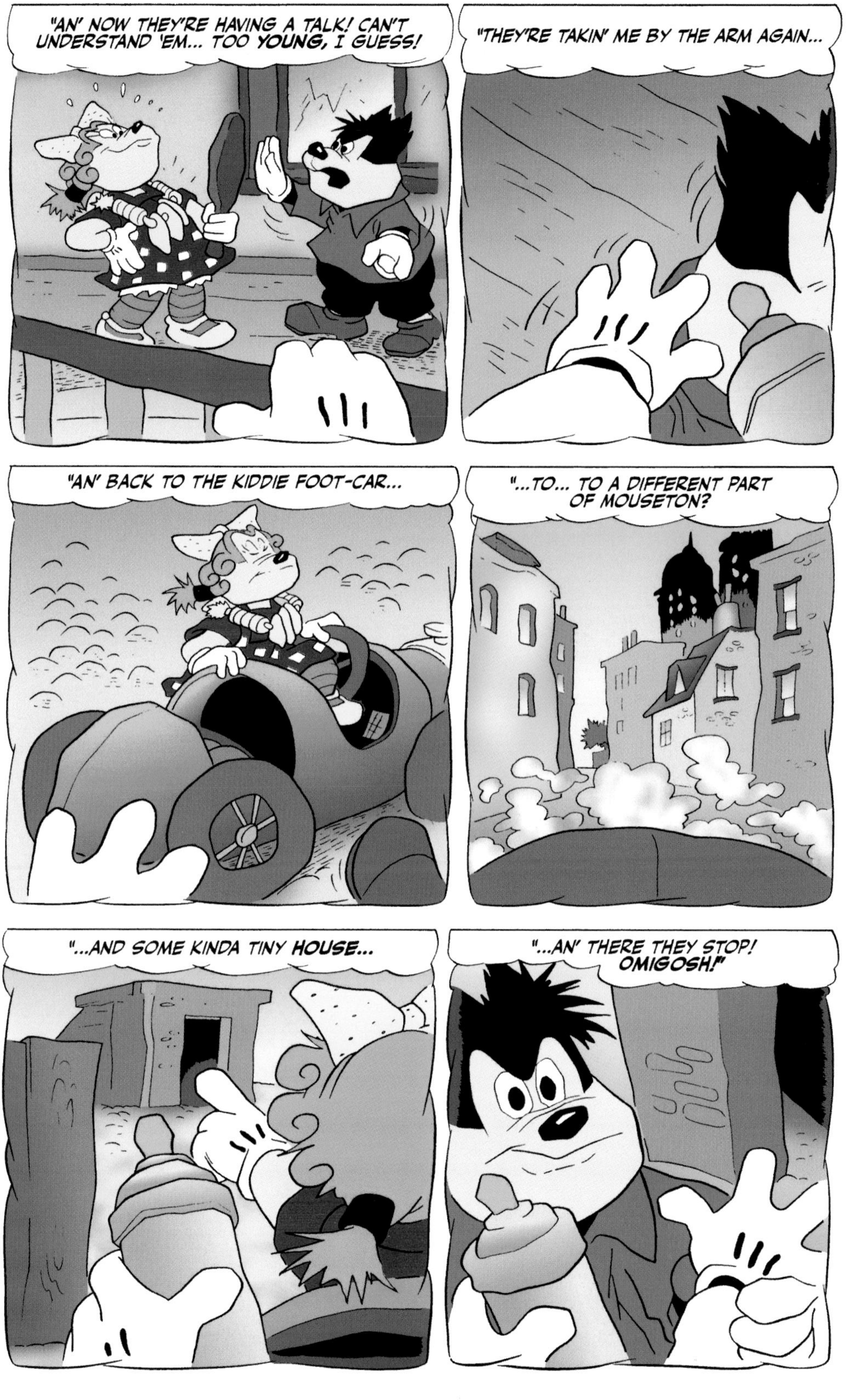
"AN' NOW THEY'RE HAVING A TALK! CAN'T UNDERSTAND 'EM... TOO YOUNG, I GUESS!
"THEY'RE TAKIN' ME BY THE ARM AGAIN...
"AN' BACK TO THE KIDDIE FOOT-CAR...
"...TO... TO A DIFFERENT PART OF MOUSETON?
"...AND SOME KINDA TINY HOUSE...
"...AN' THERE THEY STOP! OMIGOSH!"

"TH' BIG KIDS! THEY **GRABBED** ME! TOSSED ME INSIDE...

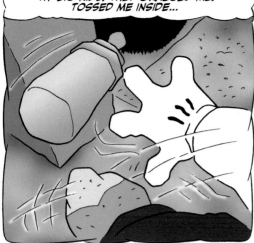

"I CAN BARELY HOLD ONTO MY BABY BOTTLE—TH' **GROUND'S** SO **SOFT!** STICKY AS A SWAMP...

"AN' **TILTY** AS A TEETER-TOTTER! ROOM'S **ROCKIN'**... GOTTA CRAWL AWAY **QUICK—**

"I'M LOSIN' **CONSCIOUSNESS**... NO! GUESS I SAVED MYSELF, BUT I'M COVERED IN **GRAY GOO**...

"AN' HERE'S AUNT MELINDA! FIRST FRIENDLY FACE I'VE SEEN IN AWHILE!"

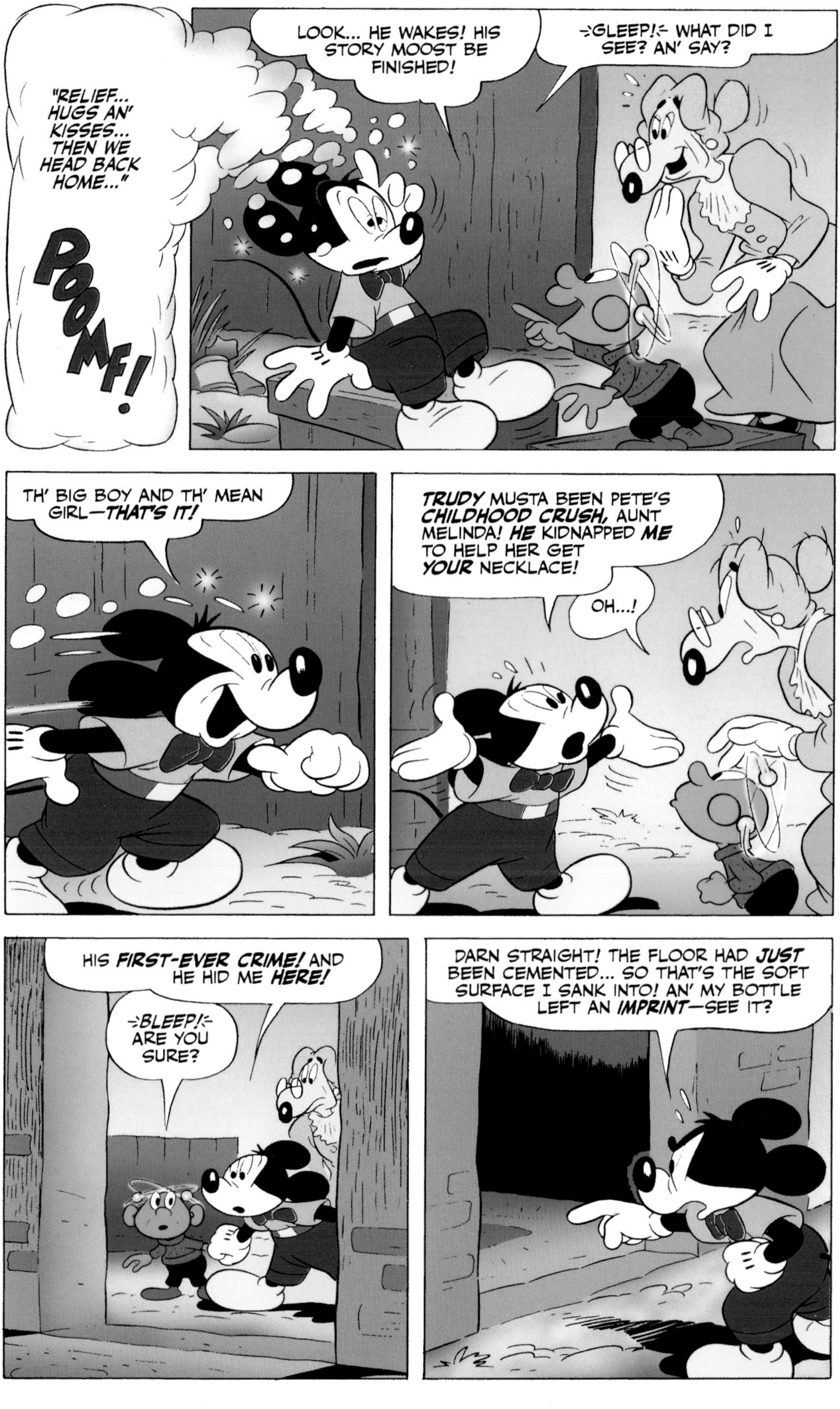
"RELIEF... HUGS AN' KISSES... THEN WE HEAD BACK HOME..."
POOMF!
LOOK... HE WAKES! HIS STORY MOOST BE FINISHED!
-GLEEP!- WHAT DID I SEE? AN' SAY?
TH' BIG BOY AND TH' MEAN GIRL—THAT'S IT!
TRUDY MUSTA BEEN PETE'S CHILDHOOD CRUSH, AUNT MELINDA! HE KIDNAPPED ME TO HELP HER GET YOUR NECKLACE!
OH...!
HIS FIRST-EVER CRIME! AND HE HID ME HERE!
-BLEEP!- ARE YOU SURE?
DARN STRAIGHT! THE FLOOR HAD JUST BEEN CEMENTED... SO THAT'S THE SOFT SURFACE I SANK INTO! AN' MY BOTTLE LEFT AN IMPRINT—SEE IT?

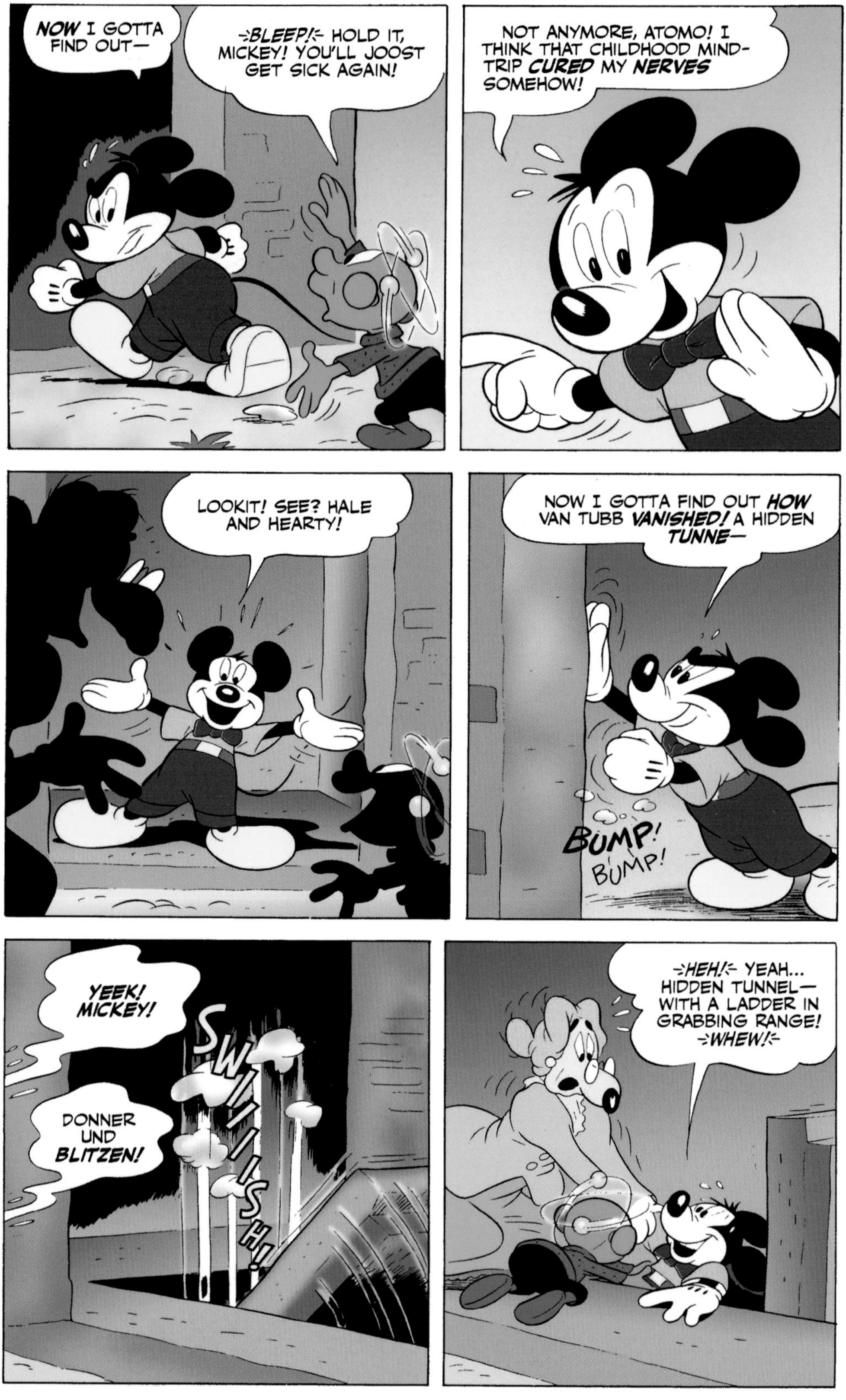
NOW I GOTTA FIND OUT—
=BLEEP!= HOLD IT, MICKEY! YOU'LL JOOST GET SICK AGAIN!
NOT ANYMORE, ATOMO! I THINK THAT CHILDHOOD MIND-TRIP CURED MY NERVES SOMEHOW!
LOOKIT! SEE? HALE AND HEARTY!
NOW I GOTTA FIND OUT HOW VAN TUBB VANISHED! A HIDDEN TUNNE—
BUMP! BUMP!
YEEK! MICKEY!
DONNER UND BLITZEN!
SWIIIISH!
=HEH!= YEAH... HIDDEN TUNNEL—WITH A LADDER IN GRABBING RANGE! =WHEW!=

UNDER A TIPPY *FALSE FLOOR!* ⇥HAH!⇤ MY *DIZZY SPELLS* WERE *FLASHBACKS* TO *THIS!*

I BET VAN TUBB VANISHED UNDER HERE, TOO!

YAH! WE MOOST GO AFTER HER!

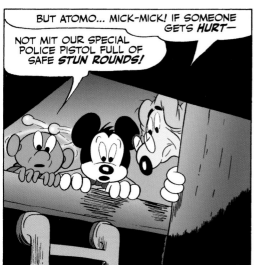

BUT ATOMO... MICK-MICK! IF SOMEONE GETS *HURT*—

NOT MIT OUR SPECIAL POLICE PISTOL FULL OF SAFE *STUN ROUNDS!*

FINE, FOR *CROOKS!* BUT FOR *OTHER* DANGER...

ATOMO'S *POWERS* CAN PROTECT US, TOO!

AN' *YOU* CAN *ALSO* BE A BIG HELP, AUNT M! THINK YOU COULD... ⇥BUZZ! MUMBLE!⇤

RIGHT AWAY, NEPHEW! GOOD LUCK!

PAL, WE'RE GOING *IN!*

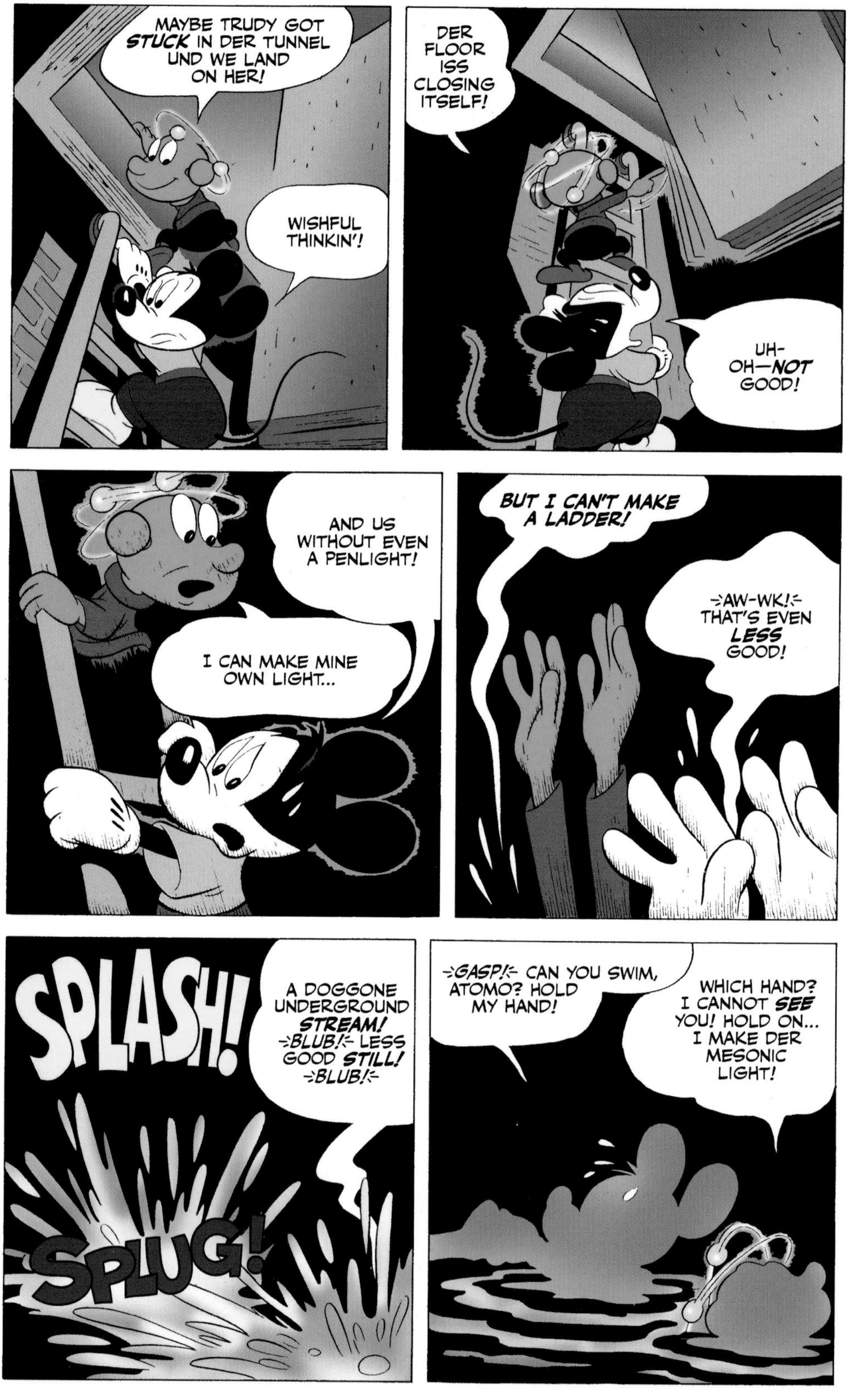
MAYBE TRUDY GOT STUCK IN DER TUNNEL UND WE LAND ON HER!
WISHFUL THINKIN'!
DER FLOOR ISS CLOSING ITSELF!
UH-OH—NOT GOOD!
AND US WITHOUT EVEN A PENLIGHT!
I CAN MAKE MINE OWN LIGHT...
BUT I CAN'T MAKE A LADDER!
-AW-WK!- THAT'S EVEN LESS GOOD!
SPLASH!
SPLUG!
A DOGGONE UNDERGROUND STREAM! -BLUB!- LESS GOOD STILL! -BLUB!-
-GASP!- CAN YOU SWIM, ATOMO? HOLD MY HAND!
WHICH HAND? I CANNOT SEE YOU! HOLD ON... I MAKE DER MESONIC LIGHT!

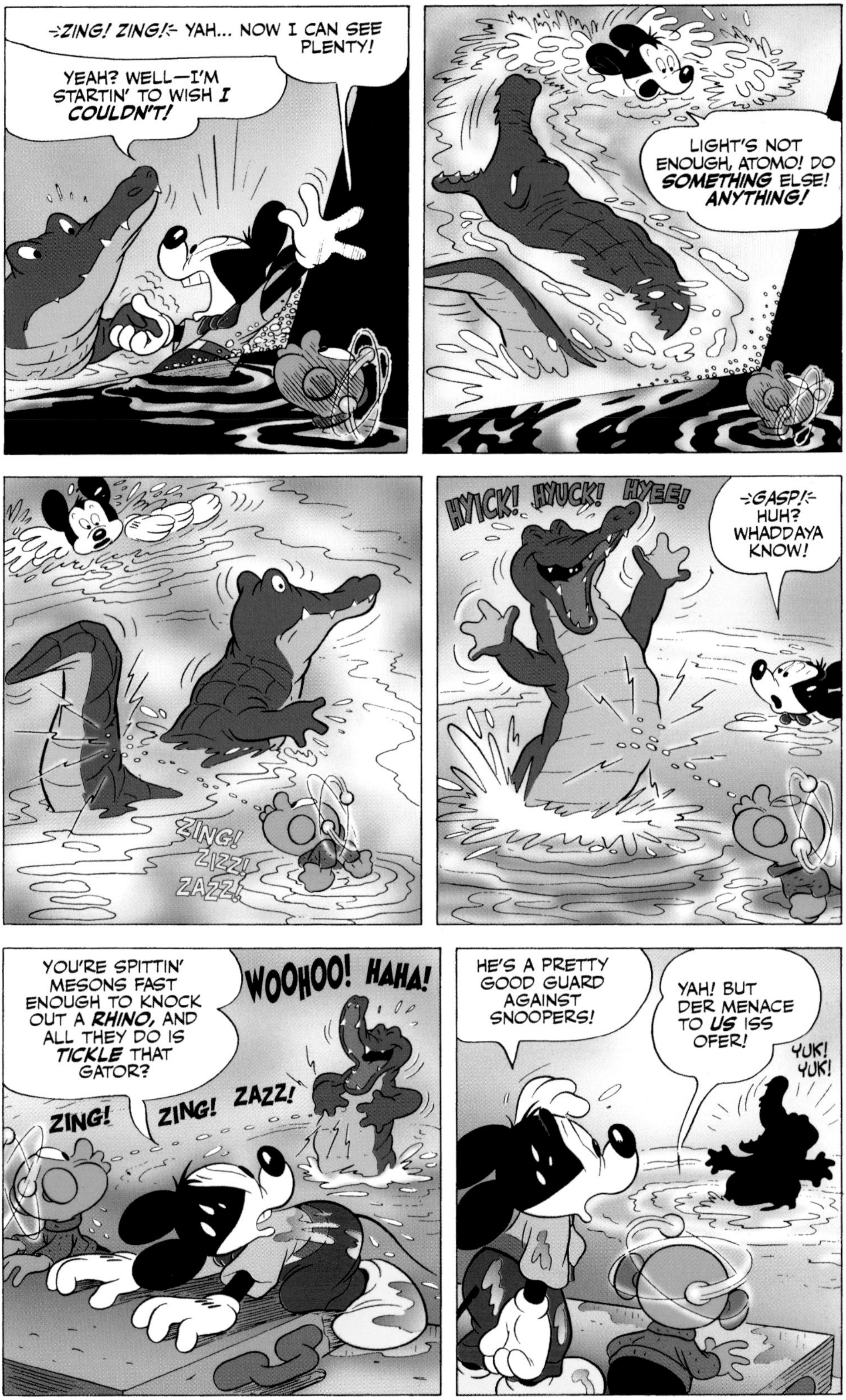
-ZING! ZING!- YAH... NOW I CAN SEE PLENTY!
YEAH? WELL—I'M STARTIN' TO WISH I COULDN'T!
LIGHT'S NOT ENOUGH, ATOMO! DO SOMETHING ELSE! ANYTHING!
ZING! ZIZZ! ZAZZ!
HYICK! HYUCK! HYEE!
-GASP!- HUH? WHADDAYA KNOW!
YOU'RE SPITTIN' MESONS FAST ENOUGH TO KNOCK OUT A RHINO, AND ALL THEY DO IS TICKLE THAT GATOR?
WOOHOO! HAHA!
ZING! ZING! ZAZZ!
HE'S A PRETTY GOOD GUARD AGAINST SNOOPERS!
YAH! BUT DER MENACE TO US ISS OFER!
YUK! YUK!

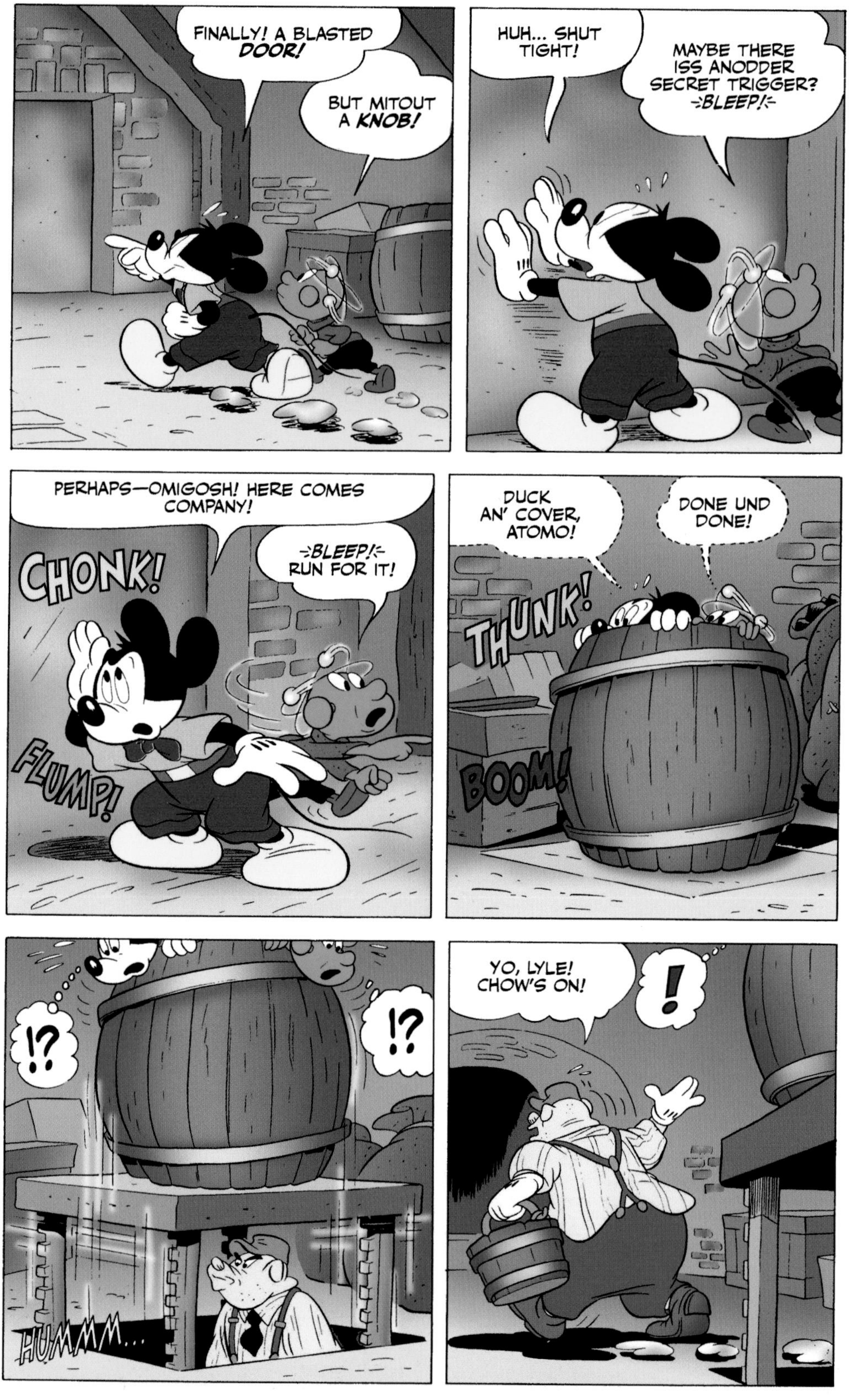

FINALLY! A BLASTED DOOR!
BUT MITOUT A KNOB!
HUH... SHUT TIGHT!
MAYBE THERE ISS ANODDER SECRET TRIGGER? -BLEEP!-
PERHAPS—OMIGOSH! HERE COMES COMPANY!
CHONK!
-BLEEP!- RUN FOR IT!
FLUMP!
DUCK AN' COVER, ATOMO!
DONE UND DONE!
THUNK!
BOOM!
!?
!?
HUMMM...
YO, LYLE! CHOW'S ON!
!

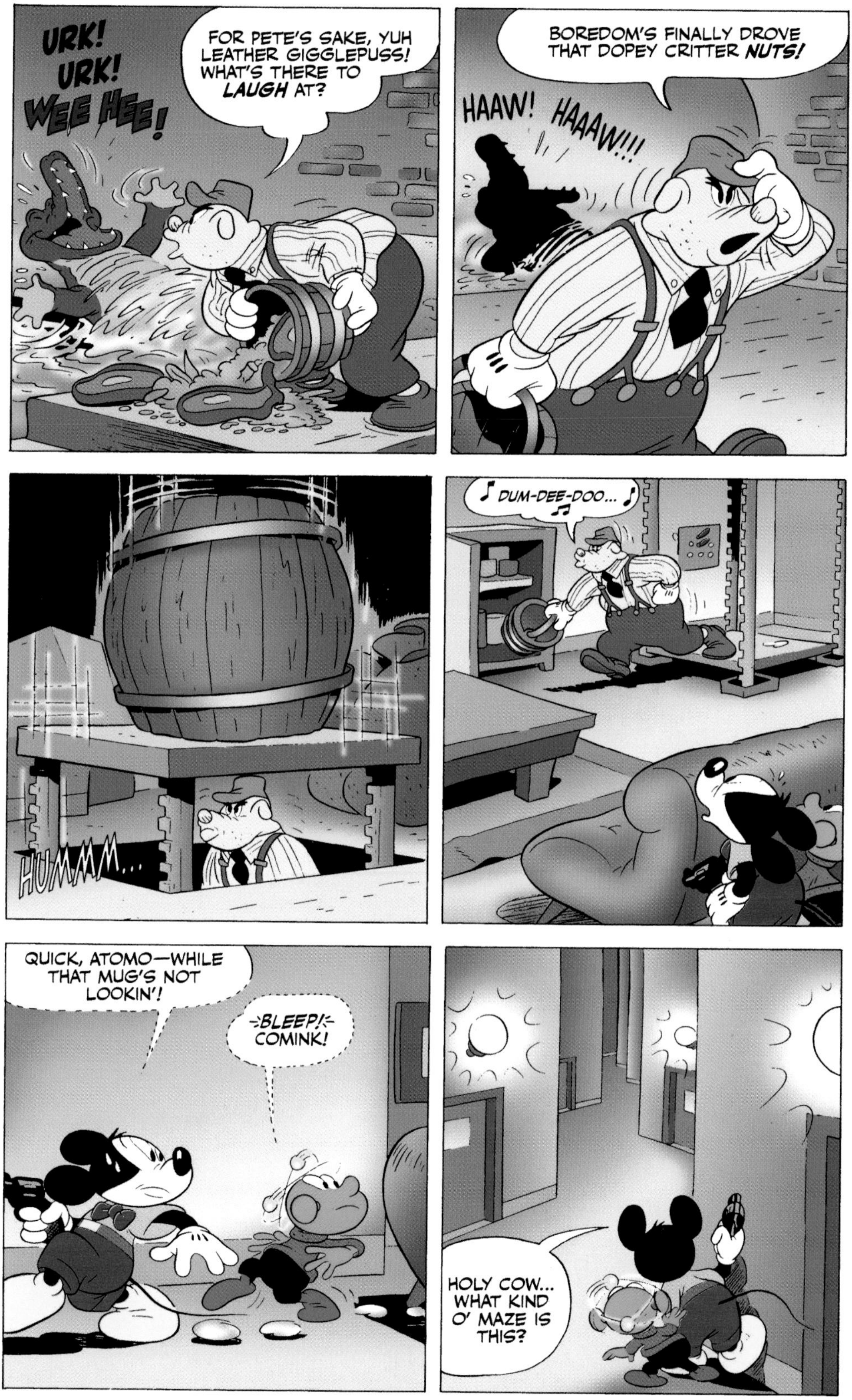
URK! URK! WEE HEE!
FOR PETE'S SAKE, YUH LEATHER GIGGLEPUSS! WHAT'S THERE TO LAUGH AT?
BOREDOM'S FINALLY DROVE THAT DOPEY CRITTER NUTS!
HAAW! HAAAW!!!
HUMMM...
DUM-DEE-DOO...
QUICK, ATOMO—WHILE THAT MUG'S NOT LOOKIN'!
BLEEP! COMINK!
HOLY COW... WHAT KIND O' MAZE IS THIS?

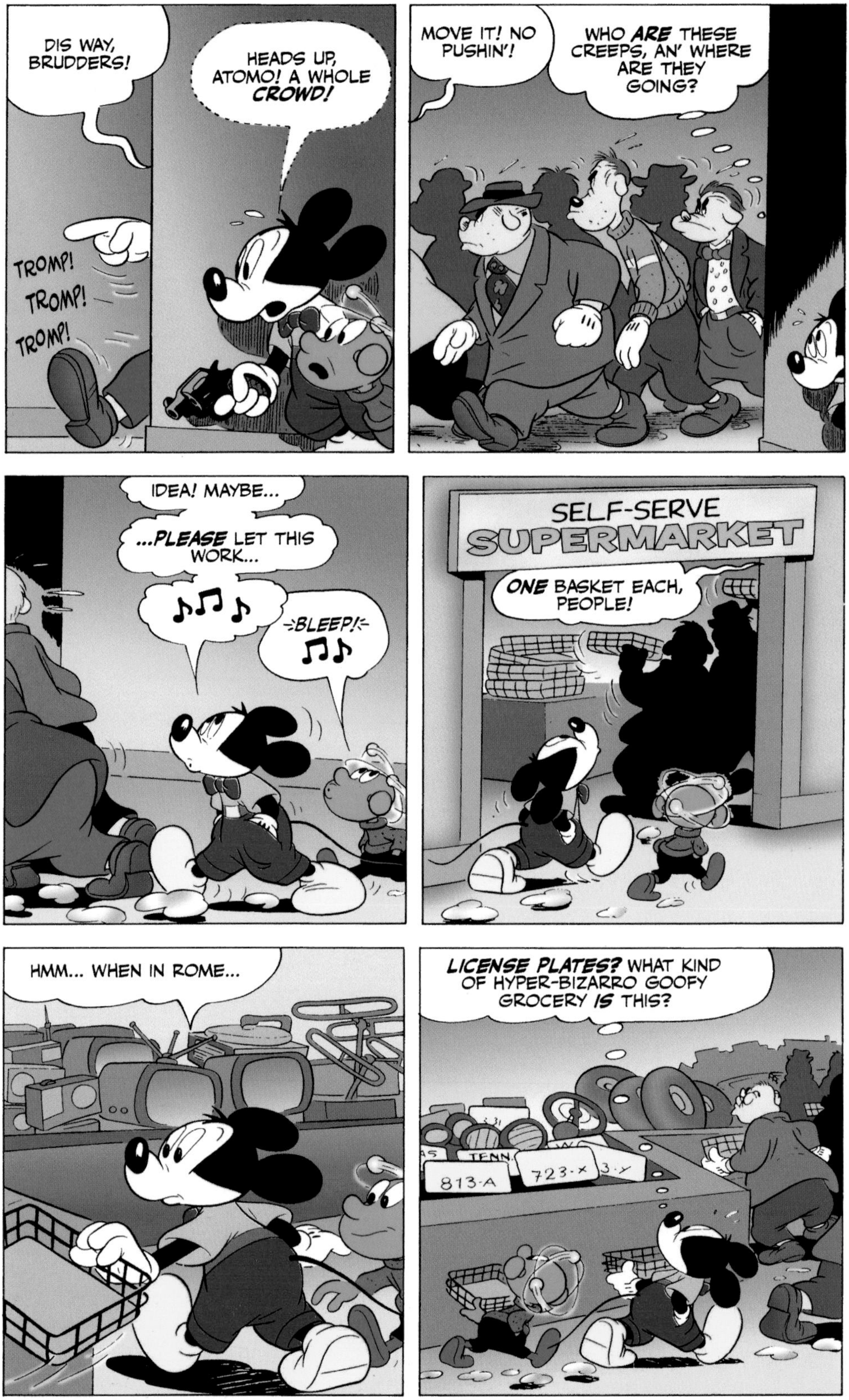

DIS WAY, BRUDDERS!
TROMP! TROMP! TROMP!
HEADS UP, ATOMO! A WHOLE CROWD!
MOVE IT! NO PUSHIN'!
WHO ARE THESE CREEPS, AN' WHERE ARE THEY GOING?
IDEA! MAYBE...
...PLEASE LET THIS WORK...
♪♫ ♪
BLEEP! ♫♪
SELF-SERVE SUPERMARKET
ONE BASKET EACH, PEOPLE!
HMM... WHEN IN ROME...
LICENSE PLATES? WHAT KIND OF HYPER-BIZARRO GOOFY GROCERY IS THIS?
TENN.
813-A
723-X
3-Y

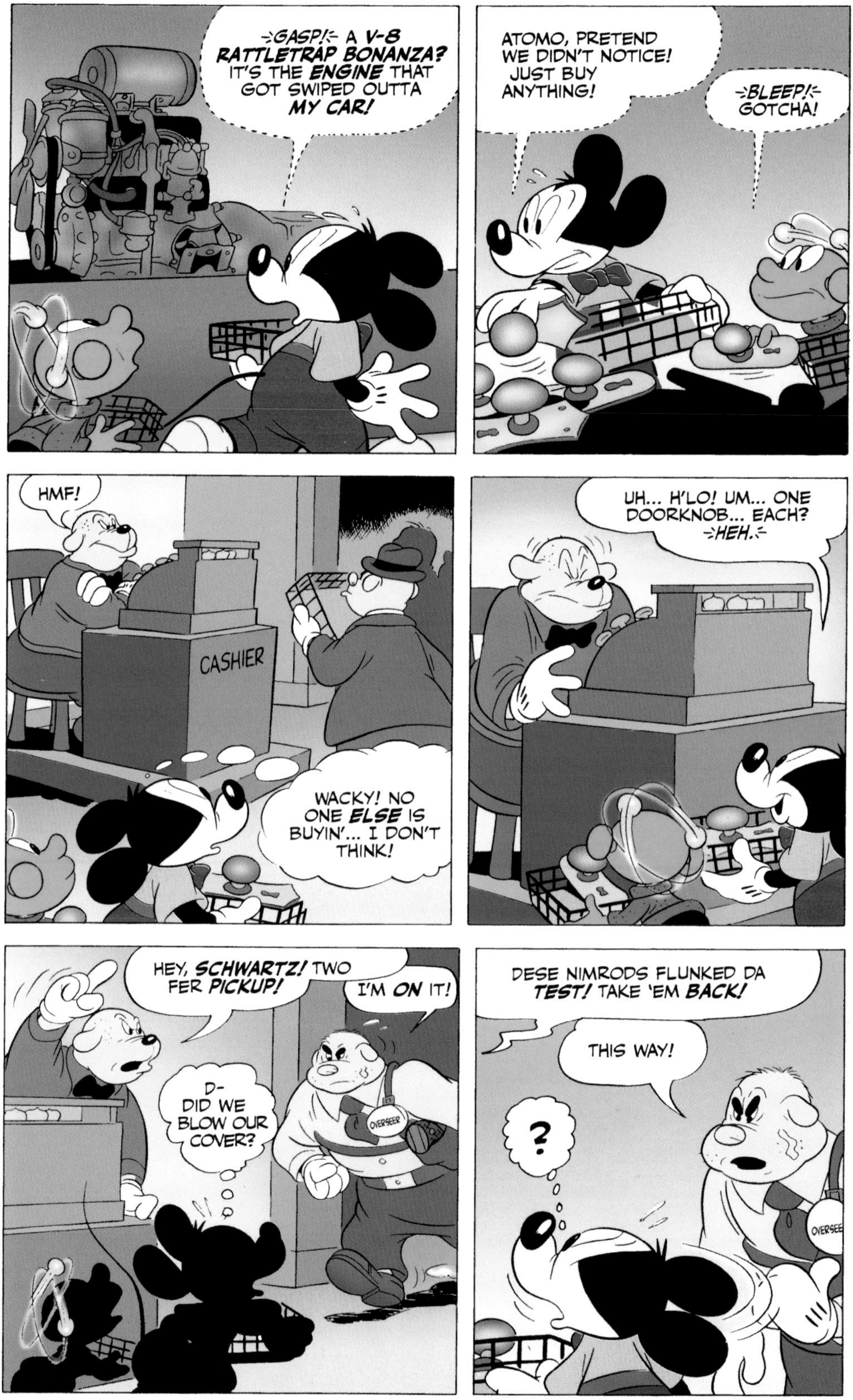

-GASP!- A V-8 RATTLETRAP BONANZA? IT'S THE ENGINE THAT GOT SWIPED OUTTA MY CAR!
ATOMO, PRETEND WE DIDN'T NOTICE! JUST BUY ANYTHING!
-BLEEP!- GOTCHA!
HMF!
CASHIER
WACKY! NO ONE ELSE IS BUYIN'... I DON'T THINK!
UH... H'LO! UM... ONE DOORKNOB... EACH? -HEH.-
HEY, SCHWARTZ! TWO FER PICKUP!
I'M ON IT!
D- DID WE BLOW OUR COVER?
OVERSEER
DESE NIMRODS FLUNKED DA TEST! TAKE 'EM BACK!
THIS WAY!
?

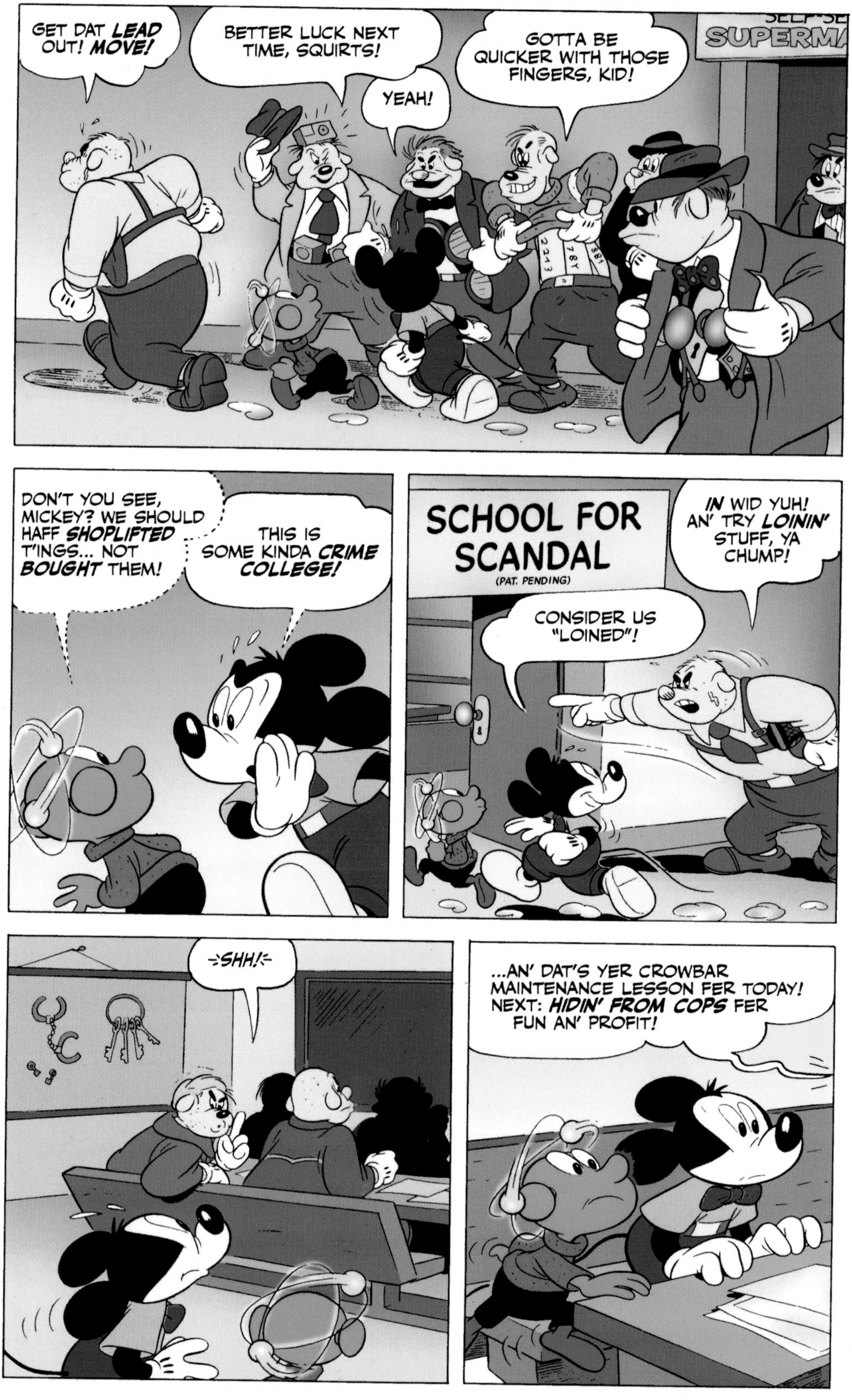

GET DAT LEAD OUT! MOVE!
BETTER LUCK NEXT TIME, SQUIRTS!
YEAH!
GOTTA BE QUICKER WITH THOSE FINGERS, KID!
SUPERMA
DON'T YOU SEE, MICKEY? WE SHOULD HAFF SHOPLIFTED T'INGS... NOT BOUGHT THEM!
THIS IS SOME KINDA CRIME COLLEGE!
SCHOOL FOR SCANDAL
(PAT. PENDING)
IN WID YUH! AN' TRY LOININ' STUFF, YA CHUMP!
CONSIDER US "LOINED"!
SHH!
...AN' DAT'S YER CROWBAR MAINTENANCE LESSON FER TODAY! NEXT: HIDIN' FROM COPS FER FUN AN' PROFIT!

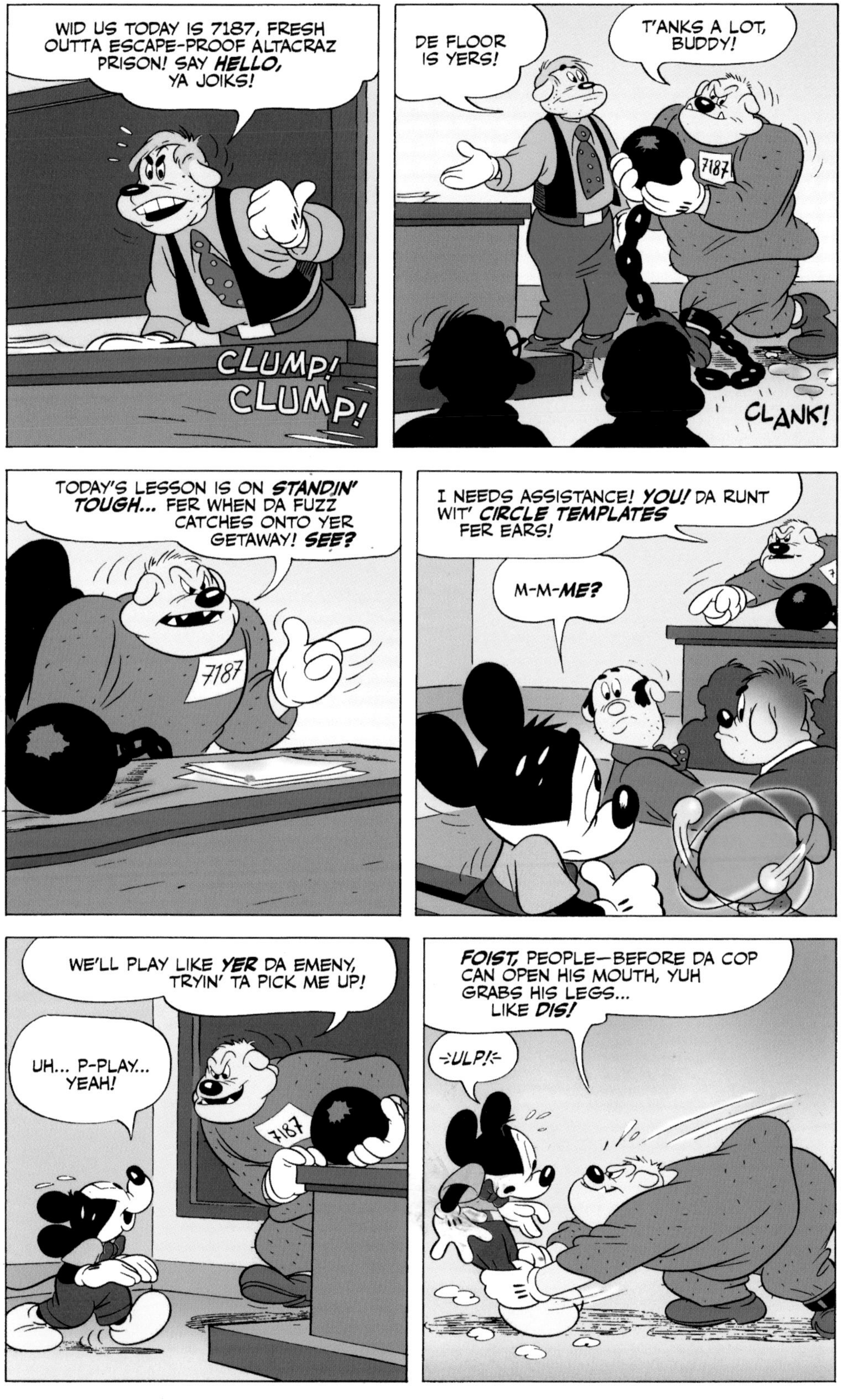
WID US TODAY IS 7187, FRESH OUTTA ESCAPE-PROOF ALTACRAZ PRISON! SAY **HELLO,** YA JOIKS!
CLUMP! CLUMP!
DE FLOOR IS YERS!
T'ANKS A LOT, BUDDY!
7187
CLANK!
TODAY'S LESSON IS ON ***STANDIN' TOUGH...*** FER WHEN DA FUZZ CATCHES ONTO YER GETAWAY! ***SEE?***
7187
I NEEDS ASSISTANCE! ***YOU!*** DA RUNT WIT' ***CIRCLE TEMPLATES*** FER EARS!
M-M-***ME?***
WE'LL PLAY LIKE ***YER*** DA EMENY, TRYIN' TA PICK ME UP!
UH... P-PLAY... YEAH!
7187
FOIST, PEOPLE—BEFORE DA COP CAN OPEN HIS MOUTH, YUH GRABS HIS LEGS... LIKE ***DIS!***
-ULP!-

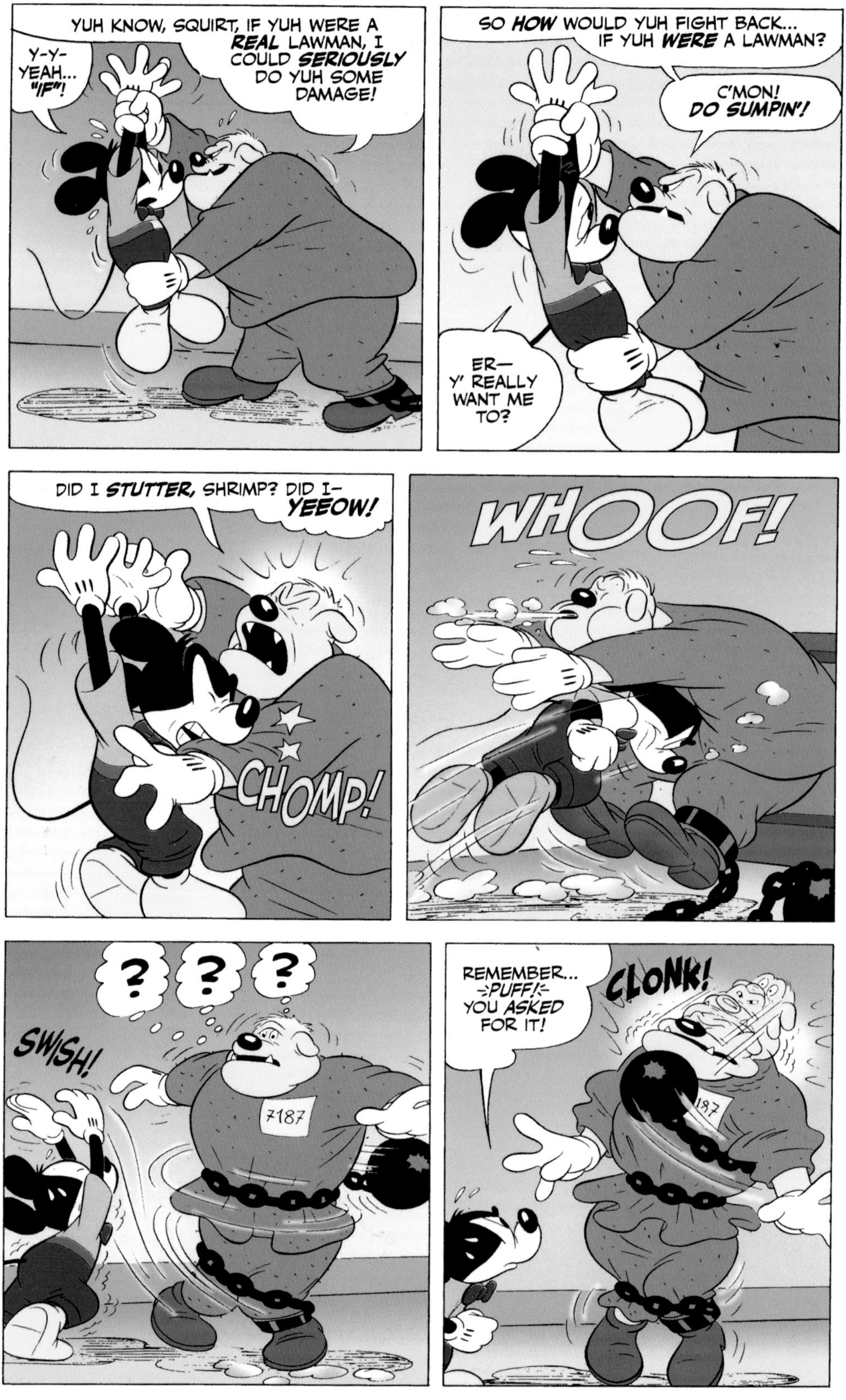
YUH KNOW, SQUIRT, IF YUH WERE A REAL LAWMAN, I COULD SERIOUSLY DO YUH SOME DAMAGE!
Y-Y-YEAH... "IF"!
SO HOW WOULD YUH FIGHT BACK... IF YUH WERE A LAWMAN?
C'MON! DO SUMPIN'!
ER— Y' REALLY WANT ME TO?
DID I STUTTER, SHRIMP? DID I— YEEOW!
CHOMP!
WHOOF!
? ? ?
SWISH!
7187
REMEMBER... -PUFF!- YOU ASKED FOR IT!
CLONK!
187

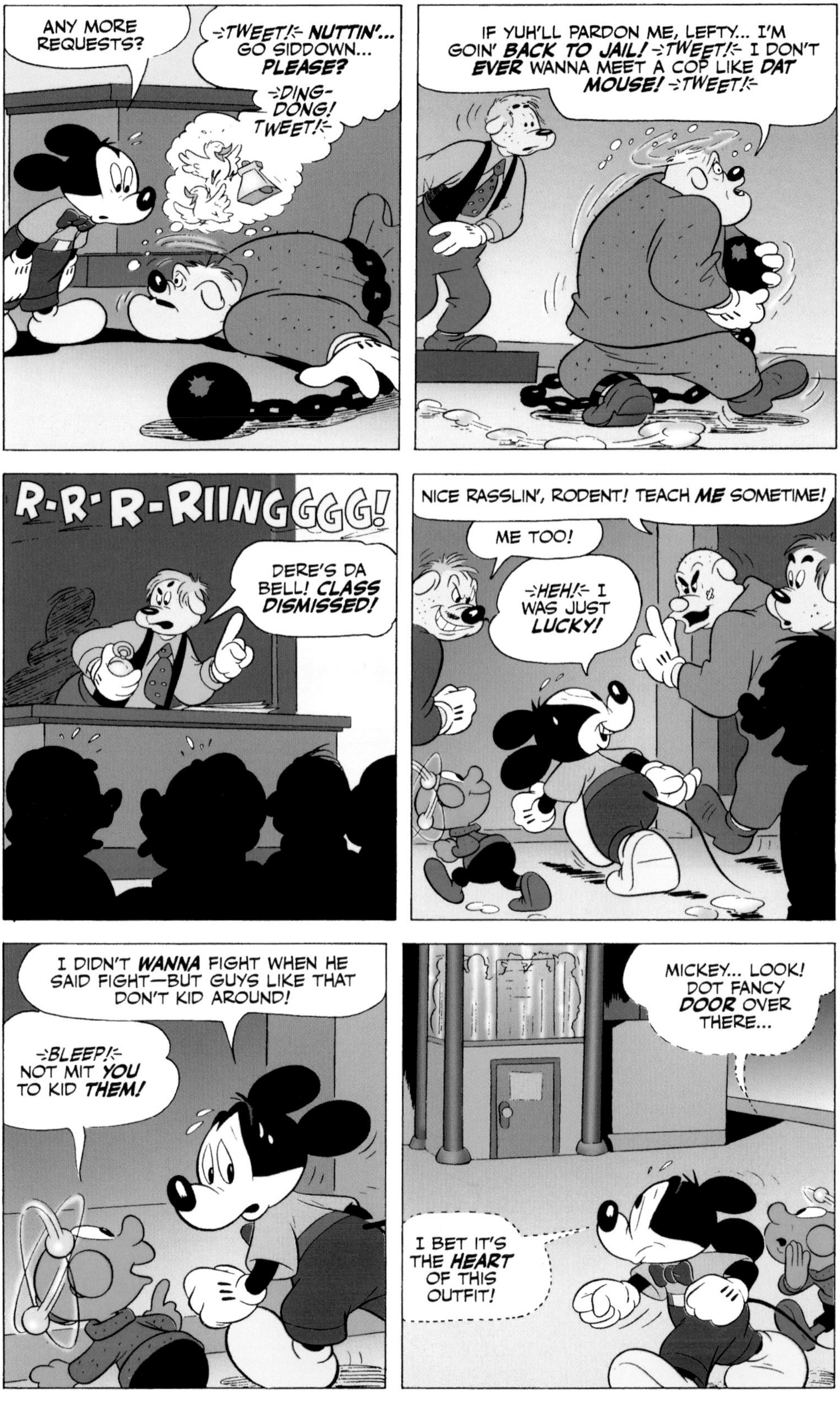
ANY MORE REQUESTS?
-TWEET!- NUTTIN'... GO SIDDOWN... PLEASE?
-DING-DONG! TWEET!-
IF YUH'LL PARDON ME, LEFTY... I'M GOIN' BACK TO JAIL! -TWEET!- I DON'T EVER WANNA MEET A COP LIKE DAT MOUSE! -TWEET!-
R-R-R-RIINGGGG!
DERE'S DA BELL! CLASS DISMISSED!
NICE RASSLIN', RODENT! TEACH ME SOMETIME!
ME TOO!
-HEH!- I WAS JUST LUCKY!
I DIDN'T WANNA FIGHT WHEN HE SAID FIGHT—BUT GUYS LIKE THAT DON'T KID AROUND!
-BLEEP!- NOT MIT YOU TO KID THEM!
MICKEY... LOOK! DOT FANCY DOOR OVER THERE...
I BET IT'S THE HEART OF THIS OUTFIT!

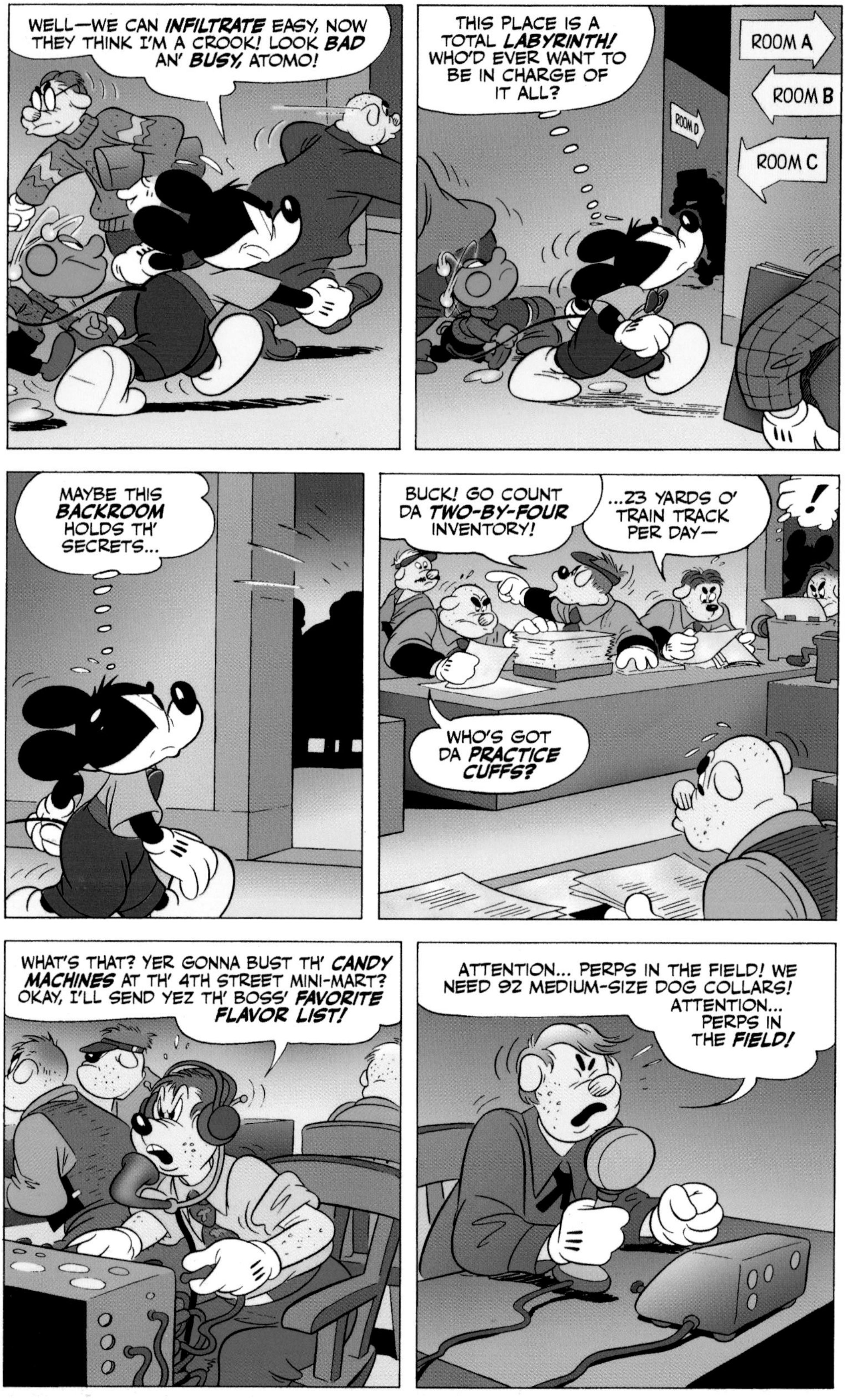
WELL—WE CAN INFILTRATE EASY, NOW THEY THINK I'M A CROOK! LOOK BAD AN' BUSY, ATOMO!
THIS PLACE IS A TOTAL LABYRINTH! WHO'D EVER WANT TO BE IN CHARGE OF IT ALL?
ROOM A
ROOM B
ROOM C
ROOM D
MAYBE THIS BACKROOM HOLDS TH' SECRETS...
BUCK! GO COUNT DA TWO-BY-FOUR INVENTORY!
...23 YARDS O' TRAIN TRACK PER DAY—
!
WHO'S GOT DA PRACTICE CUFFS?
WHAT'S THAT? YER GONNA BUST TH' CANDY MACHINES AT TH' 4TH STREET MINI-MART? OKAY, I'LL SEND YEZ TH' BOSS' FAVORITE FLAVOR LIST!
ATTENTION... PERPS IN THE FIELD! WE NEED 92 MEDIUM-SIZE DOG COLLARS! ATTENTION... PERPS IN THE FIELD!

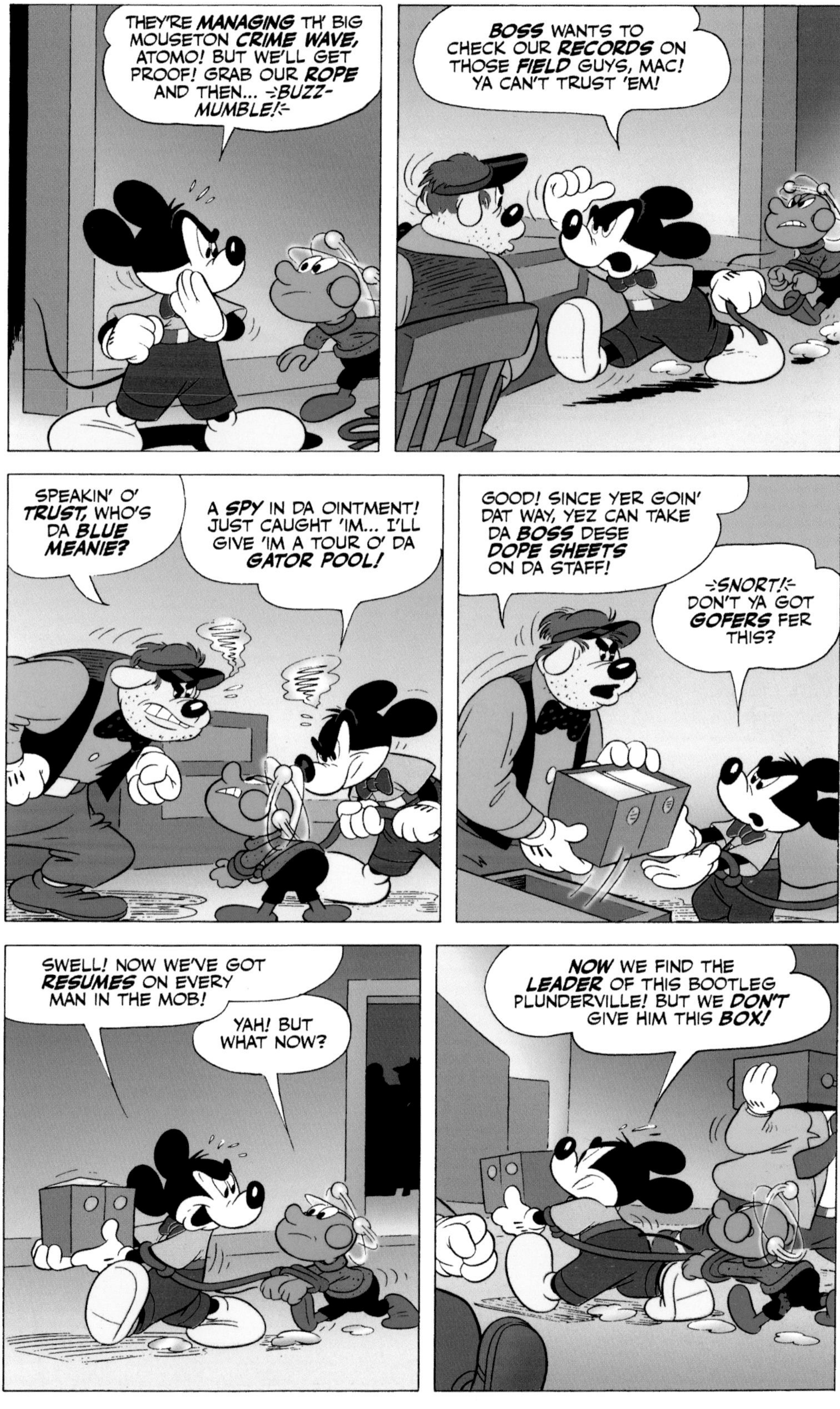

THEY'RE MANAGING TH' BIG MOUSETON CRIME WAVE, ATOMO! BUT WE'LL GET PROOF! GRAB OUR ROPE AND THEN... -BUZZ-MUMBLE!-
BOSS WANTS TO CHECK OUR RECORDS ON THOSE FIELD GUYS, MAC! YA CAN'T TRUST 'EM!
SPEAKIN' O' TRUST, WHO'S DA BLUE MEANIE?
A SPY IN DA OINTMENT! JUST CAUGHT 'IM... I'LL GIVE 'IM A TOUR O' DA GATOR POOL!
GOOD! SINCE YER GOIN' DAT WAY, YEZ CAN TAKE DA BOSS DESE DOPE SHEETS ON DA STAFF!
-SNORT!- DON'T YA GOT GOFERS FER THIS?
SWELL! NOW WE'VE GOT RESUMES ON EVERY MAN IN THE MOB!
YAH! BUT WHAT NOW?
NOW WE FIND THE LEADER OF THIS BOOTLEG PLUNDERVILLE! BUT WE DON'T GIVE HIM THIS BOX!

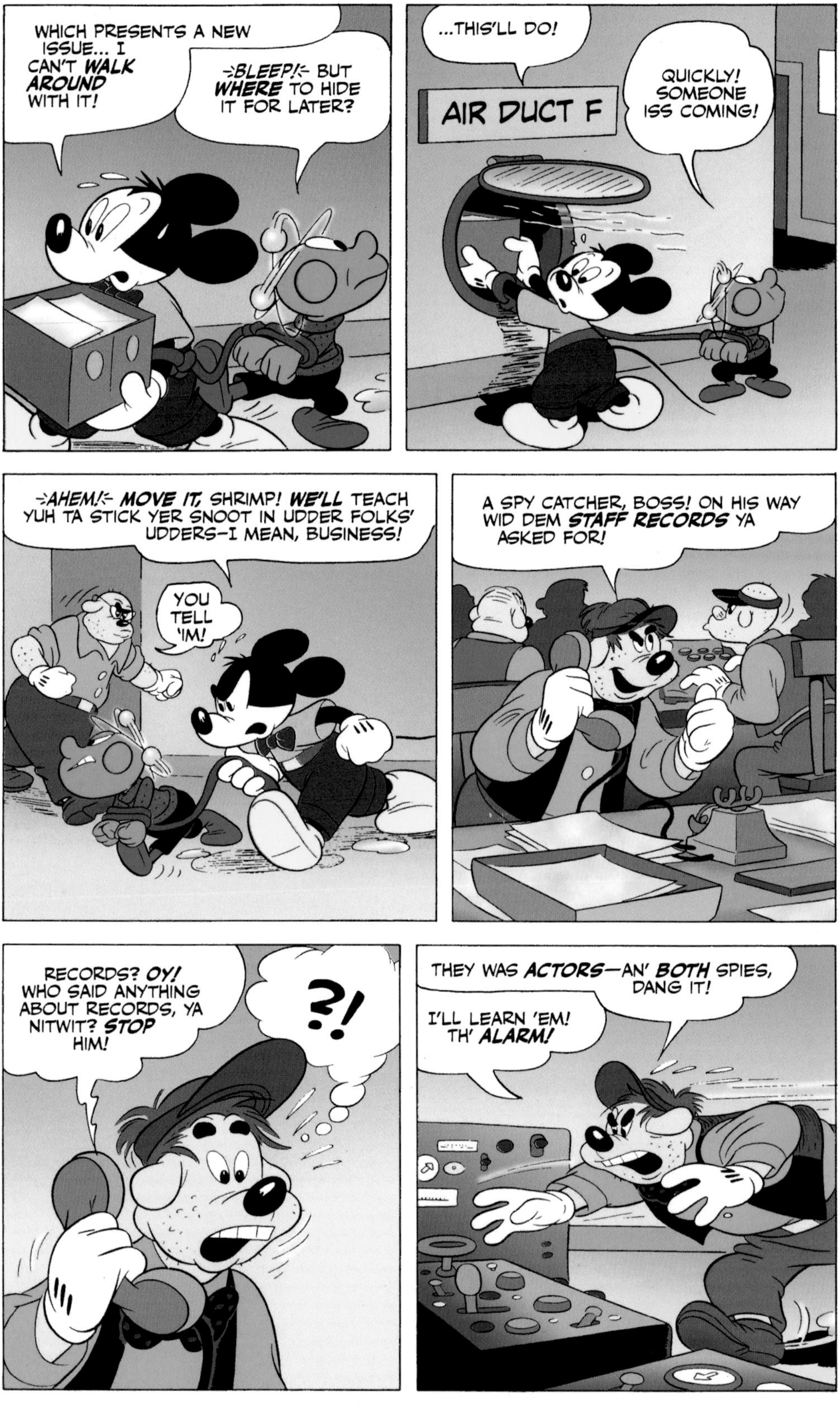
WHICH PRESENTS A NEW ISSUE... I CAN'T WALK AROUND WITH IT!
⇒BLEEP!⇐ BUT WHERE TO HIDE IT FOR LATER?
...THIS'LL DO!
AIR DUCT F
QUICKLY! SOMEONE ISS COMING!
⇒AHEM!⇐ MOVE IT, SHRIMP! WE'LL TEACH YUH TA STICK YER SNOOT IN UDDER FOLKS' UDDERS—I MEAN, BUSINESS!
YOU TELL 'IM!
A SPY CATCHER, BOSS! ON HIS WAY WID DEM STAFF RECORDS YA ASKED FOR!
RECORDS? OY! WHO SAID ANYTHING ABOUT RECORDS, YA NITWIT? STOP HIM!
?!
THEY WAS ACTORS—AN' BOTH SPIES, DANG IT!
I'LL LEARN 'EM! TH' ALARM!

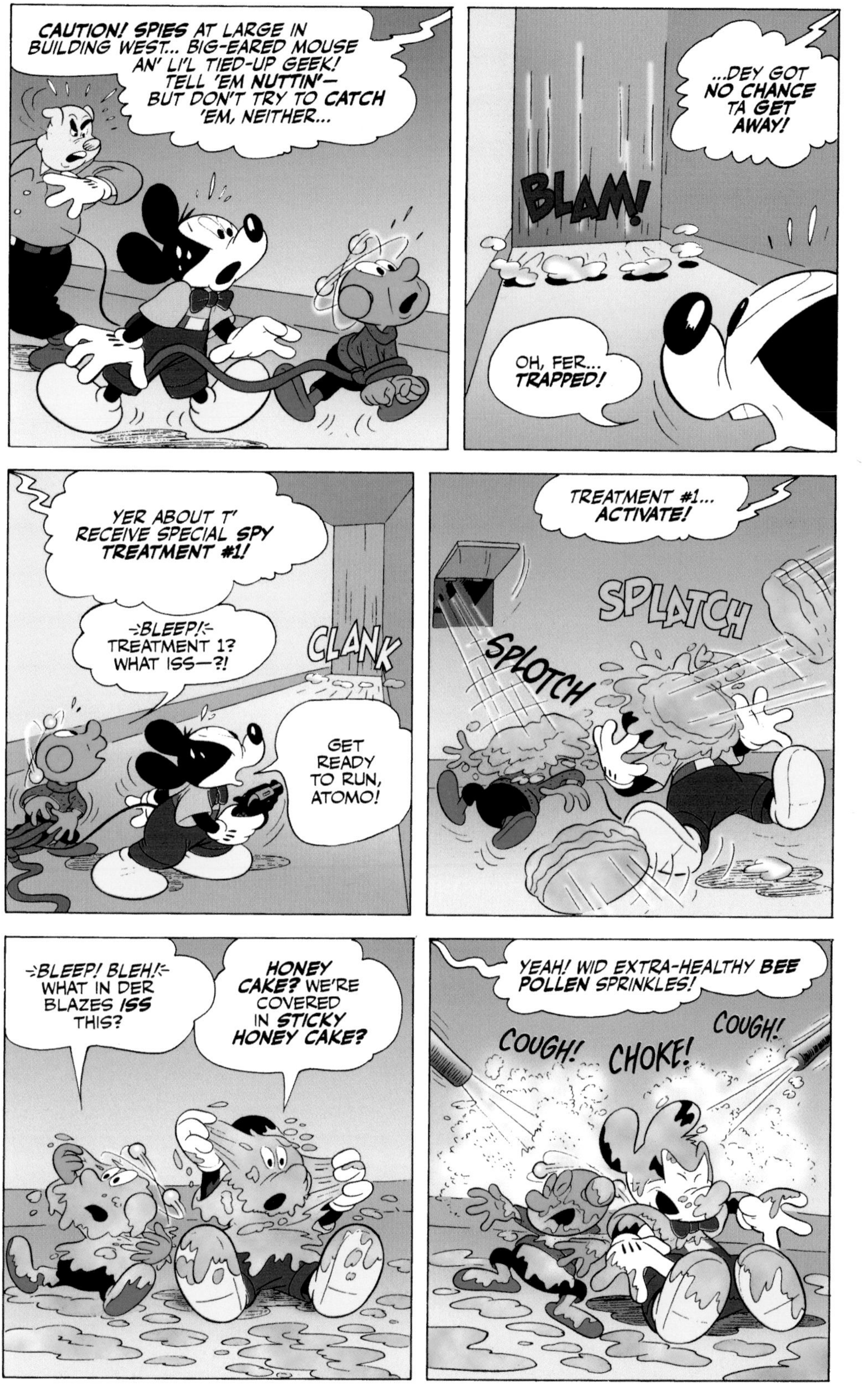
CAUTION! SPIES AT LARGE IN BUILDING WEST... BIG-EARED MOUSE AN' LI'L TIED-UP GEEK! TELL 'EM NUTTIN'— BUT DON'T TRY TO CATCH 'EM, NEITHER...
...DEY GOT NO CHANCE TA GET AWAY!
BLAM!
OH, FER... TRAPPED!
YER ABOUT T' RECEIVE SPECIAL SPY TREATMENT #1!
-BLEEP!- TREATMENT 1? WHAT ISS—?!
CLANK
GET READY TO RUN, ATOMO!
TREATMENT #1... ACTIVATE!
SPLATCH
SPLOTCH
-BLEEP! BLEH!- WHAT IN DER BLAZES ISS THIS?
HONEY CAKE? WE'RE COVERED IN STICKY HONEY CAKE?
YEAH! WID EXTRA-HEALTHY BEE POLLEN SPRINKLES!
COUGH!
CHOKE!
COUGH!

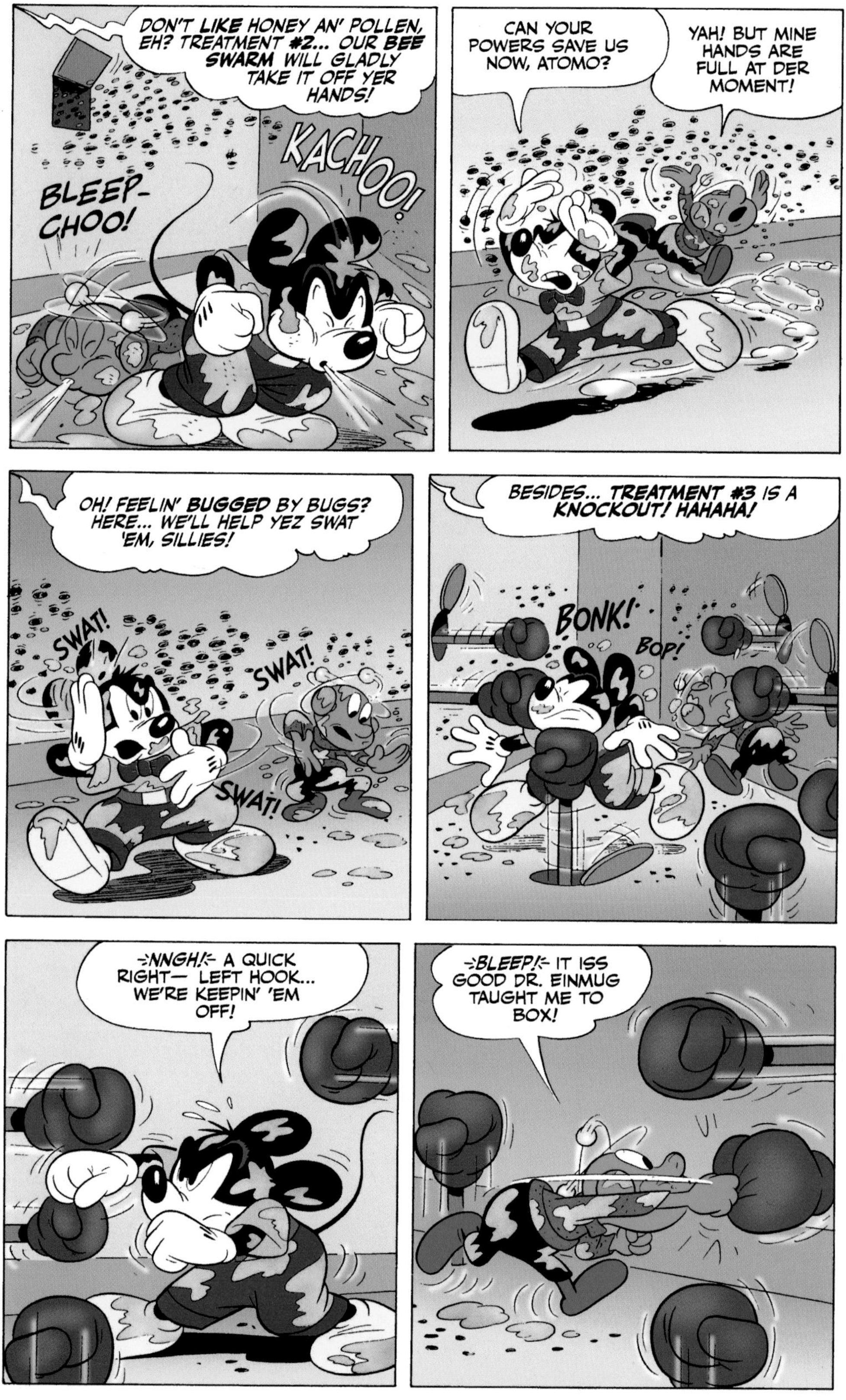
DON'T **LIKE** HONEY AN' POLLEN, EH? TREATMENT **#2**... OUR **BEE SWARM** WILL GLADLY TAKE IT OFF YER HANDS!
BLEEP-CHOO!
KACHOO!
CAN YOUR POWERS SAVE US NOW, ATOMO?
YAH! BUT MINE HANDS ARE FULL AT DER MOMENT!
OH! FEELIN' **BUGGED** BY BUGS? HERE... WE'LL HELP YEZ SWAT 'EM, SILLIES!
SWAT!
SWAT!
SWAT!
BESIDES... **TREATMENT #3** IS A **KNOCKOUT! HAHAHA!**
BONK!
BOP!
=NNGH!= A QUICK RIGHT— LEFT HOOK... WE'RE KEEPIN' 'EM OFF!
=BLEEP!= IT ISS GOOD DR. EINMUG TAUGHT ME TO BOX!

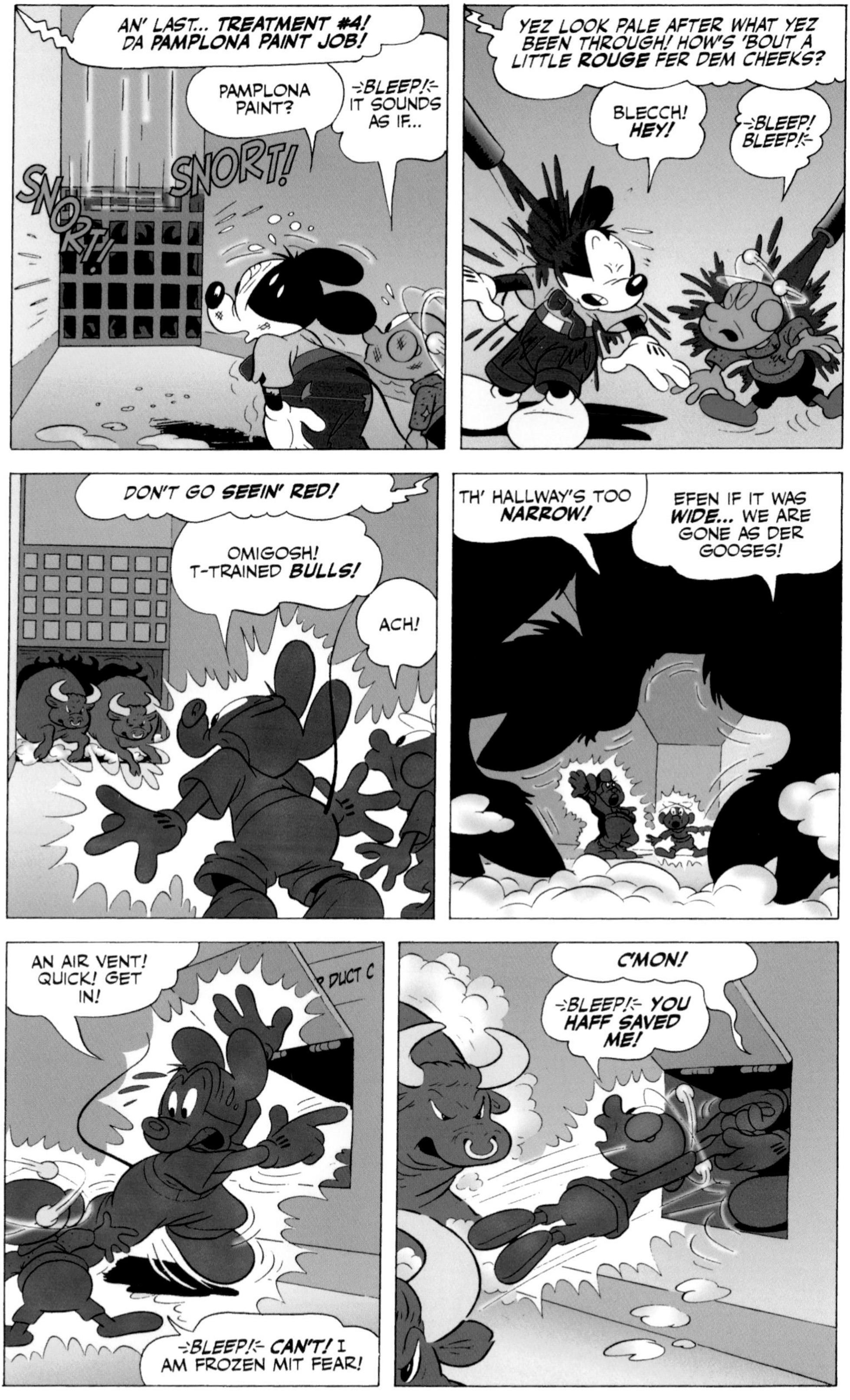
AN' LAST... TREATMENT #4! DA PAMPLONA PAINT JOB!
PAMPLONA PAINT?
=BLEEP!= IT SOUNDS AS IF...
SNORT!
SNORT!
YEZ LOOK PALE AFTER WHAT YEZ BEEN THROUGH! HOW'S 'BOUT A LITTLE ROUGE FER DEM CHEEKS?
BLECCH! HEY!
=BLEEP! BLEEP!=
DON'T GO SEEIN' RED!
OMIGOSH! T-TRAINED BULLS!
ACH!
TH' HALLWAY'S TOO NARROW!
EFEN IF IT WAS WIDE... WE ARE GONE AS DER GOOSES!
AN AIR VENT! QUICK! GET IN!
P DUCT C
=BLEEP!= CAN'T! I AM FROZEN MIT FEAR!
C'MON!
=BLEEP!= YOU HAFF SAVED ME!

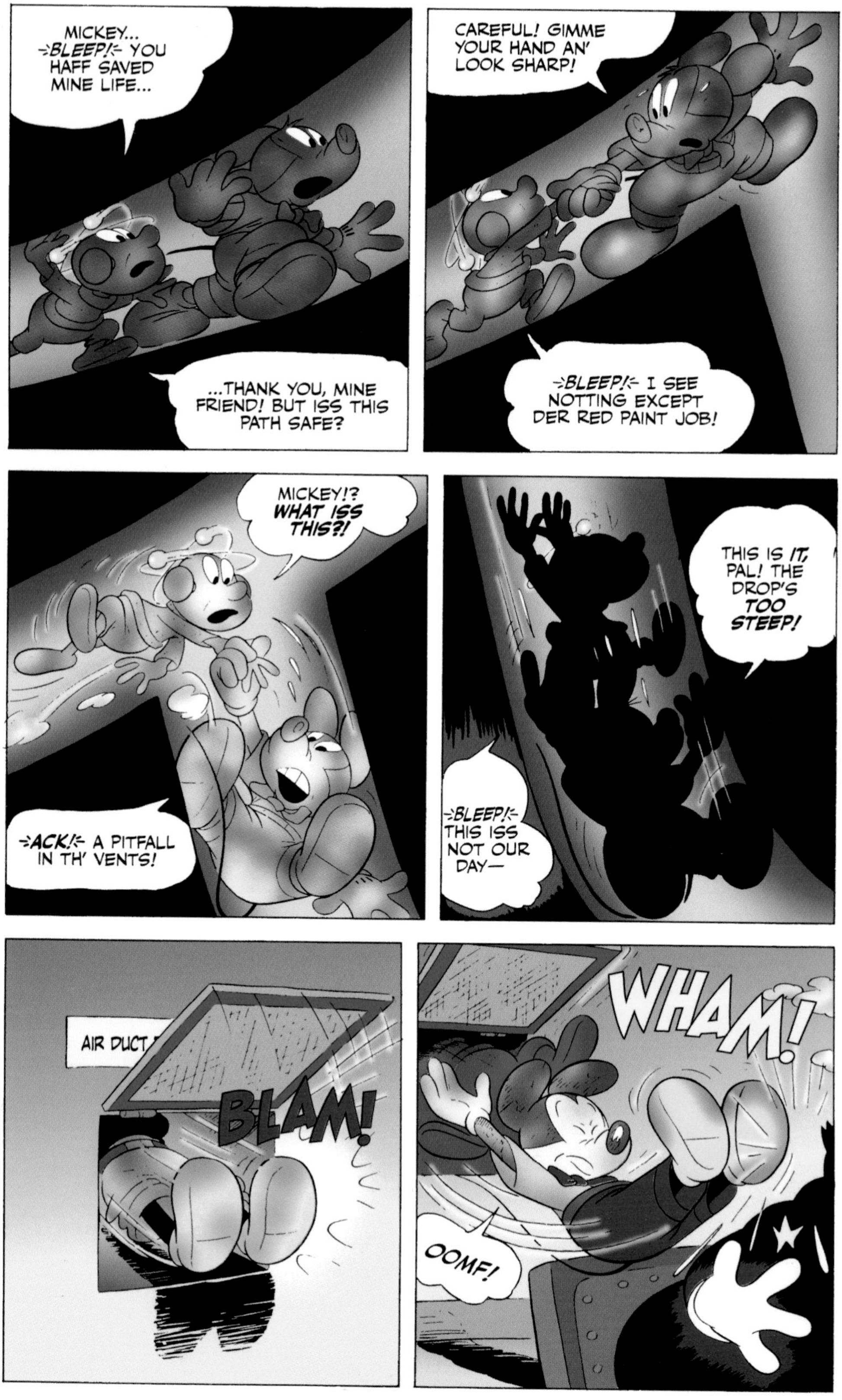

MICKEY... ⇒BLEEP!⇐ YOU HAFF SAVED MINE LIFE...
...THANK YOU, MINE FRIEND! BUT ISS THIS PATH SAFE?
CAREFUL! GIMME YOUR HAND AN' LOOK SHARP!
⇒BLEEP!⇐ I SEE NOTTING EXCEPT DER RED PAINT JOB!
MICKEY!? WHAT ISS THIS?!
⇒ACK!⇐ A PITFALL IN TH' VENTS!
THIS IS IT, PAL! THE DROP'S TOO STEEP!
⇒BLEEP!⇐ THIS ISS NOT OUR DAY—
AIR DUCT
BLAM!
WHAM!
OOMF!

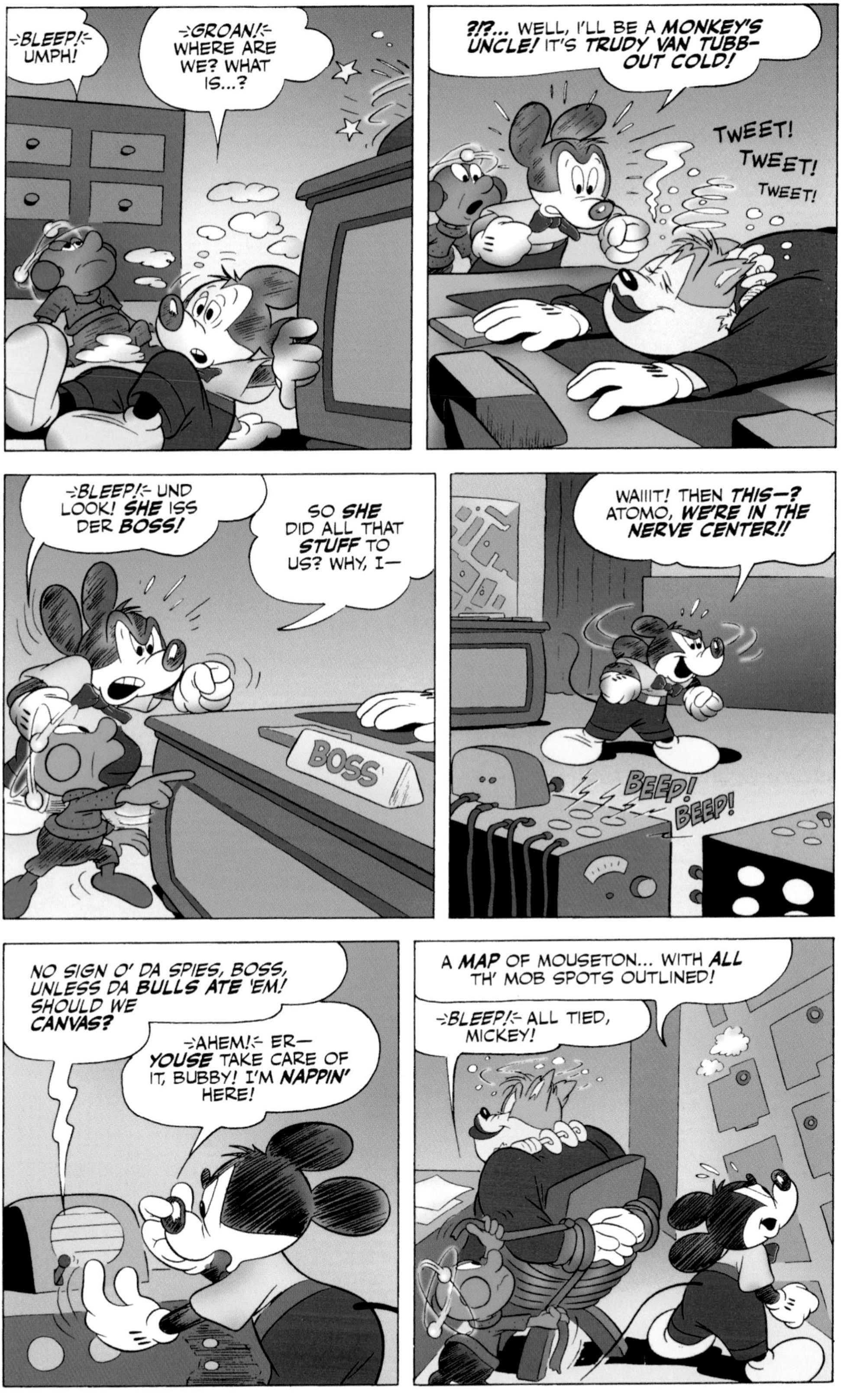

-BLEEP!- UMPH!
-GROAN!- WHERE ARE WE? WHAT IS...?
?!?... WELL, I'LL BE A MONKEY'S UNCLE! IT'S TRUDY VAN TUBB— OUT COLD!
TWEET! TWEET! TWEET!
-BLEEP!- UND LOOK! SHE ISS DER BOSS!
SO SHE DID ALL THAT STUFF TO US? WHY, I—
BOSS
WAIIIT! THEN THIS—? ATOMO, WE'RE IN THE NERVE CENTER!!
BEEP! BEEP!
NO SIGN O' DA SPIES, BOSS, UNLESS DA BULLS ATE 'EM! SHOULD WE CANVAS?
-AHEM!- ER— YOUSE TAKE CARE OF IT, BUBBY! I'M NAPPIN' HERE!
A MAP OF MOUSETON... WITH ALL TH' MOB SPOTS OUTLINED!
-BLEEP!- ALL TIED, MICKEY!

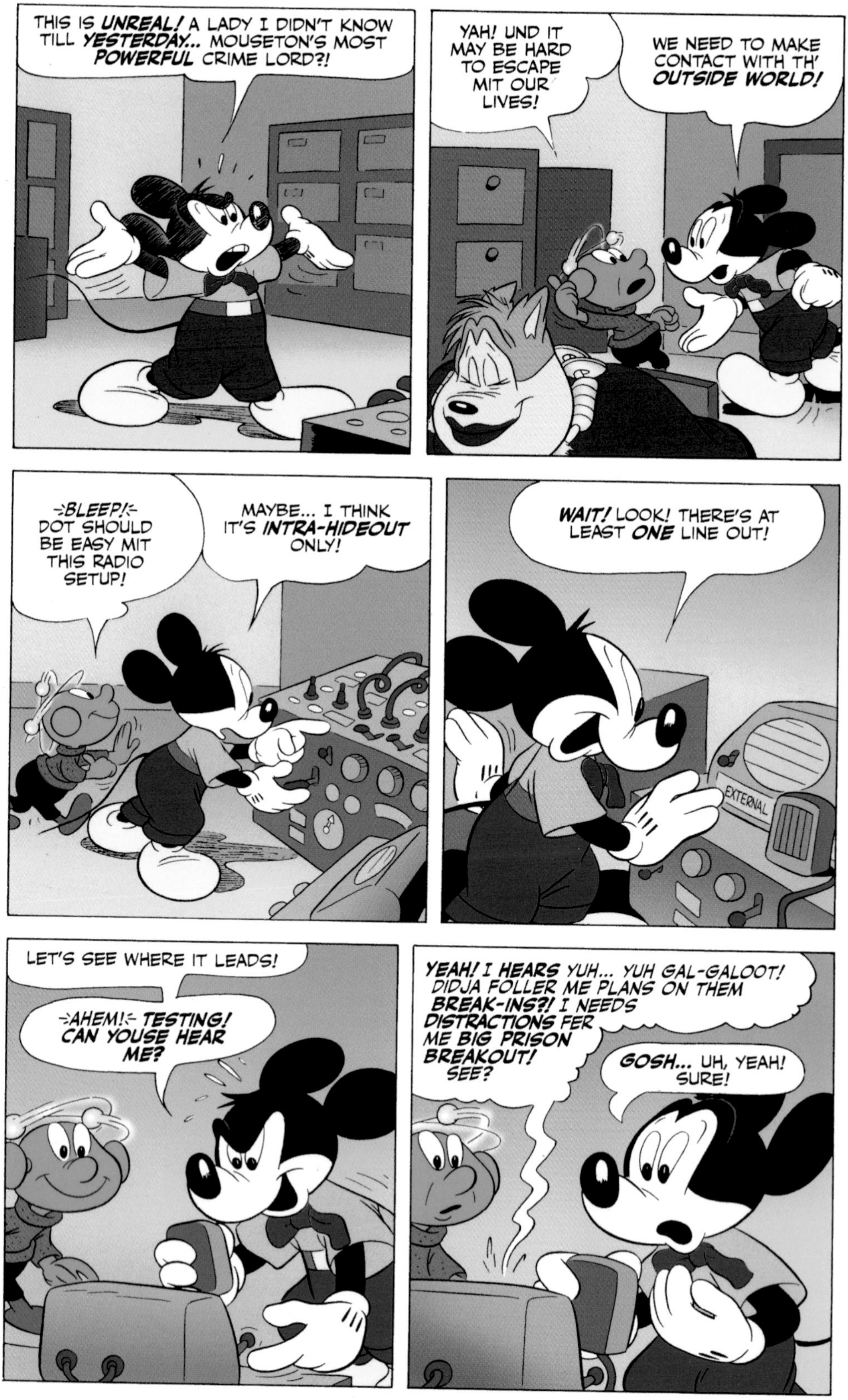
THIS IS UNREAL! A LADY I DIDN'T KNOW TILL YESTERDAY... MOUSETON'S MOST POWERFUL CRIME LORD?!
YAH! UND IT MAY BE HARD TO ESCAPE MIT OUR LIVES!
WE NEED TO MAKE CONTACT WITH TH' OUTSIDE WORLD!
-BLEEP!- DOT SHOULD BE EASY MIT THIS RADIO SETUP!
MAYBE... I THINK IT'S INTRA-HIDEOUT ONLY!
WAIT! LOOK! THERE'S AT LEAST ONE LINE OUT!
EXTERNAL
LET'S SEE WHERE IT LEADS!
-AHEM!- TESTING! CAN YOUSE HEAR ME?
YEAH! I HEARS YUH... YUH GAL-GALOOT! DIDJA FOLLER ME PLANS ON THEM BREAK-INS?! I NEEDS DISTRACTIONS FER ME BIG PRISON BREAKOUT! SEE?
GOSH... UH, YEAH! SURE!

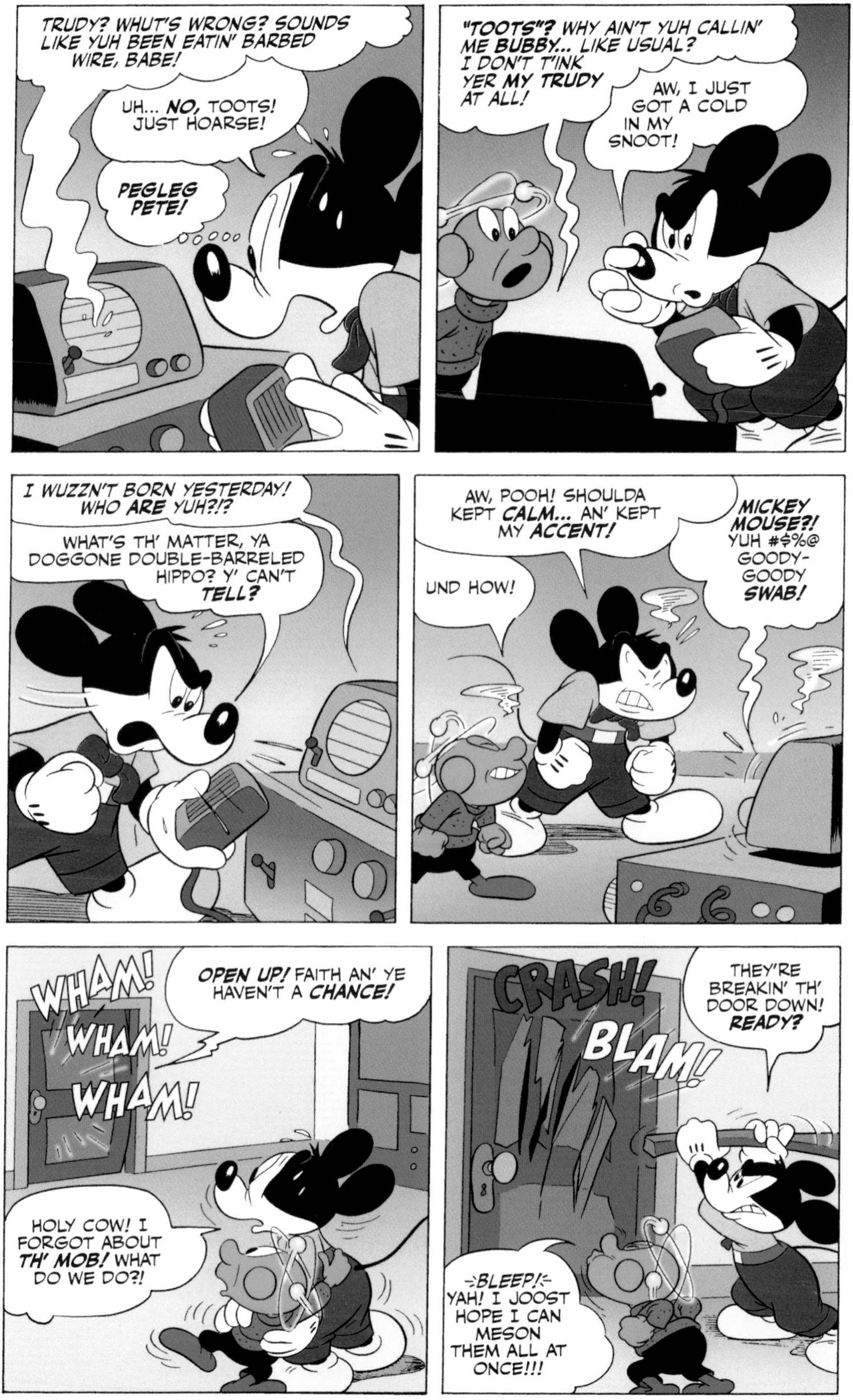
TRUDY? WHUT'S WRONG? SOUNDS LIKE YUH BEEN EATIN' BARBED WIRE, BABE!
UH... NO, TOOTS! JUST HOARSE!
PEGLEG PETE!
"TOOTS"? WHY AIN'T YUH CALLIN' ME BUBBY... LIKE USUAL? I DON'T T'INK YER MY TRUDY AT ALL!
AW, I JUST GOT A COLD IN MY SNOOT!
I WUZZN'T BORN YESTERDAY! WHO ARE YUH?!?
WHAT'S TH' MATTER, YA DOGGONE DOUBLE-BARRELED HIPPO? Y' CAN'T TELL?
AW, POOH! SHOULDA KEPT CALM... AN' KEPT MY ACCENT!
UND HOW!
MICKEY MOUSE?! YUH #$%@ GOODY-GOODY SWAB!
WHAM!
WHAM!
WHAM!
OPEN UP! FAITH AN' YE HAVEN'T A CHANCE!
HOLY COW! I FORGOT ABOUT TH' MOB! WHAT DO WE DO?!
CRASH!
BLAM!
THEY'RE BREAKIN' TH' DOOR DOWN! READY?
-BLEEP!- YAH! I JOOST HOPE I CAN MESON THEM ALL AT ONCE!!!

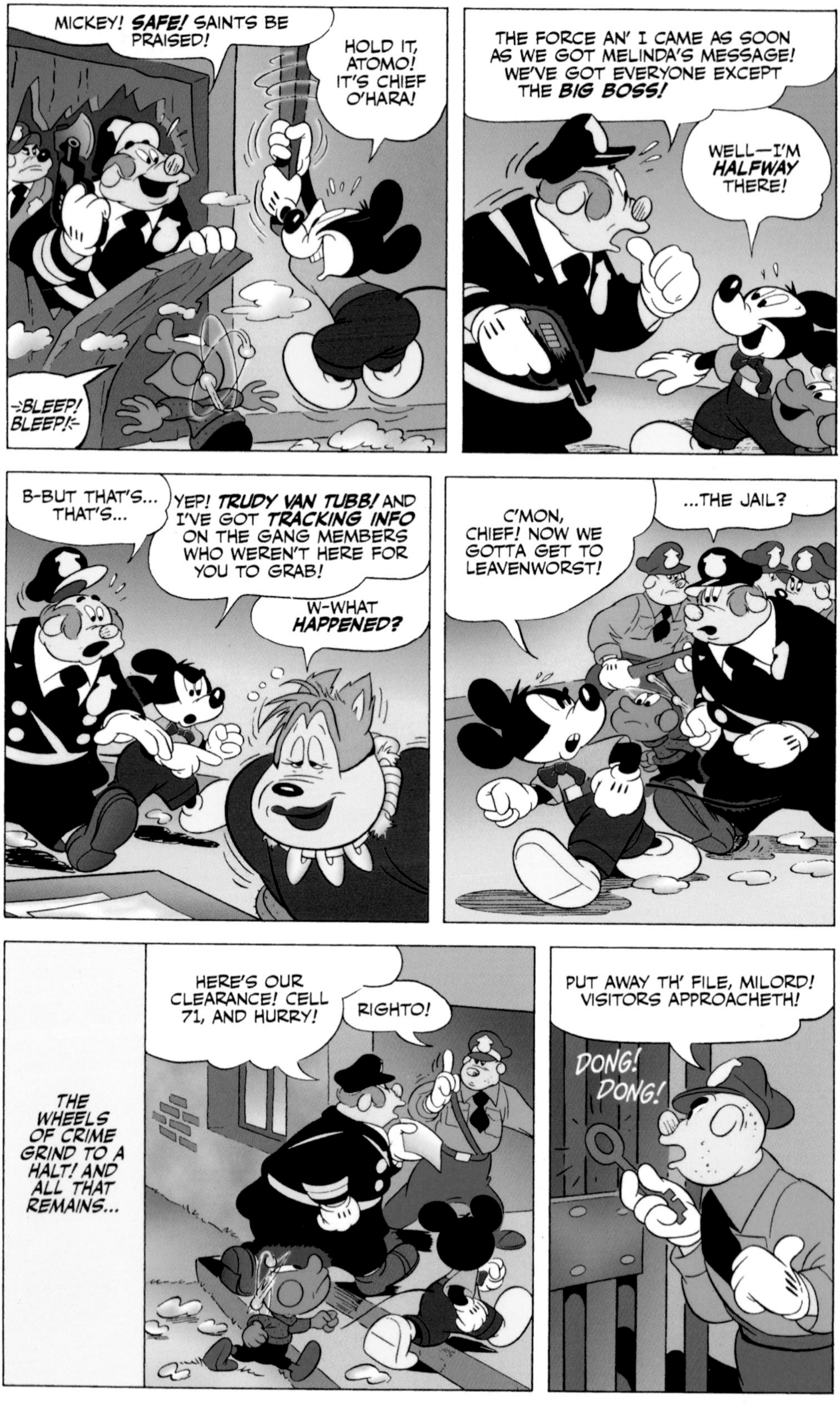
MICKEY! SAFE! SAINTS BE PRAISED!
HOLD IT, ATOMO! IT'S CHIEF O'HARA!
BLEEP! BLEEP!
THE FORCE AN' I CAME AS SOON AS WE GOT MELINDA'S MESSAGE! WE'VE GOT EVERYONE EXCEPT THE BIG BOSS!
WELL—I'M HALFWAY THERE!
B-BUT THAT'S... THAT'S...
YEP! TRUDY VAN TUBB! AND I'VE GOT TRACKING INFO ON THE GANG MEMBERS WHO WEREN'T HERE FOR YOU TO GRAB!
W-WHAT HAPPENED?
C'MON, CHIEF! NOW WE GOTTA GET TO LEAVENWORST!
...THE JAIL?
THE WHEELS OF CRIME GRIND TO A HALT! AND ALL THAT REMAINS...
HERE'S OUR CLEARANCE! CELL 71, AND HURRY!
RIGHTO!
PUT AWAY TH' FILE, MILORD! VISITORS APPROACHETH!
DONG! DONG!

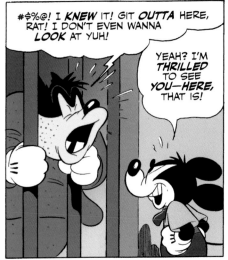

#$%@! I **KNEW** IT! GIT **OUTTA** HERE, RAT! I DON'T EVEN WANNA **LOOK** AT YUH!

YEAH? I'M **THRILLED** TO SEE **YOU—HERE,** THAT IS!

SHADDAP! I **HATE** YUH!

TRUDY'S THE **BOSS,** CHIEF... BUT SOMEONE **ELSE** ACTED AS **TACTICAL** MANAGER!

HERE? FROM HIS **CELL?**

HE'S GOT "MISS BAD MANNERS" ON A RADIO LINK! IT'S GOTTA BE HIDDEN HERE SOMEPLACE!

I CAN FIND IT MIT MINE ATOMIC POWERS!

⇥BLEEP!⇤ IT'S IN **DER RAZOR!** DOT EXPLAINS HIS UNSHAVEN SASQUATCH LOOKS!

⇥ROWR!⇤ EACH GUY'S **WORSE** THAN TH' OTHER!

*FOILED! PETE'S **BREAKOUT** IS A NO-GO... AND HE **TELLS ALL** ABOUT HIS BOYHOOD "MOUSENAPPING"!*

...SO WE TOSSED TH' LI'L RUNT IN TH' SHED—AN' **DISCOVERED** DAT TIPPY **FAKE FLOOR!** IT WUZ A GANG HIDEOUT ENTRANCE THEN, TOO!

I READ HOW TH' COPS HAD SENT TH' GANG UP TH' RIVER! THEY MUSTA **JUST** CEMENTED OVER DAT FLOOR... TH' CEMENT WASN'T **DRY,** AN' DIDN'T HOLD TH' FLOOR **STEADY—** BUT TH' COPS DIDN'T **KNOW!**

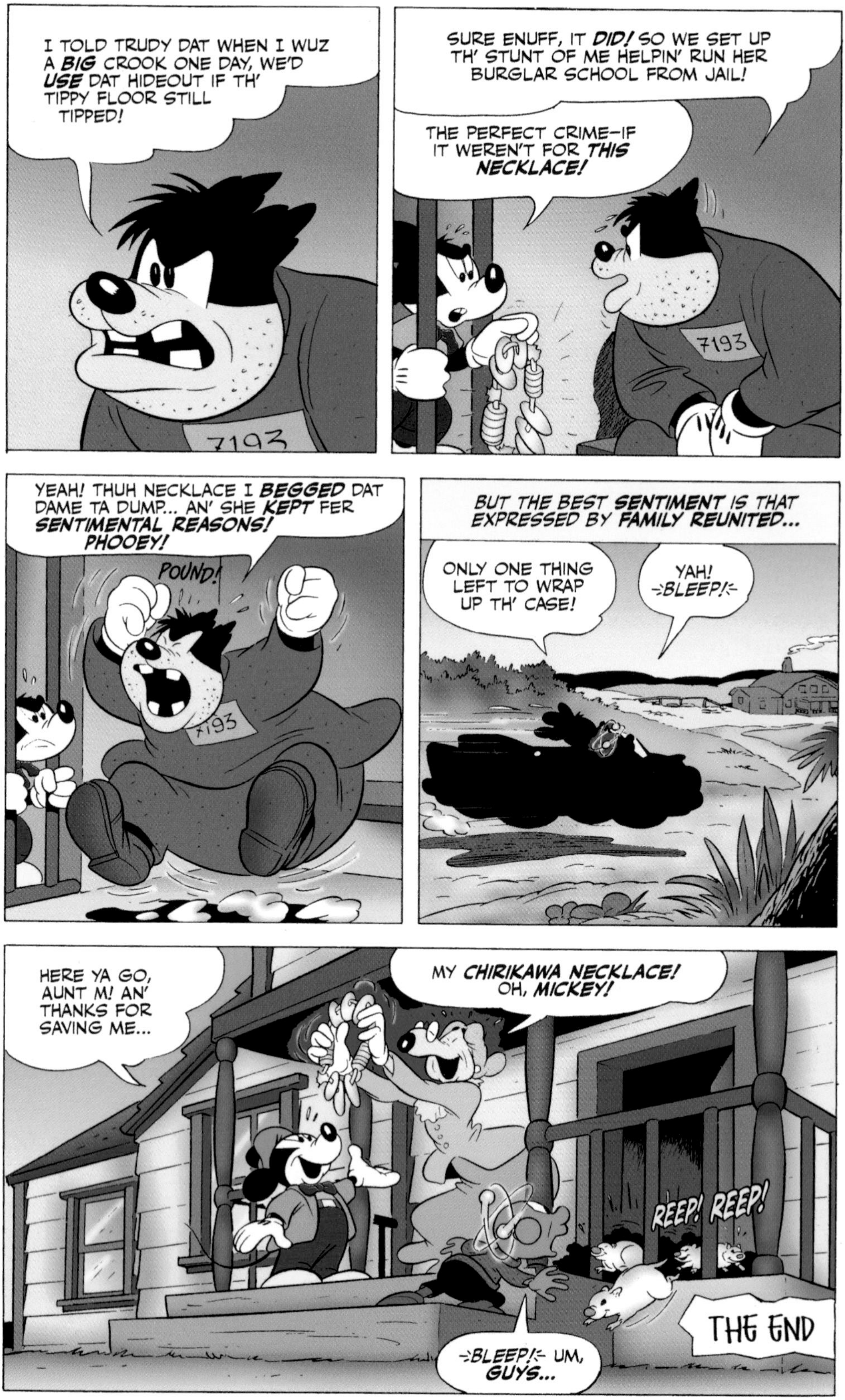
I TOLD TRUDY DAT WHEN I WUZ A BIG CROOK ONE DAY, WE'D USE DAT HIDEOUT IF TH' TIPPY FLOOR STILL TIPPED!
7193
SURE ENUFF, IT DID! SO WE SET UP TH' STUNT OF ME HELPIN' RUN HER BURGLAR SCHOOL FROM JAIL!
THE PERFECT CRIME—IF IT WEREN'T FOR THIS NECKLACE!
7193
YEAH! THUH NECKLACE I BEGGED DAT DAME TA DUMP... AN' SHE KEPT FER SENTIMENTAL REASONS! PHOOEY!
POUND!
7193
BUT THE BEST SENTIMENT IS THAT EXPRESSED BY FAMILY REUNITED...
ONLY ONE THING LEFT TO WRAP UP TH' CASE!
YAH! BLEEP!
HERE YA GO, AUNT M! AN' THANKS FOR SAVING ME...
MY CHIRIKAWA NECKLACE! OH, MICKEY!
REEP! REEP!
BLEEP! UM, GUYS...
THE END

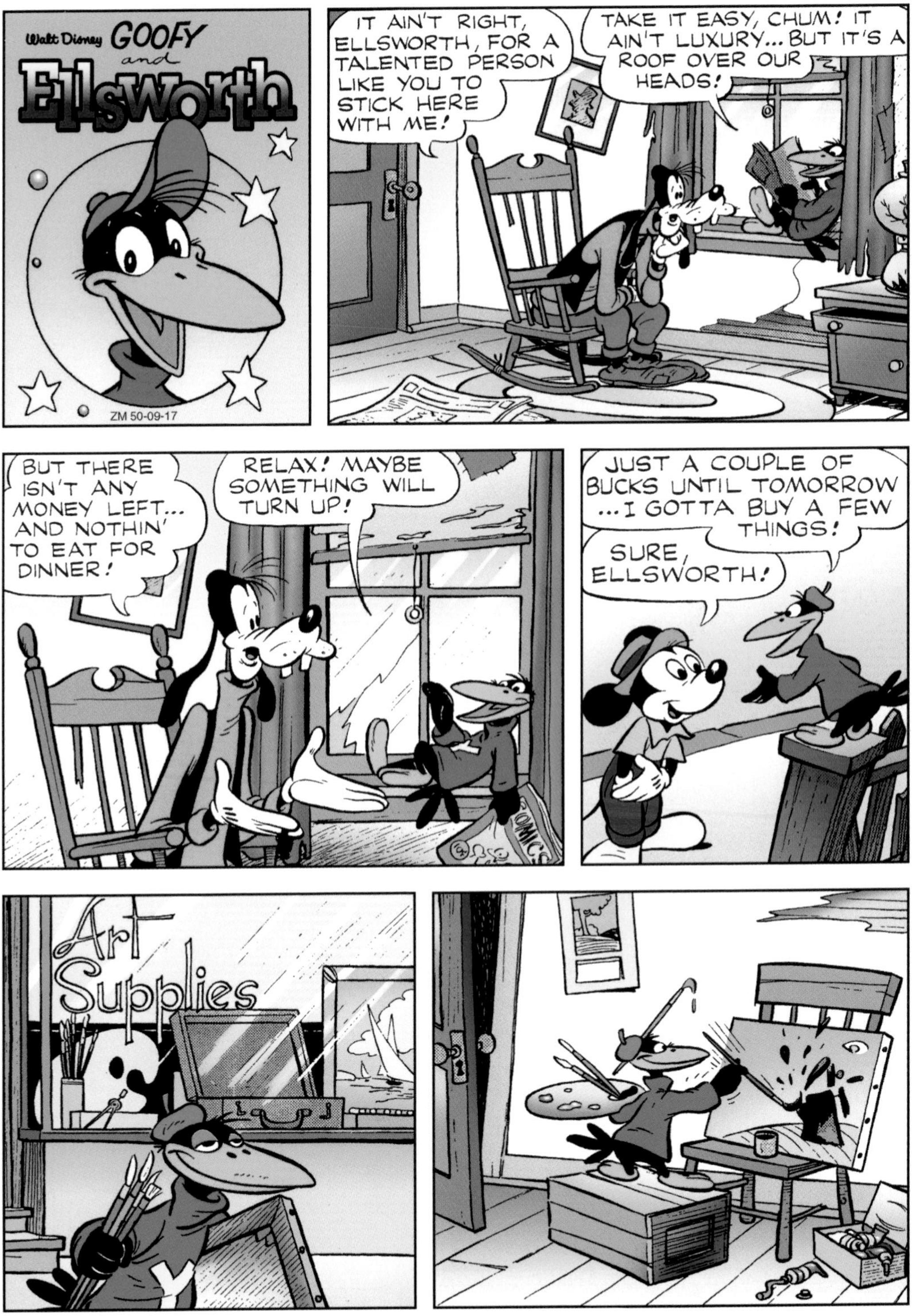
Walt Disney GOOFY and Ellsworth
ZM 50-09-17
IT AIN'T RIGHT, ELLSWORTH, FOR A TALENTED PERSON LIKE YOU TO STICK HERE WITH ME!
TAKE IT EASY, CHUM! IT AIN'T LUXURY... BUT IT'S A ROOF OVER OUR HEADS!
BUT THERE ISN'T ANY MONEY LEFT... AND NOTHIN' TO EAT FOR DINNER!
RELAX! MAYBE SOMETHING WILL TURN UP!
JUST A COUPLE OF BUCKS UNTIL TOMORROW ...I GOTTA BUY A FEW THINGS!
SURE, ELLSWORTH!
Art Supplies

Originally published in *Mickey Mouse* Sunday comic strip (USA, 1950)

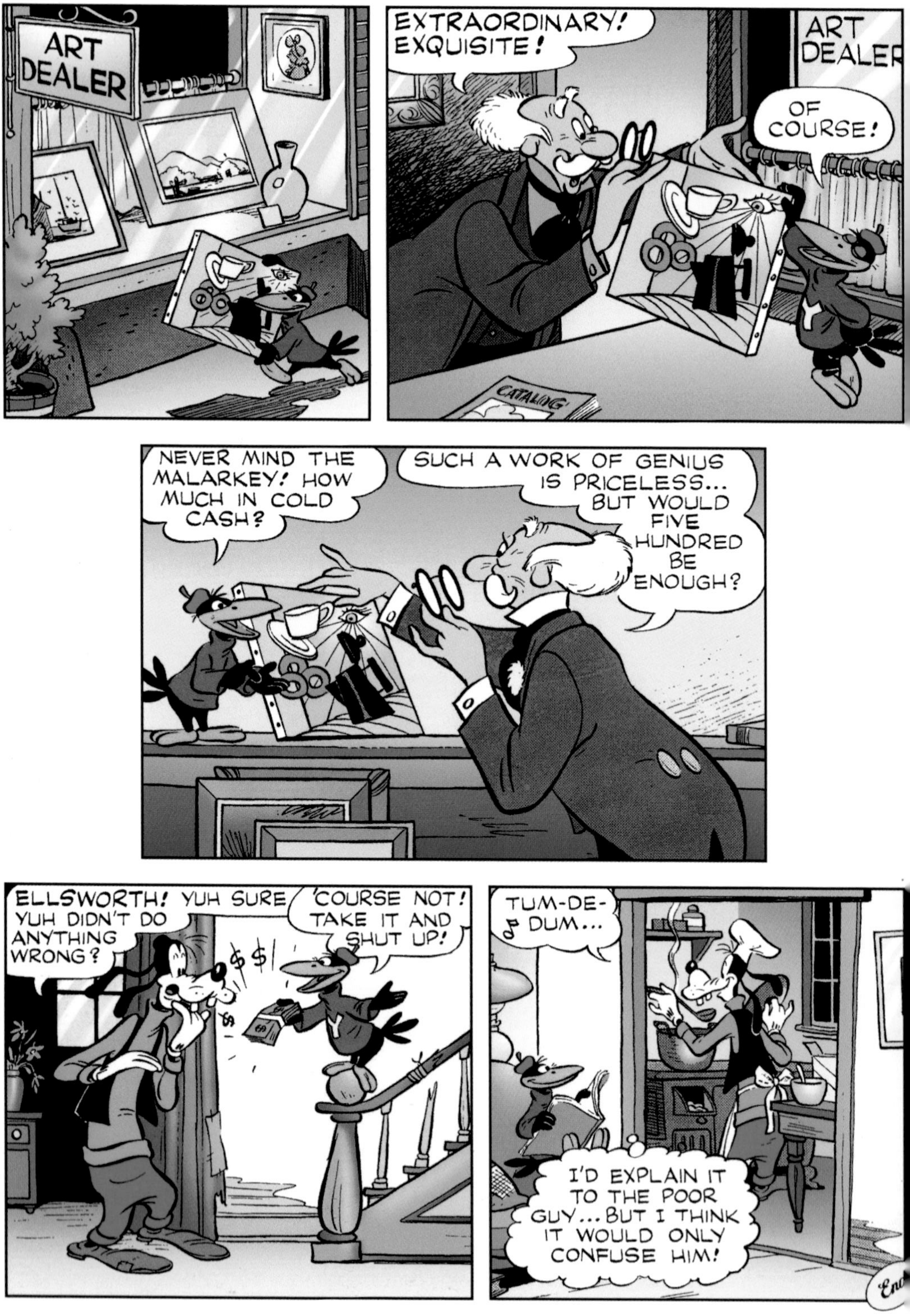
ART DEALER
EXTRAORDINARY! EXQUISITE!
ART DEALER
OF COURSE!
NEVER MIND THE MALARKEY! HOW MUCH IN COLD CASH?
SUCH A WORK OF GENIUS IS PRICELESS... BUT WOULD FIVE HUNDRED BE ENOUGH?
ELLSWORTH! YUH SURE YUH DIDN'T DO ANYTHING WRONG?
'COURSE NOT! TAKE IT AND SHUT UP!
TUM-DE-DUM...
I'D EXPLAIN IT TO THE POOR GUY... BUT I THINK IT WOULD ONLY CONFUSE HIM!

Walt Disney MICKEY and GOOFY in THE MAN WHO WASN'T THERE!

Goofy: WELL, *HOT-CHA-CHA!* IF IT AIN'T MICKEY MOUSE—MOUSETON'S *FINEST!*

Mortimer: AN' IF IT ISN'T MORTIMER MOUSE... *MR. PERSONALITY!* THEY'LL LET *ANYONE* ROAM THIS TOWN!

S-73218

Mortimer: WHERE'S YOUR *DUFUS* PLAYMATE GOOFY? *LOSE* HIM SOMEWHERE?

Mickey: GOOFY IS *NOT* A DUFUS!

Mortimer: WELL, YA *GOTTA* ADMIT HE'S NOT THE *SMARTEST* GUY IN THE WORLD...

Mickey: NEITHER ARE *YOU!* WHY DON'T YA GET LOCKJAW?

Slim: NOW, MORTIMER! GOOFY *IS* SMARTER THAN PEOPLE GIVE HIM CREDIT FOR—

Goofy: HEY THERE, MICK! HOWDY, SLIM! HI, MORTIMER!

Mortimer: —:HAH!:— IF IT ISN'T TALL-DARK-AND-*GRUESOME* HIMSELF!

Mickey: KNOCK IT *OFF*, MORTIMER!

Mortimer: HIYA, GOOFY! *WHERE ARE YOU?*

Goofy: HUH? SHUCKS, MORT, I'M RIGHT HERE IN FRONT O' YUH! SEE?

Originally published in *Donald and Mickey* #137 (United Kingdom, 1974)

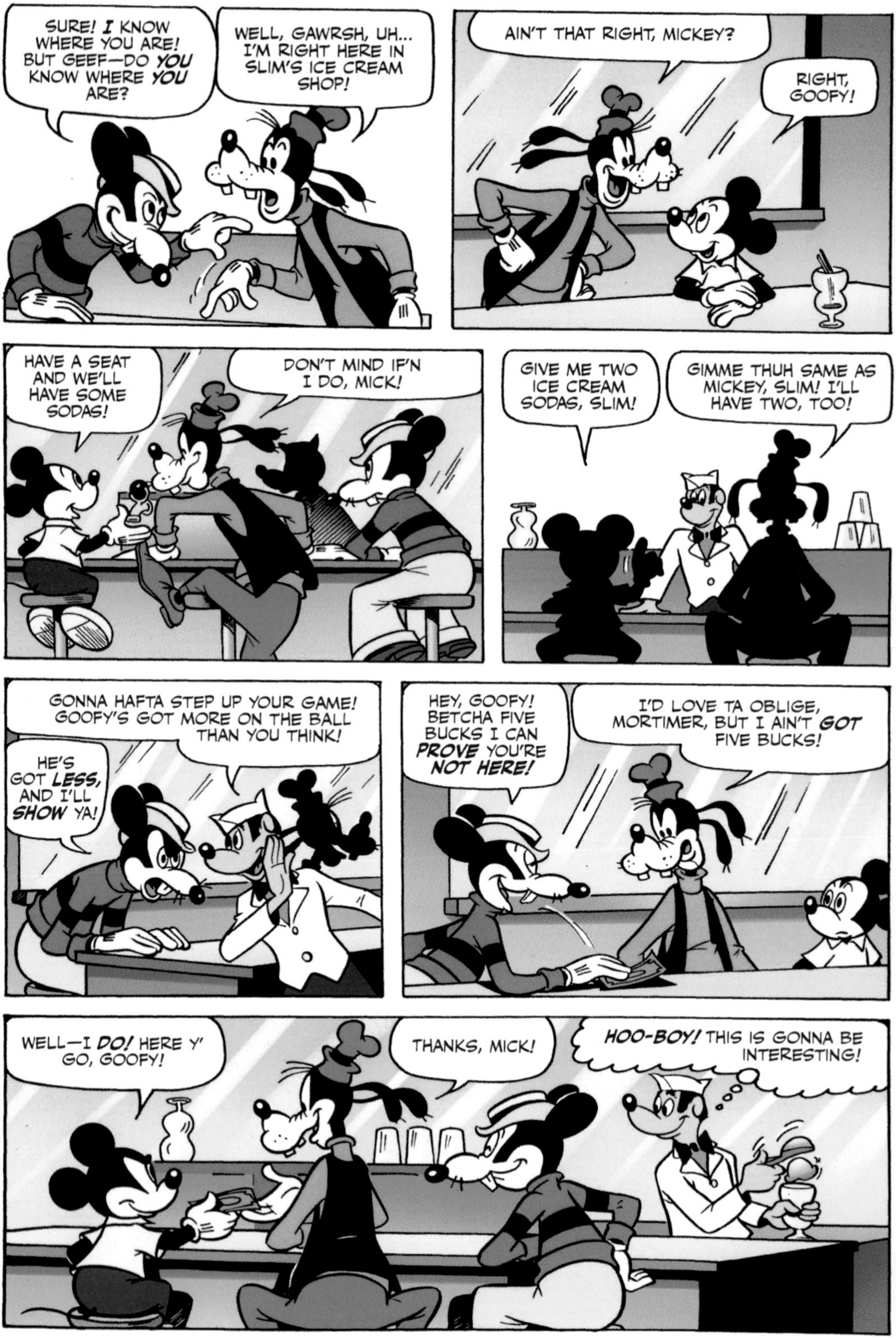
SURE! I KNOW WHERE YOU ARE! BUT GEEF—DO YOU KNOW WHERE YOU ARE?
WELL, GAWRSH, UH... I'M RIGHT HERE IN SLIM'S ICE CREAM SHOP!
AIN'T THAT RIGHT, MICKEY?
RIGHT, GOOFY!
HAVE A SEAT AND WE'LL HAVE SOME SODAS!
DON'T MIND IF'N I DO, MICK!
GIVE ME TWO ICE CREAM SODAS, SLIM!
GIMME THUH SAME AS MICKEY, SLIM! I'LL HAVE TWO, TOO!
GONNA HAFTA STEP UP YOUR GAME! GOOFY'S GOT MORE ON THE BALL THAN YOU THINK!
HE'S GOT LESS, AND I'LL SHOW YA!
HEY, GOOFY! BETCHA FIVE BUCKS I CAN PROVE YOU'RE NOT HERE!
I'D LOVE TA OBLIGE, MORTIMER, BUT I AIN'T GOT FIVE BUCKS!
WELL—I DO! HERE Y' GO, GOOFY!
THANKS, MICK!
HOO-BOY! THIS IS GONNA BE INTERESTING!

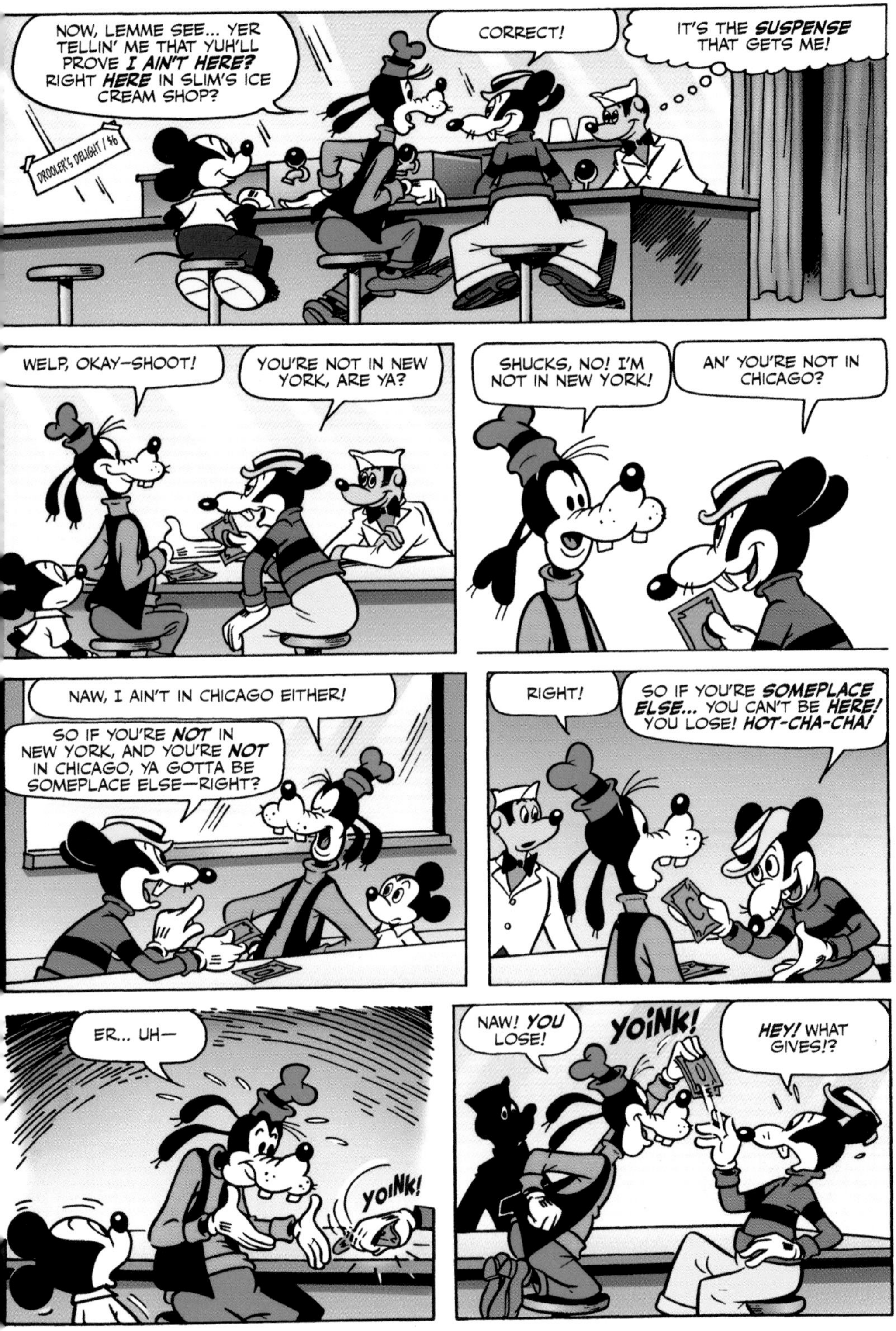
NOW, LEMME SEE... YER TELLIN' ME THAT YUH'LL PROVE *I AIN'T HERE?* RIGHT *HERE* IN SLIM'S ICE CREAM SHOP?
CORRECT!
IT'S THE *SUSPENSE* THAT GETS ME!
DROOLER'S DELIGHT / $6
WELP, OKAY—SHOOT!
YOU'RE NOT IN NEW YORK, ARE YA?
SHUCKS, NO! I'M NOT IN NEW YORK!
AN' YOU'RE NOT IN CHICAGO?
NAW, I AIN'T IN CHICAGO EITHER!
SO IF YOU'RE *NOT* IN NEW YORK, AND YOU'RE *NOT* IN CHICAGO, YA GOTTA BE SOMEPLACE ELSE—RIGHT?
RIGHT!
SO IF YOU'RE *SOMEPLACE ELSE...* YOU CAN'T BE *HERE!* YOU LOSE! *HOT-CHA-CHA!*
ER... UH—
YOINK!
NAW! *YOU* LOSE!
YOINK!
HEY! WHAT GIVES!?

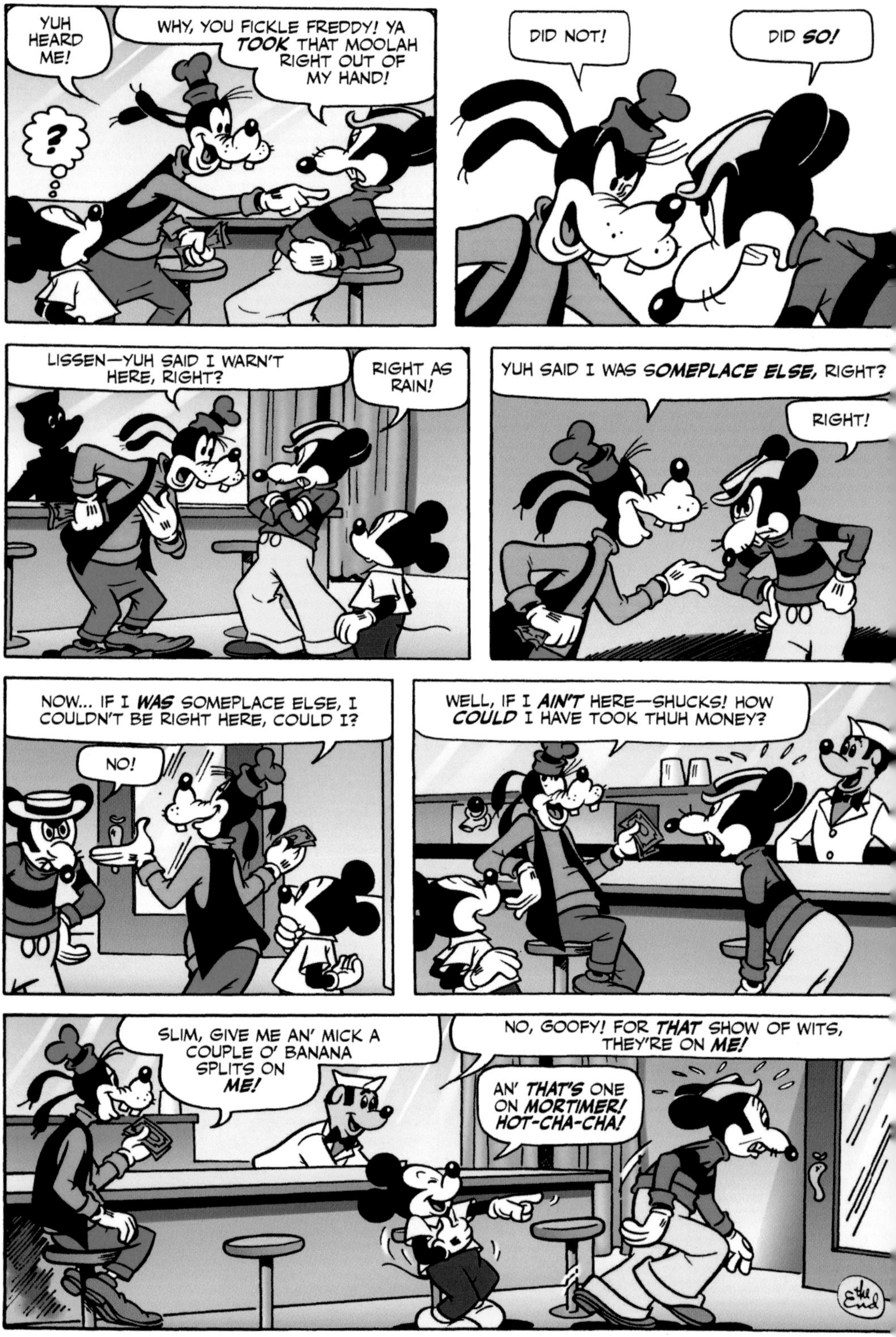
YUH HEARD ME!
WHY, YOU FICKLE FREDDY! YA TOOK THAT MOOLAH RIGHT OUT OF MY HAND!
?
DID NOT!
DID SO!
LISSEN—YUH SAID I WARN'T HERE, RIGHT?
RIGHT AS RAIN!
YUH SAID I WAS SOMEPLACE ELSE, RIGHT?
RIGHT!
NOW... IF I WAS SOMEPLACE ELSE, I COULDN'T BE RIGHT HERE, COULD I?
NO!
WELL, IF I AIN'T HERE—SHUCKS! HOW COULD I HAVE TOOK THUH MONEY?
SLIM, GIVE ME AN' MICK A COUPLE O' BANANA SPLITS ON ME!
NO, GOOFY! FOR THAT SHOW OF WITS, THEY'RE ON ME!
AN' THAT'S ONE ON MORTIMER! HOT-CHA-CHA!
the End

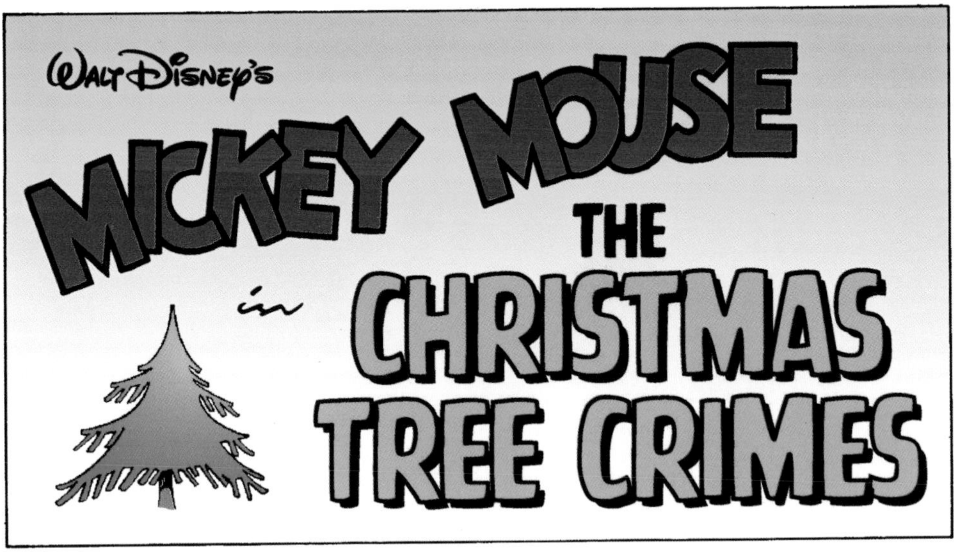
Walt Disney's
MICKEY MOUSE
in
THE CHRISTMAS TREE CRIMES

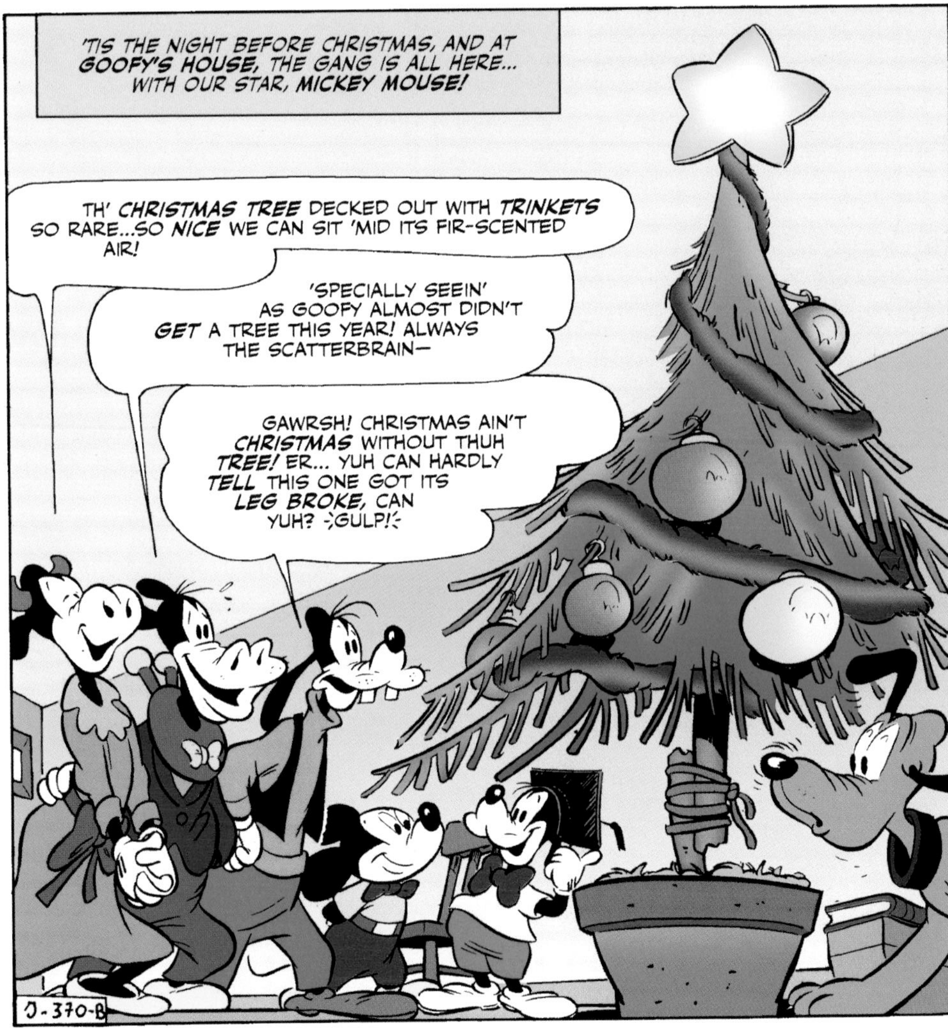
'TIS THE NIGHT BEFORE CHRISTMAS, AND AT GOOFY'S HOUSE, THE GANG IS ALL HERE... WITH OUR STAR, MICKEY MOUSE!
TH' CHRISTMAS TREE DECKED OUT WITH TRINKETS SO RARE...SO NICE WE CAN SIT 'MID ITS FIR-SCENTED AIR!
'SPECIALLY SEEIN' AS GOOFY ALMOST DIDN'T GET A TREE THIS YEAR! ALWAYS THE SCATTERBRAIN—
GAWRSH! CHRISTMAS AIN'T CHRISTMAS WITHOUT THUH TREE! ER... YUH CAN HARDLY TELL THIS ONE GOT ITS LEG BROKE, CAN YUH? GULP!
1
J-370-B

Originally published in *Topolino* #370 (Italy, 1962)

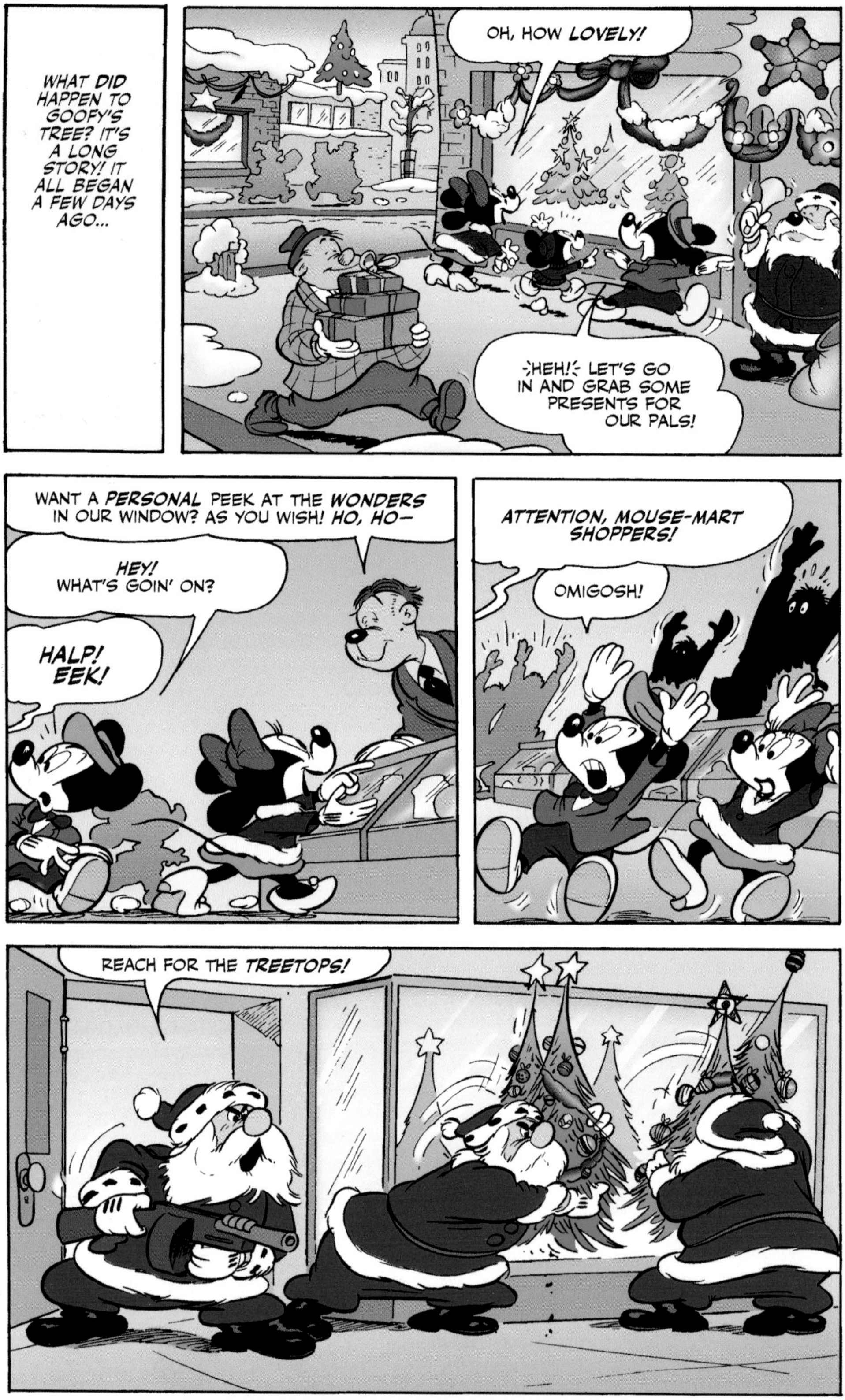
WHAT DID HAPPEN TO GOOFY'S TREE? IT'S A LONG STORY! IT ALL BEGAN A FEW DAYS AGO...
OH, HOW LOVELY!
HEH! LET'S GO IN AND GRAB SOME PRESENTS FOR OUR PALS!
WANT A PERSONAL PEEK AT THE WONDERS IN OUR WINDOW? AS YOU WISH! HO, HO—
HEY! WHAT'S GOIN' ON?
HALP! EEK!
ATTENTION, MOUSE-MART SHOPPERS!
OMIGOSH!
REACH FOR THE TREETOPS!

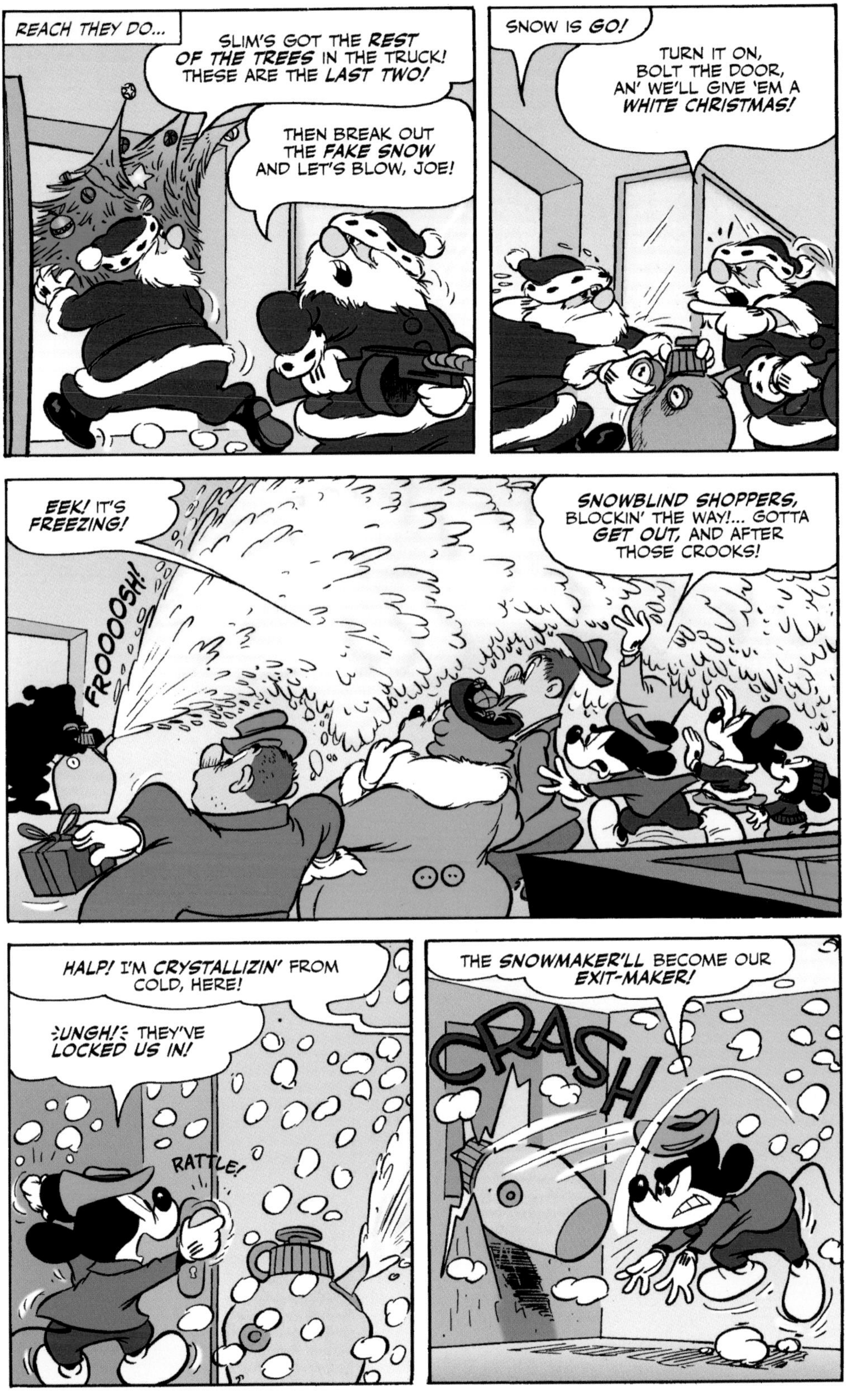
REACH THEY DO...
SLIM'S GOT THE REST OF THE TREES IN THE TRUCK! THESE ARE THE LAST TWO!
THEN BREAK OUT THE FAKE SNOW AND LET'S BLOW, JOE!
SNOW IS GO!
TURN IT ON, BOLT THE DOOR, AN' WE'LL GIVE 'EM A WHITE CHRISTMAS!
EEK! IT'S FREEZING!
FROOOOSH!
SNOWBLIND SHOPPERS, BLOCKIN' THE WAY!... GOTTA GET OUT, AND AFTER THOSE CROOKS!
HALP! I'M CRYSTALLIZIN' FROM COLD, HERE!
UNGH! THEY'VE LOCKED US IN!
RATTLE!
THE SNOWMAKER'LL BECOME OUR EXIT-MAKER!
CRASH

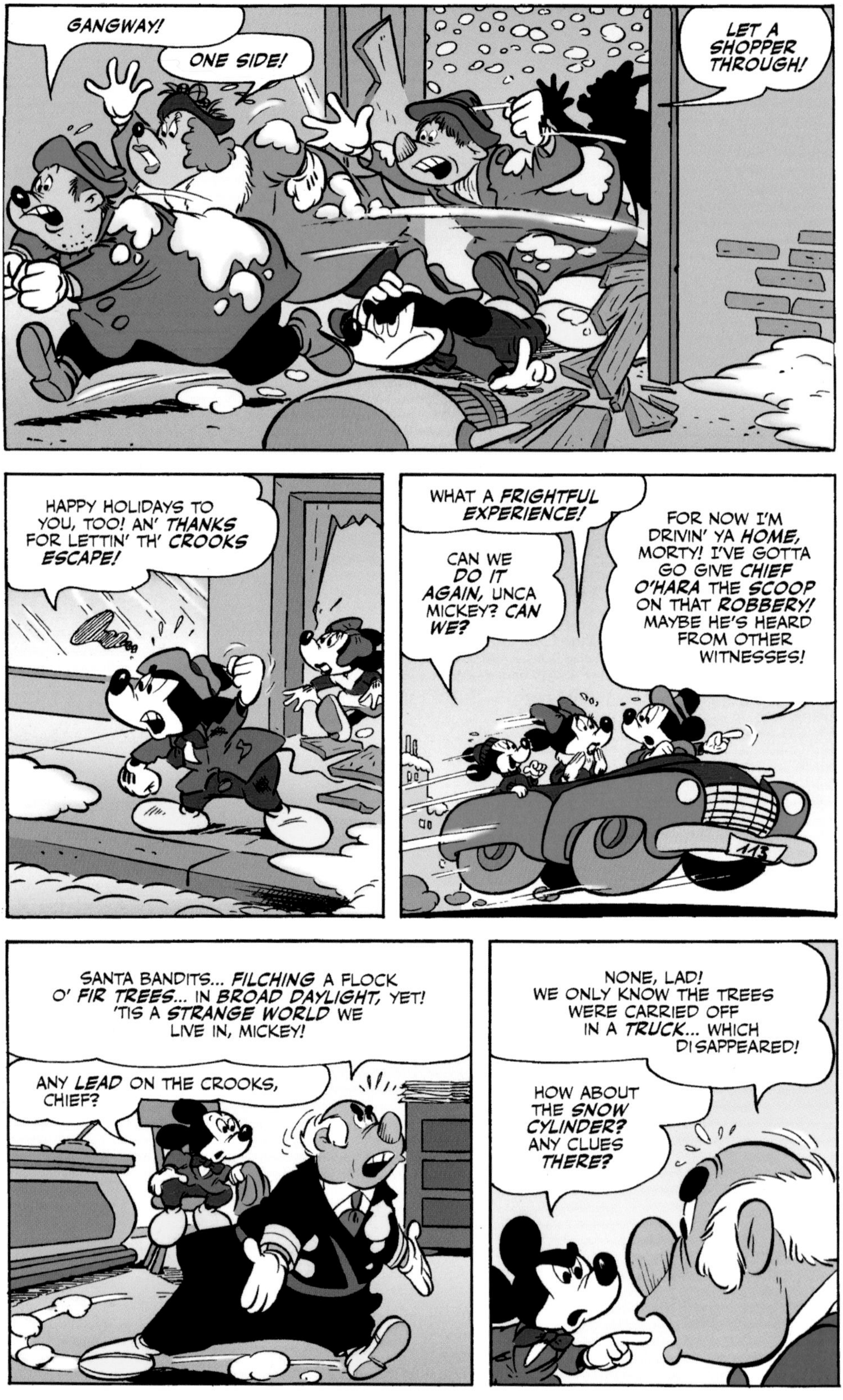
GANGWAY!
ONE SIDE!
LET A SHOPPER THROUGH!
HAPPY HOLIDAYS TO YOU, TOO! AN' THANKS FOR LETTIN' TH' CROOKS ESCAPE!
WHAT A FRIGHTFUL EXPERIENCE!
CAN WE DO IT AGAIN, UNCA MICKEY? CAN WE?
FOR NOW I'M DRIVIN' YA HOME, MORTY! I'VE GOTTA GO GIVE CHIEF O'HARA THE SCOOP ON THAT ROBBERY! MAYBE HE'S HEARD FROM OTHER WITNESSES!
113
SANTA BANDITS... FILCHING A FLOCK O' FIR TREES... IN BROAD DAYLIGHT, YET! 'TIS A STRANGE WORLD WE LIVE IN, MICKEY!
ANY LEAD ON THE CROOKS, CHIEF?
NONE, LAD! WE ONLY KNOW THE TREES WERE CARRIED OFF IN A TRUCK... WHICH DISAPPEARED!
HOW ABOUT THE SNOW CYLINDER? ANY CLUES THERE?

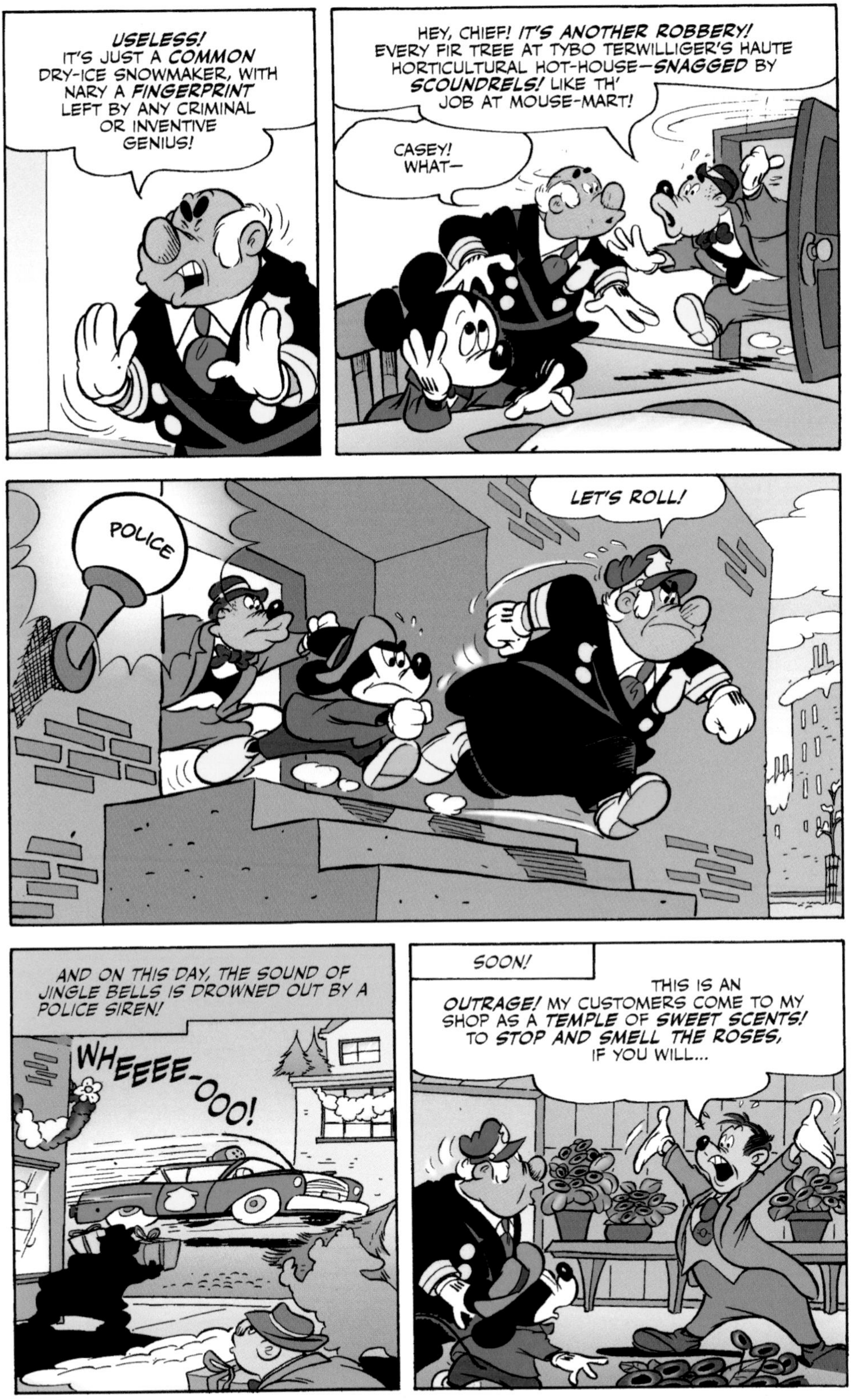
USELESS! IT'S JUST A COMMON DRY-ICE SNOWMAKER, WITH NARY A FINGERPRINT LEFT BY ANY CRIMINAL OR INVENTIVE GENIUS!
HEY, CHIEF! IT'S ANOTHER ROBBERY! EVERY FIR TREE AT TYBO TERWILLIGER'S HAUTE HORTICULTURAL HOT-HOUSE—SNAGGED BY SCOUNDRELS! LIKE TH' JOB AT MOUSE-MART!
CASEY! WHAT—
POLICE
LET'S ROLL!
AND ON THIS DAY, THE SOUND OF JINGLE BELLS IS DROWNED OUT BY A POLICE SIREN!
WHEEEE-OOO!
SOON!
THIS IS AN OUTRAGE! MY CUSTOMERS COME TO MY SHOP AS A TEMPLE OF SWEET SCENTS! TO STOP AND SMELL THE ROSES, IF YOU WILL...

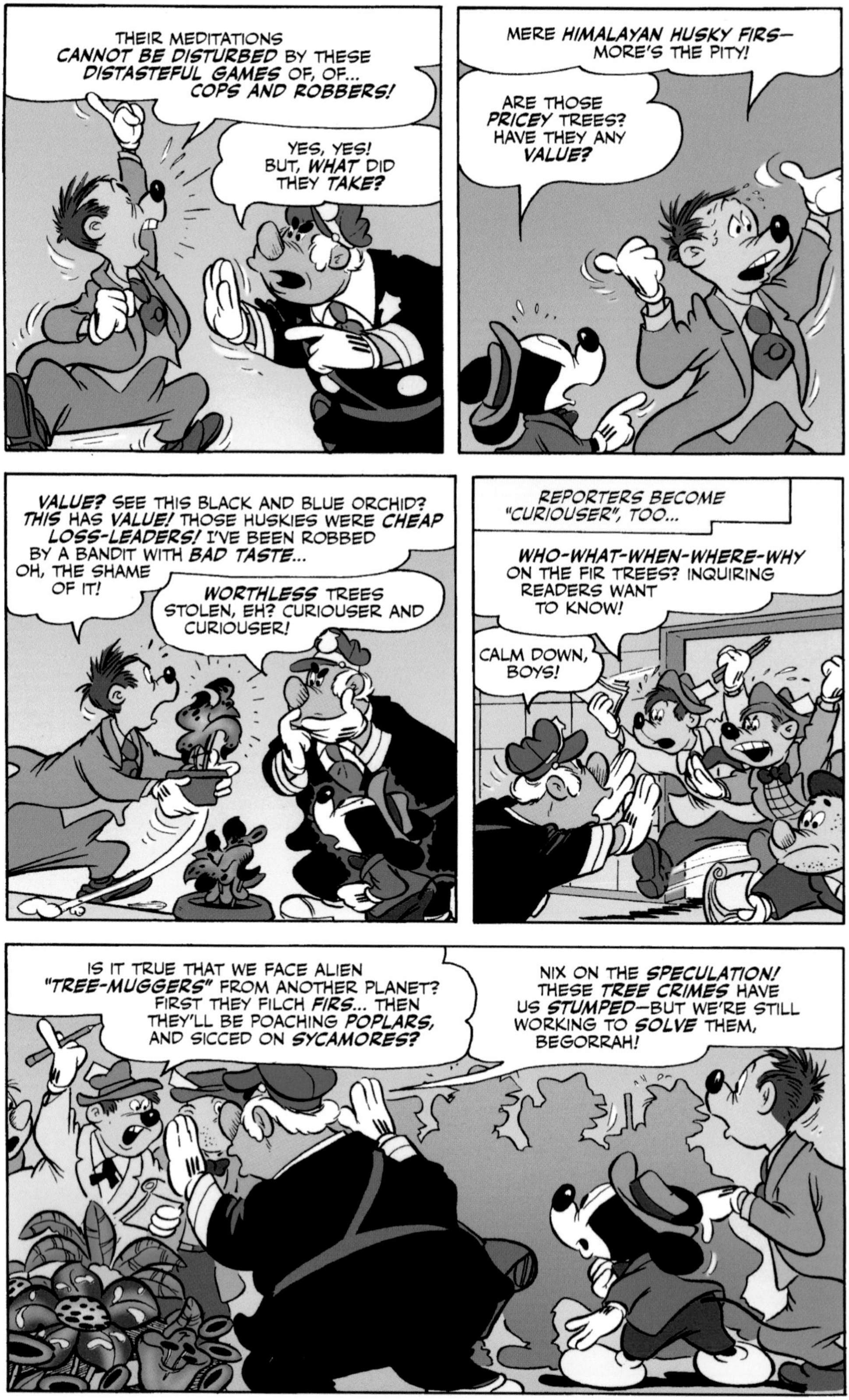
THEIR MEDITATIONS CANNOT BE DISTURBED BY THESE DISTASTEFUL GAMES OF, OF... COPS AND ROBBERS!
YES, YES! BUT, WHAT DID THEY TAKE?
MERE HIMALAYAN HUSKY FIRS— MORE'S THE PITY!
ARE THOSE PRICEY TREES? HAVE THEY ANY VALUE?
VALUE? SEE THIS BLACK AND BLUE ORCHID? THIS HAS VALUE! THOSE HUSKIES WERE CHEAP LOSS-LEADERS! I'VE BEEN ROBBED BY A BANDIT WITH BAD TASTE... OH, THE SHAME OF IT!
WORTHLESS TREES STOLEN, EH? CURIOUSER AND CURIOUSER!
REPORTERS BECOME "CURIOUSER", TOO...
WHO-WHAT-WHEN-WHERE-WHY ON THE FIR TREES? INQUIRING READERS WANT TO KNOW!
CALM DOWN, BOYS!
IS IT TRUE THAT WE FACE ALIEN "TREE-MUGGERS" FROM ANOTHER PLANET? FIRST THEY FILCH FIRS... THEN THEY'LL BE POACHING POPLARS, AND SICCED ON SYCAMORES?
NIX ON THE SPECULATION! THESE TREE CRIMES HAVE US STUMPED—BUT WE'RE STILL WORKING TO SOLVE THEM, BEGORRAH!

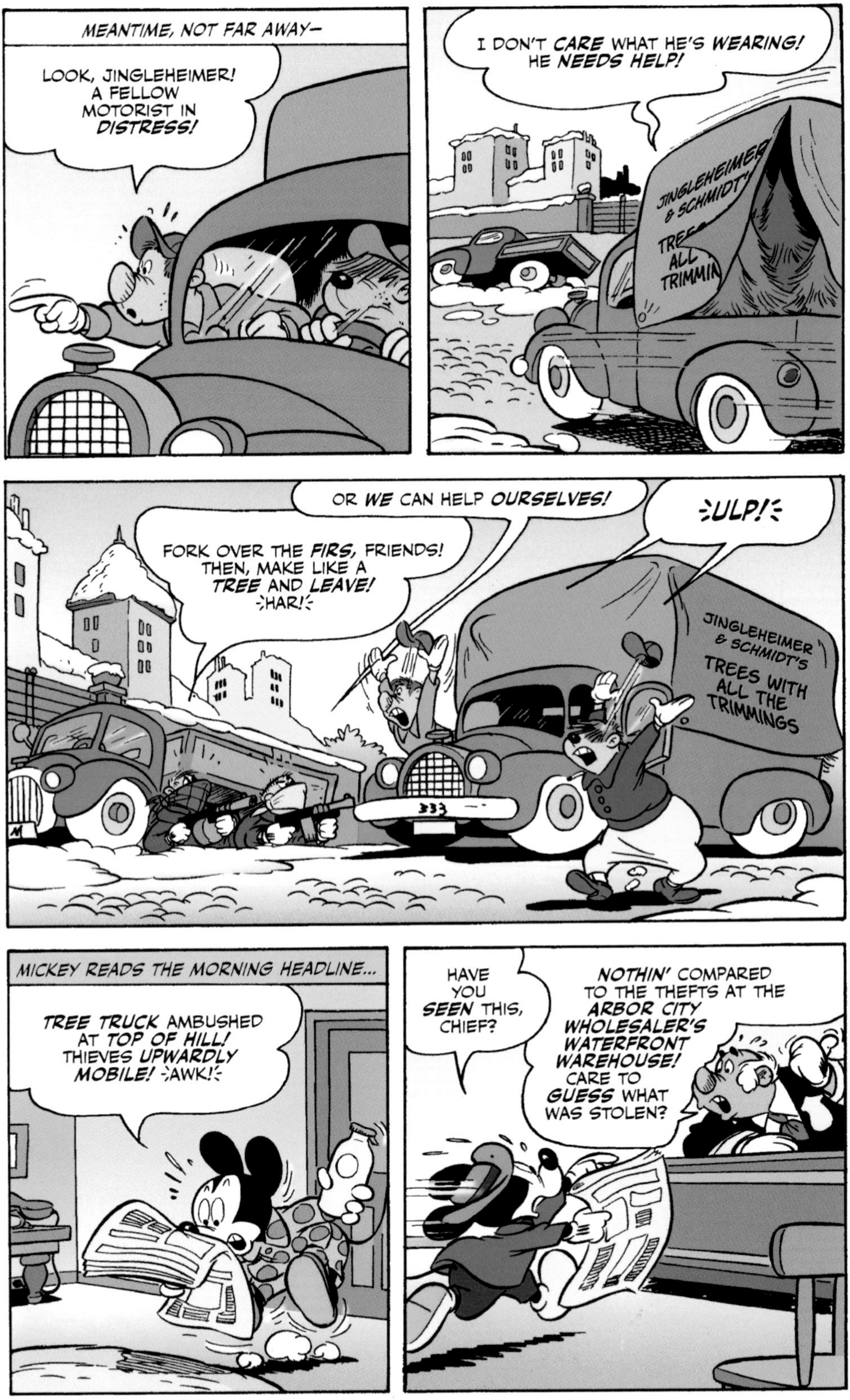

MEANTIME, NOT FAR AWAY—
LOOK, JINGLEHEIMER! A FELLOW MOTORIST IN DISTRESS!
I DON'T CARE WHAT HE'S WEARING! HE NEEDS HELP!
FORK OVER THE FIRS, FRIENDS! THEN, MAKE LIKE A TREE AND LEAVE! HAR!
OR WE CAN HELP OURSELVES!
ULP!
JINGLEHEIMER & SCHMIDT'S TREES WITH ALL THE TRIMMINGS
333
MICKEY READS THE MORNING HEADLINE...
TREE TRUCK AMBUSHED AT TOP OF HILL! THIEVES UPWARDLY MOBILE! AWK!
HAVE YOU SEEN THIS, CHIEF?
NOTHIN' COMPARED TO THE THEFTS AT THE ARBOR CITY WHOLESALER'S WATERFRONT WAREHOUSE! CARE TO GUESS WHAT WAS STOLEN?

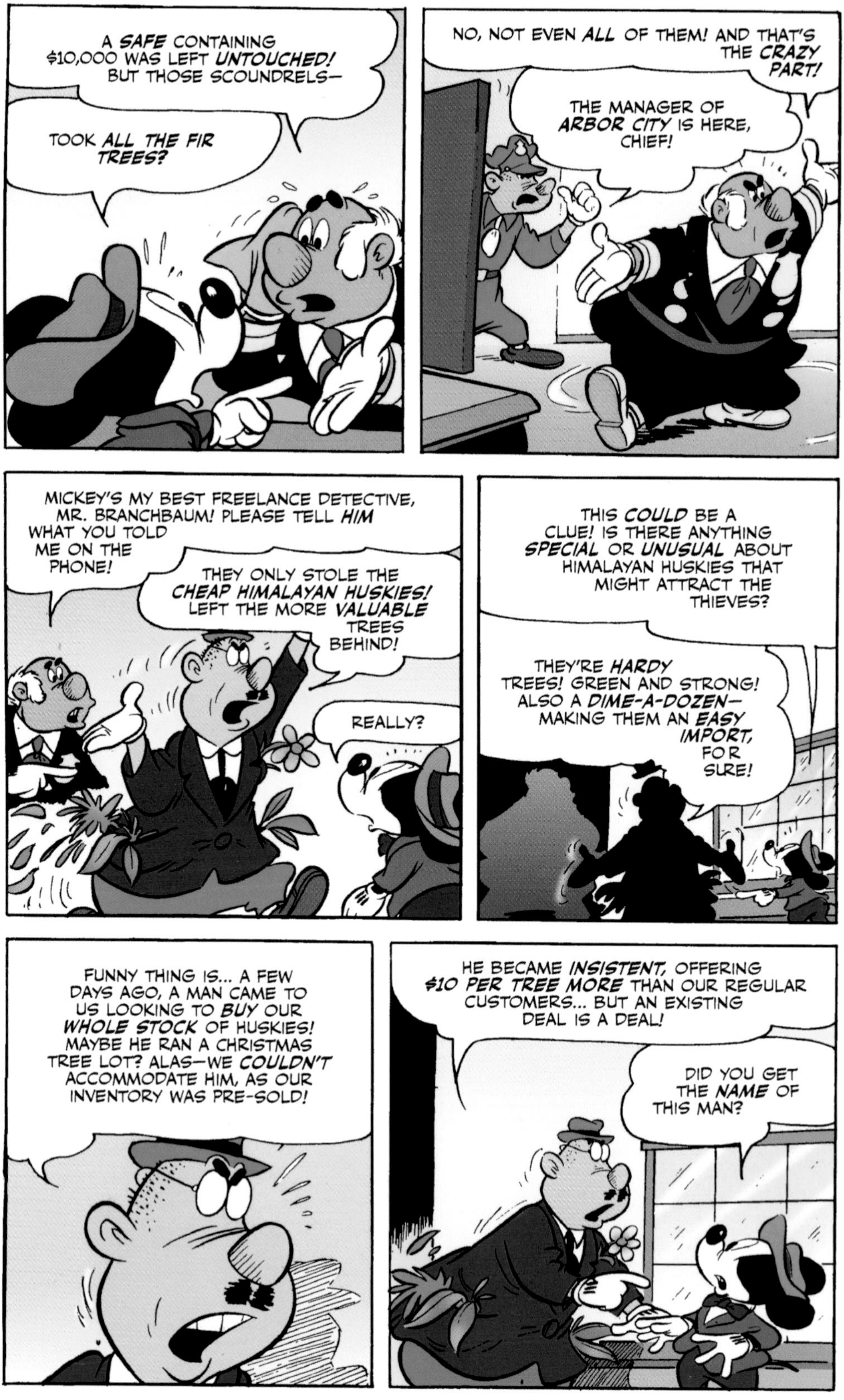

A SAFE CONTAINING $10,000 WAS LEFT UNTOUCHED! BUT THOSE SCOUNDRELS—
TOOK ALL THE FIR TREES?
NO, NOT EVEN ALL OF THEM! AND THAT'S THE CRAZY PART!
THE MANAGER OF ARBOR CITY IS HERE, CHIEF!
MICKEY'S MY BEST FREELANCE DETECTIVE, MR. BRANCHBAUM! PLEASE TELL HIM WHAT YOU TOLD ME ON THE PHONE!
THEY ONLY STOLE THE CHEAP HIMALAYAN HUSKIES! LEFT THE MORE VALUABLE TREES BEHIND!
REALLY?
THIS COULD BE A CLUE! IS THERE ANYTHING SPECIAL OR UNUSUAL ABOUT HIMALAYAN HUSKIES THAT MIGHT ATTRACT THE THIEVES?
THEY'RE HARDY TREES! GREEN AND STRONG! ALSO A DIME-A-DOZEN— MAKING THEM AN EASY IMPORT, FOR SURE!
FUNNY THING IS... A FEW DAYS AGO, A MAN CAME TO US LOOKING TO BUY OUR WHOLE STOCK OF HUSKIES! MAYBE HE RAN A CHRISTMAS TREE LOT? ALAS—WE COULDN'T ACCOMMODATE HIM, AS OUR INVENTORY WAS PRE-SOLD!
HE BECAME INSISTENT, OFFERING $10 PER TREE MORE THAN OUR REGULAR CUSTOMERS... BUT AN EXISTING DEAL IS A DEAL!
DID YOU GET THE NAME OF THIS MAN?

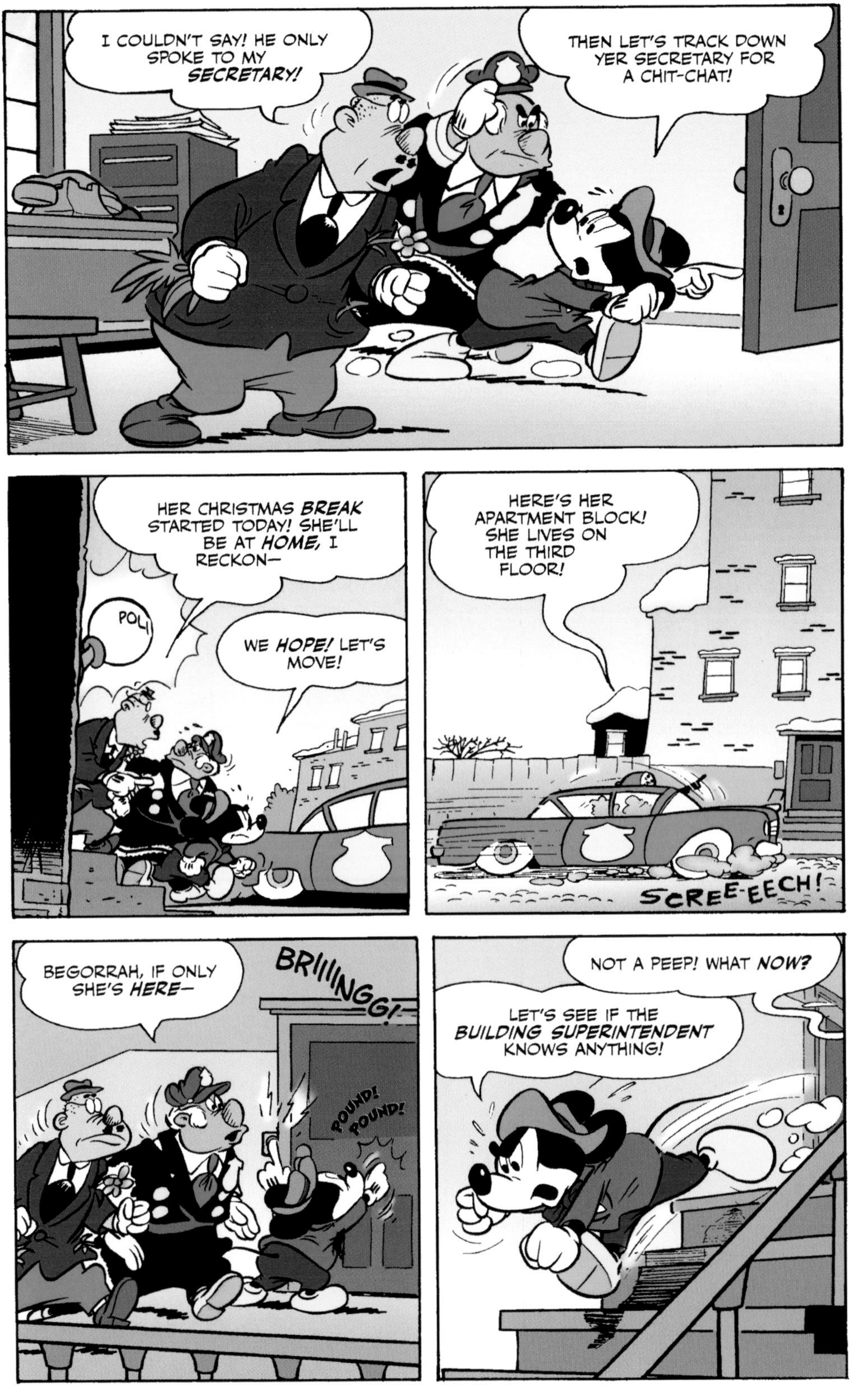
I COULDN'T SAY! HE ONLY SPOKE TO MY SECRETARY!
THEN LET'S TRACK DOWN YER SECRETARY FOR A CHIT-CHAT!
HER CHRISTMAS BREAK STARTED TODAY! SHE'LL BE AT HOME, I RECKON—
POLI
WE HOPE! LET'S MOVE!
HERE'S HER APARTMENT BLOCK! SHE LIVES ON THE THIRD FLOOR!
SCREE-EECH!
BEGORRAH, IF ONLY SHE'S HERE—
BRIIIINGG!
POUND! POUND!
NOT A PEEP! WHAT NOW?
LET'S SEE IF THE BUILDING SUPERINTENDENT KNOWS ANYTHING!

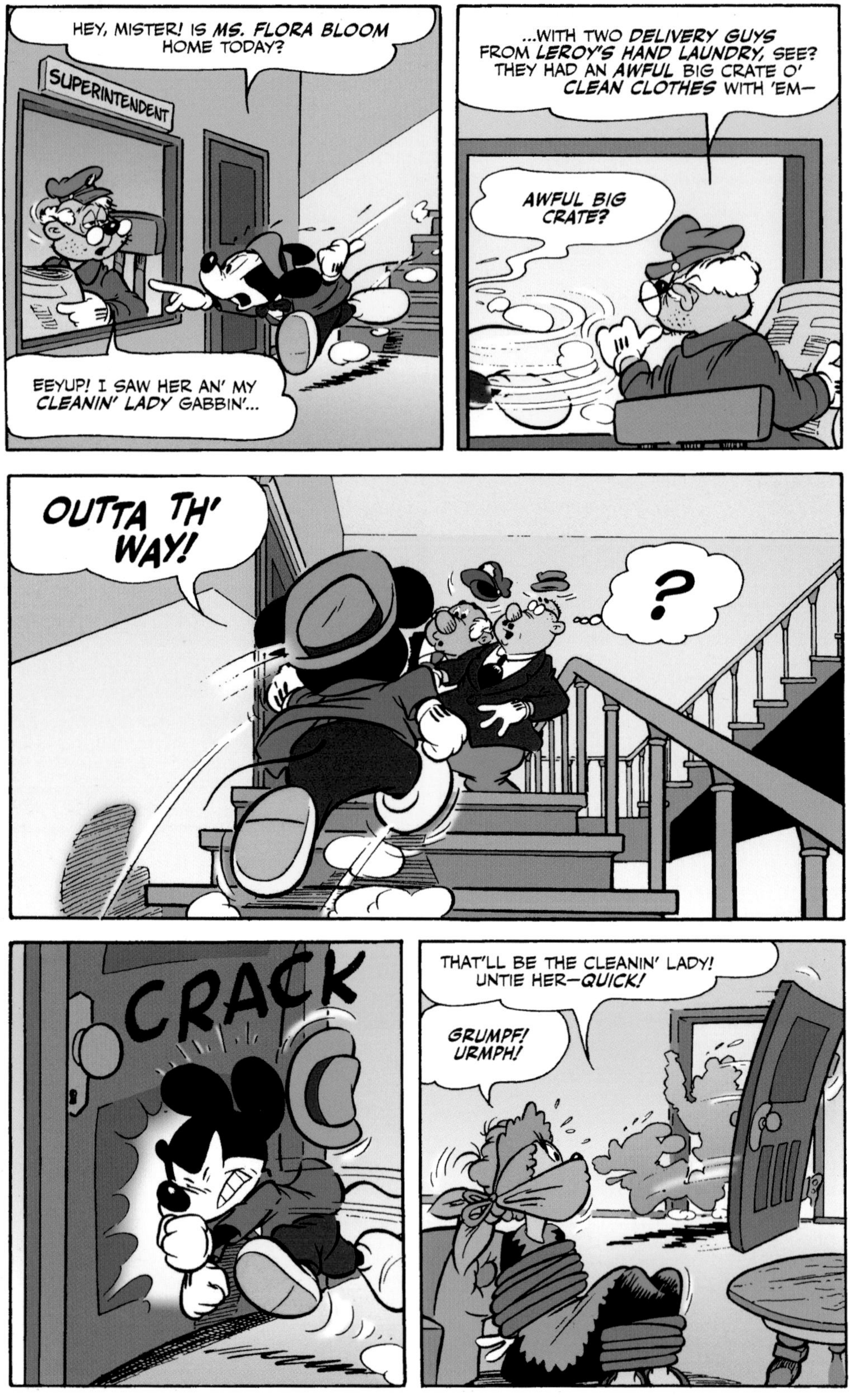
HEY, MISTER! IS MS. FLORA BLOOM HOME TODAY?
SUPERINTENDENT
EEYUP! I SAW HER AN' MY CLEANIN' LADY GABBIN'...
...WITH TWO DELIVERY GUYS FROM LEROY'S HAND LAUNDRY, SEE? THEY HAD AN AWFUL BIG CRATE O' CLEAN CLOTHES WITH 'EM—
AWFUL BIG CRATE?
OUTTA TH' WAY!
?
CRACK
THAT'LL BE THE CLEANIN' LADY! UNTIE HER—QUICK!
GRUMPF! URMPH!

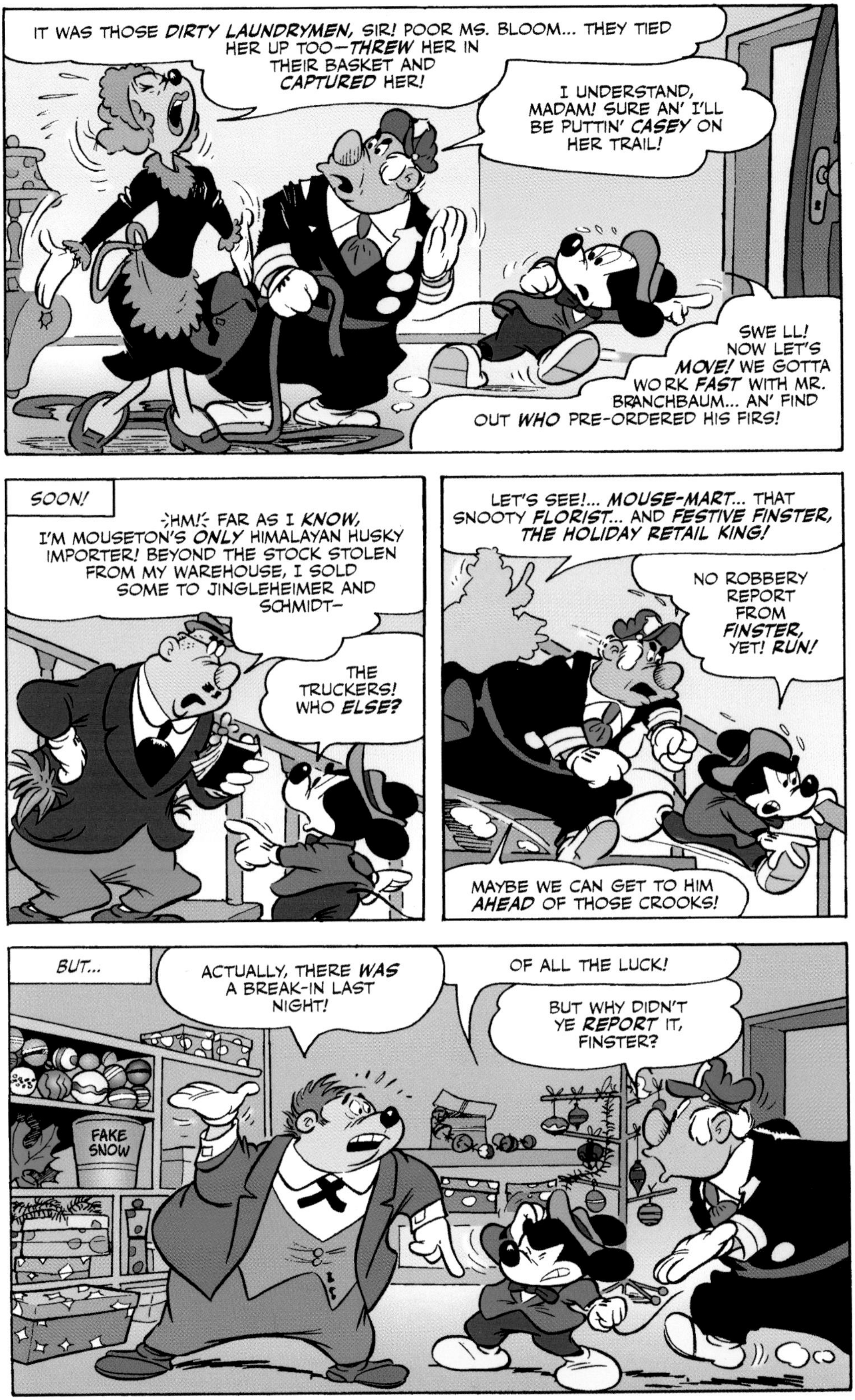
IT WAS THOSE DIRTY LAUNDRYMEN, SIR! POOR MS. BLOOM... THEY TIED HER UP TOO—THREW HER IN THEIR BASKET AND CAPTURED HER!
I UNDERSTAND, MADAM! SURE AN' I'LL BE PUTTIN' CASEY ON HER TRAIL!
SWELL! NOW LET'S MOVE! WE GOTTA WORK FAST WITH MR. BRANCHBAUM... AN' FIND OUT WHO PRE-ORDERED HIS FIRS!
SOON!
HM! FAR AS I KNOW, I'M MOUSETON'S ONLY HIMALAYAN HUSKY IMPORTER! BEYOND THE STOCK STOLEN FROM MY WAREHOUSE, I SOLD SOME TO JINGLEHEIMER AND SCHMIDT—
THE TRUCKERS! WHO ELSE?
LET'S SEE!... MOUSE-MART... THAT SNOOTY FLORIST... AND FESTIVE FINSTER, THE HOLIDAY RETAIL KING!
NO ROBBERY REPORT FROM FINSTER, YET! RUN!
MAYBE WE CAN GET TO HIM AHEAD OF THOSE CROOKS!
BUT...
ACTUALLY, THERE WAS A BREAK-IN LAST NIGHT!
OF ALL THE LUCK!
BUT WHY DIDN'T YE REPORT IT, FINSTER?
FAKE SNOW

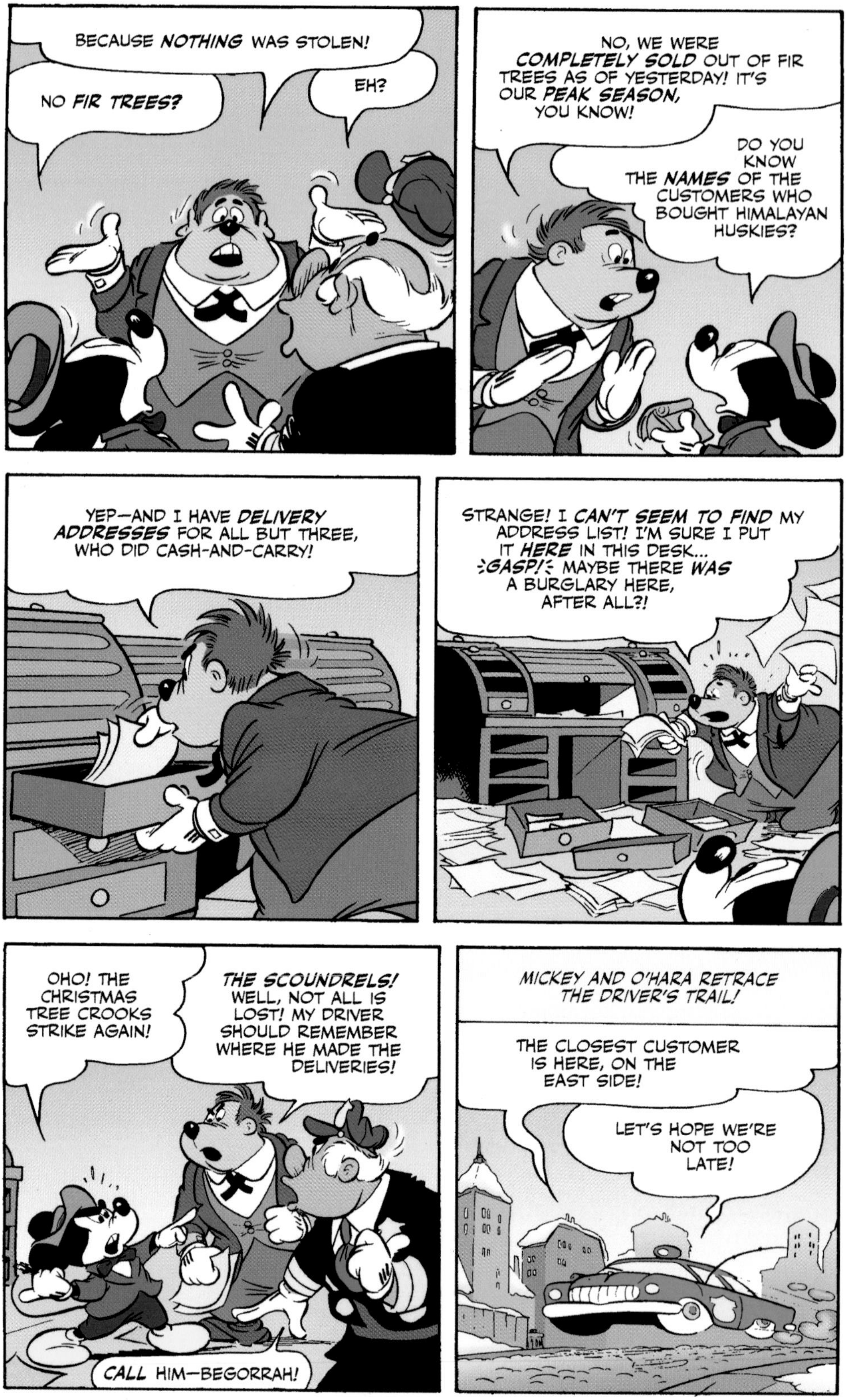

BECAUSE NOTHING WAS STOLEN!
NO FIR TREES?
EH?
NO, WE WERE COMPLETELY SOLD OUT OF FIR TREES AS OF YESTERDAY! IT'S OUR PEAK SEASON, YOU KNOW!
DO YOU KNOW THE NAMES OF THE CUSTOMERS WHO BOUGHT HIMALAYAN HUSKIES?
YEP—AND I HAVE DELIVERY ADDRESSES FOR ALL BUT THREE, WHO DID CASH-AND-CARRY!
STRANGE! I CAN'T SEEM TO FIND MY ADDRESS LIST! I'M SURE I PUT IT HERE IN THIS DESK... GASP! MAYBE THERE WAS A BURGLARY HERE, AFTER ALL?!
OHO! THE CHRISTMAS TREE CROOKS STRIKE AGAIN!
THE SCOUNDRELS! WELL, NOT ALL IS LOST! MY DRIVER SHOULD REMEMBER WHERE HE MADE THE DELIVERIES!
CALL HIM—BEGORRAH!
MICKEY AND O'HARA RETRACE THE DRIVER'S TRAIL!
THE CLOSEST CUSTOMER IS HERE, ON THE EAST SIDE!
LET'S HOPE WE'RE NOT TOO LATE!

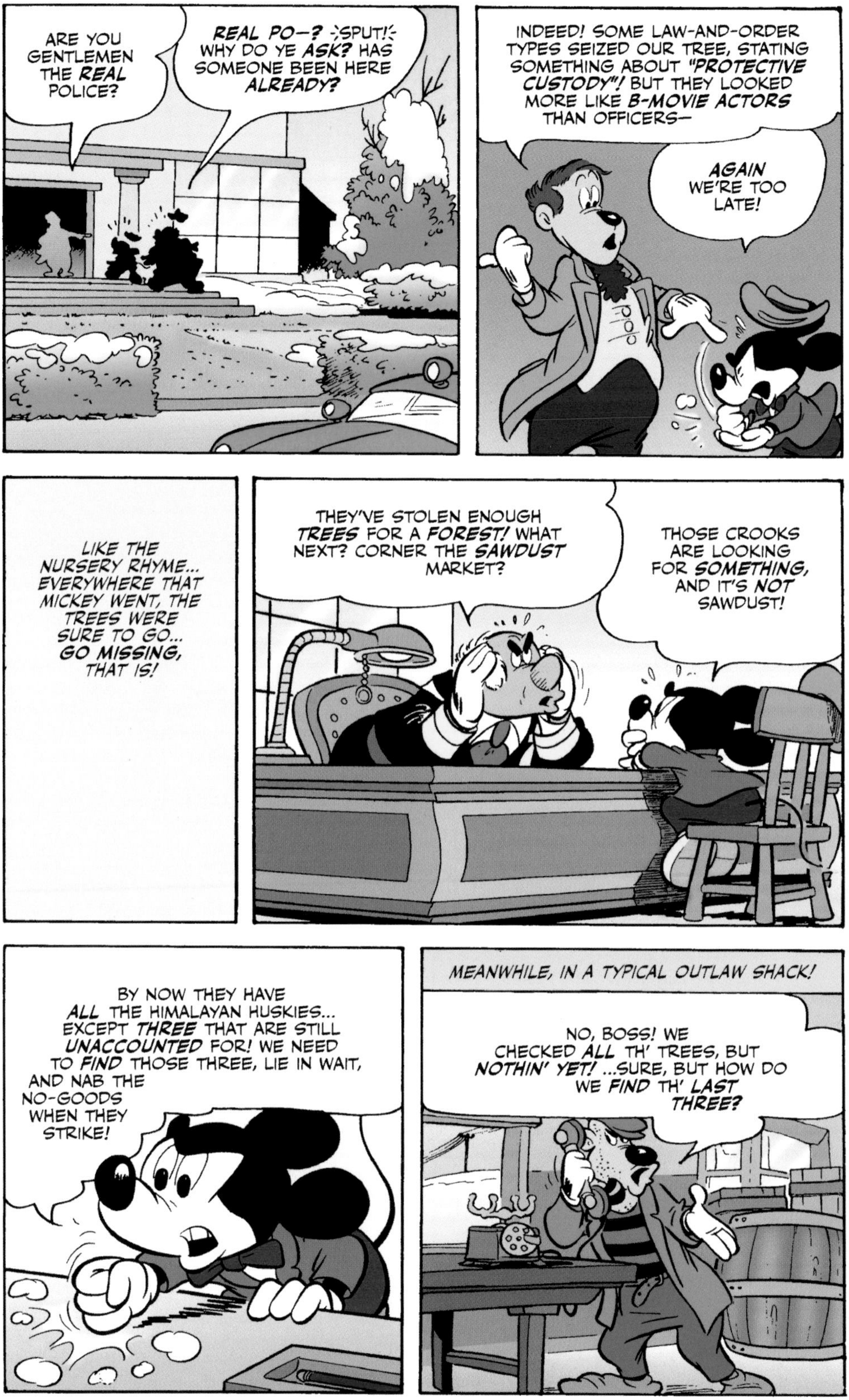
ARE YOU GENTLEMEN THE REAL POLICE?
REAL PO--? -SPUT!- WHY DO YE ASK? HAS SOMEONE BEEN HERE ALREADY?
INDEED! SOME LAW-AND-ORDER TYPES SEIZED OUR TREE, STATING SOMETHING ABOUT "PROTECTIVE CUSTODY"! BUT THEY LOOKED MORE LIKE B-MOVIE ACTORS THAN OFFICERS—
AGAIN WE'RE TOO LATE!
LIKE THE NURSERY RHYME... EVERYWHERE THAT MICKEY WENT, THE TREES WERE SURE TO GO... GO MISSING, THAT IS!
THEY'VE STOLEN ENOUGH TREES FOR A FOREST! WHAT NEXT? CORNER THE SAWDUST MARKET?
THOSE CROOKS ARE LOOKING FOR SOMETHING, AND IT'S NOT SAWDUST!
BY NOW THEY HAVE ALL THE HIMALAYAN HUSKIES... EXCEPT THREE THAT ARE STILL UNACCOUNTED FOR! WE NEED TO FIND THOSE THREE, LIE IN WAIT, AND NAB THE NO-GOODS WHEN THEY STRIKE!
MEANWHILE, IN A TYPICAL OUTLAW SHACK!
NO, BOSS! WE CHECKED ALL TH' TREES, BUT NOTHIN' YET! ...SURE, BUT HOW DO WE FIND TH' LAST THREE?

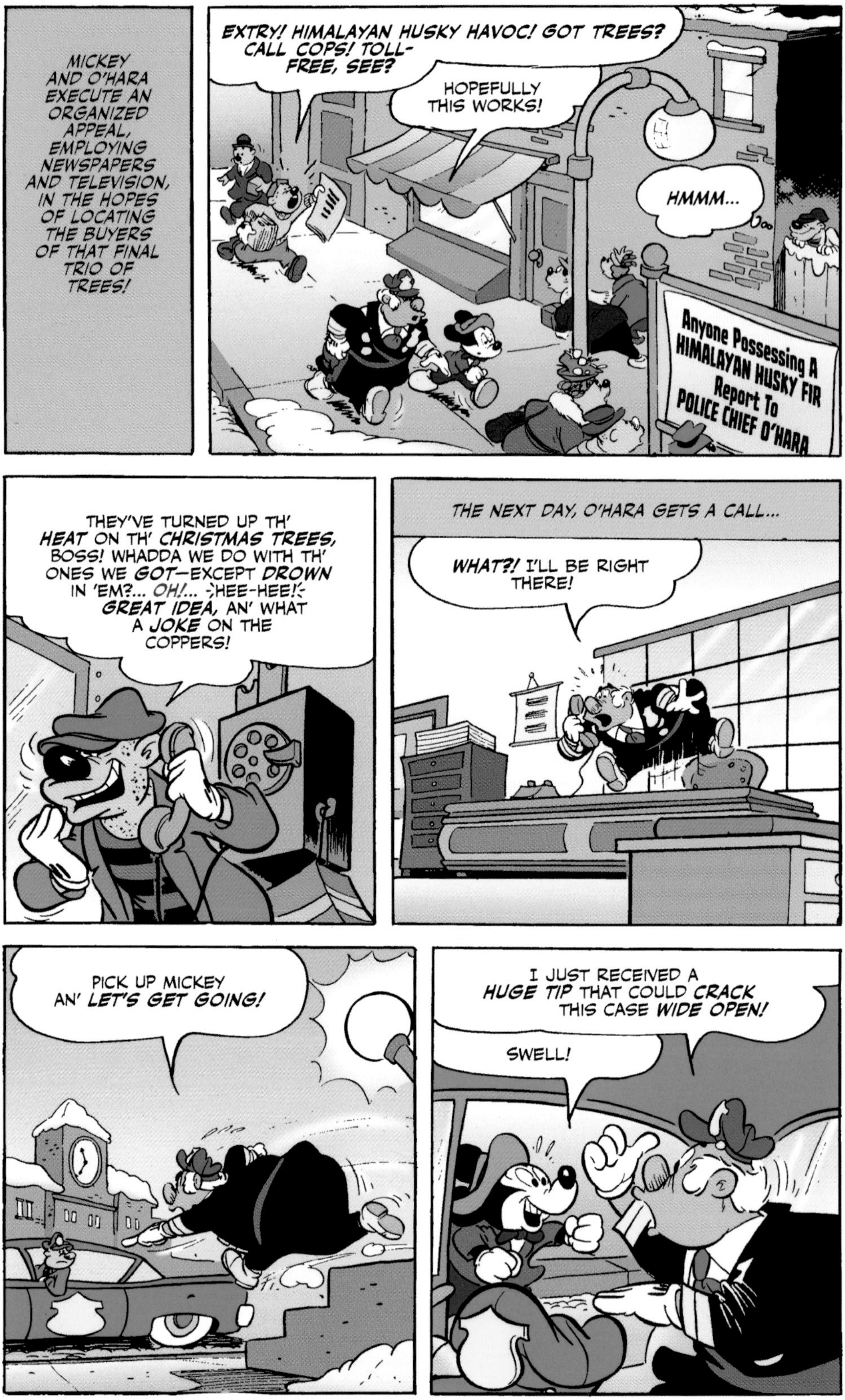
MICKEY AND O'HARA EXECUTE AN ORGANIZED APPEAL, EMPLOYING NEWSPAPERS AND TELEVISION, IN THE HOPES OF LOCATING THE BUYERS OF THAT FINAL TRIO OF TREES!
EXTRY! HIMALAYAN HUSKY HAVOC! GOT TREES? CALL COPS! TOLL-FREE, SEE?
HOPEFULLY THIS WORKS!
HMMM...
Anyone Possessing A HIMALAYAN HUSKY FIR Report To POLICE CHIEF O'HARA
THEY'VE TURNED UP TH' HEAT ON TH' CHRISTMAS TREES, BOSS! WHADDA WE DO WITH TH' ONES WE GOT—EXCEPT DROWN IN 'EM?... OH!... HEE-HEE! GREAT IDEA, AN' WHAT A JOKE ON THE COPPERS!
THE NEXT DAY, O'HARA GETS A CALL...
WHAT?! I'LL BE RIGHT THERE!
PICK UP MICKEY AN' LET'S GET GOING!
I JUST RECEIVED A HUGE TIP THAT COULD CRACK THIS CASE WIDE OPEN!
SWELL!

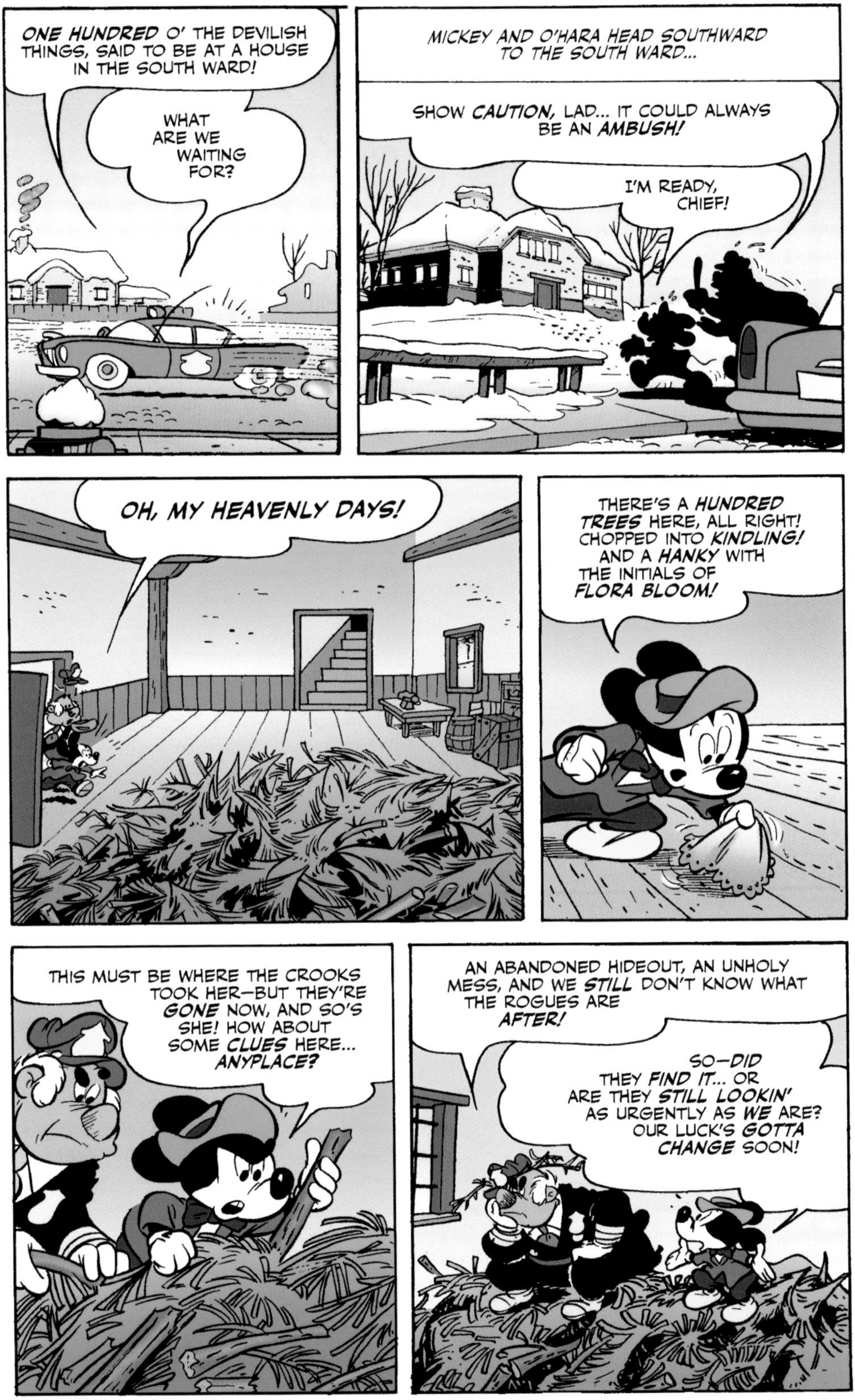
ONE HUNDRED O' THE DEVILISH THINGS, SAID TO BE AT A HOUSE IN THE SOUTH WARD!
WHAT ARE WE WAITING FOR?
MICKEY AND O'HARA HEAD SOUTHWARD TO THE SOUTH WARD...
SHOW CAUTION, LAD... IT COULD ALWAYS BE AN AMBUSH!
I'M READY, CHIEF!
OH, MY HEAVENLY DAYS!
THERE'S A HUNDRED TREES HERE, ALL RIGHT! CHOPPED INTO KINDLING! AND A HANKY WITH THE INITIALS OF FLORA BLOOM!
THIS MUST BE WHERE THE CROOKS TOOK HER—BUT THEY'RE GONE NOW, AND SO'S SHE! HOW ABOUT SOME CLUES HERE... ANYPLACE?
AN ABANDONED HIDEOUT, AN UNHOLY MESS, AND WE STILL DON'T KNOW WHAT THE ROGUES ARE AFTER!
SO—DID THEY FIND IT... OR ARE THEY STILL LOOKIN' AS URGENTLY AS WE ARE? OUR LUCK'S GOTTA CHANGE SOON!

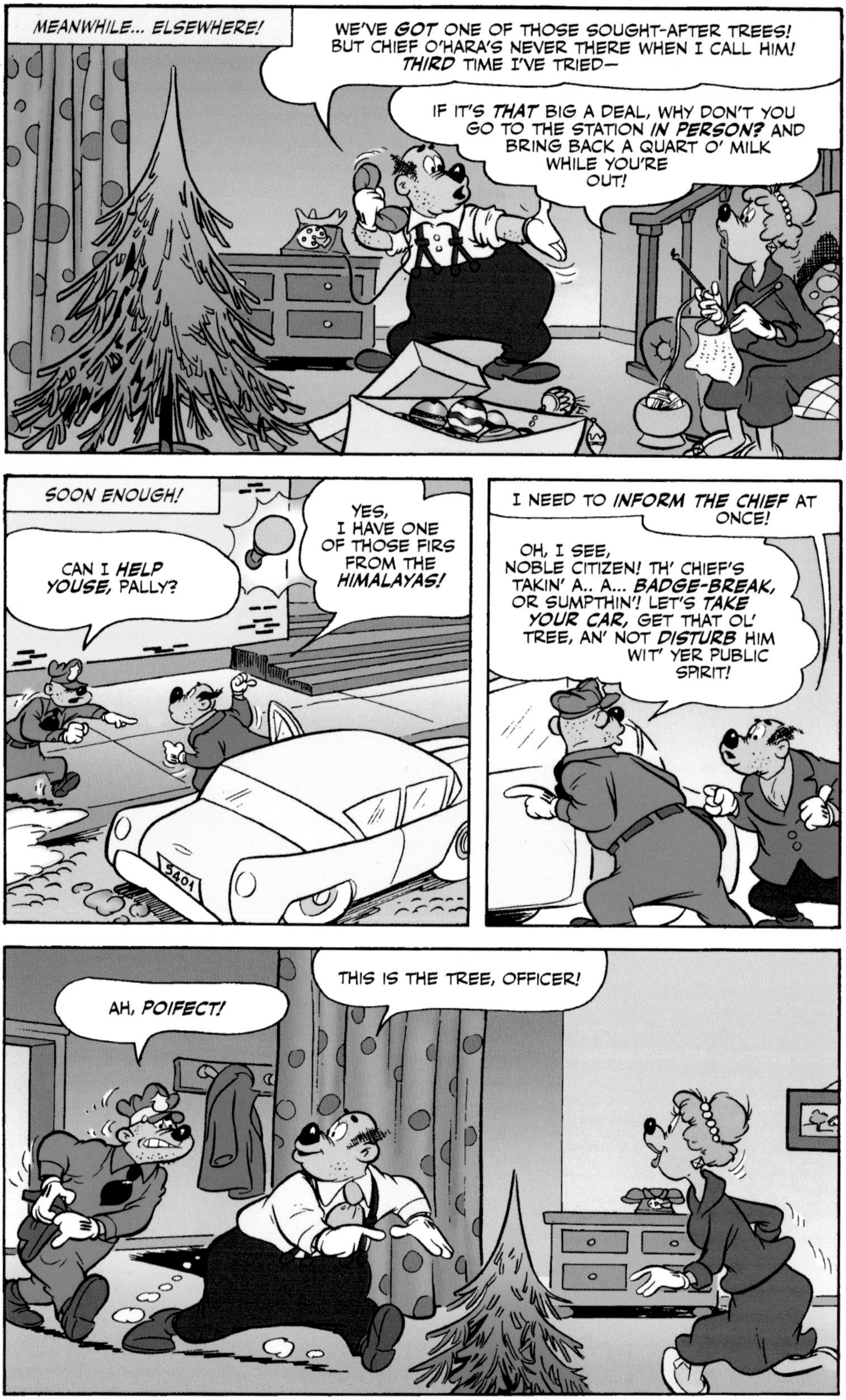
MEANWHILE... ELSEWHERE!
WE'VE GOT ONE OF THOSE SOUGHT-AFTER TREES! BUT CHIEF O'HARA'S NEVER THERE WHEN I CALL HIM! THIRD TIME I'VE TRIED—
IF IT'S THAT BIG A DEAL, WHY DON'T YOU GO TO THE STATION IN PERSON? AND BRING BACK A QUART O' MILK WHILE YOU'RE OUT!
SOON ENOUGH!
YES, I HAVE ONE OF THOSE FIRS FROM THE HIMALAYAS!
CAN I HELP YOUSE, PALLY?
5401
I NEED TO INFORM THE CHIEF AT ONCE!
OH, I SEE, NOBLE CITIZEN! TH' CHIEF'S TAKIN' A.. A... BADGE-BREAK, OR SUMPTHIN'! LET'S TAKE YOUR CAR, GET THAT OL' TREE, AN' NOT DISTURB HIM WIT' YER PUBLIC SPIRIT!
THIS IS THE TREE, OFFICER!
AH, POIFECT!

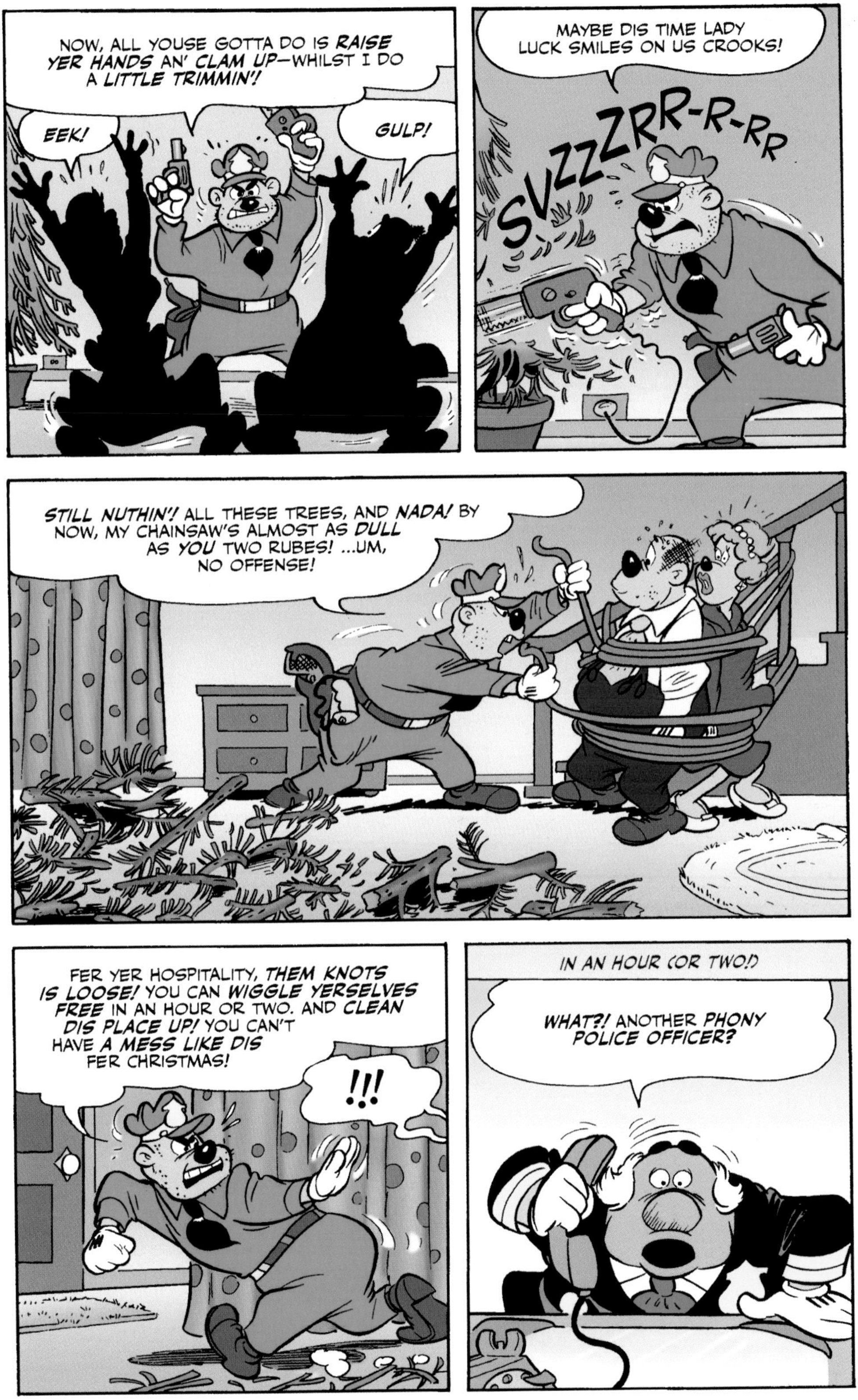
NOW, ALL YOUSE GOTTA DO IS RAISE YER HANDS AN' CLAM UP—WHILST I DO A LITTLE TRIMMIN'!
EEK!
GULP!
MAYBE DIS TIME LADY LUCK SMILES ON US CROOKS!
SVZZZRR-R-RR
STILL NUTHIN'! ALL THESE TREES, AND NADA! BY NOW, MY CHAINSAW'S ALMOST AS DULL AS YOU TWO RUBES! ...UM, NO OFFENSE!
FER YER HOSPITALITY, THEM KNOTS IS LOOSE! YOU CAN WIGGLE YERSELVES FREE IN AN HOUR OR TWO. AND CLEAN DIS PLACE UP! YOU CAN'T HAVE A MESS LIKE DIS FER CHRISTMAS!
!!!
IN AN HOUR (OR TWO!)
WHAT?! ANOTHER PHONY POLICE OFFICER?

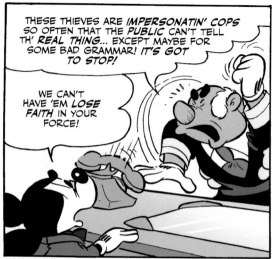

THESE THIEVES ARE *IMPERSONATIN'* COPS SO OFTEN THAT THE *PUBLIC* CAN'T TELL TH' *REAL THING...* EXCEPT MAYBE FOR SOME BAD GRAMMAR! *IT'S GOT TO STOP!*

WE CAN'T HAVE 'EM *LOSE FAITH* IN YOUR FORCE!

WHAT TO DO? HMMM... THERE MUST BE *SOMETHING IMPORTANT* HIDDEN INSIDE ONE OF THOSE *HIMALAYAN HUSKIES!* HIMALAYAN... TH' HIMALAYAS RUN THROUGH NEPAL, BHUTAN, INDIA, AN'—

...*INDIA?!*

THAT'S IT! INDIA! I'LL BE BACK, CHIEF!

?

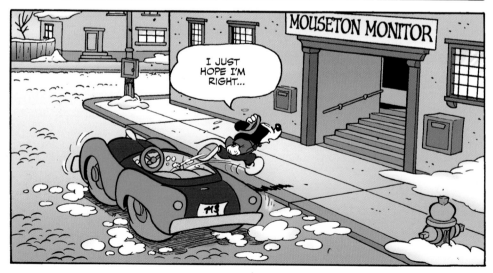

MOUSETON MONITOR

I JUST HOPE I'M RIGHT...

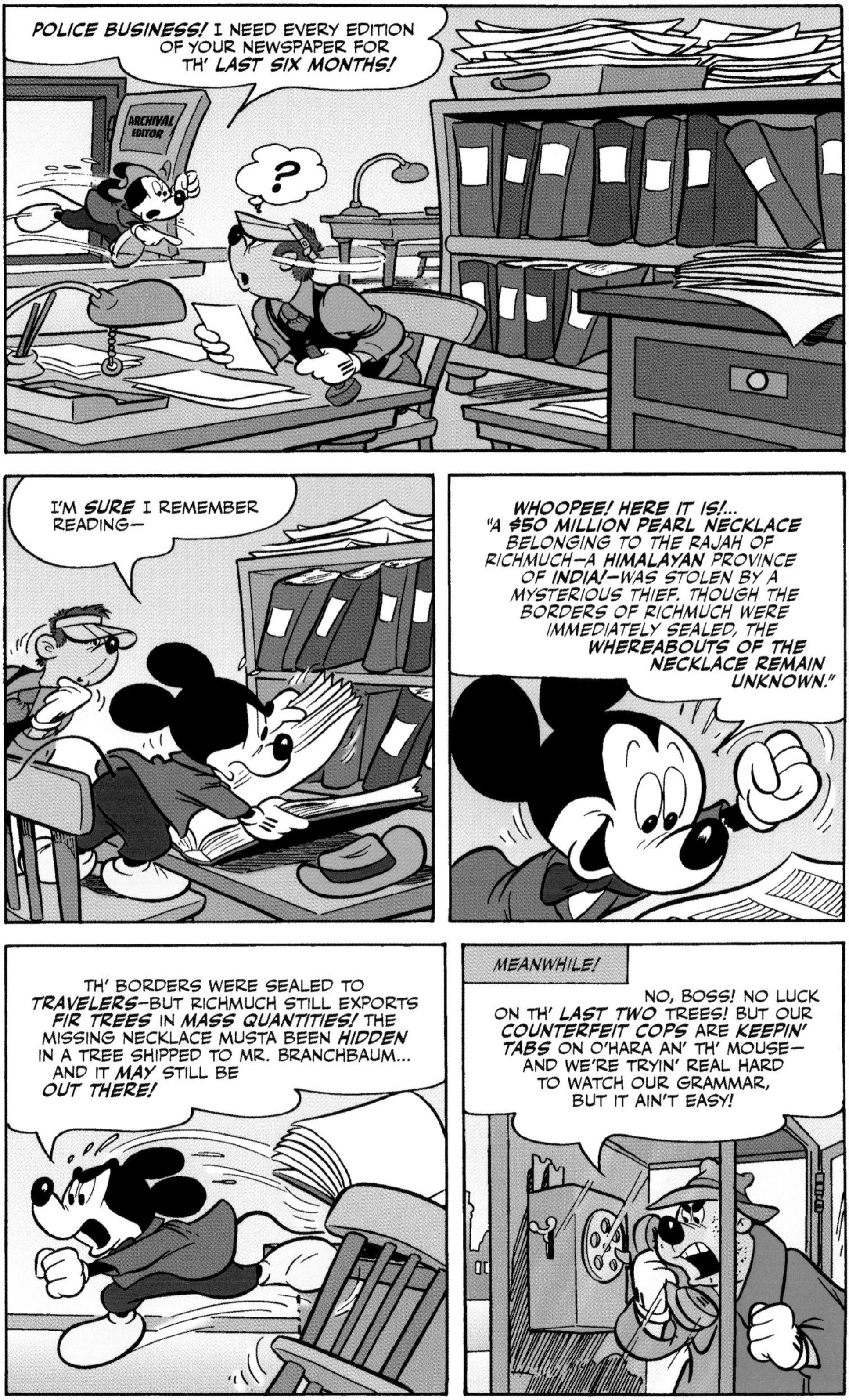

POLICE BUSINESS! I NEED EVERY EDITION OF YOUR NEWSPAPER FOR TH' LAST SIX MONTHS!
ARCHIVAL EDITOR
?
I'M SURE I REMEMBER READING—
WHOOPEE! HERE IT IS!... "A $50 MILLION PEARL NECKLACE BELONGING TO THE RAJAH OF RICHMUCH—A HIMALAYAN PROVINCE OF INDIA!—WAS STOLEN BY A MYSTERIOUS THIEF. THOUGH THE BORDERS OF RICHMUCH WERE IMMEDIATELY SEALED, THE WHEREABOUTS OF THE NECKLACE REMAIN UNKNOWN."
TH' BORDERS WERE SEALED TO TRAVELERS—BUT RICHMUCH STILL EXPORTS FIR TREES IN MASS QUANTITIES! THE MISSING NECKLACE MUSTA BEEN HIDDEN IN A TREE SHIPPED TO MR. BRANCHBAUM... AND IT MAY STILL BE OUT THERE!
MEANWHILE!
NO, BOSS! NO LUCK ON TH' LAST TWO TREES! BUT OUR COUNTERFEIT COPS ARE KEEPIN' TABS ON O'HARA AN' TH' MOUSE—AND WE'RE TRYIN' REAL HARD TO WATCH OUR GRAMMAR, BUT IT AIN'T EASY!

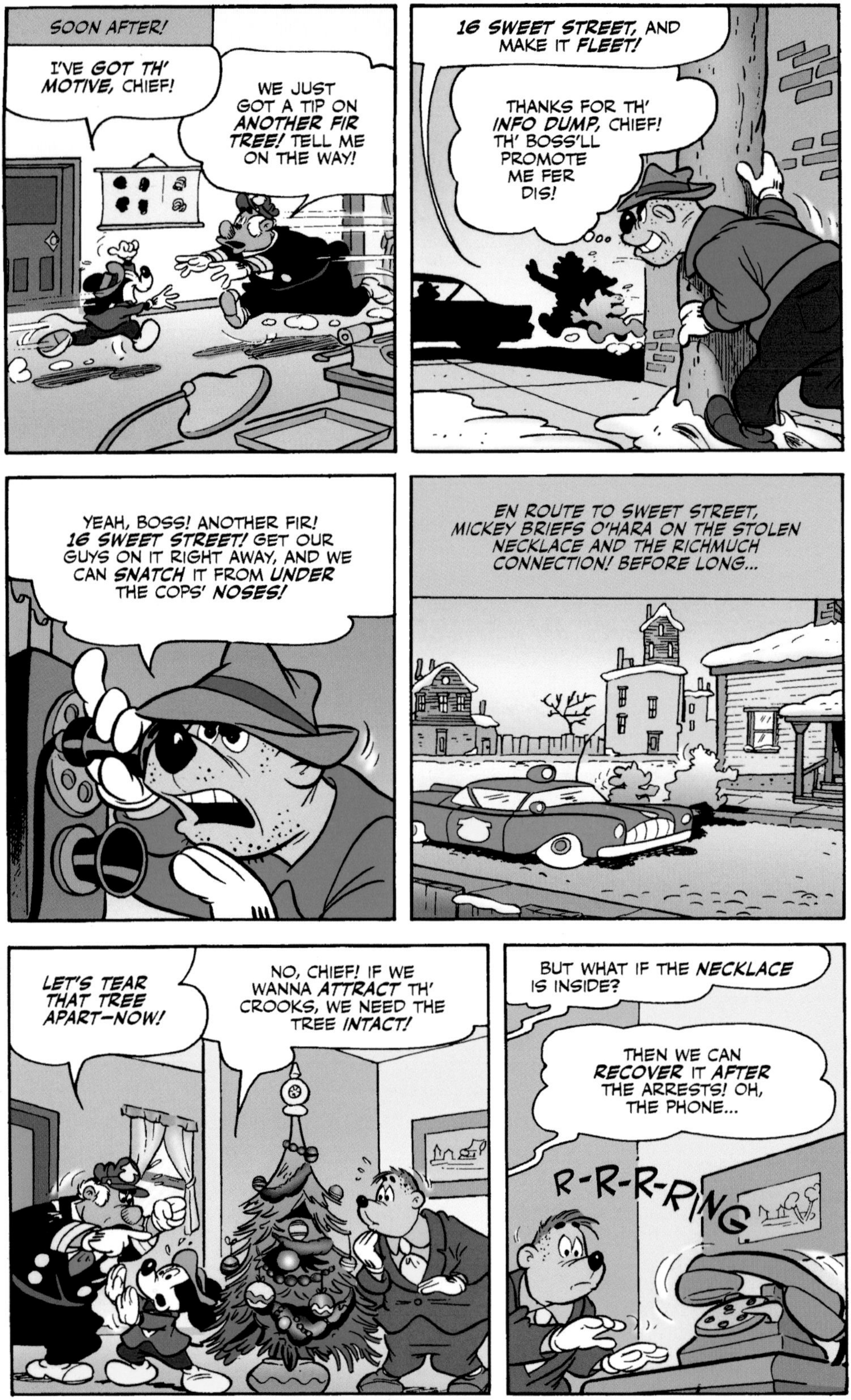
SOON AFTER!
I'VE GOT TH' MOTIVE, CHIEF!
WE JUST GOT A TIP ON ANOTHER FIR TREE! TELL ME ON THE WAY!
16 SWEET STREET, AND MAKE IT FLEET!
THANKS FOR TH' INFO DUMP, CHIEF! TH' BOSS'LL PROMOTE ME FER DIS!
YEAH, BOSS! ANOTHER FIR! 16 SWEET STREET! GET OUR GUYS ON IT RIGHT AWAY, AND WE CAN SNATCH IT FROM UNDER THE COPS' NOSES!
EN ROUTE TO SWEET STREET, MICKEY BRIEFS O'HARA ON THE STOLEN NECKLACE AND THE RICHMUCH CONNECTION! BEFORE LONG...
LET'S TEAR THAT TREE APART—NOW!
NO, CHIEF! IF WE WANNA ATTRACT TH' CROOKS, WE NEED THE TREE INTACT!
BUT WHAT IF THE NECKLACE IS INSIDE?
THEN WE CAN RECOVER IT AFTER THE ARRESTS! OH, THE PHONE...
R-R-R-RING

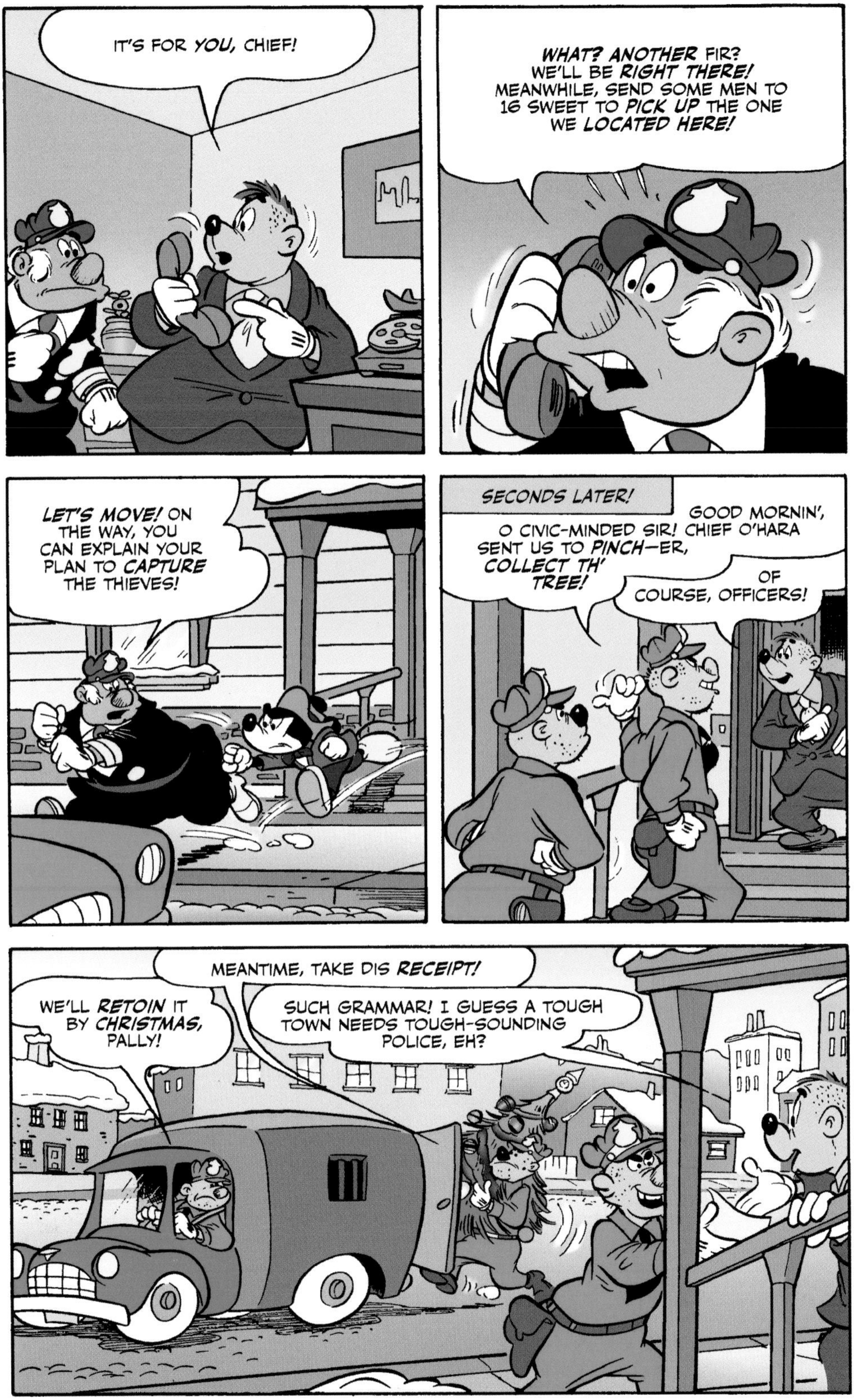
IT'S FOR *YOU,* CHIEF!
WHAT? ANOTHER FIR? WE'LL BE *RIGHT THERE!* MEANWHILE, SEND SOME MEN TO 16 SWEET TO *PICK UP* THE ONE WE *LOCATED HERE!*
LET'S MOVE! ON THE WAY, YOU CAN EXPLAIN YOUR PLAN TO *CAPTURE* THE THIEVES!
SECONDS LATER!
GOOD MORNIN', O CIVIC-MINDED SIR! CHIEF O'HARA SENT US TO *PINCH*—ER, *COLLECT TH' TREE!*
OF COURSE, OFFICERS!
MEANTIME, TAKE DIS *RECEIPT!*
WE'LL *RETOIN* IT BY *CHRISTMAS,* PALLY!
SUCH GRAMMAR! I GUESS A TOUGH TOWN NEEDS TOUGH-SOUNDING POLICE, EH?

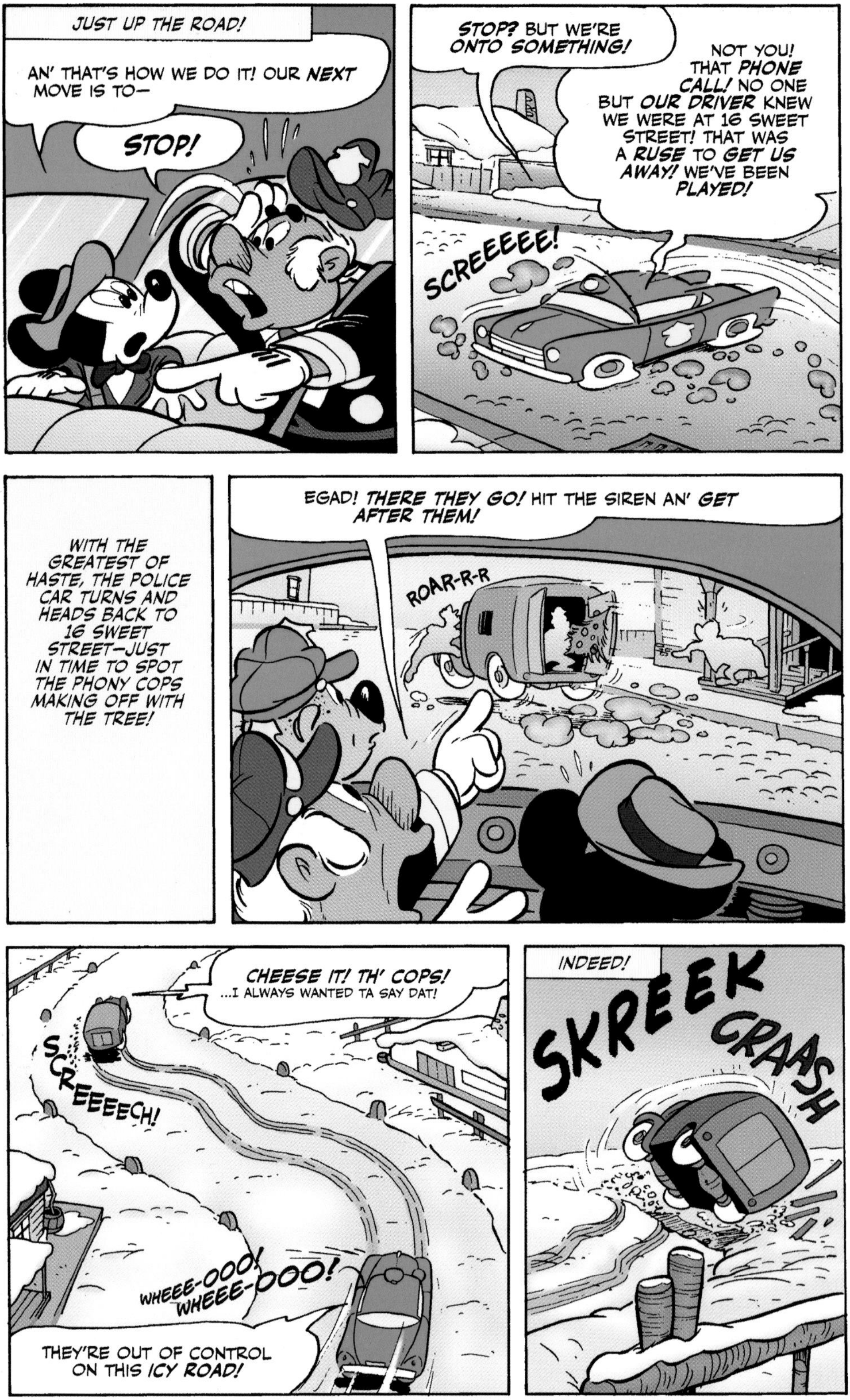

JUST UP THE ROAD!
AN' THAT'S HOW WE DO IT! OUR NEXT MOVE IS TO—
STOP!
STOP? BUT WE'RE ONTO SOMETHING!
NOT YOU! THAT PHONE CALL! NO ONE BUT OUR DRIVER KNEW WE WERE AT 16 SWEET STREET! THAT WAS A RUSE TO GET US AWAY! WE'VE BEEN PLAYED!
SCREEEEEE!
WITH THE GREATEST OF HASTE, THE POLICE CAR TURNS AND HEADS BACK TO 16 SWEET STREET—JUST IN TIME TO SPOT THE PHONY COPS MAKING OFF WITH THE TREE!
EGAD! THERE THEY GO! HIT THE SIREN AN' GET AFTER THEM!
ROAR-R-R
CHEESE IT! TH' COPS! ...I ALWAYS WANTED TA SAY DAT!
SCREEEECH!
WHEEE-OOO! WHEEE-OOO!
THEY'RE OUT OF CONTROL ON THIS ICY ROAD!
INDEED!
SKREEK
CRAASH

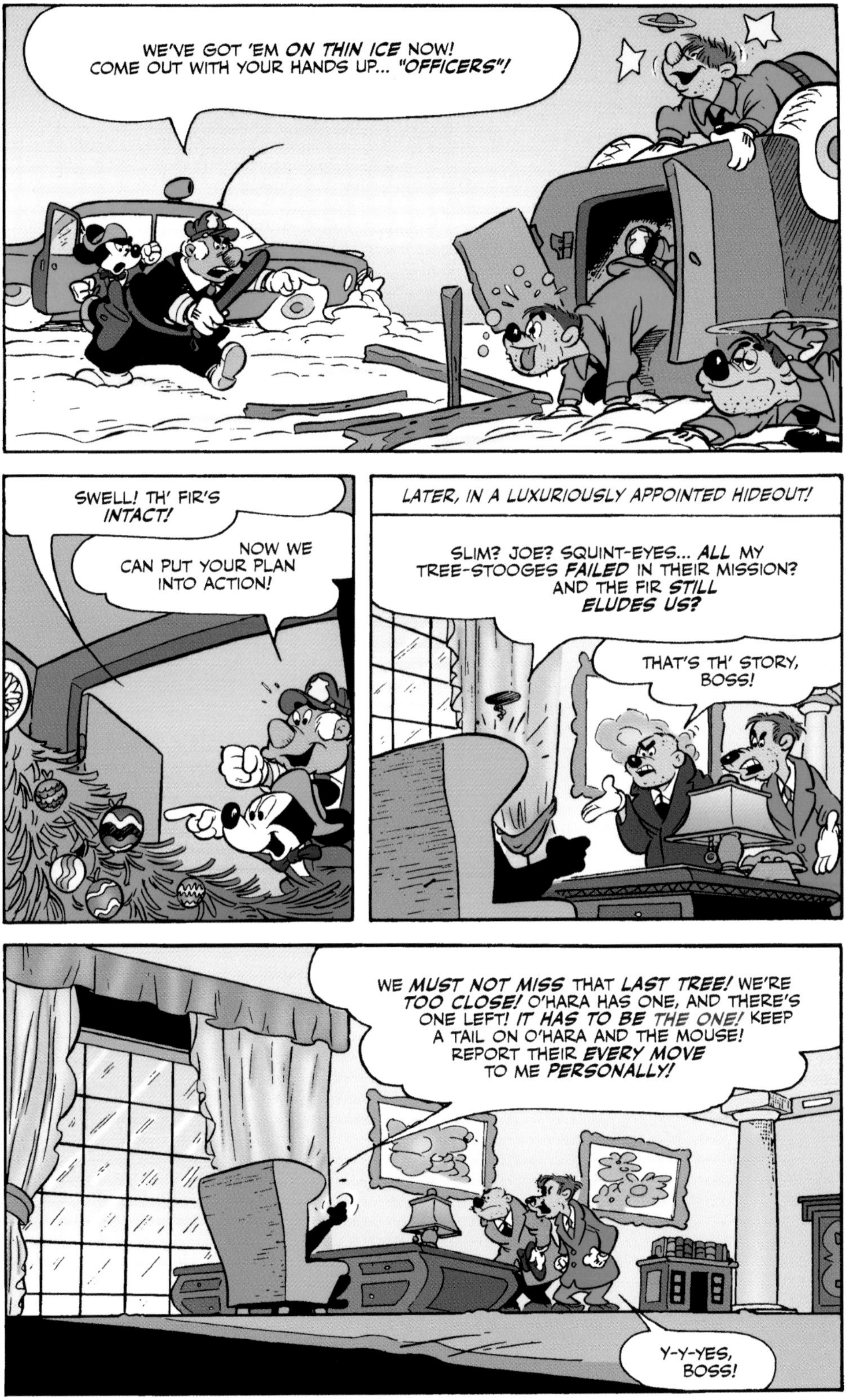
WE'VE GOT 'EM ON THIN ICE NOW! COME OUT WITH YOUR HANDS UP... "OFFICERS"!
SWELL! TH' FIR'S INTACT!
NOW WE CAN PUT YOUR PLAN INTO ACTION!
LATER, IN A LUXURIOUSLY APPOINTED HIDEOUT!
SLIM? JOE? SQUINT-EYES... ALL MY TREE-STOOGES FAILED IN THEIR MISSION? AND THE FIR STILL ELUDES US?
THAT'S TH' STORY, BOSS!
WE MUST NOT MISS THAT LAST TREE! WE'RE TOO CLOSE! O'HARA HAS ONE, AND THERE'S ONE LEFT! IT HAS TO BE THE ONE! KEEP A TAIL ON O'HARA AND THE MOUSE! REPORT THEIR EVERY MOVE TO ME PERSONALLY!
Y-Y-YES, BOSS!

Panel 1:

THAT NIGHT!

ALL RIGHT, MICKEY— *BEGIN YOUR PLAN!* OUR *CONFISCATED* TREE HAS ALREADY BEEN *PLACED* BY MY OFFICERS! I'LL GET YOU AND HEAD FOR THE SPOT... SLOW ENOUGH TO BE FOLLOWED! FAITH AND BEJABBERS... *WE ARE GO!*

Panel 2:

¿AHEM!¿ PICK UP MICKEY! WE'VE FOUND THE LAST TREE!

HEAR THAT, MAXIE? *IT'S TAIL' EM TIME!*

Panel 3:

YEAH, BOSS! O'HARA AN' TH' MOUSE! HEADIN' UP INTO THE *COUNTRYSIDE,* ALONG TH' *RIVER!* WHEN DEY STOP, I'LL REPORT TH' LOCATION!

Panel 4:

INTO THE WOODS!

BOSS! TH' PLACE IS *888 AVENUE OF THE ELMS!* GOOD! WE'LL HOLD THE FORT TILL YOU GET HERE!

WE *GOT* IT,

Panel 5:

THE *TRAP* IS SET—THANKS TO YOUR COOPERATION, CITIZEN! IN A FEW HOURS, THE *WHOLE AREA* WILL BE SURROUNDED BY POLICE!

HEH-HEH! *IN A FEW HOURS,* WE'LL ALREADY BE *FAR AWAY* WIT TH' NECKLACE!

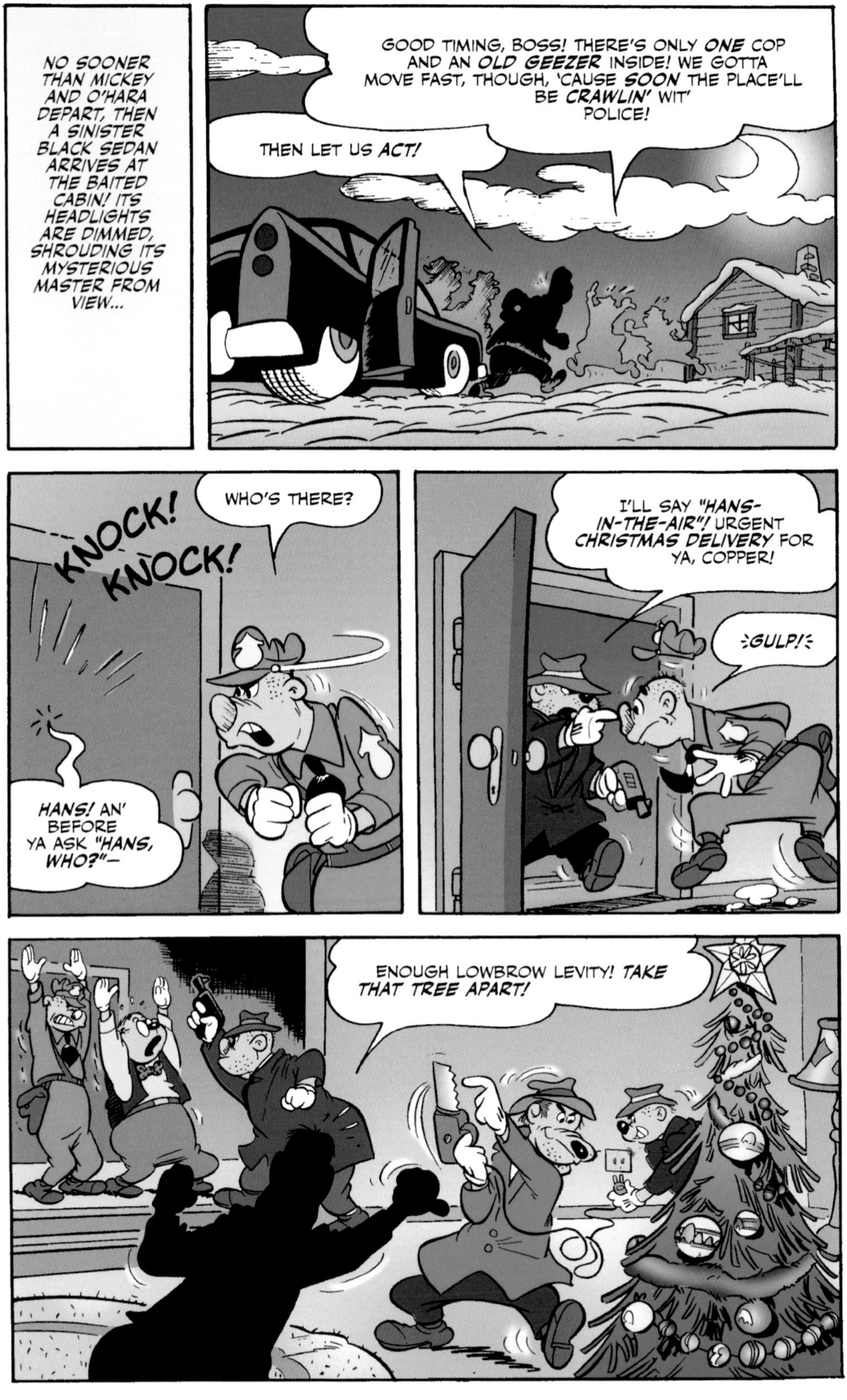
NO SOONER THAN MICKEY AND O'HARA DEPART, THEN A SINISTER BLACK SEDAN ARRIVES AT THE BAITED CABIN! ITS HEADLIGHTS ARE DIMMED, SHROUDING ITS MYSTERIOUS MASTER FROM VIEW...
GOOD TIMING, BOSS! THERE'S ONLY ONE COP AND AN OLD GEEZER INSIDE! WE GOTTA MOVE FAST, THOUGH, 'CAUSE SOON THE PLACE'LL BE CRAWLIN' WIT' POLICE!
THEN LET US ACT!
KNOCK! KNOCK!
WHO'S THERE?
HANS! AN' BEFORE YA ASK "HANS, WHO?"—
I'LL SAY "HANS-IN-THE-AIR"! URGENT CHRISTMAS DELIVERY FOR YA, COPPER!
GULP!
ENOUGH LOWBROW LEVITY! TAKE THAT TREE APART!

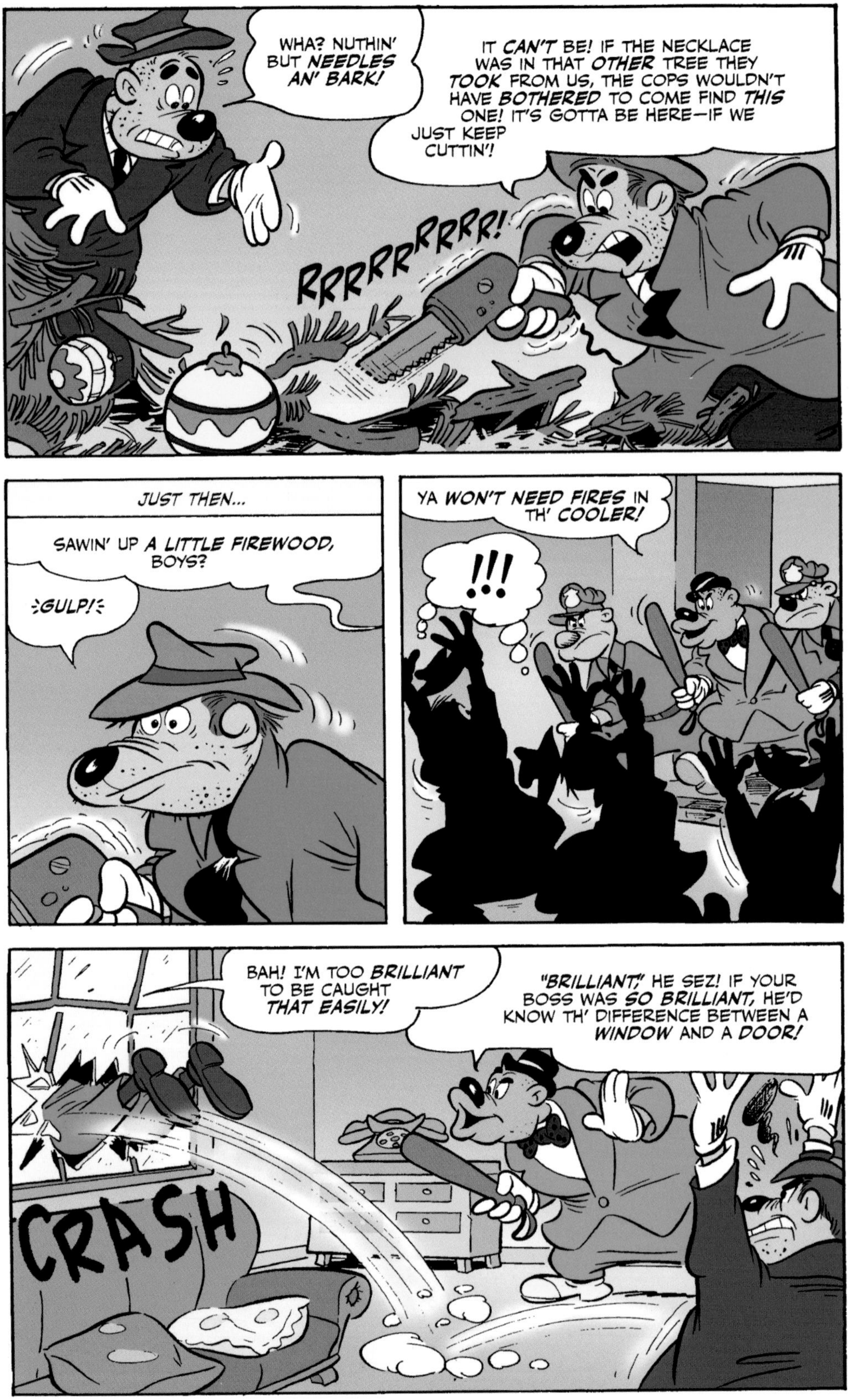
WHA? NUTHIN' BUT NEEDLES AN' BARK!
IT CAN'T BE! IF THE NECKLACE WAS IN THAT OTHER TREE THEY TOOK FROM US, THE COPS WOULDN'T HAVE BOTHERED TO COME FIND THIS ONE! IT'S GOTTA BE HERE—IF WE JUST KEEP CUTTIN'!
RRRRRRRRRR!
JUST THEN...
SAWIN' UP A LITTLE FIREWOOD, BOYS?
GULP!
YA WON'T NEED FIRES IN TH' COOLER!
!!!
BAH! I'M TOO BRILLIANT TO BE CAUGHT THAT EASILY!
"BRILLIANT," HE SEZ! IF YOUR BOSS WAS SO BRILLIANT, HE'D KNOW TH' DIFFERENCE BETWEEN A WINDOW AND A DOOR!
CRASH

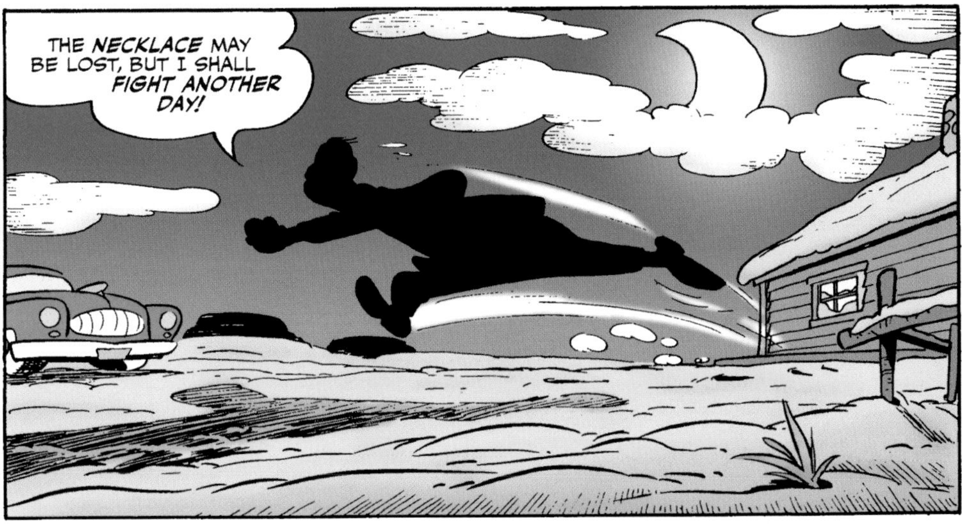
THE NECKLACE MAY BE LOST, BUT I SHALL FIGHT ANOTHER DAY!

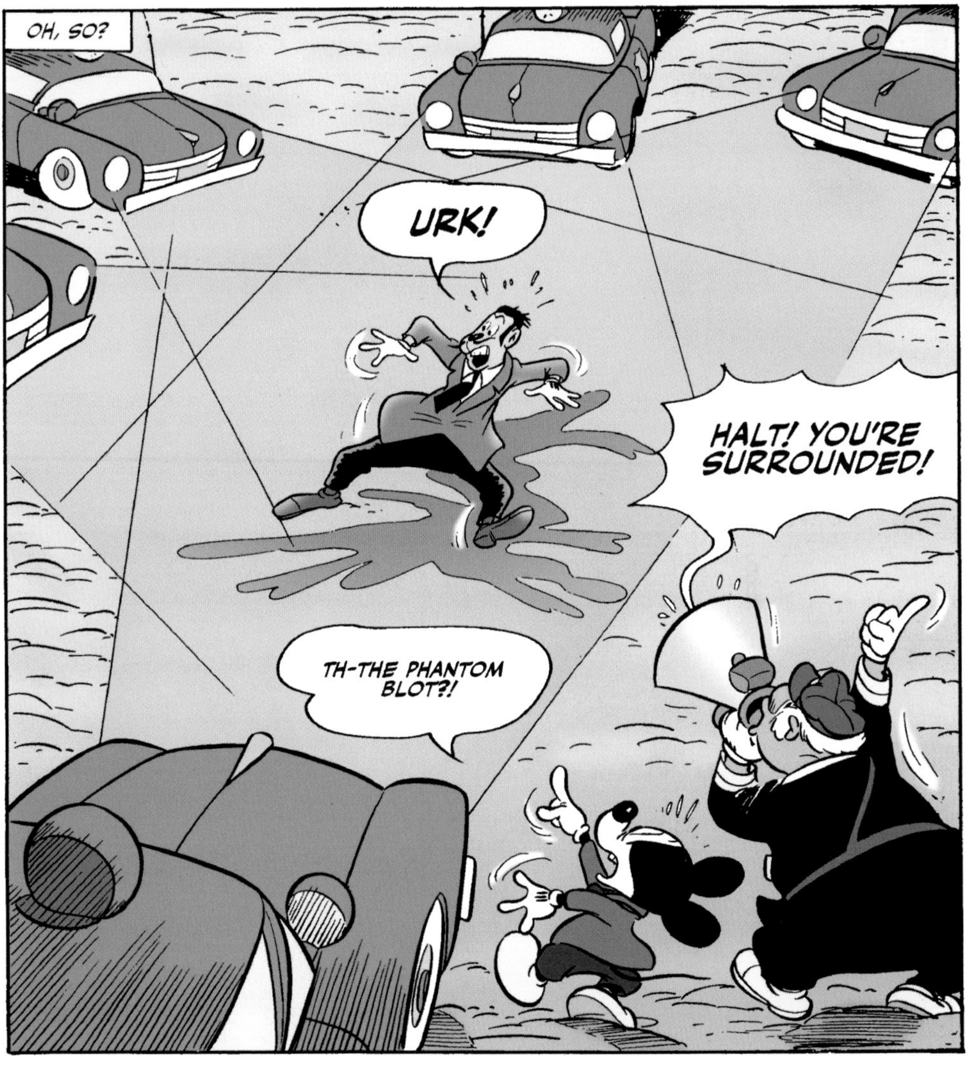
OH, SO?
URK!
HALT! YOU'RE SURROUNDED!
TH-THE PHANTOM BLOT?!

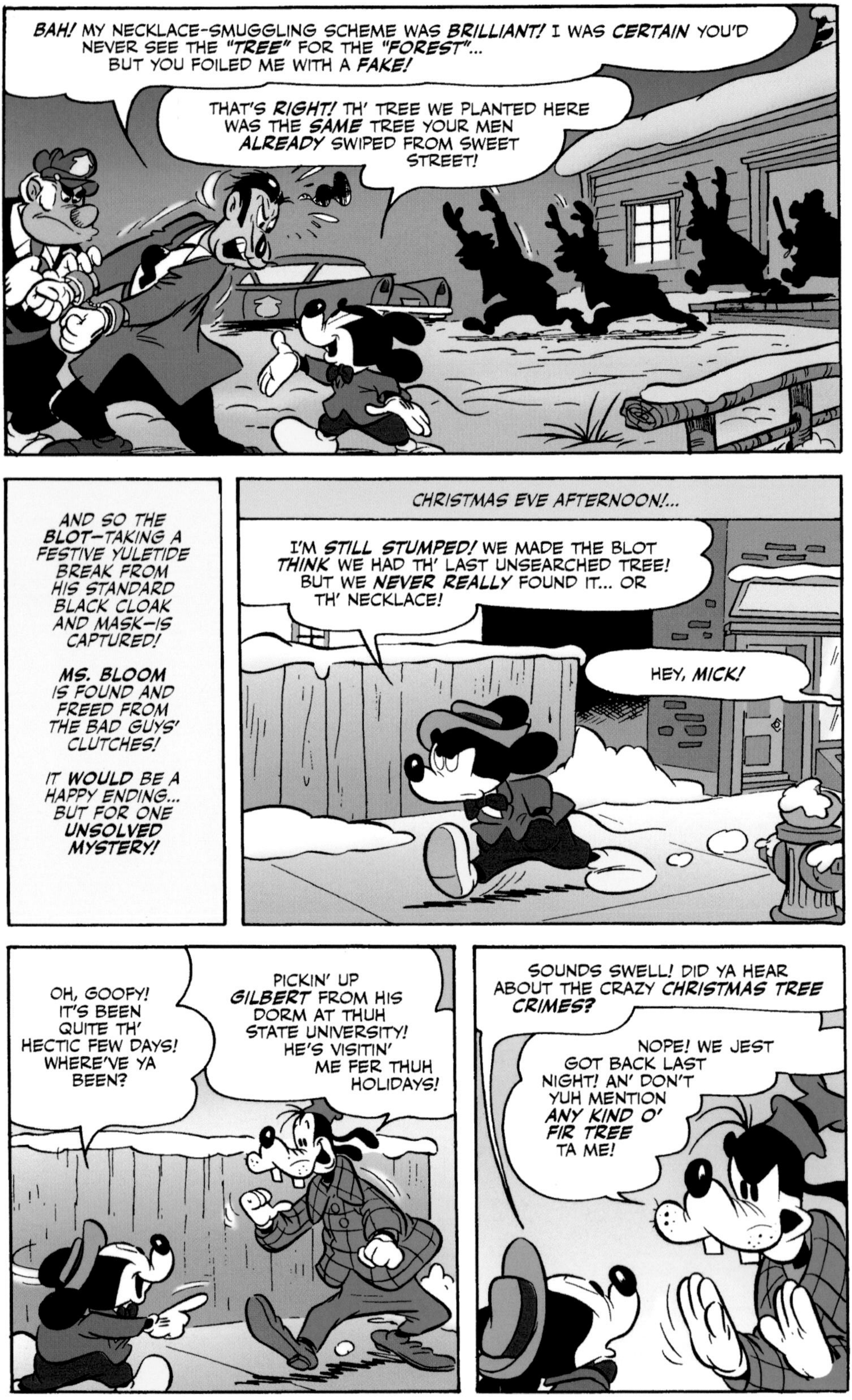
BAH! MY NECKLACE-SMUGGLING SCHEME WAS BRILLIANT! I WAS CERTAIN YOU'D NEVER SEE THE "TREE" FOR THE "FOREST"... BUT YOU FOILED ME WITH A FAKE!
THAT'S RIGHT! TH' TREE WE PLANTED HERE WAS THE SAME TREE YOUR MEN ALREADY SWIPED FROM SWEET STREET!
AND SO THE BLOT—TAKING A FESTIVE YULETIDE BREAK FROM HIS STANDARD BLACK CLOAK AND MASK—IS CAPTURED!
MS. BLOOM IS FOUND AND FREED FROM THE BAD GUYS' CLUTCHES!
IT WOULD BE A HAPPY ENDING... BUT FOR ONE UNSOLVED MYSTERY!
CHRISTMAS EVE AFTERNOON!...
I'M STILL STUMPED! WE MADE THE BLOT THINK WE HAD TH' LAST UNSEARCHED TREE! BUT WE NEVER REALLY FOUND IT... OR TH' NECKLACE!
HEY, MICK!
OH, GOOFY! IT'S BEEN QUITE TH' HECTIC FEW DAYS! WHERE'VE YA BEEN?
PICKIN' UP GILBERT FROM HIS DORM AT THUH STATE UNIVERSITY! HE'S VISITIN' ME FER THUH HOLIDAYS!
SOUNDS SWELL! DID YA HEAR ABOUT THE CRAZY CHRISTMAS TREE CRIMES?
NOPE! WE JEST GOT BACK LAST NIGHT! AN' DON'T YUH MENTION ANY KIND O' FIR TREE TA ME!

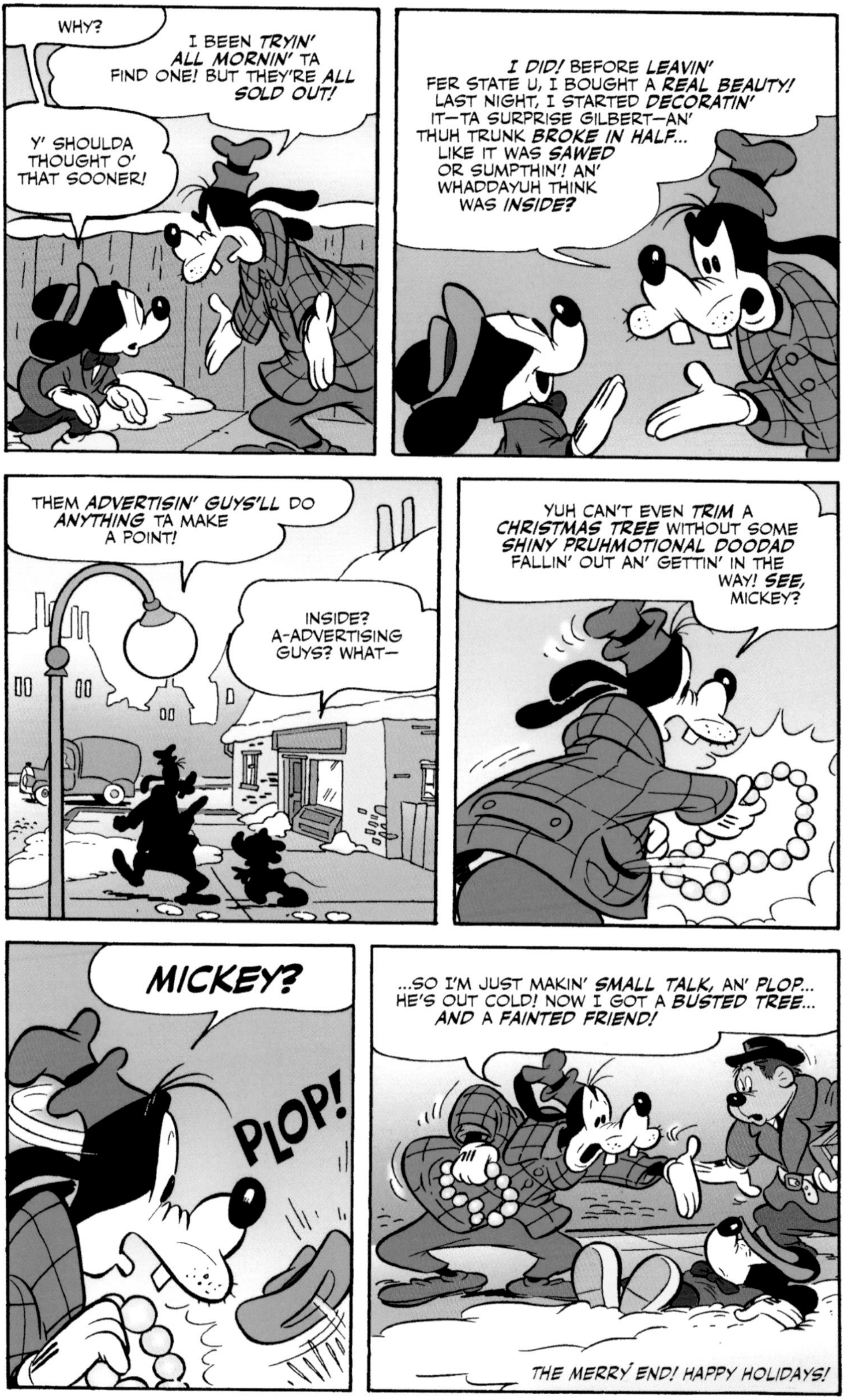
WHY?
I BEEN TRYIN' ALL MORNIN' TA FIND ONE! BUT THEY'RE ALL SOLD OUT!
Y' SHOULDA THOUGHT O' THAT SOONER!
I DID! BEFORE LEAVIN' FER STATE U, I BOUGHT A REAL BEAUTY! LAST NIGHT, I STARTED DECORATIN' IT—TA SURPRISE GILBERT—AN' THUH TRUNK BROKE IN HALF... LIKE IT WAS SAWED OR SUMPTHIN'! AN' WHADDAYUH THINK WAS INSIDE?
THEM ADVERTISIN' GUYS'LL DO ANYTHING TA MAKE A POINT!
INSIDE? A-ADVERTISING GUYS? WHAT—
YUH CAN'T EVEN TRIM A CHRISTMAS TREE WITHOUT SOME SHINY PRUHMOTIONAL DOODAD FALLIN' OUT AN' GETTIN' IN THE WAY! SEE, MICKEY?
MICKEY?
PLOP!
...SO I'M JUST MAKIN' SMALL TALK, AN' PLOP... HE'S OUT COLD! NOW I GOT A BUSTED TREE... AND A FAINTED FRIEND!
THE MERRY END! HAPPY HOLIDAYS!

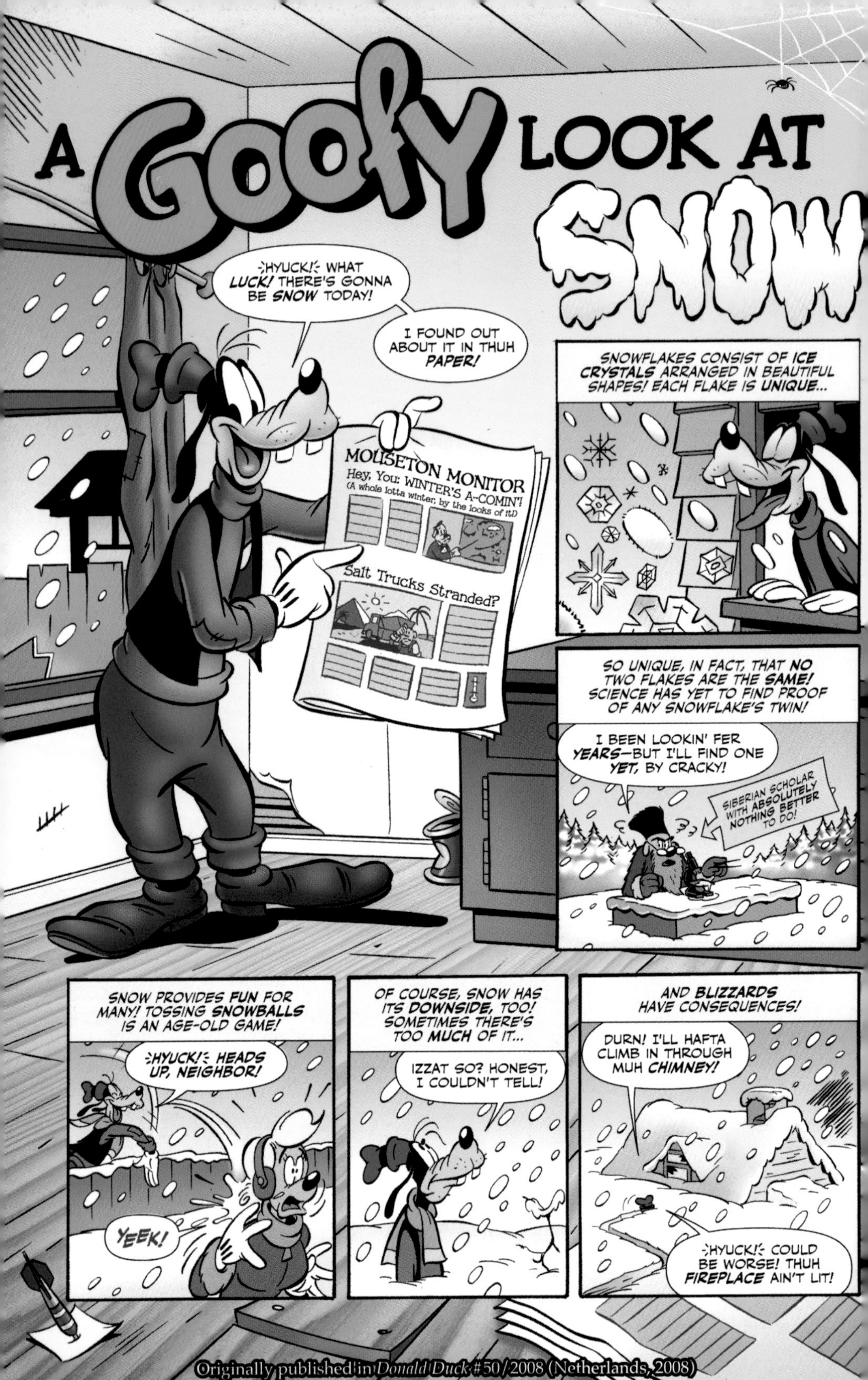
A GOOFY LOOK AT SNOW
HYUCK! WHAT LUCK! THERE'S GONNA BE SNOW TODAY!
I FOUND OUT ABOUT IT IN THUH PAPER!
MOUSETON MONITOR
Hey, You: WINTER'S A-COMIN'!
(A whole lotta winter, by the looks of it!)
Salt Trucks Stranded?
SNOWFLAKES CONSIST OF ICE CRYSTALS ARRANGED IN BEAUTIFUL SHAPES! EACH FLAKE IS UNIQUE...
SO UNIQUE, IN FACT, THAT NO TWO FLAKES ARE THE SAME! SCIENCE HAS YET TO FIND PROOF OF ANY SNOWFLAKE'S TWIN!
I BEEN LOOKIN' FER YEARS—BUT I'LL FIND ONE YET, BY CRACKY!
SIBERIAN SCHOLAR WITH ABSOLUTELY NOTHING BETTER TO DO!
SNOW PROVIDES FUN FOR MANY! TOSSING SNOWBALLS IS AN AGE-OLD GAME!
HYUCK! HEADS UP, NEIGHBOR!
YEEK!
OF COURSE, SNOW HAS ITS DOWNSIDE, TOO! SOMETIMES THERE'S TOO MUCH OF IT...
IZZAT SO? HONEST, I COULDN'T TELL!
AND BLIZZARDS HAVE CONSEQUENCES!
DURN! I'LL HAFTA CLIMB IN THROUGH MUH CHIMNEY!
HYUCK! COULD BE WORSE! THUH FIREPLACE AIN'T LIT!

Originally published in *Donald Duck* #50/2008 (Netherlands, 2008)

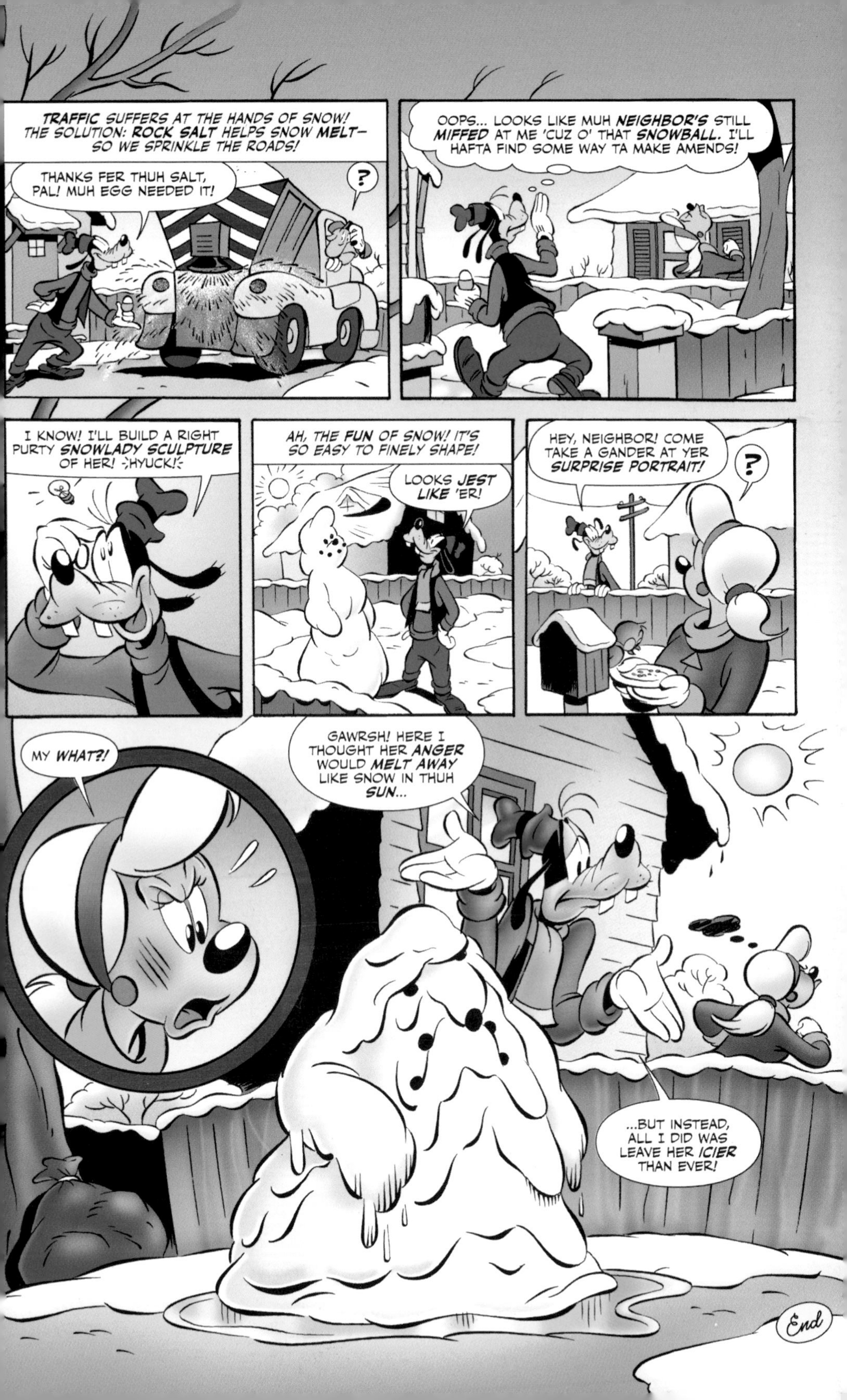
TRAFFIC SUFFERS AT THE HANDS OF SNOW! THE SOLUTION: ROCK SALT HELPS SNOW MELT— SO WE SPRINKLE THE ROADS!
THANKS FER THUH SALT, PAL! MUH EGG NEEDED IT!
?
OOPS... LOOKS LIKE MUH NEIGHBOR'S STILL MIFFED AT ME 'CUZ O' THAT SNOWBALL. I'LL HAFTA FIND SOME WAY TA MAKE AMENDS!
I KNOW! I'LL BUILD A RIGHT PURTY SNOWLADY SCULPTURE OF HER! HYUCK!
AH, THE FUN OF SNOW! IT'S SO EASY TO FINELY SHAPE!
LOOKS JEST LIKE 'ER!
HEY, NEIGHBOR! COME TAKE A GANDER AT YER SURPRISE PORTRAIT!
?
MY WHAT?!
GAWRSH! HERE I THOUGHT HER ANGER WOULD MELT AWAY LIKE SNOW IN THUH SUN...
...BUT INSTEAD, ALL I DID WAS LEAVE HER ICIER THAN EVER!
End

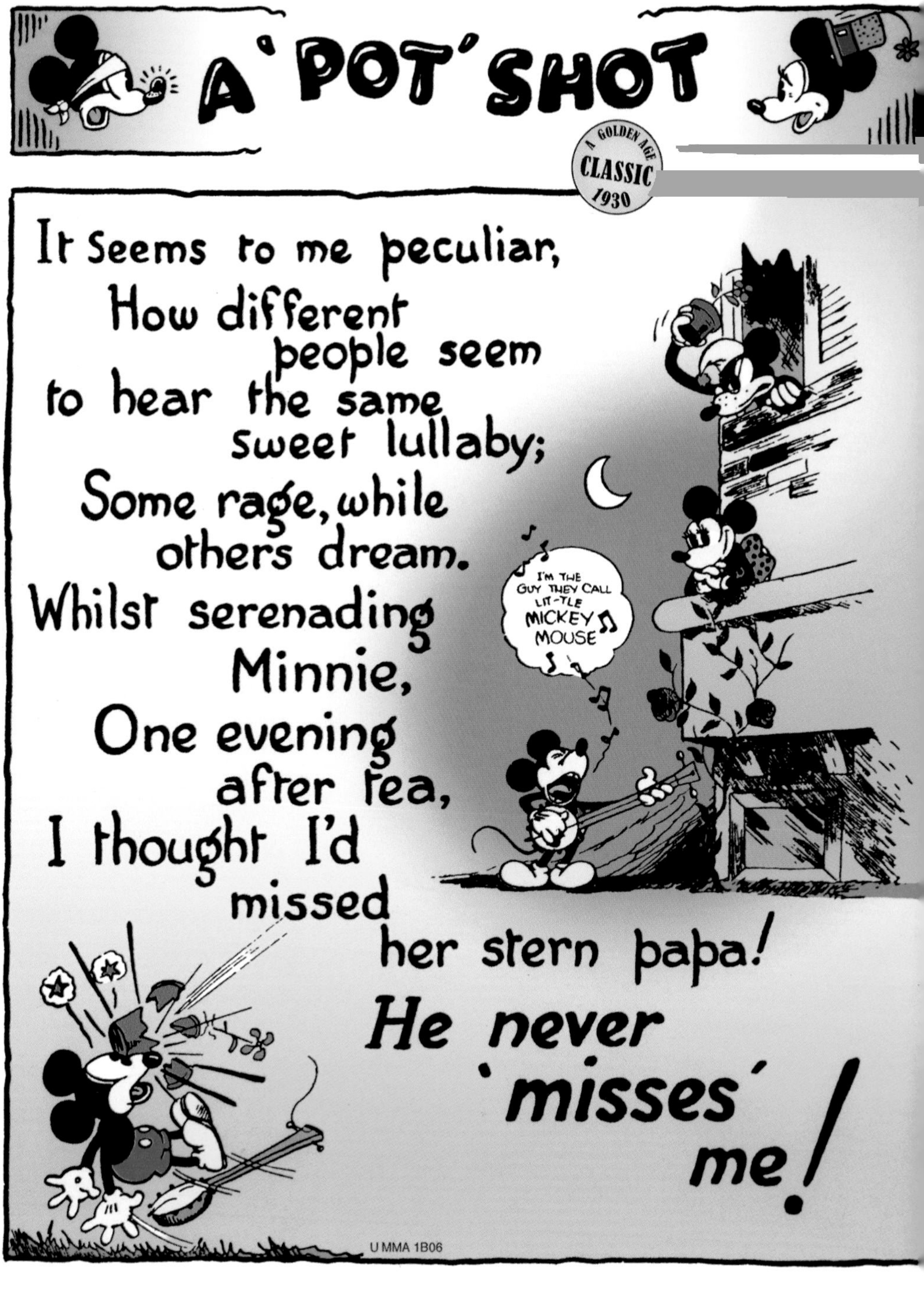
A 'POT' SHOT
A GOLDEN AGE CLASSIC 1930
It seems to me peculiar,
How different people seem
to hear the same sweet lullaby;
Some rage, while others dream.
Whilst serenading Minnie,
One evening after tea,
I thought I'd missed her stern papa!
He never 'misses' me!
I'M THE GUY THEY CALL LIT-TLE MICKEY MOUSE
U MMA 1B06

Originally published in *Mickey Mouse Annual* #1 (United Kingdom, 1930)

Walt Disney's Mickey Mouse in While We Were Waiting

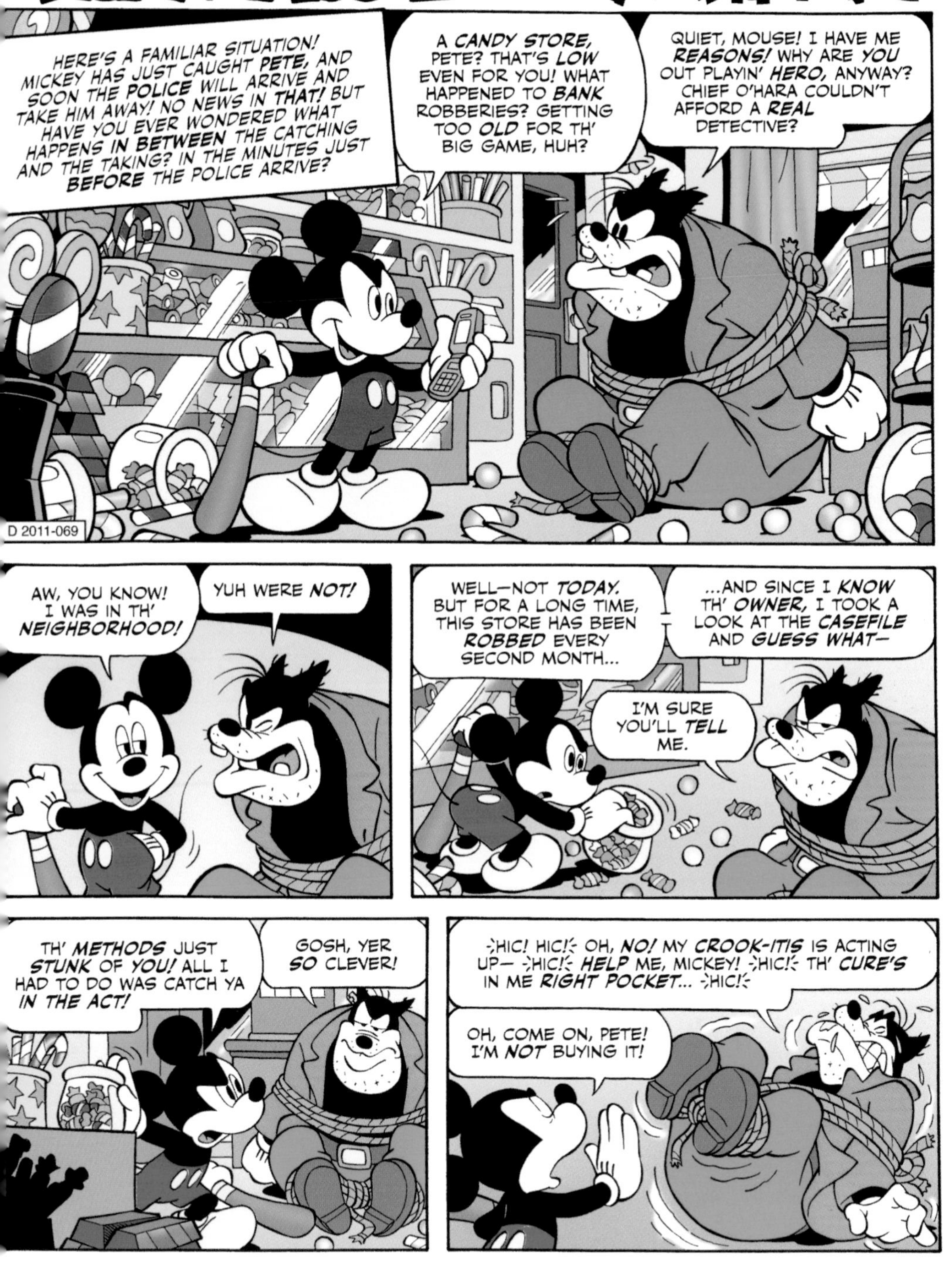
HERE'S A FAMILIAR SITUATION! MICKEY HAS JUST CAUGHT PETE, AND SOON THE POLICE WILL ARRIVE AND TAKE HIM AWAY! NO NEWS IN THAT! BUT HAVE YOU EVER WONDERED WHAT HAPPENS IN BETWEEN THE CATCHING AND THE TAKING? IN THE MINUTES JUST BEFORE THE POLICE ARRIVE?
A CANDY STORE, PETE? THAT'S LOW EVEN FOR YOU! WHAT HAPPENED TO BANK ROBBERIES? GETTING TOO OLD FOR TH' BIG GAME, HUH?
QUIET, MOUSE! I HAVE ME REASONS! WHY ARE YOU OUT PLAYIN' HERO, ANYWAY? CHIEF O'HARA COULDN'T AFFORD A REAL DETECTIVE?
D 2011-069
AW, YOU KNOW! I WAS IN TH' NEIGHBORHOOD!
YUH WERE NOT!
WELL—NOT TODAY. BUT FOR A LONG TIME, THIS STORE HAS BEEN ROBBED EVERY SECOND MONTH...
...AND SINCE I KNOW TH' OWNER, I TOOK A LOOK AT THE CASEFILE AND GUESS WHAT—
I'M SURE YOU'LL TELL ME.
TH' METHODS JUST STUNK OF YOU! ALL I HAD TO DO WAS CATCH YA IN THE ACT!
GOSH, YER SO CLEVER!
HIC! HIC! OH, NO! MY CROOK-ITIS IS ACTING UP— HIC! HELP ME, MICKEY! HIC! TH' CURE'S IN ME RIGHT POCKET... HIC!
OH, COME ON, PETE! I'M NOT BUYING IT!

Originally published in *Anders And & Co.* #39/2012 (Denmark, 2012)

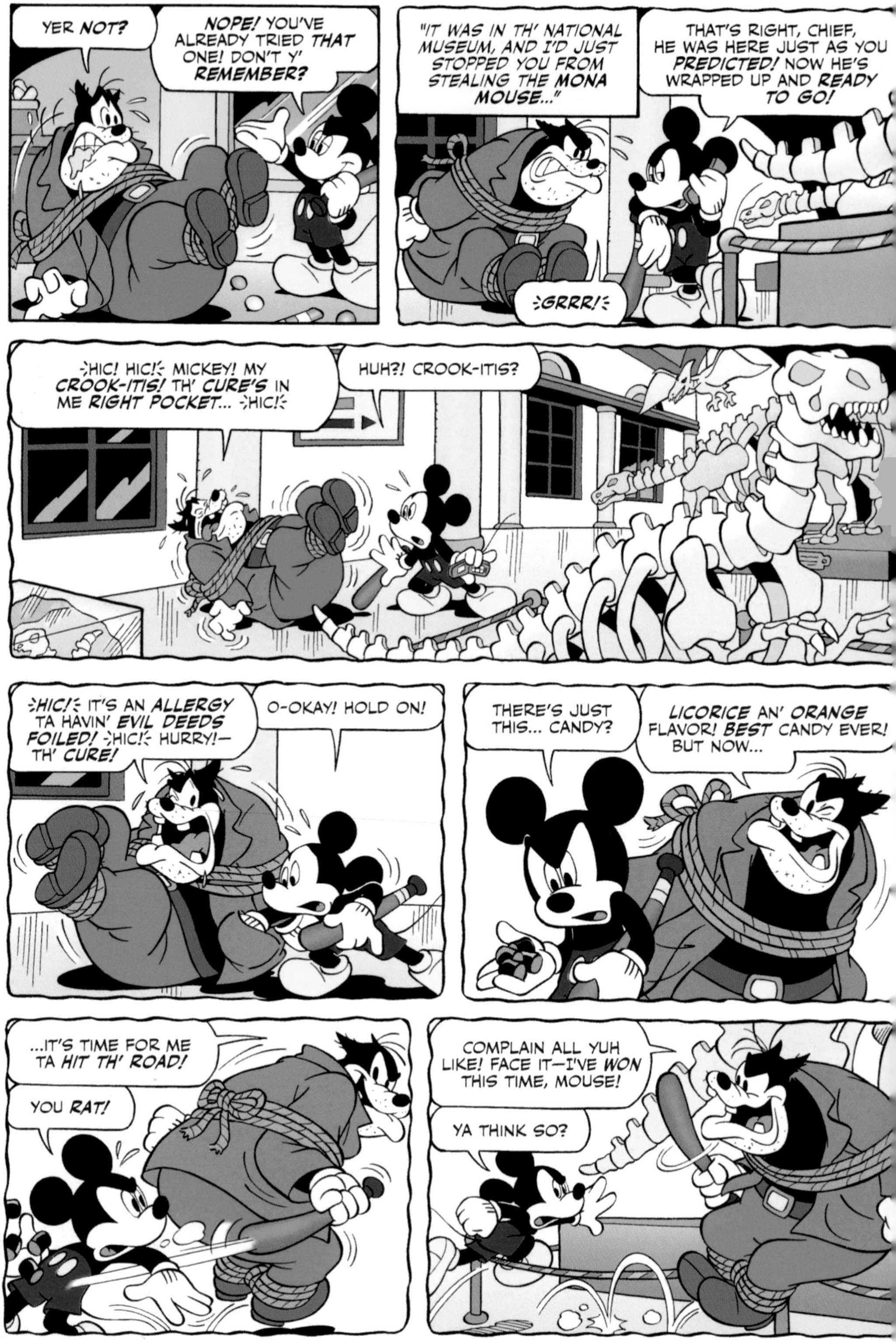
YER NOT?
NOPE! YOU'VE ALREADY TRIED THAT ONE! DON'T Y' REMEMBER?
"IT WAS IN TH' NATIONAL MUSEUM, AND I'D JUST STOPPED YOU FROM STEALING THE MONA MOUSE..."
THAT'S RIGHT, CHIEF, HE WAS HERE JUST AS YOU PREDICTED! NOW HE'S WRAPPED UP AND READY TO GO!
GRRR!
HIC! HIC! MICKEY! MY CROOK-ITIS! TH' CURE'S IN ME RIGHT POCKET... HIC!
HUH?! CROOK-ITIS?
HIC! IT'S AN ALLERGY TA HAVIN' EVIL DEEDS FOILED! HIC! HURRY!— TH' CURE!
O-OKAY! HOLD ON!
THERE'S JUST THIS... CANDY?
LICORICE AN' ORANGE FLAVOR! BEST CANDY EVER! BUT NOW...
...IT'S TIME FOR ME TA HIT TH' ROAD!
YOU RAT!
COMPLAIN ALL YUH LIKE! FACE IT—I'VE WON THIS TIME, MOUSE!
YA THINK SO?

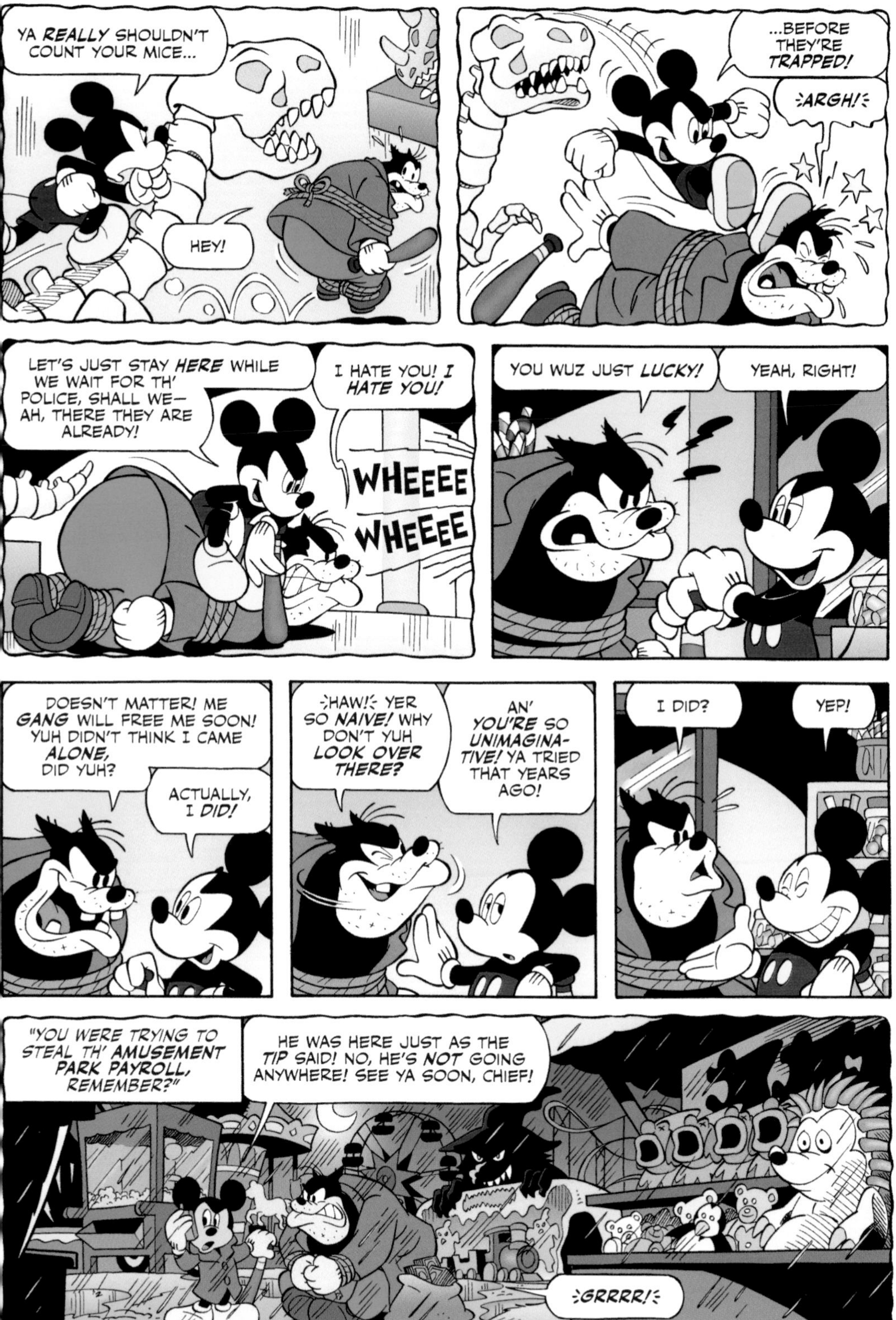
YA REALLY SHOULDN'T COUNT YOUR MICE...
HEY!
...BEFORE THEY'RE TRAPPED!
ARGH!
LET'S JUST STAY HERE WHILE WE WAIT FOR TH' POLICE, SHALL WE— AH, THERE THEY ARE ALREADY!
I HATE YOU! I HATE YOU!
WHEEEE WHEEEE
YOU WUZ JUST LUCKY!
YEAH, RIGHT!
DOESN'T MATTER! ME GANG WILL FREE ME SOON! YUH DIDN'T THINK I CAME ALONE, DID YUH?
ACTUALLY, I DID!
HAW! YER SO NAIVE! WHY DON'T YUH LOOK OVER THERE?
AN' YOU'RE SO UNIMAGINATIVE! YA TRIED THAT YEARS AGO!
I DID?
YEP!
"YOU WERE TRYING TO STEAL TH' AMUSEMENT PARK PAYROLL, REMEMBER?"
HE WAS HERE JUST AS THE TIP SAID! NO, HE'S NOT GOING ANYWHERE! SEE YA SOON, CHIEF!
GRRRR!

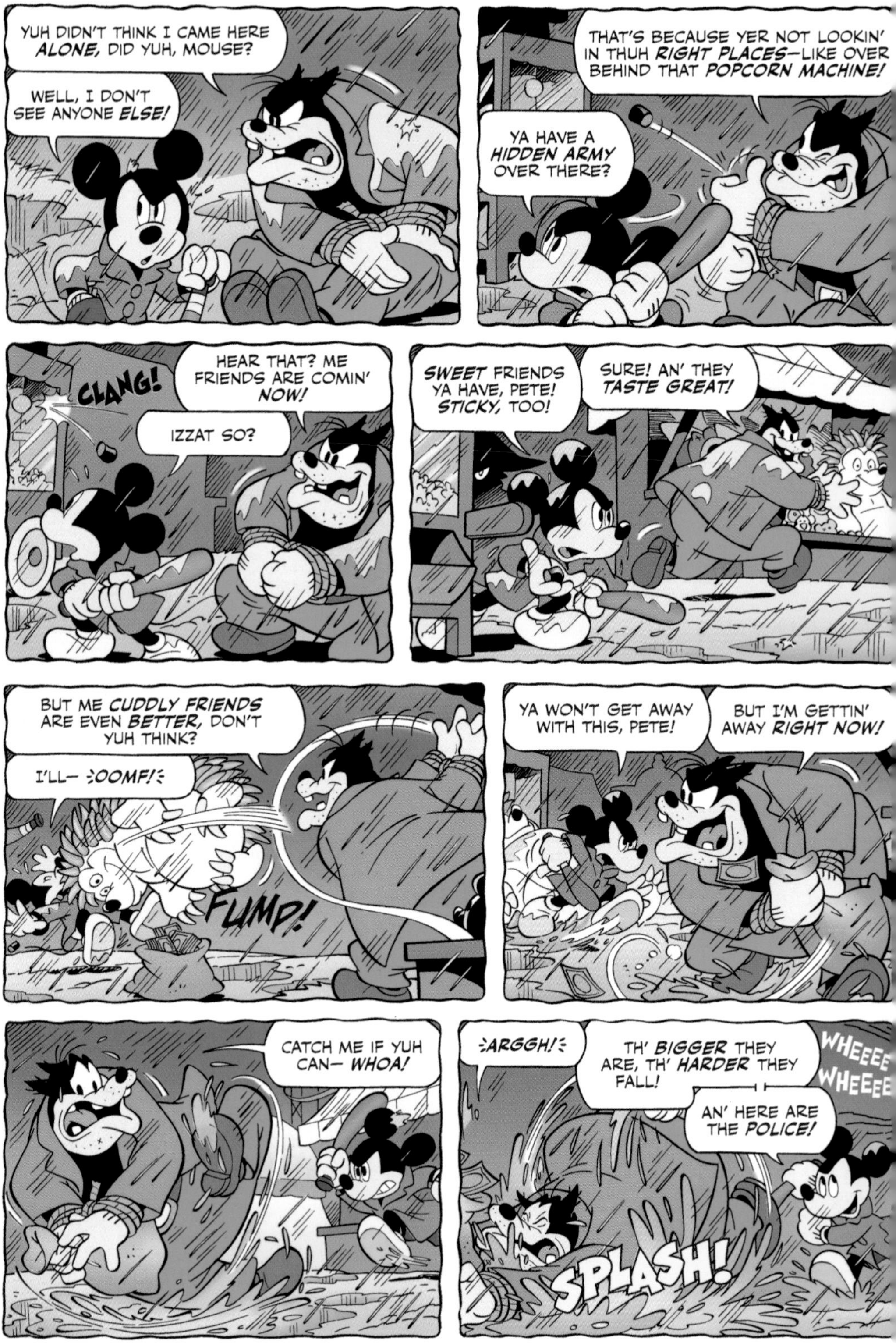
YUH DIDN'T THINK I CAME HERE *ALONE,* DID YUH, MOUSE?
WELL, I DON'T SEE ANYONE *ELSE!*
THAT'S BECAUSE YER NOT LOOKIN' IN THUH *RIGHT PLACES*—LIKE OVER BEHIND THAT *POPCORN MACHINE!*
YA HAVE A *HIDDEN ARMY* OVER THERE?
CLANG!
HEAR THAT? ME FRIENDS ARE COMIN' *NOW!*
IZZAT SO?
SWEET FRIENDS YA HAVE, PETE! *STICKY,* TOO!
SURE! AN' THEY *TASTE GREAT!*
BUT ME *CUDDLY FRIENDS* ARE EVEN *BETTER,* DON'T YUH THINK?
I'LL— *OOMF!*
FUMP!
YA WON'T GET AWAY WITH THIS, PETE!
BUT I'M GETTIN' AWAY *RIGHT NOW!*
CATCH ME IF YUH CAN— *WHOA!*
ARGGH!
TH' *BIGGER* THEY ARE, TH' *HARDER* THEY FALL!
AN' HERE ARE THE *POLICE!*
WHEEEE
WHEEEE
SPLASH!

SO YA SEE, *I'VE* LEARNED FROM MY MISTAKES! MAYBE *YOU* SHOULD TOO, HUH?

ANYBODY EVER TELL YOU HOW *ANNOYING* YUH ARE?

HEY! REMEMBER THE *SHRINKING INCIDENT?!* ⌐HAR!⌐

NO.

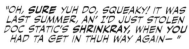

"OH, *SURE* YUH DO, SQUEAKY! IT WAS LAST SUMMER, AN' I'D JUST STOLEN DOC STATIC'S *SHRINKRAY*, WHEN *YOU* HAD TA GET IN THUH WAY AGAIN— "

⌐OOF!⌐

SO *YOU'RE* TH' ONE WHO'S BEEN *SPYING* ON DOC ALL NIGHT, HUH? GOOD THING HE CALLED *ME!*

"*YOU* WUZ *QUICK* TA BRAG TO YER PATHETIC PALS!"

YEP—I *GOT HIM*, CHIEF! SEND TH' PADDY WAGON!

WHAT ARE *YOU* SO HAPPY ABOUT? GET YOUR *HANDS* OUT WHERE I CAN *SEE* 'EM!

OKAY! *ENJOY!*

⌐AIEE!⌐

IT'S THUH BEST CANDY *EVER*, MOUSE! AN' NOW IT'LL *LAST YOU* EVEN LONGER! ⌐HAR-HAR!⌐

NO!

ZAAP!

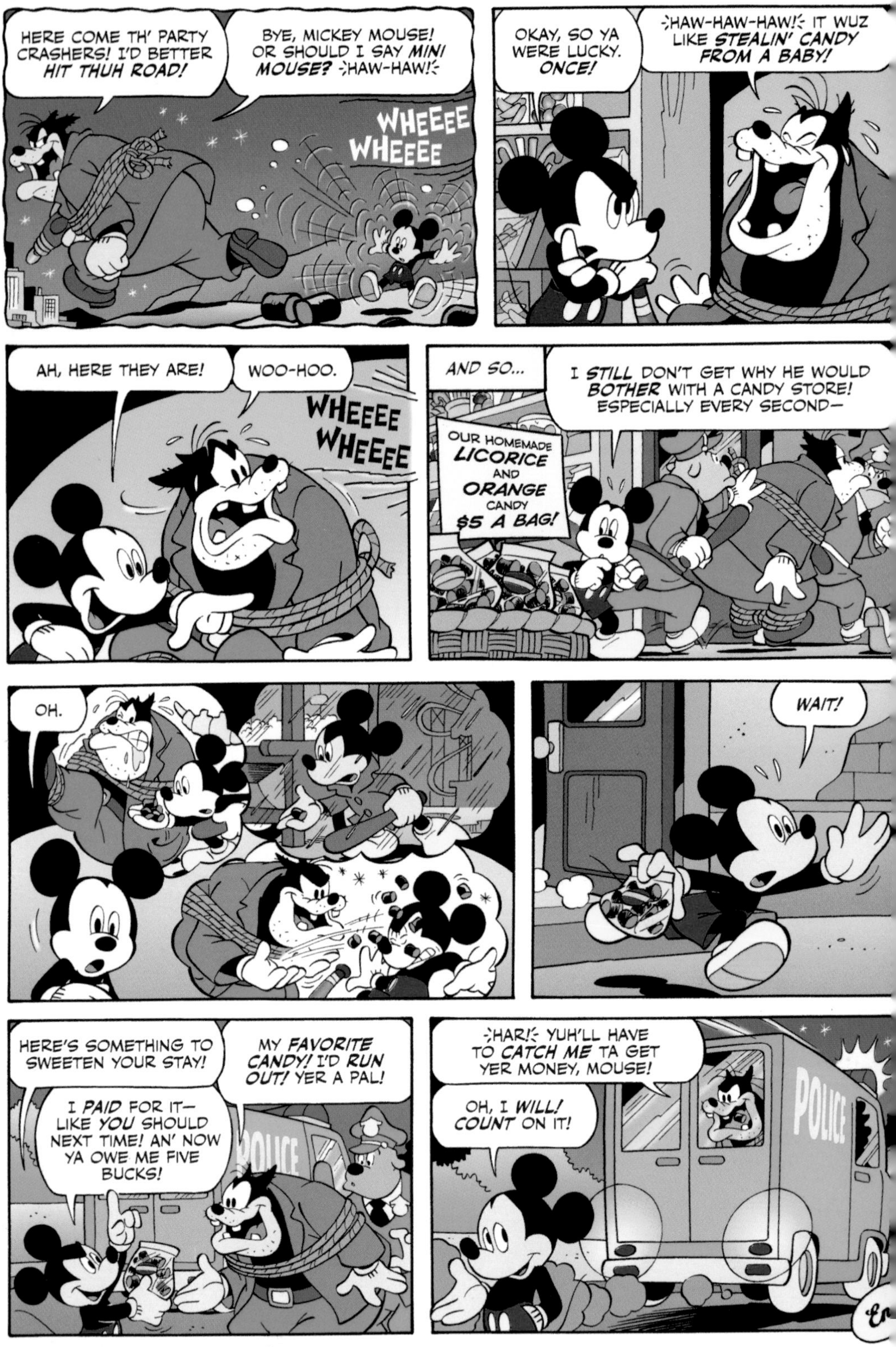
HERE COME TH' PARTY CRASHERS! I'D BETTER HIT THUH ROAD!
BYE, MICKEY MOUSE! OR SHOULD I SAY MINI MOUSE? HAW-HAW!
WHEEEE WHEEEE
OKAY, SO YA WERE LUCKY. ONCE!
HAW-HAW-HAW! IT WUZ LIKE STEALIN' CANDY FROM A BABY!
AH, HERE THEY ARE!
WOO-HOO.
WHEEEE WHEEEE
AND SO...
I STILL DON'T GET WHY HE WOULD BOTHER WITH A CANDY STORE! ESPECIALLY EVERY SECOND—
OUR HOMEMADE LICORICE AND ORANGE CANDY $5 A BAG!
OH.
WAIT!
HERE'S SOMETHING TO SWEETEN YOUR STAY!
I PAID FOR IT— LIKE YOU SHOULD NEXT TIME! AN' NOW YA OWE ME FIVE BUCKS!
MY FAVORITE CANDY! I'D RUN OUT! YER A PAL!
POLICE
HAR! YUH'LL HAVE TO CATCH ME TA GET YER MONEY, MOUSE!
OH, I WILL! COUNT ON IT!
POLICE

Cover
Gallery

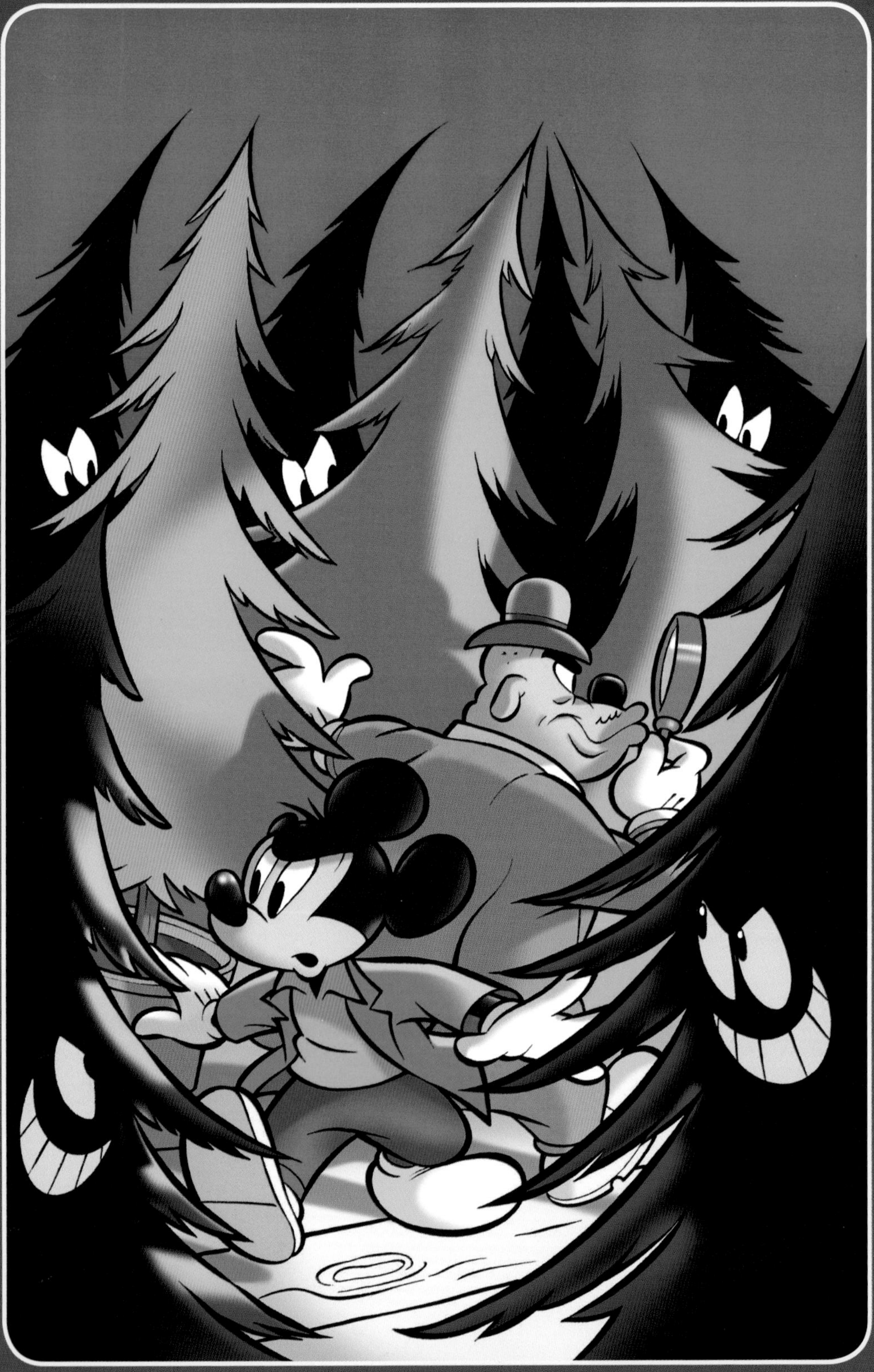

Art by Andrea "Casty" Castellan

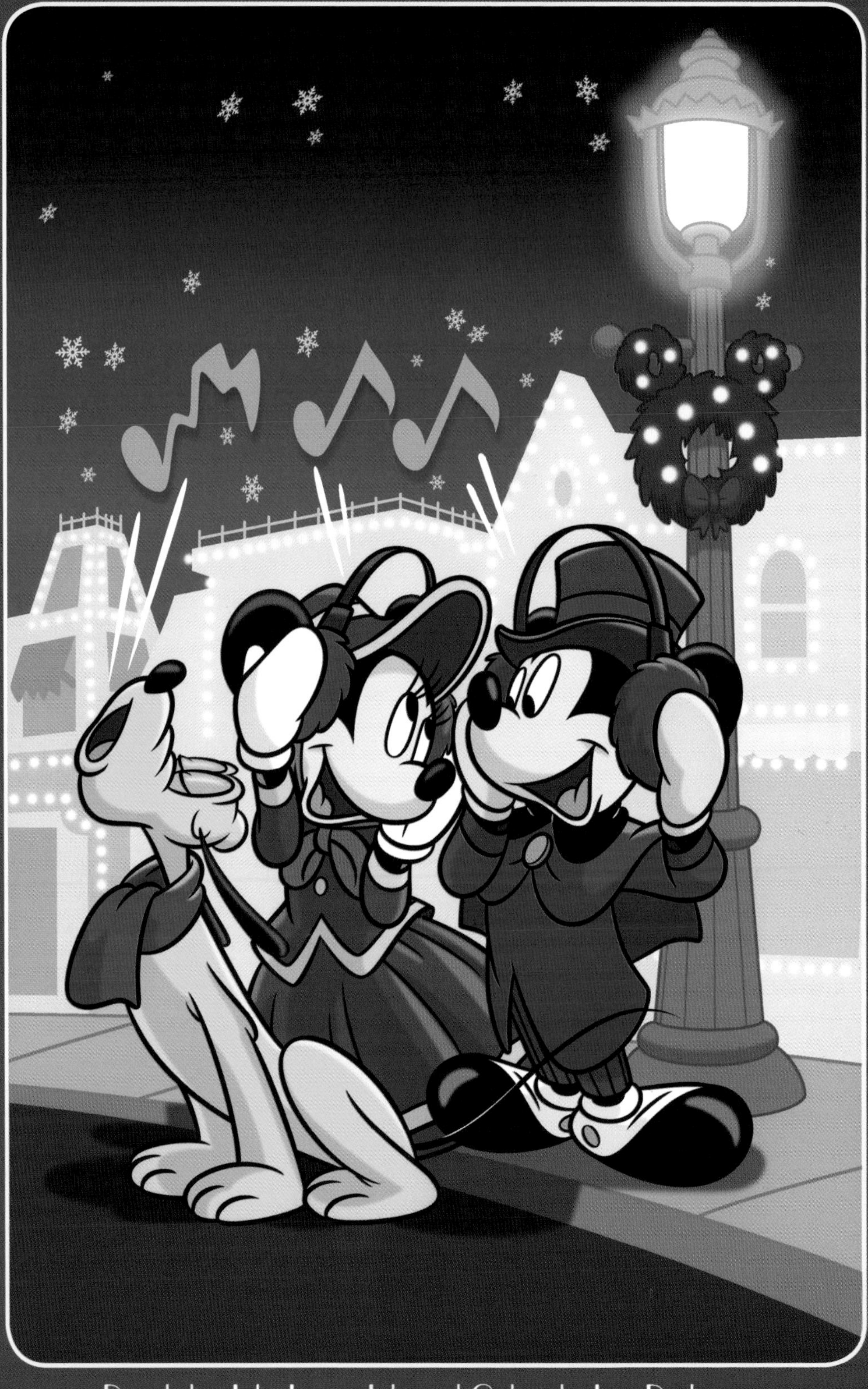

Pencils by John Loter, Inks and Colors by Lou Rodriguez

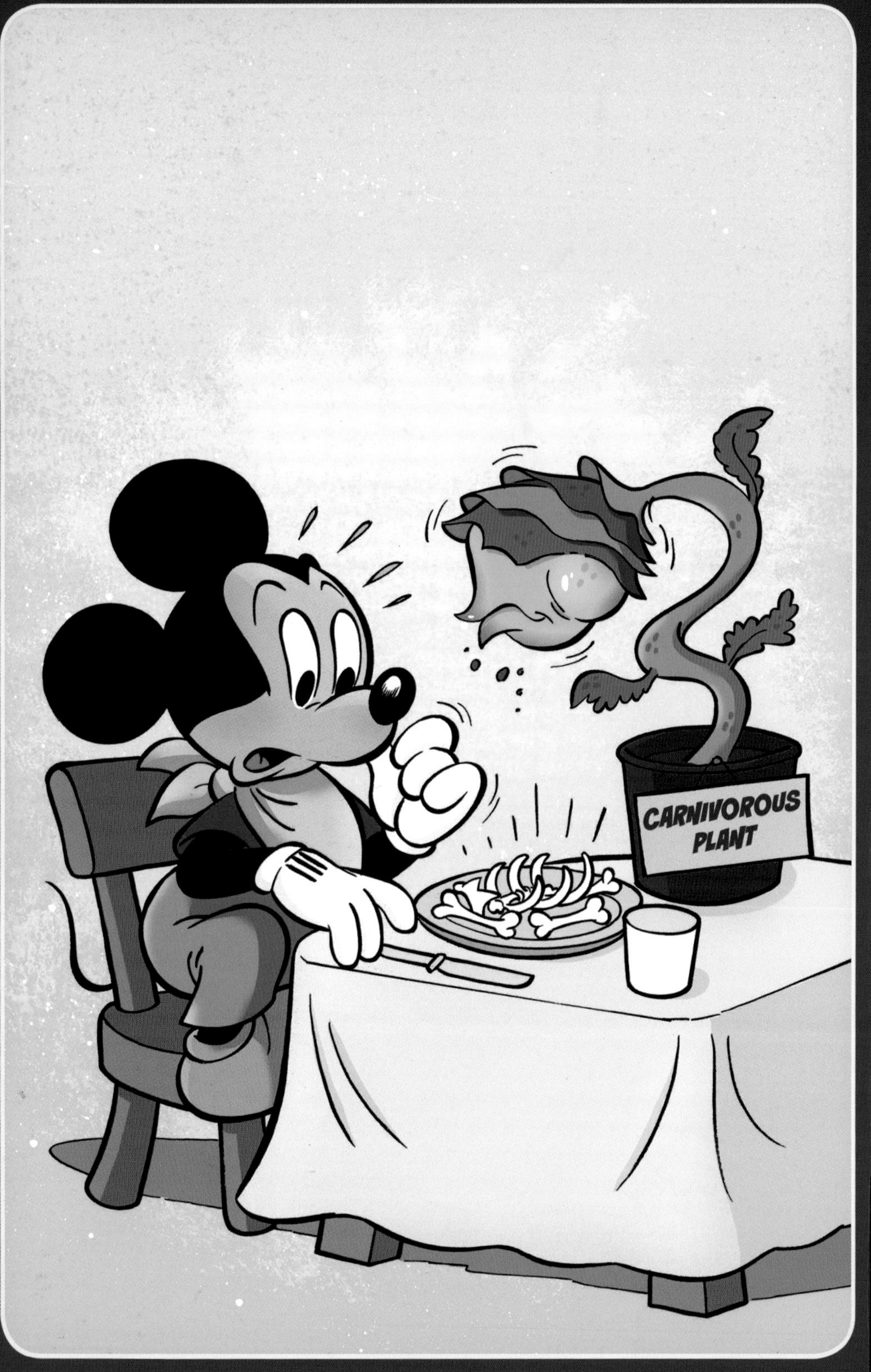
CARNIVOROUS PLANT

Art by Marco Rota, Colors by Derek Charm

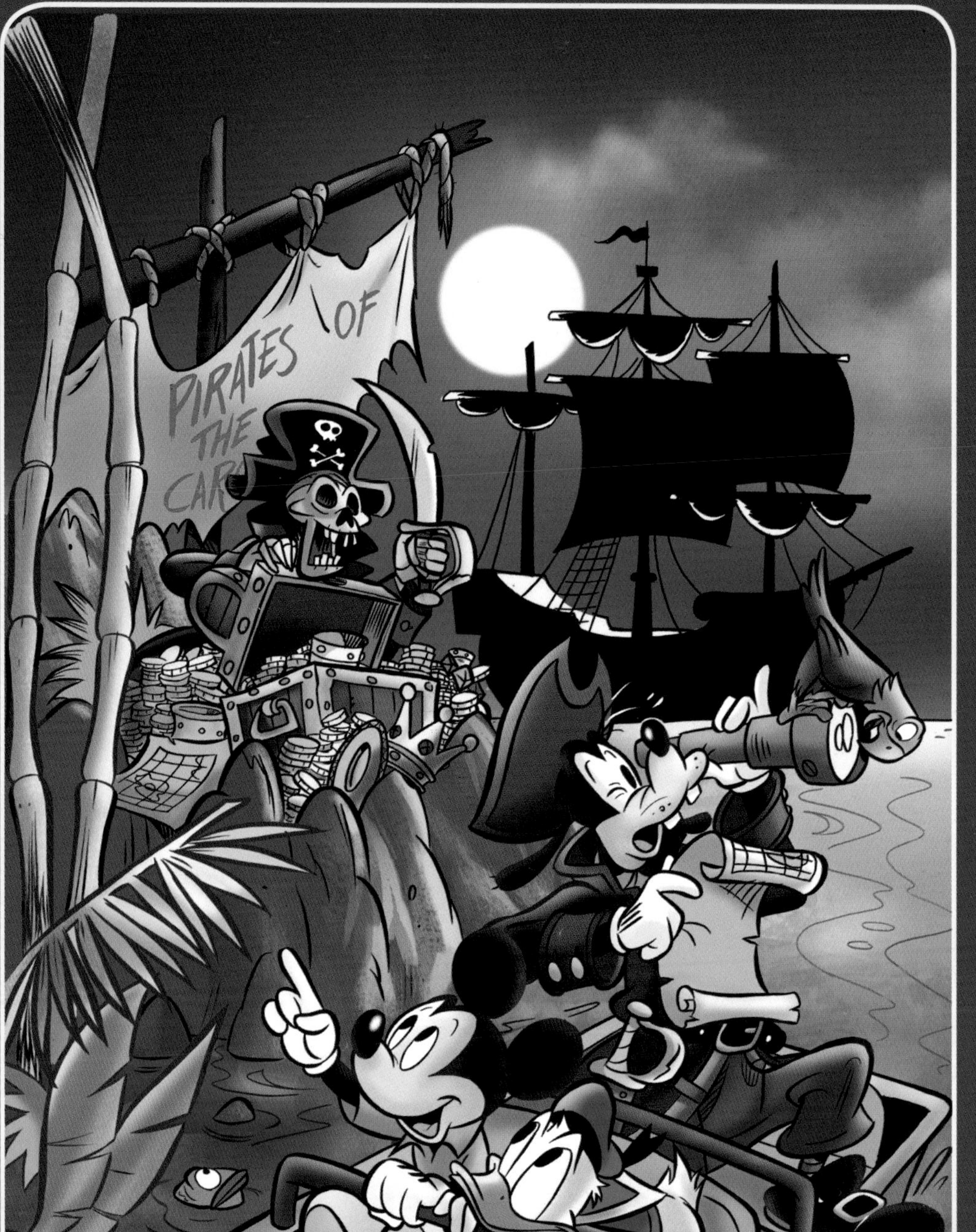
PIRATES OF
THE

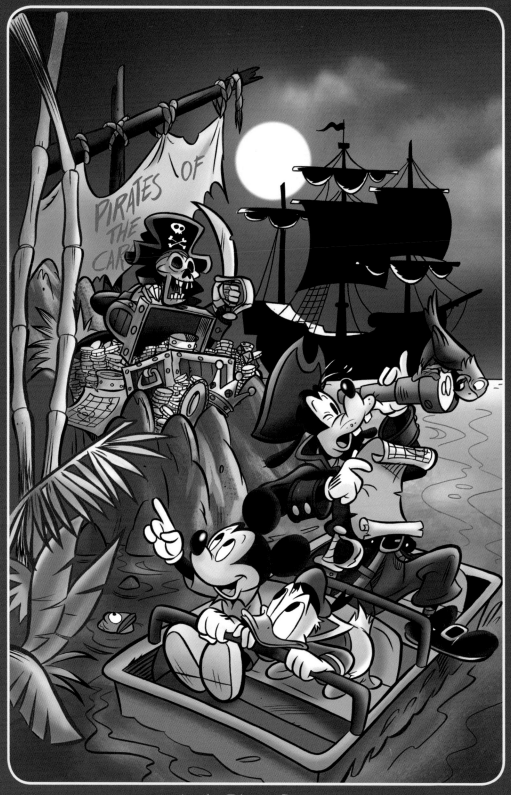

Art by Fabrizio Petrossi

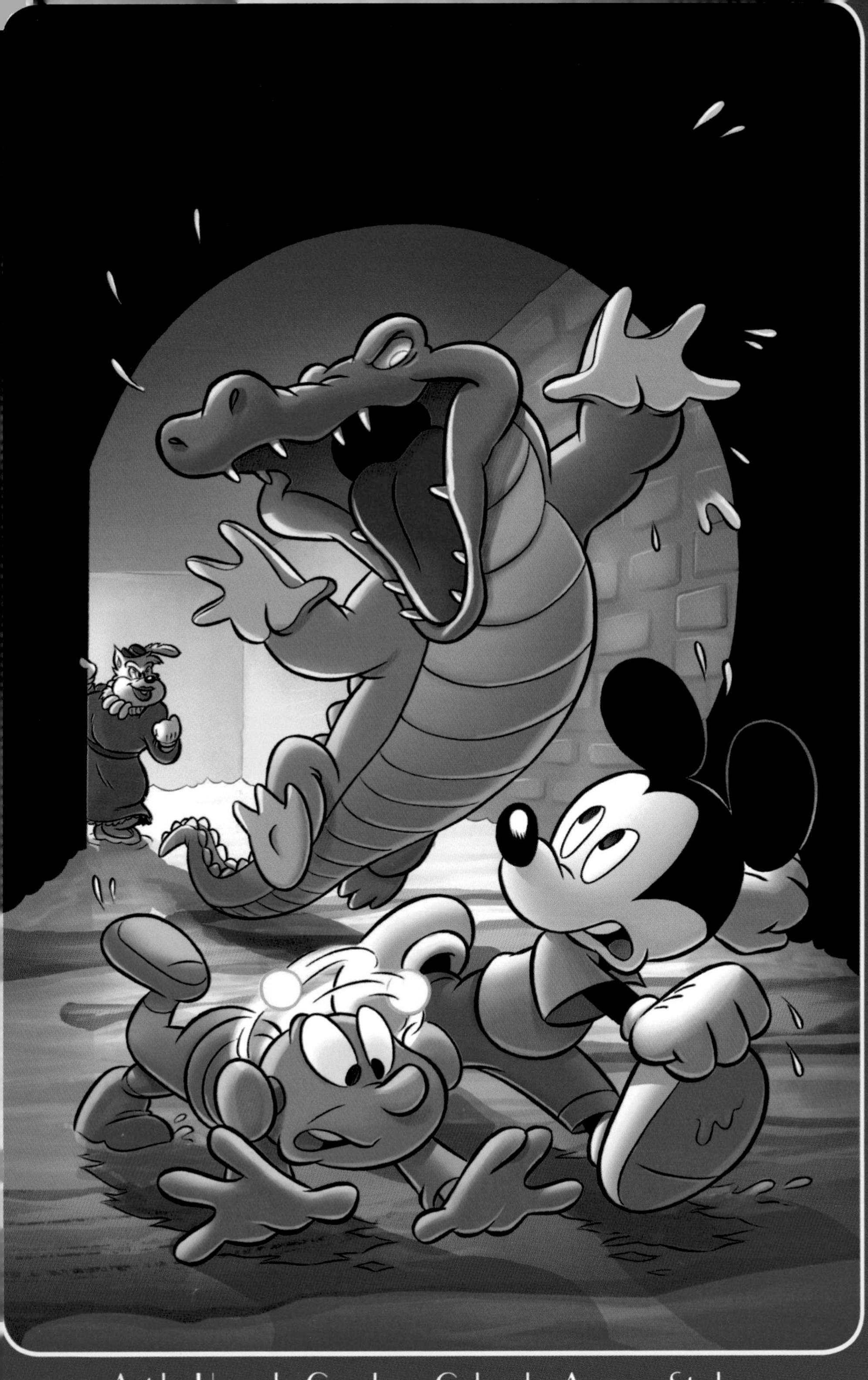

Art by Henrieke Goorhuis, Colors by Arancia Studios

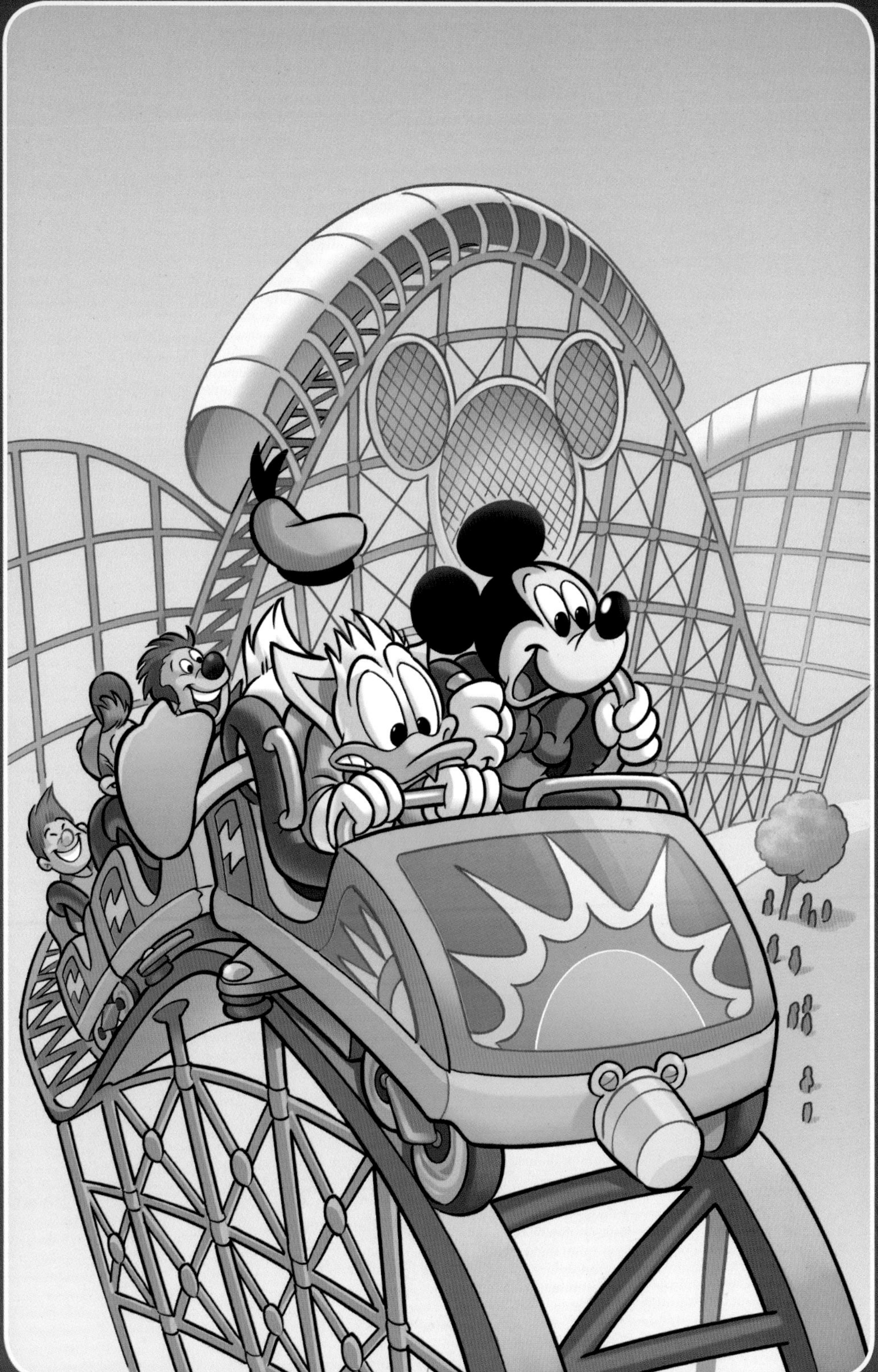

Art by Alessandro Perina, Colors by Mario Perrotta

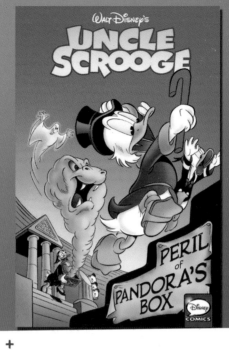

WALT DISNEY'S
UNCLE SCROOGE

PERIL of PANDORA'S BOX

Disney COMICS

+
741.5 M

Mickey Mouse.
Floating Collection GN
06/16

TYCOONRAKER

Disney COMICS

DONALD DUCK
TYCOONRAKER
ISBN: 978-1-63140-553-2

Disney COMICS

IDW